PRAISE FOR
THE FBI YELLOWSTONE
ADVENTURE SERIES

"The characters are entrancing, and Weaver describes scenery like a poet, slipping the reader into the comfort of a Yellowstone cabin where one can almost feel the heat from the nearby hot springs or hear the pound of bison footfalls."

—*Arkansas Democrat Gazette*

"Loved it! Awesome book that flat-out rocks! It really honors park rangers, FBI agents . . . [shows them as] real people with real strengths and weaknesses. Great descriptions of the scenery and pure adventure! Can't wait to see what happens next!"

—Central District Ranger Kevin Moses, Shenandoah National Park

"Read the book in two days! Absolutely loved it, especially how it depicted the problems (and successes) between agencies and different groups within the FBI. Can't wait for the next one!"

—Diane O., FBI, retired

"*A Noble Calling*: Mysteries, mayhem, and the maturation of an FBI agent. Win [Tyler] remains determined to honor his sacred oath as an FBI agent, even at the cost of his own physical and emotional well-being."

—*Philological Review*

"*A Sacred Duty* matches its predecessor, *A Noble Calling*, in presenting a fast-paced narrative . . . a spellbinding series of mysterious occurrences

. . . suspenseful developments . . . startling revelations . . . a first-rate mystery novel."

"*A Sacred Duty* goes even beyond her initial success . . . reads like a John Grisham novel . . . this book kept me guessing. I'm already looking forward to the third installment."

—*Arkansas Democrat Gazette*

ALSO BY RHONA WEAVER

The FBI Yellowstone Adventure series:

A Noble Calling
A Sacred Duty

Awards for *A Noble Calling*:

2021 Bill Fisher Award for Best First Book in Fiction
(Independent Book Publishers Association)

2021 Best Action/Adventure Novel (Next
Generation Indie Book Awards)

2021 Best Christian Fiction (Next
Generation Indie Book Awards)

2021 Finalist for Best Thriller (Next
Generation Indie Book Awards)

2021 Finalist for the Eric Hoffer Award for
Commercial Fiction (Eric Hoffer Foundation)

2021 Finalist for the Christy Award for First Novel
(Evangelical Christian Publishers Association)

2021 Bronze Medalist in Regional Fiction
(Independent Publisher Book Awards)

Awards for *A Sacred Duty*:

2023 Grand Prize for Fiction (Next
Generation Indie Book Awards)

2023 Best Christian Fiction (Next
Generation Indie Book Awards)

2023 Best Second Novel (Next
Generation Indie Book Awards)

2023 Finalist for the Eric Hoffer Award for
Commercial Fiction (Eric Hoffer Foundation)

2023 Gold Medalist for Religious Fiction
(Independent Publisher Book Awards)

2023 Finalist Action/Adventure Novel
(Next Generation Indie Book Awards)

A JUST CAUSE

A JUST CAUSE

◆ AN FBI YELLOWSTONE ADVENTURE ◆

RHONA WEAVER

Two Oaks Press

This is a work of fiction. Names, characters, organizations, places, events, and incidents are either products of the author's imagination or are used fictitiously.

Published by Two Oaks Press, Little Rock, Arkansas
www.rhonaweaver.com

Edited and designed by Girl Friday Productions
www.girlfridayproductions.com

Design: Paul Barrett
Project management: Sara Addicott
Editorial production: Kylee Hayes
Image credits: Front and Back Cover © Bill Temple

ISBN (hardcover): 978-1-7347500-6-5
ISBN (paperback): 978-1-7347500-7-2
ISBN (ebook): 978-1-7347500-8-9

Library of Congress Control Number: 2024920207

First edition

To Mother . . .

My mother introduced me to the magic of Yellowstone National Park through the pages of World Book Encyclopedias when I was six years old. She took on two extra jobs to pay for those books. "Good things usually require sacrifices," she often said. This novel is dedicated to her memory.

CHAPTER ONE

It was farther away than it looked . . . and it exploded into a fireball just as they topped the dirt-and-gravel berm high above the Snake River. All four stumbled to a stop, staring in shock as the sound wave and then the blast of heat slammed into them. Another burst of flames erupted from the rear of the vehicle and Win Tyler instinctively ducked, his arm flying up to shield his face and his labored breath catching in his throat. He reckoned the others had reacted the same. The car, or SUV, or whatever it had been, was fully engulfed in flames—that was his first thought as he took it in, and that would be the terminology he'd use when he wrote his report. He was standing alongside his two brothers and his best friend less than one hundred yards from the burning wreckage.

Win fished his phone out of his waterproof belt bag and called 911. The call with the Park Service Dispatch Office was quick: a vehicle wreck, a fire, victims unknown. He wasn't real sure where they were, some dirt road on the west side of the Snake River. A remote spot with one of the most iconic backdrops in America—the jagged granite peaks of the Grand Tetons towered over the landscape. Nothing like it. Absolutely breathtaking, stunning vistas. The boiling black smoke was rising almost straight up into the crystal-blue sky. It seemed odd that there wasn't any breeze. There was always a bit of wind in this wild western country. . . . A series of sharp pops from the burning vehicle snapped his attention back to the awful situation. It occurred to him that he was thinking about the scenery, the wind, the surreal nature of the thing, to take his mind off the near certainty that a person had just died here—maybe more than one.

"Tucker, Blake, you wanta come with me?" Win looked down at Will, his fifteen-year-old brother. A look of horror was etched on the boy's face. Win used his FBI tone of voice. "You stay put, Will. We'll check this out."

They took off at a fast trot across uneven ground that was studded with knee-high sagebrush and buffalo grass; the low scrub scraped their bare legs. Win dodged to the side at the sound of gunshots coming from the black, twisted pile of metal. Blake grabbed for his arm and they stopped, still a good fifty yards away from the wreckage.

"It's rounds goin' off . . . they had bullets in there!" Blake shouted. They all flinched again as more shots erupted from the carnage.

"Lots of rounds. Damn." Tucker had to nearly yell to be heard over the roar of the fire.

Win nodded, but he kept his troubled reflections to himself. *Whoa! Geez! Bullets exploding in a fire can happen—lots of folks have guns— but so many rounds? And did I heard shots before we hit the plateau? . . . before the fire? . . . before the explosion?* He'd learned at Quantico that bullets could explode in a fire, that they could fly in any direction but they generally didn't travel far, that they usually had low velocity— rarely caused harm. But knowing that and acting on that knowledge were two different things; the sound of gunshots caused him to hesitate. Finally, he shielded his face and moved closer. "Let's make sure no one got thrown clear. Y'all check that side." He raised his voice over the popping, cracking, and occasionally roaring sounds. "I'll go around." He could see nothing inside the overturned blackened vehicle except orange and yellow flames.

The men circled the inferno in a wide ring, then a tighter one; they found no one. Win raised a hand to signal them away from the fire, back toward Will and the riverbank. Someone had died here. Win had no idea who or even how many. All he knew was that someone had died and there wasn't a thing he could have done about it. They were too late.

He got back on the phone with the dispatcher and explained that he was on a raft trip on the river, that they'd pulled over to the opposite bank to photograph a moose when they'd heard, more than seen, the wreck. He told her that they'd crossed the river, left the guide in the raft, and climbed the bank . . . told her they'd been too late. He turned away from the fire and walked back toward his brothers and Tucker. They just stood around and watched the flames begin to die back.

There wasn't much to be said. "Y'all go on back to the raft." Win nodded toward the berm and the river below. "I'll wait for the rangers to show up. It might be a while."

Blake, Win's twenty-seven-year-old brother, drew himself up to his full six-foot-four height. He let out a long sigh and held up a hand. "We need to pray . . . uh, pray . . . for their families, for their friends."

"Yeah. Yeah, right," Win agreed, ashamed that he hadn't said those words himself. So Blake prayed and Win raised his head as the shrill sound of a distant siren cut the air.

They'd just said their *Amens* when another small group of rafters joined them. The lead guy wasn't tall, but his girth was considerable, and the gray T-shirt with its big Georgia black-and-red *G* was stretched tight. A Bulldogs ball cap and long black-and-red shorts completed his look. He was flushed and huffing from the steep climb up the bank. He reached down and hooked a finger in the jersey of the young boy next to him. "Whoa . . . whoa, son. Don't be goin' any further," he said in a deep, slow drawl. A woman and another man struggled over the top of the bank and stared at the fire. The woman pulled the little boy back to her and held him tight. And again, Win thought that there should be something they could do. Instead they all just stood there watching the black smoke roll, trying to shut the thoughts of death out of their minds. Each coped with the passing of strangers in their own way—for Win Tyler there was a deep sadness, as if a void had been created in this world with the passing of someone, even though he didn't know who.

The siren grew louder. It was coming from the south. The red-faced man from Georgia finally cleared his throat. "Them shots have quit poppin' off . . . we need to move in and make sure nobody got thrown clear of the wreck."

"We've already done that," Win said.

"Alright, ain't nothing else to do till the EMTs get here. I'll take charge. You people can go on about your rafting." The tone said it was an order.

Win shifted his focus from the wreckage to the stranger. He felt his brothers' eyes on him as he cleared his throat and spoke. "You have some jurisdiction here? Mister . . . ?"

The portly man drew himself up at the perceived challenge. "I'm Deputy Donnie Sawyer. Chattooga County—"

Win cut in. "Lemme guess, Georgia?"

The man raised his eyebrows in a suspicious look. "How'd you know that?" Apparently he'd forgotten his getup for the day.

"University of Georgia fan." Win nodded down at the huge *G* on the bulging shirt.

"Oh yeah, that."

Win moved to shake hands. "I'm Win Tyler, FBI resident agent for Yellowstone National Park. I'm here on leave for a few days."

The man returned the handshake and sized Win up with narrowing eyes. Win knew what the guy was thinking: *He doesn't look like a Fed, looks like a college kid on summer break.* The deputy dropped the handshake, reached in his pocket for a business card, and handed it to Win. "We're staying at the Frontier Inn in Jackson. Glad this is your problem." Maybe Deputy Sawyer hadn't had good relationships with federal law enforcement officers in the past, or maybe he was just anxious to get on with his interrupted vacation. Whatever the reason, he nodded to the rest of his party, and they retreated down the steep bank toward the river without another word.

Win turned his attention back to Tucker and his brothers. "I'll get a ride back with the rangers when they finish up. The deputy is right—there isn't anything else for y'all to do here." Tucker and Blake nodded and turned to follow the others down the gravel incline, but Win noticed that his youngest brother stood for several more seconds, staring at the wreckage. Will's face was pinched and pale; Win sensed that the boy was seeing something other than the sputtering fire.

* * *

"Hey, bud." Win let his hand trail over Will's shoulder as he straddled the bench on the picnic table outside Dornan's riverfront restaurant. He eased down beside his little brother and tested the table to make sure their combined weight wouldn't flip it. Will didn't speak, he just glanced down at his phone when it vibrated against the wooden tabletop.

Win tried to lift his brother out of the gloom. "Some girl reachin' out?" he asked with a grin.

"Naw, it's recruiters blowing up my phone. I don't know how to get 'em to back off . . . it ain't like I'm graduating next year."

Win raised his eyebrows. "Seriously? College recruiters? You're just going into tenth grade."

"Yeah, yeah. They've been calling ever since the Razorback Camp in early June. But it ain't 'bout me so much—just that I've got an older brother who ended up an All-SEC receiver, ended up settin' SEC scoring records . . . so it isn't really about me."

"Uh-huh." Win wasn't sure how to respond. He knew it would be hard on Will, coming up in his shadow. He'd been a high school football standout, a four-star recruit. The pressure to perform had been bad enough those many years ago; he knew it was much worse now. Even in junior high, Will Tyler had shown he was a legitimate talent, but living up to the lofty expectations of big-time college coaches would be daunting. It was a discussion they'd need to have, but not now. Now there was another hard conversation at hand.

"You okay?"

The youngest member of the Tyler clan glanced down at his phone again, then stared off toward the wall of mountains that stood beyond the fast-moving green river. He barely nodded.

"I hate that you had to see that . . . hate that—"

"You're thinkin' I'm a little kid. Can't handle the heavy stuff. Can't deal with it."

"You're fourteen—"

"Fifteen." Will's phone buzzed again. He silenced it.

"Barely fifteen."

"Doesn't matter. It happened and I'm so sorry for those people. . . ." Will's voice trailed off.

"I didn't mean to treat you like a little kid. Maybe it's the big-brother protection thing. I reckon I shoulda been more sensitive." *Sensitive isn't something I do real well.* Win drew a deep breath and followed Will's gaze across the tops of the cottonwoods that lined the Snake River to the towering mountains that stood three miles to the west. Then his eyes swept the lunch crowd of tourists milling around outside the popular restaurant's door. The postcard view, the smell of pizza and bread, and the murmur of happy voices in the background were a stark contrast to the horror they'd witnessed less than three hours ago.

"Yeah, everyone comes here to get away from real life, but an accident and tragedy found some folks today." Win hesitated before he continued. "There were two people in the vehicle. It was horrible."

Will closed his eyes tight and finally spoke. "Kinda brought back Jim Bob's wreck. The smell . . . the sounds."

Win had heard about the high school senior's death last spring. *"Drag racing,"* he remembered his dad saying during a phone call. It wasn't like there were a bunch of Jim Bobs around; Heber Springs, Arkansas, was a small town. Something clicked in Win's consciousness. *How does Will have personal knowledge of that awful wreck?* Win had been told that Jim Bob Tanner was drag racing in the middle of the night on one of the few straight stretches of highway in Cleburne County. He turned on the bench to face his little brother. "How would you know about those sounds and smells? Dad told me Jim Bob was killed at two a.m. on the road to Drasco." Win had switched to his investigative tone.

"Heard about it is all." Will quickly glanced away. His jaw twitched and he swallowed hard. He knew he'd been caught in a lie.

"That isn't what I'm hearin' in your voice. That isn't what I'm seein' on your face," Win softly replied. "You were there?"

Wasn't any need to deny it. Will nodded but kept his eyes averted. "Don't go telling me how stupid that was—I don't need to hear that right now. I ain't snuck out since." The boy drew in a breath. "You gonna tell Dad?"

Win paused a long moment and studied his brother. He saw a muscular young man nearly six feet tall—not the skinny, awkward teen that Win still pictured in his mind. Will Tyler had grown up while Win was away, and Win was shocked to realize he hardly knew the brother sitting beside him.

Win was almost twenty-nine years old; he was a freshman in high school when Will was born. While he was tight with Blake, it had never been that way with Will. Win tried to dismiss a stab of regret over that lack of closeness, as his rational self pointed out that it wasn't his fault. But he wondered how he could have missed the child growing into a man, wondered how that time had gotten away from him. He'd lived enough life to know there was no getting it back.

"No, I'm not gonna tell anyone," Win said. "This is between you and me. Hard way to learn a lesson, but I'm glad you learned it. Not much good happens with a bunch of teenagers out at two a.m. Everyone was drinkin'?"

Will shrugged. "I wasn't."

"Okay." Win started to rise. He was going to drop it, try to salvage the rest of the spectacular day, when it hit him. "You said it was just like with Jim Bob . . . but he was drag racing. Today the poor folks just lost control—"

"No. There was a truck racing them, there were two vehicles. I shot it as we were goin' down the river." Will held up his phone and pulled up the video he'd taken from the raft. He adjusted the objects' size with his fingers. There were clearly two plumes of dust. The sun glinted off the lead car—looked like a light-colored midsize SUV—but the sun was also gleaming off a second, larger vehicle closing on the first one. Then the view was obstructed by trees along the bank, and then just seconds more of the two vehicles on the distant dirt road, now nearly side by side. The chaser was a dark pickup of some sort. The video ended just before the crash, when the higher riverbank blocked the view. Win stared at the shaky reel in shock.

That's a pursuit, not a race.

*   *   *

Win pulled out his Bureau phone and recorded the date, the time, and some basic evidentiary facts before airdropping his brother's video to himself. He typed a quick email and sent it to his boss. Just over a minute later, Jim West was on the phone. "Tell me what's going on. You're thinking a chase, some sorta crime?"

"Maybe. We'd pulled off the river to photograph a moose, we heard the crash, the guide said there was a gravel road up there. We had to climb a sixty-foot bank to get to the plateau where the wreck was. I thought I heard gunfire as we were climbing, but . . . I'm really not sure. My little brother had been watching and videoing the vehicles as we floated. I didn't even know there was a road above the river. Honestly, I was just lookin' for a moose."

"You're on leave, Win, I wouldn't expect anything else," Jim replied.

Still, it bothered Win that he hadn't seen the chase, wasn't sure about the gunshots.

Jim was still talking. "Since we closed the Jackson office, we've got no one in that area. Our Lander office is two and a half hours out from you, and we need to stop the Park Service folks from moving the vehicle or disturbing the scene until we figure this out. Can you handle that? Can you get to a ranger station and get a ride back out there?"

"Yes, sir. We're at a riverside restaurant at Moose. The ranger station is just across the bridge. The ambulance was still at the site when I left—it was looking like two adults, but it was a mess. They were gonna wait for the fire to cool down, wait for the coroner. I gave my statement to the first ranger on the scene . . . I thought it was just a car crash. I left before they removed the bodies. I . . . uh . . . I didn't . . ." Win sighed.

"There was no reason for you to think anything was suspicious, Win. Just get out there and see what you can find. I'll handle the Park Service. Maybe we'll luck out and they'll have a special agent or two that they can call in, get you back on your vacation."

"Yes, sir. I'm staying here in the Jackson area for a few nights. You can pull me in if you need to."

* * *

It was nearly six that evening when the ranger dropped Win off at Tucker's aunt's house in the gated, and guarded, community on a hilltop just northwest of Jackson. Win stood there for a minute and took it in. There weren't any trees up here, not real trees anyway. Just four multimillion-dollar houses artfully designed to hug the summit of the high ridge and face the wall of mountains that stood five miles away. The soaring peaks seemed close enough to touch. It was a type of optical illusion, Win knew; he'd read about it. The highest mountains climbed straight into the sky; they were 12,500 to nearly 13,800 feet in elevation, no foothills stood between him and the range. The lack of scale caused the peaks to appear much closer and taller—they seemed to pierce the heavens. Win stood there, breathed in the crisp air, and stared at the surreal landscape. He was forcing his mind to go to the mountains, trying to use their overwhelming beauty to chase away the competing thoughts of violence and death. He shook his head and sighed. His efforts to compartmentalize the horror he'd seen weren't working for him just yet.

He was still standing there in the home's circular driveway when the massive front door opened and a spry Hispanic man in a white jacket stepped out. "They called from the gate, Mr. Win. The others are on the patio. Mr. Tucker asked that you join them when you're ready. I'm sure you'll want to freshen up. . . . I can show you to your room."

Win moved toward the man and tried again to shift his mind from the carnage he'd seen—from the death of two individuals—to the expansive home before him, to his friend and his brothers inside. He'd nearly reached the front door when Aunt Martha appeared from the depths of the house, rushed past her employee with arms wide, and pulled Win into a hug.

"Oh, Win, bless your heart! Tucker told me about the horrible accident . . . terrible, just terrible! It breaks my heart for those poor souls." She pulled back a little to look up into his dirty face, then took his arm; she didn't seem to notice the grit and the smell. But of course she did—Win knew she simply had too much class to mention it. "Oh, goodness," she said softly, "what you've been through." He wasn't sure if she was talking about today's crisis or his growing list of life traumas.

She introduced José, and Win went through the expected recital of pleasantries and thanks for her hospitality. He remembered to compliment her magnificent house, the blooming pots of red petunias near the entry, the lovely silk suit that brightened her eyes. He might have been grungy and disheveled, but Miss Martha's delighted smile told him his sincere compliments would have made his mother proud.

"José will take care of you. He'll clean everything. You just let him know what needs to be done." The man nodded as she continued to talk. "I wish I could stay—I'm going home for a few days." Win wondered which home. He knew Tucker's aunt had several. She was wearing a summer jacket and skirt with a soft-pink scarf; she was dressed more for the big city than for this casual tourist town. As she held his arm and led him toward the doorway, he refocused on her words.

"I'm so glad y'all can make good use of the place. I wish I could stay and visit. Win, I haven't seen you in years—that last time was, ah, at Moriah . . . you brought that lovely Shelby to the farm to visit. My, it's probably been two years."

Nearly three years ago . . . at Tucker's family home on the Moriah Plantation in Louisiana . . . an engagement party—my engagement party—nearly three years ago.

"Such a delightful girl." She beamed up at him. "Ah, y'all were getting engaged! Your career with the FBI had just taken off. I'd love to hear—"

A white Mercedes pulled behind them into the circular drive and caught her attention, saving Win from an awkward explanation of how his life had recently gone off the rails.

"Oh, time to go already!" She glanced back at the house wistfully. "I don't get out here often. Sometimes only two or three times each summer."

The driver stepped out of the car and moved around it to open the trunk. Another man materialized from the house and handed the driver several shopping bags and Martha's luggage. He opened the back passenger door and held out his hand for her to enter.

She nodded to him and turned back to the man in the white jacket. "José, thank you for everything. You take good care of these boys!" She looked up at Win with a quick smile. "Tucker's going to be here several more days than we originally thought—he said he could work out some property matters for me. He is such a dear." She smoothed down her scarf and took Win's hand again. "You're welcome to stay as long as you can . . . please say that you will. Tucker will try to convince you to practice law with him." She lowered her voice as if her words were a secret. "He's doing real well for himself in Oxford, but he hasn't met anyone yet . . . you could be such a good influence on him, Win."

And with that she slid into the back seat, the door closed, and she was gone.

CHAPTER TWO

He was up well before dawn, and he followed the aroma of freshly brewed coffee into the opulent marble kitchen. José was pulling something that smelled even more amazing from the oven. He looked up at Win and smiled. "It is Miss Martha's pecan cinnamon rolls. She made them yesterday afternoon so you young men could enjoy them today. All I had to do is turn on the oven and now drizzle on the glaze." He placed the large tray of pastries on the cooling shelf and turned back to the coffee.

"How do you like your coffee, Mr. Win?"

Win started to correct him on the *Mr. Win* thing, but he knew better. He just smiled as he accepted the mug. "Thank you, black is perfect for me. You're up early."

"Ah, Mr. Tucker is up too. He wants to take your brothers out to look for bears and lions this morning before the full light, before the wildlife watchers are all out."

Win breathed in the aroma of the coffee and watched José use a piping bag to stream sour cream icing on the warm buns. "I wish I could go—"

"Maybe tomorrow." Tucker's voice came from behind him. "I rousted your brothers and they'll be here in a minute. Since we're playing hooky from church, we'll get into the backcountry real early. You got time to eat before you go?"

"Naw, I better get moving. My supervisor texted me late last night and I'm supposed to meet another agent up near Jenny Lake. It'll take me more than half an hour to drive there. Since the Bureau closed the Jackson Hole Resident Agency last month, the nearest FBI office is in Lander, down in central Wyoming. I don't know where this other agent is out of." Win sighed, then took a long sip of coffee. "Could be a long morning." He leaned against the counter and eyed the cinnamon rolls before he turned back to Tucker. "Will y'all be in cell phone range this morning?"

"Off and on. I'm gonna take them up past Moran, up along Pacific and Pilgrim Creeks. There's almost always a grizzly bear or two in those areas. Want to try to touch base around noon? Maybe we could meet for lunch at the Jackson Lake Lodge or back here in Jackson." Tucker moved to refill his coffee. "That is if I haven't worn those boys out."

Win nodded. As he turned to go, José handed him a sack. "There's a thermos of coffee and cinnamon buns in the bag. Miss Martha wouldn't stand for you leaving without breakfast," he said with a smile.

"Alrighty then." Win eyed the bag of goodies. "Thank you!" Win saluted with his mug and took two more long sips before he set it on the counter and walked toward the foyer. Tucker walked him to the door and they stepped out into the cold air as the multitude of stars were beginning to fade and the first hints of light were dancing off the high mountains. "Geez, what a place," Win said. "What a view."

"I'll be seeing it a few more days than I expected," Tucker said as he opened the SUV's door for Win. "Aunt Martha wants me to handle the legal work on some of her real estate acquisitions—her Wyoming attorney is retiring. Soooo . . ." He shrugged with his eyebrows and smiled at the stunning view. "A man could get used to this every morning."

"'Cept it gets twenty below zero in the winter, and I'll bet the wind comin' off those mountains is horrific," Win countered.

"Well, there is that," Tucker conceded. His gaze caught the Glock on Win's belt as the cold breeze blew his light jacket back. "First time I've ever seen you dressed as an FBI agent in the field. You really look the G-man part in a suit and tie, but somehow you look it even more today—hiking boots, T-shirt, safari jacket, Indiana Jones hat . . . kinda the Jack Ryan look." Tucker grinned.

"Jack Ryan was CIA."

"You know what I mean." Tucker shook his head and the grin widened. "Man, it's no wonder you have to beat off the girls."

Win ignored the teasing, but he hesitated before he got into his old Explorer. "Speaking of which, I hate that I'm dumpin' the boys on you, plus you'll have to get ready for the cookout, for Tory and Lauren to get here. No tellin' when I'll get back."

Tucker shrugged with a smile. "In case you haven't noticed, I've got plenty of help here at the house. And you know how I love to hunt—me and the boys will just be doin' our huntin' with cameras instead of rifles today."

"Yeah, maybe you can snap Will outa his funk." It bothered Win that his little brother had continued to be withdrawn and pensive, even during the meal at the best Mexican restaurant in Jackson last night.

"Will's got that football recruiting mess on his mind, plus the wreck yesterday really shook him. He's on his phone constantly—who knows how many girls are after him." Tucker shrugged again. "He's a teenager, Win. Being moody goes with the territory. Gotta let him grow out of it in his own time."

Win nodded, waved his goodbye, slid into the seat, and started the ignition. He watched Tucker turn and take in the view of the mountains again; they were glowing in the dim light. It felt odd to get relationship advice from his best friend. Win studied the man's silhouette as he put the Explorer in reverse. Tucker Moses was way shorter than Win and kinda homely in a pleasant sort of way. Win knew Tucker was self-conscious about his thinning sandy-blond hair, his narrow shoulders, and the line of freckles that dotted his face. No amount of time in the gym could add muscle to his thin frame; he just wasn't built that way. He wasn't made to be an athlete, but he'd walked on at Ole Miss and been their primary kicker for three of his four years of undergraduate school. Some folks had the God-given gifts to be exceptional at their craft—Win knew he was one of those fortunate ones. Tucker had no such benefits, but he'd succeeded all the same. Win Tyler had tremendous respect for that type of effort and perseverance.

Win pulled around the circle drive, glanced in the rearview mirror, and saw Tucker still standing there staring at the Tetons. They'd been best friends since they'd shared an apartment for their three years of law school at the University of Arkansas. But something had recently changed, and Win wasn't sure what to make of it. Tucker was an only child. He was a year older than Win, nearly thirty. Win knew Tucker was being pushed by his family to put down roots, carry on the family legacy. Win had no such issues. His brother Blake had joined his dad on the family farm after college; Blake and his wife, Rachel, had produced the grandchildren his parents had hoped for. No, he wasn't feeling the same pressure that Tucker was under to find a suitable wife and take over the reins of the family business. *Maybe that's all it is.*

Neither he nor Tucker was big on discussing emotional topics. In all the time they'd known each other, Win could count the times on one hand when they'd dug deep on any issue that evoked strong feelings. Well, other than sports, business, or politics . . . certainly not relationships. *But here he is giving me advice on my little brother.* A gut feeling told him to heed that advice.

*   *   *

Win wound down the high ridge, cut through the outskirts of Jackson, and headed up Highway 89 into Grand Teton National Park. It was only a few miles north of town, and the drive to the park headquarters at Moose took less than twenty minutes. It was still early, not quite 5:30, but he needed to touch base with the rangers and see where things stood. There was no news from the Teton County Coroner, not that Win was expecting anything this soon. He was surprised to hear that an agent had gotten to the wreck site before daybreak and met with the park ranger who'd had the unpleasant duty of standing guard over the blackened hulk all night.

Win sat in his vehicle in the rangers' station parking lot, finished up Miss Martha's second pecan cinnamon roll, and drank another cup of coffee from the thermos as he rechecked the text that Jim West had sent him late last night: **Tomorrow am—reach out to Cst. Alex Lindell. ATF may have agents at the scene. Let me know what you need once you assess situation.** It didn't tell him much, but it did tell him that his vacation was fixing to get interrupted again. He punched in the contact number that Jim had forwarded to him. A woman answered, and it didn't sound like he'd awakened her. She sounded intense.

"Who's calling?" That was her curt opening. It was not a friendly voice.

"Win Tyler with the FBI. I'm calling for Alex Lindell. Can you get him on the phone, please?"

There was a long pause, then an angry tone. "Where are you?"

"Look, maybe I've got the wrong number. I need to speak to Alex Lindell. Is he there or not?" Now Win's voice had a bit of an edge. Yeah, it was 5:35, early for a call, but no need for her to be rude.

"This *is* Alex Lindell. Do you think I'm *his* hookup for the night? That I'm *his* answering service? It's nearly six, why aren't you out here at the site?"

Whoa! Didn't see that coming!

Win tried to regroup. "I'm . . . uh, sorry—"

"Meet me outside the Jenny Lake Store at 0615 hours." The call went dead. Win sat there for a few seconds and stared at his phone. He took another sip of coffee and tried to tamp down the anger he felt toward the woman. What had Jim's text said? *Cst. Alex Lindell. What's a Cst.?* Jim said ATF might be involved somehow. He didn't know much about the Bureau of Alcohol, Tobacco, Firearms and Explosives . . . maybe it was an analyst or evidence response team title? Darned if he knew. He confirmed the area code on her cell phone. Yeah, 406—that was Montana. So maybe she was some kind of local law enforcement. He capped the thermos, pocketed his phone, and started his truck. *I'll find out soon enough.*

*   *   *

She had her long dark hair pulled back tight in a ponytail and she was facing away from him, watching the traffic roll into the main parking lot. A sweat-stained blue ball cap and a gray fleece jacket were on the bench beside her, along with a daypack. She wore an olive-drab T-shirt under an equally drab long-sleeve shirt, dusty cargo pants, and dirty hiking boots. She could have been just another of the many hikers settling in for a respite on the picnic tables or benches beneath the big spruce and pine trees near the log building that housed the Jenny Lake Store. She almost looked the part. Almost. But as he walked toward her, he could see the slight bulge of the handgun under her open shirttail, he could smell the ash on her boots. She smelled of death. He knew he'd found Alex Lindell.

He sat down on the opposite end of the shaded bench and took off his hat. He glanced over at her and nodded. She didn't say anything at first, just watched him with a gaze he couldn't quite interpret.

"We got off on the wrong foot," he began.

"You think so?"

"I was told to contact Alex. . . . I'm sorry if I made the wrong assumption. The folks I've known who go by male names are generally men." It wasn't much of an apology, and he knew it. He didn't even look her in the eye when he said it. He wasn't into playing games, and he was sick and tired of being politically correct. There were two deaths to be solved, and she was uptight over an honest mistake. She needed to get over it. He was willing to let it go if she was, but she made no move to shake hands, to say anything conciliatory. She just nodded, and her dark eyes turned back to the steady stream of traffic. He had the feeling she was watching for someone.

Win made another stab at it. "I'm here on annual leave. . . . I don't have any background on the situation, but my supervisor indicated that ATF has been called in for some reason. You're with ATF?"

She glanced back his way. "No. I'm RCMP."

Win's mind flew through the seemingly endless string of federal agency acronyms but got no hits. The confusion was apparently on his face.

She drew in a breath. "Royal Canadian Mounted Police. Are you really that slow."

He knew it wasn't a question and he didn't like her tone, but of the myriad of agencies she could have named, the Mounties weren't anywhere on that list. Before he'd been exiled to Yellowstone National Park three months earlier, he'd spent his first three years with the FBI in Charlotte, North Carolina, working white-collar crime and public corruption. He'd had no interaction with Canadian police agencies and hadn't given them a thought. Montana's border with Canada was nearly 550 miles long, he did know that much, but that border was hundreds of miles north of where they sat in northwestern Wyoming. He knew the surprise was evident in his voice. "So why are you here?"

Her tanned face turned back to him, but she didn't answer his question. "It's getting crowded. Let's take a walk," she said as she stood. She stuffed her jacket and cap in the daypack, hoisted it over one shoulder, and weaved through the throng of tourists going in and out of the general store. It was early, but the place was already busy on this holiday morning, and the murmur of voices in English and other languages blended together in the background. She paused at the low stone wall and seemed to be reading the signage. Three asphalt paths diverged, and she chose the one headed toward Jenny Lake. Win walked a few paces behind her as they made their way through the sunlit evergreen forest along a trail flanked by smooth boulders and bright-yellow arrowleaf balsamroot flowers. The number of tourists quickly began to dwindle as they left the store and parking areas behind.

Her gait was steady and fast for a person of her size; she was maybe five five and thin as a rail. Too thin, he was thinking. Maybe she'd been sick, maybe she was a distance runner, or maybe she just didn't eat. Win was hoping he wouldn't be around her long enough to find out. There was something about Alex Lindell that bothered him, and he didn't think it was just her surly attitude.

She paused at a spot overlooking the glistening blue lake that nestled up against the soaring mountains. He wondered how many folks had stopped here for the ultimate vacation photo: smiling faces framed by the picturesque lake, the cobalt sky, and the jagged granite peaks. He knew he and Alex Lindell wouldn't be among them.

She turned abruptly and took a left along the path marked *Boat Dock*. Win's vision of a marina from his time on the big lakes in the Arkansas Ozarks didn't fit in this high alpine place. The Jenny Lake Boat Dock was a three-boat slip where tourists paid a fee and lined up to board a thirty-five-foot covered aluminum boat for the twelve-minute scenic ride to the hiking trails on the opposite side of the lake. A sign said the first boat departed at seven.

Win followed Alex past the waiting tourists and across a log pedestrian bridge over Cottonwood Creek. Icy water was flowing out of the lake and under the bridge and tumbling down through the forest. He slowed to watch her back, wondering again where she was going. That question got answered when she crawled through a pole fence on the other side of the bridge and sat down on a large rock beside the stream. She unlaced one of her hiking boots and dipped it in the water. She was cleaning away the fire's ash, washing away the smell of death.

Win moved to a smooth log and sat down near her with his back against a stump. He wanted to be able to watch her and still have a view of the people who were arriving for the short boat ride. No one seemed out of the ordinary—about a couple dozen expectant hikers, most of whom looked like city folks excited to have a day in the woods. One couple carried overnight gear and looked the part of seasoned backpackers. There were few children, but it was probably a bit early for most parents to wrangle their kids here. Nothing struck him as odd or out of place, except maybe the woman beside him. Her brooding expression and thin, slouched shoulders contrasted with the upbeat vibe coming from the tourists and the boat's crew, who were selling tickets a few yards away. It was as if she carried her darkness with her.

He'd managed to unintentionally insult her twice already; it wasn't a great start. He'd always prided himself on getting along with most everyone, but for some reason that wasn't happening today. He'd never met a Canadian, he reasoned, so maybe it was a cultural thing, or a gender thing, or a social thing. He knew that it likely had nothing to do with him.

He noticed that she was still watching the crowd. He wondered who she was looking for, what was going on. And he was getting real damn tired of guessing. No one could hear them here, with the rush of the fast stream as a backdrop, so he reached into his jacket pocket, pulled out his credentials, and flipped them open in front of her. "Win Tyler, FBI. And you?"

She glanced at his creds as she unbuttoned her shirt's front pocket, pulled out a lacquered fold-over card and held it up. He read it quickly, but it gave him few answers. "Are you going to tell me what's going on? Why you were at the wreck site? What jurisdiction do you have here?" he asked.

She turned her attention back to rinsing her boot while she spoke. "I'm working a case in cooperation with your ATF. The case is based out of Salt Lake City and Calgary." She cut her eyes to his. "That's Calgary, *Canada*."

She was still baiting him, but he wasn't biting. He kept his expression neutral. "Okay, that explains the ATF connection—"

She interrupted him. "And before you ask, I've got an exemption through ATF to carry a firearm in the U.S. You can check that if you want."

"I will." He watched her glance back at the growing line of tourists. "So how is this vehicle wreck connected?"

She continued to slosh her boot in the water. She didn't make any effort to meet his eyes. "Not sure that it is, but an informant and an undercover ATF agent have dropped out of sight. They missed a contact last night." She paused for a minute and took the other boot off. She still didn't meet his eyes.

"You're thinking—"

"I'm not thinking anything. I don't know anything for sure. We've got nothing new back from the coroner. I looked at the chase video you sent in . . . gave it a hard look. We're having it enhanced, as I'm sure your agency is. You were there yesterday before they took the bodies away. What do you know?"

"I was there at 9:22 a.m. when we thought it was just an accident. I stayed on-site about ninety minutes, then got back out there just after one, right as they were removing the bodies. Two adults in a midsize SUV—the EMTs were guessing males, but they were just guessing. The fire was intense. Nothing much survived."

She swallowed hard but her expression never changed. "You found the brass?"

"Yeah, twenty-three along the dirt road, in the brush. They were either .223 or 5.56, so an AR-15 type rifle, all the way back to the highway turnoff, over two miles. That's what I found, and I could have missed some—it's rough terrain. We need to do an extended grid search this morning. The fire caused a lot of ammo blowoff from within the vehicle. Numerous rounds. We'll have to see if any of those casings survived the fire. And one odd thing, there were six .45 caliber casings near the car—could have been blown out when the rounds discharged in the flames, but I don't think so, they were tight in one spot. The rangers helped me flag them after I put a stop to the vehicle recovery . . . after they removed the bodies. You saw the flagging? What's going on?"

She nodded, her eyes scanned the line of tourists near the boats, she dipped the second boot in the fast water again. "I'm not authorized to tell you any case details," she said. "This is all preliminary . . . but the rangers are holding the vehicle at the incident site for ATF's Evidence Response Team out of Salt Lake City. They should be there by mid-morning at the latest. There's no reason to go back out there until then. They'll handle any grid search that needs to be done."

Win started to ask a question, but Alex kept talking. "There'll be a briefing later today. I don't have a location yet—probably somewhere in Jackson, since I assume that's where they'll transport the vehicle. We should have something back from the coroner by then. Maybe some initial results from the evidence team on-site."

"Whoa, slow down. *If* there's a briefing, the FBI should be holding it. If a crime has been committed in a national park, the FBI has jurisdiction, not ATF, and certainly not Canadian law enforcement. Who gave you the authority to call in an evidence response team? Who's running this show?"

She focused on lacing up her boot, then glanced back toward the line of tourists waiting to board the first boat. She didn't look at him when she spoke. "I can't discuss case details with you. It's really none of your business. I suppose you'll know more *if* you get called into the meeting." She pulled on the second boot. "You've given me the intel I need. You're free to go."

Free to go. . . . Now he was getting a little hot. There was way more going on here than he'd been told. He forced down a harsh reply and spoke calmly. "I need to get back with my supervisor, see where—"

His Bureau phone buzzed, and he pulled it out. She was still piddling with her boot, watching the crowd. The text from Jim West was short: **Be at briefing at NPS HQ in Moose at 1:00—I am coming. Assist Cst. Lindell until I arrive.**

He typed in a **10-4**, then turned to her and held out the phone so that she could read the messages.

"Well, you're stuck with me till the briefing. So how 'bout you tell me why we're at the marina, what's going on here." He motioned toward the crowd with his chin. "You're looking for someone. Expecting someone to be on that first boat."

She didn't look happy with his comments, and she paused for so long that he didn't think she would answer, but she finally did. "Our informant used the area across the lake as a drop site to get messages to me related to the case. He didn't trust the phones—or your law enforcement people. He's been trying to infiltrate a gang of gunrunners for several months. He . . . ah, our informant, thought the gang was using the national park roads as a route into Canada, so he and an ATF undercover agent have focused on the park roads the last few weeks. I've been in the area monitoring them. In Jackson, here in Grand Teton, even up into Yellowstone."

She paused and bit her lip before she continued. "And . . . and in the last few days, things were suddenly looking promising. Our guys had stopped most communication with us . . . with me. It was looking like they might be in touch with the gang. . . they were going to try to set up the sale of firearms to the bad guys, lure them in. They may have set something up . . ."

Or they may have driven into a trap. "So why are we here?" Win asked again.

"I thought there might be another info drop. Sometimes he . . . ah, our informant, he used a drop point across the lake near Hidden Falls. I thought it might be worth checking. Maybe someone made a drop yesterday afternoon . . . or will show up this morning."

There was an inflection in her voice that he found unusual. She was desperately hoping someone would show up, hoping there would be a message that had been left after the wreck occurred, hoping someone was still alive. He knew he wasn't getting the full story, but he decided to play along. "They'd use the same drop site more than once?" he asked.

She shrugged. "Yeah, yeah, they do. The Evidence Response Team won't be at the incident site until mid-morning and the briefing isn't till one. . . . This might be worth checking." She switched to a more casual tone. "You up for acting like a tourist and riding to the other side? Or we could hike it, it's about five miles round trip to the falls and back around the south end of the lake. Takes longer is all. The shuttle boats run every fifteen or twenty minutes." She stood and took a step toward the bridge.

Two people had died in the last twenty-one hours and they had next to nothing to go on. He glanced at his watch: 6:44. *What the heck.* "Okay, let's take a boat ride."

CHAPTER THREE

I t was early—just coming up on 6:45, but Dex Pierson had already concluded that he wasn't having a good day. He leaned back against the front fender of his nearly new black Dodge Ram pickup and watched as the sun cleared a cloud bank over the Mirror Plateau of the Absaroka Range just east of Yellowstone's Hayden Valley. He pulled a cigarette out of the pack and slid the pack back into his heavy canvas jacket. The cigarette hung from the corner of his mouth, but he didn't light it. It was a habit he was trying to break, which unfortunately brought to mind other bad habits he needed to break. Like not flossing his teeth every night, smoking the occasional joint, not spending enough time with his boy, hanging out with rough men, robbing convenience stores, going to prison. His mother always said that one bad habit leads to another. He sighed, pulled out his BIC, and shielded the flame from the cold breeze as he lit the cigarette. Hell, his life's downward spiral probably started with not flossing his teeth.

His clients were late. He pocketed the lighter and glanced at his watch again: 6:48. They were real late. It had been full light for over an hour, and the ridgetop parking lot beside the Grand Loop Road was full. He'd parked at the end of the lot, up next to the trees, but several kids had already asked to look through the scopes he'd set up on the tripods beside his truck. He'd obliged them because he didn't want to appear out of place, but they'd all retreated after their parents got a good look at him and called them away. A shame really, since he liked kids and letting them use the scopes to better see the small pack of wolves in the valley below was a treat. He watched as another young mother grabbed a child by the back of his jacket as soon as he started toward one of the scopes. She whispered something in his ear and the little kid stared up at him in alarm. He reckoned he must have *shady ex-con* written across his forehead, or maybe it was the prison tats on his neck and face, or the wild hair. Maybe he should put on a hat.

He'd set his camp chair and two scopes in the space next to his truck so they blocked other cars from parking too close. Not real ethical given the Yellowstone code of *first-come, first-served* when it came to parking spaces, camping spots, or whatever in the national park, but he wanted the clients next to him. Well actually, he didn't want the clients here at all. Meeting out in public was definitely not his idea and he'd argued against it, but he wasn't the one calling the shots in this deal. Jesse was giving the clients some sort of geyser/wildlife tour before the real action began. That's what Jesse had told him. So he'd drug the scopes up here and tried to blend in with all the other tourists looking for wildlife at daybreak. He didn't like it, but the money was good and he'd agreed.

And here they finally were. An imposing gray Infiniti SUV nosed in beside his truck. He grabbed the scopes and camp chair and made room for it to park. The passenger doors flew open before the driver got it completely stopped; two small, slender men jumped out and pulled on their caps. Dex sized them up in one quick sweep as they moved toward the front of his Dodge: both five four, maybe, with expectant looks on their faces, both dressed head to toe in black—expensive black from the looks of it, right down to the high-dollar hiking boots. The gray-haired man in front hesitated when he spotted Dex, and the driver moved in to take over the introductions. There was lots of head nodding and fake smiles among the four of them as they got the pleasantries out of the way.

Jesse guided them to the spotting scopes that Dex had repositioned overlooking the Hayden Valley. Dex gave them an overview of what they were seeing below the backdrop of deep-blue sky and dark-blue mountains. The shimmering azure Yellowstone River serpentined through the valley; sandhill cranes and Canada geese were standing on its banks. Several small herds of bison, pronghorn, and elk were grazing the bright-green grass near the water. Mint-green sagebrush covered the sloping terrain that climbed away from the river toward the forest of dark lodgepole pine. The lounging wolves still lay in the sun just below the tree line. The tapestry in shades of blues and greens was teaming with wildlife, proof of Yellowstone's title of America's Serengeti.

Dex settled himself against his truck's grill and pretended to watch the wildlife; instead he was focused on his partner in this deal, Jesse Gibbs. Jesse was smooth, always had been. His designer clothes, sharp haircut, trim beard, and manicured hands fit the image he was trying to project—same as the luxury vehicle he was driving. He'd even used a bit of the clients' language, whatever it was, as he did the introductions. Dex knew that under the slick facade, Jesse was a class A con man. They had grown up around each other in small-town Rock Springs, Wyoming, and had both managed to get into a fair amount of trouble. At the end of their junior year of high school, Jesse's family moved to North Dakota with the first oil field boom, and Dex joined the Army the minute he turned seventeen. They'd lost touch for many years until one day the previous summer, when Dex typed his old friend's name into Instagram and was amazed to find that they lived only miles apart. It had been a lucrative reunion. Gotta love social media.

He lowered the field glasses when Jesse moved closer. "Dex, as much as I'm paying you for this gig, maybe you coulda cleaned up a little, lost some of the grunge factor, used somethin' to cover the tats. You look scary as hell."

"You're worried about appearances? When you brought in those two oriental dudes who look like they've been cast directly out of some Japanese mobster movie?"

The other man sighed. "It's *Asian*, not *oriental*, and they're Chinese, not Japanese. But the mobster thing isn't too far off, so mind your manners. Mr. Zhào, the gray-haired man, is the client. He probably speaks more English than he lets on, but Mr. Yé is his business manager and he'll do the translating."

They both watched the valley with their binoculars for a minute. The wolves were moving toward a couple of big bison bulls. It wasn't likely that four wolves would really attack the bulls, not this time of year, but they might annoy them enough to provoke a fight. Things were going to get interesting.

Jesse dropped his binoculars to his chest and turned toward Dex. "You're still thinking later today, early tomorrow? Mr. Zhào has to be back in San Francisco by midweek. You've got the bull picked out?"

"Yeah, yeah . . . you know what I've told you. Many of the biggest solitary bulls won't join the herds for another week or two. They're at their prime now—they've lost the winter coat, good horn length. I've been following one who's a dandy. He's hanging out with two younger bulls; they were about a mile above the South Cache Creek split yesterday. Good grass up there, so they won't likely stray too far from that spot for few days. I'm set for late this afternoon if your guys are good to go."

Jesse pretended to watch the wildlife in the valley as he cut his eyes to Dex. "Yeah, that'll work. I've planned to switch vehicles just after lunch. Everything's on ready." He paused and drew a breath. "Was hoping you'd come up with a spot outside the park, maybe national forest . . . or private land. We're gonna get heat if we keep workin' the park."

Dex just shrugged. "High risk, high reward. Your people are wantin' the biggest and the best. The cow herds are congregated in the valleys in the park now. The biggest bulls will be moving in to claim their harems, lots of them already have. Just a few of the best are still up in the foothills. That's what I'm goin' for. That's what you want, ain't it?"

The other man still seemed hesitant. He nodded slightly. Dex continued to talk. "It ain't like we're kids spotlighting deer and shootin' from the highway like we used to back in junior high. We'll do this the same way we handled it last week. We hike in, do an overnight camp, then go out before light—*well before light*. We scout the bull, get set up, get the shot. We get a video, a few nice photos of Mr. Zhào with the kill, then you handle the trophy haul out. Same as last time. . . . We good?"

Jesse frowned, but he nodded his agreement. Dex scanned the valley again and spotted a herd of twenty-something elk quickly trotting

down from the tree line not far above the wolves. *Not a smart move.*
Then he saw the reason for their dangerous route. A good-size blond
grizzly was loping out of the trees directly toward the elk. Given its
size, it was amazing how quick the bear was; it was closing in fast on a
yearling. Dex moved to point out the bear to the two Asian gentlemen
and left them to the spotting scopes. Now everyone at the overlook
was pointing or calling out, *"Bear!"* The scopes were helpful, but the
animals were less than a thousand feet away, and the action could be
seen plenty good with the naked eye. Dex knew it was developing into
one of those moments in the wild when something would probably
get killed. He glanced down the row of entranced tourists; they were
going to find out that this wasn't Disneyland—real blood was gonna
get spilled. The cycle of fragile life and sudden death was a constant in
Yellowstone National Park.

Dex turned his back on the action and wandered toward his truck.
He pulled out another cigarette. He lit it, then dropped it to the ground
and crushed it out before he even pulled a drag. *Need to lose some bad
habits.*

* * *

Win squeezed his six-foot-three frame through the rustic pole fence
that separated the stream bank from the trail and the footbridge, then
he joined Alex at the end of the ticket line. The enthusiastic young
man who was collecting money and scanning credit cards ushered
them forward. "Welcome aboard! We'll dock at the foot of Teewinot
Mountain—what a beautiful day to hike Cascade Canyon! You'll be
able to see forever from Inspiration Point! Hidden Falls will be roaring!"

Alex slid into the last bench seat available, next to two young girls
who were complaining about the cold and the early hour. Win took
a back crew seat when the boatman signaled him down. The skipper
went through the safety talk. He got Win's attention when he said the
1,190-acre alpine lake was 456 feet deep and forty-eight degrees. Win
looked around for the life jackets while he did another check of their

fellow passengers. He counted twenty-four tourists and a two-man crew. Everyone looked legit.

As the boat started moving, Alex pulled the gray fleece jacket out of her daypack; Win wished he'd brought his heavier coat along. It was downright frigid when the boat turned the corner out of the marina's sheltered inlet and headed into the wind. Win pulled off his hat to keep it from blowing away. He ran his hand through his thick brown hair and made a mental note to get a haircut. Every time the boat hit a wave and icy spray shot into his face, he made another mental note never to be the last one on board to choose a seat. He watched Alex out of the corner of his eye and thought she seemed more relaxed after the boat pulled away from the dock. But maybe it wasn't calm he was seeing, maybe it was resignation—as if she'd accepted the reality that whatever she was seeking would either be there, or not. There was nothing she could do to change the outcome.

They were the first two off the boat when it docked at the foot of the towering peaks. Alex didn't even glance around at him as she headed up the well-worn trail into the canyon. He figured she knew he was there, about five yards behind, watching her back. It was obvious that Alex knew exactly where she was going, that she'd been this way before—he had the feeling it was far more than once. She didn't even hesitate at the numerous path junctions; she didn't bother to read the brown wooden signs. He wondered if her review of the signage at the Jenny Lake Store had been for show, just in case someone was watching. And even though she moved as if she were on a single-minded mission to get to the drop point, she still paused occasionally to quickly scan her surroundings, to look for someone. He wished he knew who.

He would tell anyone it was a great short hike—the sweeping views back across the lake, log bridges over rushing streams, massive boulders scattered among majestic evergreens. If there hadn't been an undercurrent of tension about it, Win would have enjoyed the walk. At least it was succeeding in taking his mind off the carnage of the wreck, off his little brother's issues, and off this evening's date with Tory. He was having a hard time getting his mind off Tory Madison, about their plans for tonight. He was nervous about seeing her and he thought he knew why.

It'd been Tucker's idea to invite Tory and her friend Lauren to his aunt's house for a Fourth of July cookout. As soon as he'd told Tucker that Tory would be in Jackson for a two-day wildlife seminar, Tucker had needled him to invite them over. Blake thought it was a great idea as well. It wasn't lost on Win that Blake and Tucker both wanted to help him "move on from Shelby," as Blake put it. He had to concede that getting over Shelby wasn't happening real fast. Something deep inside told him he had to focus on the future, not the past. It sounded simple, but he was discovering an age-old truth: moving beyond loss, beyond grief, isn't a straight-line process; often it's two steps forward and three steps back. There was nothing easy or simple about it. He'd been with Shelby for nearly five years when she walked out of his life back in February. They'd finally talked about it in May, and she'd returned the engagement ring in June. Here it was early July, and he thought he should be free, but not a day went by that he didn't think of her. He drew in a deep breath and reviewed that last thought. *Who am I kidding? Not an hour goes by without her floating through my mind, without me seeing, hearing, or touching something that reminds me of her, without me aching to pick up the phone and call her. Not an hour goes by.*

Win's attention shifted back to Alex when she suddenly slowed. She didn't stop, she just dropped her right hand to signal him to turn aside as they neared two huge trees that hugged the trail. He sat down on a log that had been carved into a makeshift bench and pretended to check his boot. She stopped next to one of the huge Douglas fir trees and pulled her metal water bottle from her pack to take a drink. The two backpacker types he'd noticed on the boat nodded a greeting and hiked on past. Alex had set a pretty good pace on the half-mile trek from the boat dock, and no one else was in sight.

Alex's body language told him she was nervous, or anxious, or scared. He wasn't sure which. He could hear the roar of a waterfall; he reckoned it must be just beyond the rockslide that he could glimpse on the far side of the big trees. His eyes took in the surrounding forest and trail; he sensed no danger. He saw only the boulders and the lush foliage, heard only the restful sounds of the rushing water, felt the cool touch of the breeze. He had the sensation that they were alone in the deep forest; its canopy of green even covered the sky.

Alex had moved to the side of one of the massive trees. He saw her eyes sweep the woods and the trail for a moment, then she dropped her stainless steel water bottle, reached behind a draping fern, and pulled an identical bottle from below the tree's moss-covered roots. She switched them quickly and effortlessly. If he hadn't been really dialed in, he would have missed it. She held the new bottle to her side as she casually walked away from the tree and moved on up the trail. He watched until she disappeared near the rockslide. He stood and slowly followed.

She was hard to spot at first. Then he saw her about forty feet above the trail, sitting in the sun on a large block of granite that looked like it had been casually tossed down the slope. There was a good quarter mile of jumbled gray rock stretching above the trail at a sharp pitch. Win guessed this was what Westerners called an avalanche chute, but he didn't know for sure since he'd only seen one actual avalanche and it had been composed of snow. Whatever this was, it was hundreds of yards of boulders and rock that ended right above the trail.

Alex's slender shoulders were slumped again, and her head was bowed a little. He could tell she hadn't opened the water bottle, but he couldn't tell much else. He carefully climbed up two good-size boulders, scanned the trail again, and sat down near her. Most of the shuttle boat's passengers had approached the base of the rockslide and were beginning to file past below them. Win knew he and Alex would be hard to see from their perch above the path; no one even glanced up at their concealed spot in the rocks. He eased back on a still-cold granite boulder and was immediately scolded by a small tan-and-gray furball that sat on the rocks five feet above his head. *Eeeek! Eeeek! Eeeek!* The little creature kept up the sharp shrieking until Win stared it down.

"It's a tribble," Alex said softly. It was a tone of voice he hadn't heard her use. The little creature glared back at him, still angry at the trespassers. *A tribble? Naw, those were on Star Trek.* Then it occurred to him. *She's trying to cope. But cope with what?*

Alex turned her attention back to the water bottle. He watched her don a pair of clear latex gloves and open the container. He watched her face as she looked inside, then shook the contents out into her hand. A draping fern frond, bright and green; a dirty rock that was less than half the size of baseball; a marble-size golden stone; a wilted leaf; and a single yellow flower—one of the multitudes of arrowleaf balsamroot blossoms that covered every sunlit spot of dirt in this high mountain country. That was it. No written note, no SD or SIM card, no flash drive. Just five common items that were picked up off the trail.

Her face was impassive as she interpreted the collection in a clinical tone. "The fern tells me he left this yesterday morning—it was our code. See the prongs on the left side? There are seven, and on the right side three have been torn away, so seven-three: July 3rd. It was always a bracken fern for the morning drop." She drew a long breath before she continued. "If it had been afternoon, it would've been a lady fern. The small yellowish stone tells me the shipment was headed to Yellowstone Park. The leaf tells me it's bound for Canada. No small stone or leaf would have meant the destination was undetermined. The size of the second rock is medium, so the shipment is under fifty weapons and over twenty-five."

Win frowned down at the items. "How in the world would anyone know that? Everything you've just told me is totally subjective."

"It's a code we worked out, ah . . . it's subjective on purpose. It's about as low-tech as it comes, but it works. If you found this water bottle, what would you think?"

"That someone had been fooling around with a discarded water bottle, putting random stuff in it, screwing around with the plants and rocks on the trail. Probably kids bored to death on an outing in the woods."

"Yeah, that's why we used this code. No one would guess, so only we would know." She was staring down at the bottle's contents, all neatly laid out on the top of the boulder. He noticed that her face was pinched and pale; he noticed that she wasn't scanning the trail any longer, she wasn't looking for anyone anymore.

"Who is *we*? And what does the flower mean?" he asked. But as he watched her fight to contain her emotions, saw her bite her lip to maintain control, he knew the answer to those questions. He wasn't surprised when she didn't answer, when she busied herself replacing the items, putting the canister in a clear evidence bag in her backpack, stuffing the gloves in her pocket. She did those things quickly and moved out of the rocks, back down the trail that led to the waterfall. Movement caught his eye and the little furball, which he knew was a pika and not a tribble, bit off a blade of grass and began chewing, seemingly pleased that one interloper had gone. As Win started to rise, he saw the discarded yellow flower lying below the big rock where Alex had sat. He gently picked it up, wrapped it in his bandana, and put it in his pocket.

* * *

He didn't really talk to Alex the rest of the morning. He followed her along the trail toward the thundering waterfall that was less than a hundred yards beyond the rockslide. The faded brown sign said *Hidden Falls on Cascade Creek*, but he couldn't figure out where they'd come up with that name. The waterfall wasn't the least bit concealed—the sucker dropped a hundred feet from the mouth of Cascade Canyon in sharp layers down to the spot where he stood. The power of the water sent spray and mist floating through the air, forming prisms of vibrant red, yellow, green, blue, and violet that danced within the walls of falling water. It was mesmerizing—a sight to behold. You could hear its roar for a good quarter mile. There wasn't anything hidden about it, but there were several secluded vantage points where folks were sitting and taking in its wonder. Alex Lindell was sitting in one of those spots, on a moss-covered rock under a mist-drenched Engelmann spruce. She seemed to be watching the falls; he couldn't see her face clearly, but he reckoned there was pain and sadness etched there. He had enough sense not to join her.

After fifteen minutes she stood and acknowledged him with a lift of her chin. She motioned with her hand back down the trail the same way they'd come. He followed from behind, same as before. They caught the shuttle boat, and this time he chose a seat under the awning that kept him out of the cold spray. He saw her look back once at the canyon, at the high point that the boatman had referred to as Inspiration Point.

It was the first time he'd really focused on her features. Her hair was very dark brown, but not quite black, and although she now had it pulled back tight, it likely fell well below her shoulders. Her tan face held the potential for roundness, but tension had pulled her skin taut. She had a wide forehead, and her dark, watchful eyes were framed by black brows. Her lips were tight and thin, and again suggested too much stress, too little laughter. It was a face that seemed to have aged beyond the thirty-four years he'd garnered from the Canadian police credentials she'd shown him earlier. It was a face that told him Alexandria Lea Lindell had hit some rough spots in her life. He knew she was smack-dab in the middle of another one.

CHAPTER FOUR

He'd just pulled into the parking lot at Moose next to the large sign that said *National Park Service* when his personal phone buzzed. He answered it on the second ring, thinking it might be Tucker or one of his brothers, but that wasn't it.

"Hey, Win, it's Trey. Hate to bother you on your vacation, but you got a minute?"

"No problem. Sure." Win noticed the words *Unknown Caller* on his phone, the ranger's clipped tone. This wasn't just a call between friends to catch up.

"It looks like we've had a poaching incident in the park. Big-time poaching based on what I'm hearing. There's nobody covering the FBI office. Agent Johnson is in Denver for at least two weeks according to his voicemail. When are you gonna be back?"

"Tell me what you've got." Win stifled a sigh as he listened to Trey Hechtner, Yellowstone National Park's Mammoth District Ranger, give a concise report of a dead bison bull that had been spotted yesterday morning by backcountry hikers on Specimen Ridge. Win could tell Trey was angry, maybe even a bit shaken. Win hadn't been in Yellowstone long, and he'd had no experience with wildlife violations. But he did know that normally those violations were carried out by small-time opportunists, someone trying to fill their freezer with deer or elk meat. He also knew those infractions were generally handled by the Park Service law enforcement rangers—no need to get the FBI involved. As he listened to Trey's brief report, Win refocused on those words: *big-time poaching.* He sighed. *Yep, my vacation is fixin' to get even shorter.*

Win was guessing that Trey was calling from someone's office at the National Park Service's HQ in Mammoth Hot Springs. He was also guessing that one of Trey's bosses was standing nearby. Trey was all business. Win ran through his schedule. "I'm putting my brothers on a flight back home outa Jackson Hole right after noon tomorrow. I was planning to take a couple more days of leave with a friend down here, but my supervisor has pulled me into a case today—we should have more boots on the ground this afternoon, and I figure they'll cut me loose on this deal. Unless nothing changes, I can be back in Mammoth by tomorrow afternoon, early Tuesday at the latest."

"I hate to ask you to cut your leave short."

"No problem," Win replied. "I'll make it work."

"All right. I'll take the helo up there today and do the preliminary incident investigation. Do I have your approval on that?" Trey didn't even pause. "If that's okay with you, I'll touch base with you tonight. Does that work?"

"Sounds good. Go check it out and I'll wait to hear from you." Win closed out the call and wondered what all the formality was about—that wasn't normally Trey's style. He pocketed the phone and stared out the windshield. *Whatever it is, it ain't good.*

*   *   *

He sat in his vehicle in the Grand Teton National Park headquarters parking lot, downed a coke, and ate a protein bar for lunch as he waited for the FBI contingent to arrive. He'd responded to several texts from Blake and Tucker—the morning's wildlife-watching trip had been a success, and the guys had eaten an early lunch at the Jackson Lake Lodge's diner. Blake had left a voicemail saying that the morning had been amazing, both the animals and the lodge, but he'd also said that Will had slipped back into his funk as soon as they'd returned to civilization and had cell and Wi-Fi connections. Win sent his regrets that he was missing the fun and fought down a stab of guilt. He knew he should be out there with Will, encouraging him, being the big brother he sensed the boy badly needed. Instead he was working. Hadn't this been the same pattern that contributed to the breakup with Shelby? *Yes.* Hadn't he promised himself he'd end his workaholic tendencies? *Yes.* Had it happened? *No.*

He frowned at his phone and sighed as he turned his attention to an unexpected text from Tory. He knew she'd been in Jackson at a seminar on wildlife conservation the last two days and that her college friend, Lauren, was joining her there today. He knew his pulse went up a few notches whenever he saw Tory's name on his phone. He also knew both girls planned to be at Tucker's tonight. What he hadn't known was that the girls were hoping he could meet them in downtown Jackson at one o'clock and hit the numerous art galleries for an hour before they set off for an afternoon of Fourth of July shopping. The text said they'd hang around one of the antler archways at the downtown square to see if he could break free and come. He glanced at his watch: ten till one. He saw his supervisor's SUV pull into the lot. He breathed another deep sigh as he texted back. **Can't make it, work meeting. Have fun. Looking forward to tonight.** *Lordy, I hope I'll make it tonight.*

Supervisory Special Agent Jim West and another man were getting out of the SUV in the crowded parking lot. Win's supervisor ran his hand through his short brownish-blond hair as he leaned back on the GMC Yukon. Jim was about Tucker's height, barely five feet ten. He was in his mid-forties, and he normally wore a pleasant expression. Not today. Today he looked stressed.

Jim waved Win over as the other man came around their vehicle. The guy Win didn't recognize looked young, maybe not even Win's age. His reddish-brown hair was longer than Win usually saw on a street agent, and he seemed nervous—he kept fooling with his sunglasses. He wasn't any taller than Jim, and he had a pale, soft look about him, as if he never ventured outside. Probably a computer guy, Win thought.

"I brought Kirk Hampton with me, but we're shorthanded in Lander. Sure appreciate you helping out, Win . . . sorry to pull you in on this." Jim's tone was subdued, his face strained.

"Not a problem, Boss," Win said as he nodded and shook hands with the other agent, taking in their crisp suits and ties. He wished he'd had time to get back to Miss Martha's place and shower; after half the morning at the wreck site, he knew he looked like a mess.

"Whata you got from this morning?" Jim asked.

"I wasn't expecting Alex Lindell to be a Mountie."

"Yeah, I didn't have a heads-up on that last night—or on much else in this deal." Win could hear the edge in Jim's voice. "ATF has been playing this one close to the vest. No issue with that as long as it's *their* case in *their* jurisdiction, but the national parks are *our* jurisdiction, and we should have been in the loop long before now. If we'd known ATF was running an operation through here, we might have been able to prevent two deaths."

"Do we know who the victims are?" Win asked.

"This is preliminary, but it's lookin' like one was Trent Beckett, an undercover agent with ATF. Beckett has a real good reputation . . . a wife and two kids. The second guy was an informant Beckett was working with—mostly in northern Utah, up into Idaho and western Montana, I think. Alex Lindell was the handler for the informant, has been for several months. We think he was Canadian, but the Mounties are keeping that intel to themselves." Jim frowned down at his shoes. "I saw Constable Lindell at the autopsy about an hour ago, met her then. She identified a few personal effects of the informant that the fire didn't get." He met Win's eyes again. "The fire got most everything."

Whoa, glad I wasn't called in for that. . . . And that explained where Alex went after she suddenly left the wreck site nearly three hours earlier.

Jim kept talking. "Your thoughts on those six .45 caliber casings near the wreck were correct. The coroner's initial results show both passengers in that vehicle were hit, they each took at least two .45 caliber slugs in head shots." Jim's jaw tightened, and he paused as he forced his emotions down. "It's lookin' like the pursuit vehicle caused the wreck, stopped, and someone popped our guys just to make a statement. The wreck may have killed them."

He paused again. "Then there's the fire . . . evidence is still out on that, but ERT is thinkin' the shooters used an accelerant or something like a flare gun to set it off. Maybe they were carrying packaged gunpowder in the vehicle—we're not sure why it burned so hot. Results are still coming in, we should get more of an update in the briefing."

More vehicles were pulling into the lot. Holiday or not, it was starting to look like all hands on deck. Jim glanced at the newcomers, then looked back at Win. "You and Constable Lindell went back to the site this morning?"

"Yes, sir, we checked out a drop site on the west side of Jenny Lake early, then got to the incident site around 9:30. ATF's Evidence Response Team was just getting there. The Park Service kept the site secure all night. ATF had a bunch of folks out there, they were starting a grid search for more casings near the wreckage. They were gonna work the two miles up that dirt-and-gravel road, all the way back to Teton Park Road. There was a transport truck on-site, so I assume they'll be bringing what's left of the vehicle back to Jackson."

"Yeah, the Teton County Sheriff's Office has an impound lot and shop they'll be using." Jim started moving toward the doors. "Anything new jump out at you while you were out there?"

"Yes, sir, the whole thing just seems off. A vehicle pursuit in the middle of the morning, in the height of tourist season, in one of the busiest parks in the country? It's not like they were quiet about it either. Over twenty shots fired from a rifle, six .45 caliber, then Lord only knows how many rounds went off in the fire. And on a rough, one-lane dirt-and-gravel road? The rangers told me there is hardly ever any traffic on that road, just an occasional wildlife watcher. The road used to go to a couple of dude ranches in the area and had access to the river, but those features are long gone. There are easier spots for an ambush . . . if that's what this was."

"How far off the paved road, uh, how far off Teton Park Road is the incident site?" Jim asked.

"About two miles. Teton Park Road leaves U.S. Highway 89 here at Moose, then goes past the Jenny Lake and Jackson Lake areas for twenty miles before it junctions with Highway 89 again just north of

Jackson Lake. Two of the park's main lodges are on that road—Signal Mountain Lodge is only four miles as the crow flies from the wreck site. There are two scenic turnouts on the paved road within two miles of the incident site. I sat in one of those on Teton Park Road this morning just before 9:30—about the same time as yesterday's incident. There was a steady stream of traffic on the paved road, and lots of cars in the turnouts. If we put out the word with the tourists, we could probably pick up photos of the vehicles, maybe even more videos of the pursuit. There were lots of folks on that highway. Somebody saw something."

Jim stopped at the door of the building to let the other agent enter. He turned back to Win. "I'll get with the Denver office and see what they want to do on putting the word out in the press. You need to get back on your leave. . . . I want you to take off early today. Why don't you sit in on the briefing for the highlights, then bug out and check in with some of the businesses in Jackson. No one knows the when and where of Agent Beckett's comings and goings when he got to this area."

"Yes, sir. I appreciate the time off."

Jim wrapped it up. "Constable Lindell said she'd hadn't talked with her informant since last Thursday evening. She said she'd report on some limited intel she picked up from the drop site this morning— she'll cover everything in the briefing."

Win nodded and held the glass door open for his boss to enter. *Nope, she won't cover everything. No way that she can.*

*   *   *

Win followed Jim into the Park Service's conference room and took in the cramped space with one practiced sweep. The building was modern, but the meeting space was utilitarian at best: mismatched metal chairs, long plastic tables that had seen years of wear, whiteboards and posters stacked in one corner of the drab room. The buzzing of fluorescent lights competed with the groaning of a lazy overhead fan. Two law enforcement park rangers were lounging near the open windows, trying to catch a breeze. The sounds of traffic on the park's busy road were floating in. A box fan in the corner was cranking away, but it was still stifling in the room. Win was constantly amazed that this part of the country had little to no air-conditioning.

Three somber guys in blue ATF T-shirts were huddled in the far corner, drinking coffee out of Styrofoam cups. They all glanced toward the FBI group when they entered. A woman in a bright floral dress was sitting in a plastic chair, intent on her phone. Win was guessing she was with the coroner's office. Jim and Kirk moved toward the huddle of men; Win moved toward the only other person in sight. Alex Lindell was leaning against the wall on the far side of the room, holding a stack of papers. She had that look in her eyes. He'd been fortunate enough in his young life to have seen that look only a few other times—a thousand-yard stare, he'd heard it called. Another human being's retreat deep into themselves when the trauma was too great to face. He tamped down his emotions and walked her way, then stopped a few feet from her and waited for her to acknowledge him. To nod or to speak. She did neither. He moved toward her slowly, as he might with a wounded animal. Tentative, cautious.

"My supervisor told me who . . . uh, I'm sorry," he began.

Her focus snapped back. "About what? What are you sorry about?" came the sharp reply.

He mentally pulled back at the unexpected question. *What am I sorry about?* That list could get a little lengthy given his current situation, so he figured he'd just address the matter at hand.

"I'm sorry about Trent Beckett's death . . . and about your informant's death. I don't know his name. Sorry you had to be involved in the autopsy, to see that." Win was standing above her now, towering over her. He expected her to lower her eyes, to shrug, maybe shed a tear . . . some acknowledgment of her loss. But she didn't. Her face was impassive.

In an instant she was all business. "They were under deep cover, and we've had no phone or in-person contact from either of them since Thursday at 11:00 p.m. My informant used our drop site early yesterday morning, before the pursuit . . . before the incident, so they were likely in this area overnight. We'll need to backtrack—find out where they were, find out who was onto them, who they were meeting."

Win nodded as she handed him a copy of a black-and-white surveillance photo from the stack she was holding. "Last photo we have of
them together with the vehicle on July 1st in Provo, Utah. We need to
get this out, run something down."

He nodded again and turned away. Several more folks had entered
the room, and it was now crowded. A couple in cowboy hats looked
to be Sheriff's office or local police, the ERT leader arrived still wearing his ash-covered utility vest, and a middle-aged woman in a park
ranger uniform closed the door. Jim West and another man moved
to the front of the room. Win figured the meeting would be heated
and intense—ATF had lost one of their guys. He also figured it would
be contentious and frustrating—the Bureau and ATF would fight for
jurisdictional control, the Park Service would be sidelined, the locals
would be ignored. He was right about all of that, and after eighteen
minutes he slipped out of the oppressive room and began the real work
of tracking down the killers.

* * *

Win pulled into an open parking space at Jackson's two-story Frontier
Inn. It was an old-style motel where all the rooms faced the parking
lot and exterior stairs led to the second floor. The young man at the
desk didn't bat an eye when Win showed him his Bureau credentials
and asked for Donnie Sawyer's room number. The clerk said he'd seen
the family's truck pull into the lot just after two. Win was stopping by
on a whim, he hadn't called ahead, but he had nearly two hours to kill
before he had to meet Tucker and the guys at Miss Martha's house. He
knew there weren't that many inexpensive places to stay in Jackson; he
figured it was worth a shot.

He climbed the metal stairs to the second level, moved down the
open walkway, and knocked on the bright-blue door. The paint was
beginning to peel and the metal room number was slightly off-center;
he wondered how many years this vintage place had welcomed guests
to this mostly upscale tourist town. He knocked on the door a second

time and waited. He could hear children yelling from the small swimming pool at the end of the parking lot.

The old motel reminded him of places his family had stayed on
those rare vacations during his childhood. They hadn't had the money
or the time to get away from the farm often—the zoo and a Cardinals
game in St. Louis, the Mid-South Fair in Memphis, Razorback games
in Little Rock, Silver Dollar City in Branson—his mind continued to
add up the infrequent trips as he waited. He'd just raised his hand to
knock again when the door swung wide open and he was face-to-face
with Deputy Sawyer and his considerable bulk. The guy was wearing a
huge white T-shirt and blue running pants with flip-flops. His hair was
disheveled, and his eyes were squinted tight. He looked like he'd just
crawled out of bed.

"Sorry to bother you, Deputy. . . . I'm Win—"

"I remember who you are. Do y'all need my statement on the
wreck?"

Okay, right to the point. "Yes, sir, that needs to be given at the
National Park Service Headquarters in Moose. That's thirteen miles
north of town, just west of Highway 191/89. They'd like it today if
possible." Win held out a card with the Park Service address on it. "It
shouldn't take long; you can ask for whoever is handling the incident.
I'm not sure who's running the case on their end."

"On their end?" The guy scoffed, accepted the card, then wiped
a hand across his ruddy face. "You didn't stop by to bring me a card.
There's more to that car crash. What's goin' on?"

Win paused. *This guy is sharp.*

Just as he started to answer, a convoy of kids came clamoring up
the stairs toward the rooms, pool floaties, diving masks, and wet tow-
els in tow. The woman he'd seen by the river was shepherding them
forward. "Not so loud, Dad's trying to sleep. Hold it down, please," she
was quietly pleading to no avail. Two little girls began banging on the
door to the next room, and an older boy, who looked to be nine or ten,
tried to squeeze past his father. The deputy reached down and stopped
the kid's forward momentum with a hand on his head; he ruffled the
boy's hair as he asked, "Have fun?"

"You bet!"

"Alright, go get in the shower."

"Yes, sir!"

Win stepped away to avoid being clocked by a pool float. The woman gave him an apologetic smile, then suddenly recognized him. "Oh, you were at that awful wreck. Did they find out what happened, who it was? We've been praying for them and their families." She never even paused. "There was barely a mention of it in the news last night. Two victims was all they said. Donnie was thinking something wasn't right."

There were all sorts of things about the car chase that *wasn't right*, but Win couldn't tell her any of them since a case had now been opened. He touched the brim of his hat and nodded down to her. "Can't say yet, ma'am, but prayers are always helpful."

The deputy moved to the walkway as she entered the room. The woman turned back to Win before the door closed. She nodded and spoke softly. "I understand, you can't talk about it. Be careful out there." The words sounded just like his mother.

The girls next door had finally gotten someone's attention, and that door opened wide enough for them to enter. He and Deputy Sawyer were alone.

Win pulled the surveillance photo out of his jacket pocket and handed it to Sawyer. The man studied it for only a few seconds.

"Yeah, they were staying here—same vehicle. Different plates. I noticed them come in night before last, right 'bout the same time we got here. That would've been nearly ten, just gettin' dark. We were hauling our stuff in, they were too. Same two men as in the photo, last room on the end down below. Is this the vehicle that exploded?" he asked as he handed the photo back.

"Maybe. Notice anything else?"

"Me and my boy were gettin' the bags outa the truck, and they were carrying a long metal box into their room. Looked like it had come outa their SUV. From the way they were lifting it, it was heavy."

"You thought that was unusual?"

He narrowed his eyes and looked up at Win. "I've been with the Chattooga County Sheriff's Office since I got outa high school, goin' on twenty-three years now. I think I know the difference between usual and unusual."

That was exactly what Win was counting on. An old-timer in law enforcement who would consider most anything suspicious and might just check it out.

The guy shrugged and leaned against the metal walkway railing. He finished his thought. "They had that look 'bout 'em: watchful, cagey, in a hurry. The box looked to be aluminum, handles on both ends and top, maybe three by six. Like I said, they were carryin' it like it was heavy."

"Anything else?"

"Well, I started to walk down and get their plates, have someone back home run 'em for me. But I told myself I was here on vacation. That I was here to get away from all that. First vacation since . . . uh, first vacation in a long time. Not my problem. That's what I told myself."

"But you ran the plates anyway," Win said and hoped it was true.

The portly man gave a rueful smile. "Plates were reported stolen outa Provo, Utah, on Thursday, July 1st. Utah plates, one of them *In God We Trust* slogans, N259R. I was gonna call the local cops that night, but those guys left before we turned in and the vehicle wasn't here when we headed out to go on our Snake River raft ride early the next morning. Never saw the men except that one time. Figured they was up to no good and they'd moved on."

Win nodded. *Yeah, they moved on . . .*

"You gonna quiz the clerk, check for any cameras, surveillance video?" the deputy asked.

"Yeah, I'll work on all that, but I noticed that they don't even have cameras in the motel's reception area; they seem to be big into privacy in this town." He shrugged with his eyes. "I wasn't even sure these guys had stayed here until I met with you just now." Win looked back down at the photo. He figured Sawyer knew he was staring at dead men. "What do you think they were up to?"

The deputy studied him for several seconds. "Not used to the Feds being interested in what I think."

"Well, I am."

"Alright. Heavy aluminum box in their vehicle . . . stolen license plates, sketchy men at a cheap motel. Then there was them rounds going off in the fire—lots of rounds. If that inferno was the same vehicle that was at the motel, and I'm betting it was or you wouldn't be standing here, then that adds up to big-time theft, drugs, or gunrunnin'. I'd put my money on gunrunnin'." He paused again. "Or it could be me just jumpin' to conclusions . . . makin' something outa nothing."

One of the little girls stuck her head out of the door down the walkway. "Uncle Donnie! You gotta get dressed!" she pleaded. "We're gonna go eat pizza!"

"Be just a minute, sister," Sawyer called to her with a wave.

Win smiled toward the pouting child and lowered his voice when he spoke. "You've seen a lot of gunrunning?"

"It's becoming a real problem along the East Coast—Georgia state troopers are pickin' up cases of stolen or illegal guns at traffic stops. Either movin' north into those gun-control cities and states up I-75 or I-95, or goin' west toward Mexico along Interstate 20 to the drug cartels. We got good ole boys in Georgia makin' hundreds of thousands of dollars just buyin' guns up at gun shows, filing off the serial numbers, and reselling them to black market gunrunners." Sawyer waved at the persistent child again, then turned back to Win. "Thugs gravitate toward the money, and there's a boatload of money in illegal guns right now . . . is that what this is?"

The girl gave up and slammed the door. Win nodded. "It's likely, but it's early on. We'll see where the evidence leads. You see anything else? Anyone watching them?" The deputy shook his head and Win moved to shake hands with him. "I appreciate your help. I'm sorry that I've had to interrupt your time off."

"As I recall, you told us you were on vacation too," Sawyer said as they shook hands.

"Yeah, I'm taking some annual leave here in Jackson."

The deputy gave him an understanding nod as he turned toward the door. "Uh-huh, and how's that workin' out for you?"

CHAPTER FIVE

Whoa. . . . That was his first reaction when he saw her step through the tall glass doors above the flagstone patio. She paused there and took in the stunning view. Tory Madison was wearing a soft-blue sundress; her brunette hair was swept up on her head in a loose bun . . . he didn't know what to call it, but it looked great. The hairstyle accentuated her neck and made her look even taller than her five-eight height. Wisps of dark hair framed her face, and her gold drop earrings gleamed in the fading sunlight. She had a dark-blue sweater draped over an arm and sunglasses in one hand. She said something to José, then she turned and saw him. She smiled that beautiful smile and he felt his breath catch in his throat. This woman enchanted him. He blinked to try to clear his mind as he waved to her. All he could think of was how lovely she was, how special she was. *She is totally amazing.*

Lauren, Tory's college friend from Vanderbilt, almost skipped down the flagstone steps with her hand on José's arm. She called out, "Hey, Win!" and snapped him out of his trance. He didn't know Lauren well—heck, he didn't even know Tory well—but he was thinking that the two girls were a lot like he and Tucker were, opposites in so many ways. Their wavy chestnut-colored hair was the only physical similarity. Tory was the tall, strikingly attractive one; she was quieter and more reserved than her friend. And Win knew Tory was a planner, organized and methodical. Lauren was very different. She was barely five feet tall, even in the platform sandals she was wearing. She was petite and cute, and her yellow sundress highlighted her dark tan. Win had been around her enough to know that she was fearlessly loyal to her friend, that she was extremely talented as an artist, and that she had an engaging spontaneity. He figured she could be the life of the party.

José was leading them down the steps toward the smoking grill, the shimmering infinity pool, and the upscale outdoor dining area. Win introduced Tucker and his brothers as José went to get drinks for the girls. He hadn't seen Tory except for a couple of brief lunch dates in the last two weeks; this was their first real date in what seemed like ages. He wanted it to be special. As soon as she touched his hand and spoke to him, he knew it would be.

Tucker had given most of the staff the afternoon and evening off, and he was solely in command of a stainless steel grill that could have held an entire hog. Win helped him with the chopped pork and ribs. It felt good to slip into this role. He wondered if it was just a Southern thing: the men did the barbecue, the women never touched the uncooked meat. As he turned another slab of ribs, he thought that it all seemed a bit sexist, but Lauren and Tory didn't seem to mind. The girls were cutting up the watermelon that Tucker's aunt had flown in from Smith County, Mississippi. Win figured it wouldn't top the Hope or Cave City melons that he'd grown up with in Arkansas, but he knew it'd be close. People took their watermelon seriously where he came from.

Win helped Tucker turn the roasted corn on the cob, listening as the girls filled Blake and Will in on their adventures in Yellowstone's wilds. The second phase of Tory's internship with the Interagency Grizzly Bear Research Project was fixing to begin. She said she'd be deep in Yellowstone's backcountry for most of the month of July. Lauren mentioned that she'd been invited to stay in Jackson for a few weeks. One of the town's art galleries wanted to sponsor her current project sketching Northern Rocky Mountain songbirds; she said she was considering it. The girls talked about their shopping trip in town that afternoon. Tory said she hadn't thought she'd need dressy clothes during her weeks in the Yellowstone wilderness or during her days of

sitting through wildlife seminars and workshops. Win started to mention how incredible her long legs looked in that dress, but he thought
better of it and just told her she looked lovely. He was thinking she
could wear a tow sack and still be pretty.

The meal was fantastic, and afterward they sat beside the pool and
watched the sun set behind the mountains. Will had been on his best
behavior all evening and had even managed to stay off his phone a
good deal of the time. He was good-natured enough to take on the job
of adding the rock salt and ice and hand-churning the ice cream. He'd
pointed out that "normal people" had electric ice cream churns, he'd
groused just a little about how old-school everyone suddenly became
on holidays, but he'd said it with a smile. The homemade peach ice
cream was a perfect finish to the wonderful dinner.

It was nearly ten when they walked out of the massive front door
and across the circular drive to a sitting area on the opposite side of
the ridge overlooking Jackson. The town's Independence Day fireworks
show would start as soon as dark fully descended. The streetlights and
neon signs were already twinkling in the valley far below them. Tucker
was handing out cashmere throws to the girls to keep the cold breeze at
bay. Win eased behind Tory and gently sat his chin on her soft hair—it
smelled like flowers. He stood close to her and wrapped the soft throw
tighter around her. She squeezed his hand just as the first booming
rockets streaked high into the night and burst into dazzling streams
of red, white, and blue. As the flickering ribbons of colored light softly
fluttered from the sky, Will, Blake, and Tucker whooped it up. Lauren
clapped as more rockets shot upward.

"What a great start!" Tory exclaimed. "I love fireworks!"

Win pulled her closer to him and smiled as he looked into the sparkling sky. It was a promising start for what Win Tyler hoped would lead
to a different kind of fireworks.

* * *

It was early and he'd just finished a five-mile run. The others had put
in a moderately paced three miles—couldn't get too aggressive given

the altitude. Jackson was at 6,237 feet, and Miss Martha's house sat
about 700 feet higher than the town. Win had experience with altitude
sickness; he wouldn't wish that on anyone. Will had already gone into
the house for a shower, and Blake was standing near the steps to the
infinity pool on a FaceTime call with his wife, Rachel.

The steam was rising from the heated pool and obscuring the
lower slopes of the mountains. The rising sun was beginning to hit the
higher peaks square on, and again Win had the sensation that he could
reach out and touch the mountains. He leaned back in the cushioned
lounge chair, sipped his coffee, and marveled that anything could be
that beautiful. Well, Tory was that beautiful, he mused with a sigh.
And Tory had dropped some things on him last night that were a little
too heavy to be dealt with at 5:25 a.m. He sighed again.

Tucker arrived with his coffee and sat down in the swivel chair
beside him. "I know that sigh. Didn't go well?"

Win wiped a hand across his sweaty brow and glanced at him.
Tucker knew him better than most anyone—Tucker would sniff it out.
There wasn't any point in fudging. "Most of the night was perfect. You
couldn't have done better with the cookout . . . the town's Fourth of July
fireworks were great. But after that. . . ." He paused, then took another
sip of the coffee. "After that it coulda gone better. She called me out for
not being over Shelby, on her being my rebound, on not making her a
priority."

Tucker was direct. "Did she end it?"

Win took another slow slip of his coffee before he answered. "No
. . . no, but maybe I should. Maybe she's right, and if that's so, it isn't fair
to her." He said the words matter of fact. No one could hear the pain
he felt upon saying his thoughts out loud. Well, no one except Tucker.

"Hmmm. . . ." Tucker sat there drinking his coffee. He drummed
his fingers on the arm of the chair; Win knew he was thinking of something serious whenever he did that. "You can't expect to quickly be over
someone you spent most every free hour with the last several years. But
Win, I was there much of the time you dated Shelby—it was clear to
me that y'all were falling apart over a year ago. You were livin' together

. . . just hanging on to the comfortable, I get that. But man, in so many ways you'd both moved on."

Tucker shifted in the chair and tried to meet Win's eyes. "I also get that it doesn't make the pain of the breakup any less." Win looked away, but Tucker kept talking. "Hearing you talk about Tory these last few weeks, then seeing y'all together last night, it's clear that you're falling for her. I'm thinkin' that may be scaring you some. You got hurt bad—real bad. Maybe you're subconsciously pulling back, maybe Tory sensed that last night."

Win still didn't meet Tucker's eyes. "When did you get so introspective?"

Tucker drew a deep breath. "It probably wouldn't hurt either one of us to aim for a little more depth in our relationships. We aren't getting any younger, as Aunt Martha pointed out to me at least ten times during the last few days. Maybe you oughta think about how to make Tory feel special, feel cherished, to keep moving things along slowly."

Blake was coming toward them, and Tucker rose from the chair. He gave Win one last parting bit of advice. "Don't you always tell me to pray about it and trust? Well, I'd be doing that if I was you. Tory seems really special, I don't think you want to lose her." He pulled his running jacket off and stood there. "Oh, and I'm gonna ask Lauren out."

Win blinked up at him in surprise. "You're kidding?"

"Nope. I had a good time with her last night . . . not that you noticed, since you couldn't get your eyes off Tory." He shrugged. "She seemed interested in me. *In me.* Not in these things." His free hand moved across the beautiful pool, the expansive glass windows of the multimillion-dollar house, the world-class view.

Tucker stared off into the distance for another moment. Win could barely hear him when he spoke again. "You may not get it . . . you've always had the looks, the smarts, the confidence. I just have things . . . and things are never enough."

* * *

He wiped the sleep from his eyes and stared across the dark room at his sleeping partner. The guy's snores had awakened him, and he was ticked. First chance to sleep a solid eight hours in weeks and that fool was sawing logs at 5:25 a.m. He rolled over and stretched as he ran a hand over his face. *Dammit.* Once he was awake, there was no use trying to drift off again.

They'd lucked out and snagged a cancellation on a room with two queen beds at the Signal Mountain Lodge on Jackson Lake. They'd decided that laying low right under the cops' noses was the best play. He figured they were less than five miles from where they'd run their competition off the road; couldn't be any more under the cops' noses than this national park lodge. It was one of the most economical accommodations in Grand Teton, but it still wasn't cheap. Roadie had groused about splitting the $400 for the room and the $275 to rent a boat for a day of fishing. He frowned up at the ceiling as he tried to give the kid the benefit of the doubt. Roadie was young and new at this; he wasn't thinking it through. These small incidental expenses were just the cost of doing business. They had lifted maybe $30,000 in handguns from the losers they'd taken out yesterday. The goal now was to disappear for a while and let the dust settle so they could move the new additions to their inventory. Their goal now was to not get caught being stupid. He was a little concerned that Roadie had a tendency to be stupid.

The boss had swung the black pickup around and driven north to Yellowstone with their newly acquired guns as soon as he'd dropped them off in the lodge's parking lot just after ten yesterday morning. He and Roadie had switched to different caps and jackets, secured a room, rented a small fishing boat, bought some bait, and gone out on Jackson Lake for six hours of fishing. It had actually been fun.

Early on they'd heard sirens. The wail of sirens was uncommon here, and on one run back to the dock, he'd introduced himself and asked a ranger what was going on. The ranger said there'd been a bad vehicle accident down south of Signal Mountain Road, down a dirt road near the Snake River. She'd heard there were fatalities. He'd shaken his head at the sad news and remarked that folks needed to be more careful in the park, he'd said it was such a shame, that bad things can happen anywhere. Then he'd gone into the dock's small office, where he knew they had a surveillance camera, and bought another couple of energy drinks and a candy bar.

They'd caught a boatload of lake and cutthroat trout, most of which they'd released back into the cold waters. They'd motored in for lunch on the dock, and they'd offered their first batch of three-to-five-pound fish to other fishermen to get them off their hands. All morning they'd taken phone photos of the beautiful lake with its backdrop of vertical peaks, of their catch, of bald eagles and osprey on patrol, of other fishermen—those date and time stamps on the pictures could come in handy. They'd visited with boaters at the dock, talked with several of the employees there, built themselves as much of an alibi as possible. *Just down this way, fishing this lake, just takin' a couple of days off.* That could work. But again, the key was to not get to the point of needing an alibi, to not get to the point of someone asking questions. He yawned and stretched again. *That is the point.*

His eyes flicked to the only light in the room—the single green orb on the smoke detector that was screwed into the old wood-paneled wall. He heard groaning in the pipes from the bathroom and figured someone next door was up and about. People didn't come out here to sleep in, they came here to gasp at the jaw-dropping scenery, see the fascinating wildlife, and check out of their day-to-day routines. He heard the thump of old wooden coat hangers banging against the wall of the closet in the next room. That would've woke him up if Roadie's snoring hadn't. *I'll bet nicer hotels don't have that damn "hangers knocking on the adjoining room's wall" issue,* he thought. But since he'd never stayed in a really nice hotel, he wouldn't know. He heard the door close on the adjoining room and footsteps moving down the hall. At least their neighbor hadn't slammed his door.

He realized that there was a shaft of dim light beginning to peek through the thin gap in the curtains. He heard the man in the next bed rustling; he was waking up. "You awake?" he asked into the near darkness.

"Uh . . . uh . . . what time is it?"

He heard Roadie shift in the bed.

"It's almost 5:30. Let's get on up and get over to the buffet for breakfast . . . they open at six. The guy at the dock said they had a real good breakfast here."

"Okay," was the weak answer, but Roadie didn't move.

"The light will be hittin' the mountains soon, it should really be pretty. On the drive back we oughta see lots of animals . . . they have nice elk and some big bears down this way." He tried to sound encouraging.

"I had awful dreams about the . . . uh . . . about the fire . . . the thugs we killed," the younger man said.

His answer was hard. "They killed themselves messin' with us, messin' in our business. It's done. Get over it." He paused. "If you hadn't drunk half a fifth of whiskey last night, you woulda slept like a log. Drinking, drugs, they ain't smart moves when you need your wits about you, when you're in the middle of a job. It's the same reason we use street names, have separate roles, use burner phones and codes . . . it's part of the job."

Roadie made no response.

"I told you not to drink, you gotta be smarter than that."

"The job was over" was the feeble answer.

"Like hell it was, the job ain't over till you're totally in the clear, till you get the payout, till you've moved on to the next job. We ain't anywhere near that point yet. You better keep it together." He knew his voice carried a threat, and he softened his tone as he continued talking. "Hey, you get in the shower first—no TV, so it's not like we can watch the *Today* show. I'll pack up. You'll feel better once you're movin' . . . once you eat."

He saw the dark form of the guy swing his legs off the bed and sit up.

"Is this normal? You've done this before. Is it normal, me feelin' bad about it and all?"

"You've got a hangover—"

"No . . . no, this is different, this is about those men that were killed."

He tried to sound reassuring. "Yeah, yeah . . . everyone feels bad about hurtin' another person—about killing—even when it can't be helped. Everyone feels something."

Except I never do, he thought as his hand found the Colt 1911 he kept under the other pillow. He smelled the faint scent of Hoppe's Gun Oil; he'd cleaned the weapon last night. The touch of the hard waffled grip and warm metal was oddly comforting. *Wonder why I never feel nothing?*

* * *

"You're suddenly so good with this touchy-feely stuff, why don't you tell me what to do about Will other than just wait it out." Win was fuming. He'd finished packing and joined Tucker in the walnut-paneled den. He'd just had the third confrontation with his little brother since their very-early-morning run. The last exchange had been loud enough for the entire household to hear. Win was starting to count down the minutes till he dropped him off at the airport.

José walked through the room and handed Tucker the mail. The small man paused at the doorway to the Western-themed room. "Mr. Tucker, I'm putting out an early lunch since they don't feed anyone on airplanes anymore." He started to leave the room, but he hesitated by the door and turned back. "I don't mean to interfere, Mr. Win, but that young one, *tu hermano pequeño*—your little brother. He is troubled . . . is not good. He is disrespectful of you and of your job . . . perhaps jealous, perhaps overwhelmed." He shook his head. "It is not a good place. He needs maybe a different place for a while."

José disappeared toward the kitchen. Win stood near Tucker, feeling angry and defeated. They should be spending their last hours of the six-day vacation sharing their gratitude for Tucker's hospitality and enjoying their remaining short time together, but instead the last hours had descended into a family feud. Will had been snarky all morning. He hadn't been rude to Tucker or any of the staff, thank goodness, but he'd crossed the line everywhere else. He'd disparaged Win's ten-year-old

SUV, his low-level government job, even his morning Bible-thumping, as Will had called it. It was getting out of hand.

A few minutes ago, the kid had jumped Win over some internet news story on FBI mismanagement of a case in California. Win had told him that in an organization with more than ten thousand agents, there would inevitably be a few bad apples. He'd tried to point out that ninety-nine percent of the Bureau's folks were great people who were sacrificing to make a positive difference in the world. Win thought he'd won the argument, but the boy wasn't finished. Will was still arguing his case as he swung down the hall and dropped his bag near the door to the den. He leveled a parting shot at his oldest brother: "You just work with a bunch of draconian losers who can't get *real* jobs, in the *real* world, just takin' taxpayer money to promote the Dark State!"

It's Deep State, you little punk! You can't even get your insults correct! Win had to force himself to hold his tongue, to control his anger. He was seething as Will turned his back on him, took a call on his phone, and walked back down the hall toward the patio door.

Blake was standing in the hallway by their bags, listening to the exchange. "Calm down, Win. Just chill, Bubba. Will knows all your triggers . . . he's hitting all those buttons this morning. He doesn't wanta go home, doesn't wanta deal with football recruiters or girls or social media or whatever it is fifteen-year-olds are dealing with these days. Just ignore his crap."

Tucker got up and moved toward them, a thoughtful look on his face. "Will's good with the horses," he said.

Where'd that thought come from? Win wondered.

"Uh-huh. Goes with how we grew up. Where'd you get the horses?" Blake asked, eager to get the subject off their insolent younger brother.

Tucker shrugged. "Aunt Martha bought them in a package deal when she got that two-hundred-acre farm you pass on the way up this ridge. She wants me to see what we've got—get them ready to sell, decide which ones to keep." He shook his head. "She seems to think they're simply lawn ornaments. Real expensive lawn ornaments. The exercise boy broke his leg and can't ride for weeks. I've got to find someone to work with the trainer and the foreman. . . . What about Will?"

"What?" Win and Blake both answered at once.

"Get him away from his surroundings for a few days, let him accomplish something different. Lose the phone. I think José is right. Maybe that's all he needs." Tucker looked pleased with his plan. "I'll be here at least two more weeks, and Will said that college football showcase camp he's scheduled to go to isn't until the last of the month. I've got a cool backpacking trip lined up. He could go."

Blake looked at Win. "That could work. We don't need him on the farm right now, so Dad won't mind. Mom's been worried sick about him; she'll go along with it. This could work."

"You really think so?" Win asked.

Blake nodded toward Tucker. "Will thinks Tucker is epic."

He used to think that about me, Win thought to himself. "Alright, I'm done. I don't care. Y'all work it out and deal with him. I've gotta be back in Yellowstone late this afternoon. I'm gonna go eat lunch."

*   *   *

Win had called Tia, his weekly housekeeper, as soon as he'd dropped Blake off at the Jackson Hole Airport. She'd been stopping by his house to feed his cat while he and the guys were at Miss Martha's. He needed to let her know that he'd be coming home a few days earlier than planned. It was her parting comment that caught his attention. He thought about it while he waited for the traffic to move forward during the early afternoon bear/moose/bison (or whatever) jam in Grand Teton National Park's upper reaches near Colter Bay. He wasn't in the mood to wildlife watch, but it wasn't optional—driving the 140 miles to Yellowstone's headquarters in Mammoth Hot Springs from the Jackson Hole Airport was not a quick trip during the height of tourist season.

"Oh, Win, I'm so sorry you've had to cut your trip short. I know how badly you needed that time away." That's what Tia had said. Win only saw his kind, middle-aged housekeeper once a week, if that often. Many times Tia just swooped in, cleaned the house, deposited his groceries in the fridge and pantry, hung up his dry cleaning, and did the ironing. She always played with Gruff. Tia was a lifesaver. She did the hour-long drive from Mammoth Hot Springs to Livingston, Montana, once or twice a week for Win and several other folks who didn't have the time or desire to drive that far to shop in the nearest large town. No, he didn't see the woman often. So why did she think he needed the time off—*"needed it badly,"* wasn't that what she said? *Am I wearing my stress on my face, in my voice? Is it obvious to everyone that these last few months have been too intense? Have they been too intense? Maybe. Yeah . . . maybe.*

Today was Monday, July 5th. He'd reported to the Yellowstone National Park FBI Satellite Office on April 8th. It had been less than three months since he'd been banished to the nation's premier park— where nothing ever happened and where he knew the powers that be in the Bureau hoped he'd soon grow bored and quit. But it hadn't worked out that way.

His first few weeks had been consumed with renovating the out-dated FBI office, then finding himself in the middle of a firestorm with a self-proclaimed prophet, a murderous militia, and a determined assassin. He'd barely come out of it alive, and he'd been forced to kill. He'd found out firsthand that it wasn't like the TV shows or the mov-ies, where the good guy takes out the bad guy and never looks back. Those horrific events in May had caused a shift in his being, a crack in his soul. He knew the reality of that now. He knew he was still strug-gling to repair it; he didn't know if he ever could.

He was reeling from that trauma when his next assignment in Eastern Russia went totally haywire. Since that case wrapped up a few weeks ago, he'd been wrestling with the truth that he'd let his bias and his prejudices drive part of that investigation, that he'd nearly missed the real demon. The Bureau had put out the word that his casework was exemplary on both of those high-profile cases—he wasn't so sure he agreed. And to make matters worse, he wasn't allowed to talk to outsiders about it; the espionage parts of the last case were off limits even with his buddies in the FBI. The concept of *need to know* was stretching out indefinitely.

After the shootout in mid-May, the FBI had assigned him an in-house shrink. Even though the Bureau had ruled that his shots were justified, he was required to attend counseling—it wasn't optional. He'd done quite a few sessions with a therapist on the office's secure video-conference system. It was helping, and working through the ins and outs of parts of the last case with his supervisor was beneficial, but in those rare moments when he was totally honest with himself, he knew he was still on edge, still conflicted. *Maybe that's why my fuse was so short with Will today. Maybe that's why his stupid teenage taunts rattled me.*

Win sucked in a deep breath and scanned the open sagebrush fields and sparse woodland to his left and right. Nothing to see. The traffic was stopped both ways, had been for several minutes. Some fool honked his horn, like that would do a lot of good. The folks who'd gotten out of their cars to look at whatever it was were slowly returning to their vehicles. He tapped his fingers on the steering wheel. His impatience was showing.

He sat there in the stalled traffic and tried to pray about it. But it just wasn't happening. It bothered him that he wasn't consistently praying for Will, or for his relationship with Will, at least not in a meaningful way. He had his routine of exercise, Scripture reading, and prayer every morning—well, most every morning—but part of that routine had become just that—*a routine.* His prayers often weren't deep conversations with God. Instead they were recitals of his wishes, hopes, and pleas. *God isn't Santa Claus,* he reminded himself as he put the SUV in gear and moved forward a few feet.

He leaned back in the seat and closed his eyes for a moment. He'd hated leaving Will on bad terms, but that's what he'd done. Blake had tried to reassure him at the airport, had told him it wasn't his job to fix his little brother's issues. Win tried to focus on the positives of the visit. The four of them had crammed a lot into those six days, but this region's long hours of summer sunlight made it easier. Most of their time together had been great. They'd seen all the famous sites in Yellowstone, hiked some of the most scenic trails, spent time at Win's house in Mammoth, made one of his flag football games, gone fly fishing with Trey Hechtner, and helped a friend build a tree house for his two young kids. They'd joked and laughed and had fun. He'd tried to set the example he felt that a big brother should be setting. He'd always been the steady one, the strong one. He'd always seen things in black and white. Now he wasn't so sure.

The vehicles in front of him began to move again, and as he inched forward a few spots, both his phones suddenly dinged, so he eased off the road into a now-empty turnout. He knew he likely wouldn't have cell service for much of the ride though the John D. Rockefeller, Jr. Memorial Parkway and into Yellowstone, he knew better than to pass up the chance to check his phones. A steady stream of SUVs, cars, and RVs pulled past him, every driver eagerly gathering speed before the next inevitable slowdown.

He lowered his window, turned off the engine, and combed through his text messages and nonsecure emails. Most were routine, thank goodness. Trey Hechtner's poaching issue seemed to be heating up, but he'd get a briefing on that after he got into Mammoth later this afternoon. Tucker had texted that Will had agreed to notify everyone except his immediate family that he was going dark for a couple of weeks. Tucker said it had been like pulling teeth to get the boy to cough up his smart phone. Win knew the allure of working with those horses must have been powerful to separate that teenager from the internet. Blake had texted that his plane was on time, that he'd touch base when he got back to Arkansas. The Bureau phone was remarkably quiet; then Win reminded himself that today was July 5th, a federal holiday—maybe some folks actually took time off. He breathed a deep sigh and turned his head just in time to see her.

Whoa! Sheeeesh! She was just across the road, barely fifty feet away, and she was staring right at him. A glance in his mirror told him the road behind was totally clear. There were no cars in sight in front of him either, which likely meant other animal jams were holding up the traffic both ways. There was always traffic this time of year on Highway 89 leading to Yellowstone. But not at this moment. At this moment, there was no one there except Win Tyler and a very large grizzly bear.

Nope, wrong about that. . . . A fluffy brown head bobbed above the sagebrush, then another, and another. Three cubs, and not tiny little ones—these were maybe 125 to 150 pounds. They were handsome little guys: the same soft-brown and golden color as their mother, the same prominent shoulder hump, the same penetrating, rust-colored eyes. When they neared the side of the road, the cubs stood on their hind legs and gave him a stern once-over. He almost missed the photo of a lifetime, but he managed to get a few pictures and a short video on his phone. He shifted in the seat and mama bear gave him a look that warned, *Don't even think about it.* She stopped her brood at the asphalt; she even looked both ways. Then the big bear seemed to give the word, and the youngers raced across the two-lane highway. She trotted along behind them as the cubs entered the cover of the sagebrush on the opposite side of the road. Win nodded his approval. *Mission accomplished.* He could have sworn she glanced back at him and smiled.

CHAPTER SIX

Trey Hechtner eased into the antique oak chair across from Win's desk, dropped his flat straw hat into an empty chair, and ran his hand through his short blond hair. He placed a stack of file folders on the floor and sighed. It was coming up on five o'clock and Trey looked stressed and drained. *Been a lot of that going around lately,* Win thought. But something was off. This wasn't the easygoing ranger's style.

Win dispensed with the pleasantries and cut to the chase. "What's goin' on?"

"Hikers found a dead bison bull up on—"

"Naw, I mean with you. What's up?"

Trey was normally calm and cool. He could be the poster boy for a National Park Service ranger: clean-cut, athletic, polite, and friendly, with an air of confidence about him. He hadn't made the rank of Mammoth District Ranger in Yellowstone National Park at the age of thirty-two by being a slacker. The guy was the real deal. And something was wrong.

Trey straightened in the chair and sighed again. "We've got the Park Service's Office of Professional Responsibility, OPR, here . . . sorta like the Gestapo. They came in on Friday, no advance notice. Over the Fourth of July holiday of all times! There are three of them, goin' through every file related to the missing persons, the deal with Prophet

Shepherd, all of it. There's stuff you and I did . . . well, stuff that's off the record. . . ." He let that trail off.

Uh-oh. "That could get messy."

"You think?" Trey leaned back in the chair. "They haven't removed me from duty, but you know as well as I do if anyone looks real close they'll see plenty of things that could have been done differently during those cases, during the last three months—and for me, during those years before." He shifted again. "We've been told to cooperate fully, but to continue with our current cases. Still, they've pulled several rangers off fieldwork to fill out endless interrogatories, to run their errands. The only reason I'm not stuck in my office is this poaching deal. A hiker posted photos of the dead bull on Instagram, and it made the national news yesterday." He shrugged. "So they cut me loose to deal with it. That's why I called you. I'm so shorthanded I can't do a proper investigation on . . . anything."

"Johnson's out on medical leave till who knows when. And could we rely on him to do anything constructive if he was here?" Win stopped himself and backtracked. "I shouldn't say that . . . that was out of line. Johnson's just ready to retire."

Trey cocked an eyebrow and shrugged. They both knew that Spence Johnson, the second agent assigned to Yellowstone's FBI satellite office, had a less-than-impressive work ethic.

"Can't y'all get a Park Service special agent or pull in someone from another park?" Win asked.

"It's July 5th, Win, every park in the country is covered up with visitors right now. This is our busiest time of the year and it'll be that way until Labor Day. You know our law enforcement branch is overtaxed to begin with—we've got fewer than thirteen hundred law enforcement rangers in the whole country, only fifty here in Yellowstone. We don't even have a rescue helicopter assigned here full-time anymore. Resources are tight." Trey looked away for a moment, then locked eyes with Win as he finished his thought. "Technically, the FBI has sole investigative jurisdiction in Yellowstone, and *technically* that includes poaching. I need a little help here." He glanced at his watch. "And I've gotta be back over at the Administration Building in twenty minutes to meet with one of the OPR inspectors."

"Okay, okay, I get it. I'll see who I can pull in. Let's go over the file . . . let's see what you've got."

Fifteen minutes later, Win stared out his second-floor window and watched Trey cross the divided street to the crowded sidewalk leading to the park's administrative headquarters—a huge stone building that in the late 1800s had housed cavalry officers. Win whispered a prayer that Trey would find favor with whoever he was meeting. He felt a little guilty asking the Lord for favor, considering the number of rules he and Trey had broken during their short time together. That number was somewhere off the charts. But he asked anyway. He figured the Holy Spirit could sort it all out.

Then he turned his attention to the files Trey had left on his desk—how to solve a big-time poaching case, as Trey had called it. This wasn't some yahoo shooting an elk to feed his family; nope, this was professional trophy killing. According to Trey, the park hadn't seen this type of offense in at least ten years. The photos that the hikers had taken Saturday morning were graphic: a big bison bull shot through the heart, its entire neck and head expertly cut away. Trey suspected the trophy had been lifted from the site by a helicopter; there didn't seem to be any other logical explanation. Much of the carcass had been consumed by animals by the time the rangers arrived at the site yesterday, and Trey could find no slug—it had either been removed, been eaten by a scavenger, or traveled through the beast. Trey thought he'd found the spot where the shooter had stood, but there was no brass there, nothing to tie a weapon to the kill. The poachers were careful. These guys were pros.

Win punched in the number for his supervisor. After Jim West's comment about how shorthanded they were in Lander, Win didn't think he'd get an offer of help, and he was right.

"There is no way I can spare anyone right now, Win," his boss said. "Johnson won't be back from his knee surgery for at least two more weeks—"

"What about pulling an agent out of the Salt Lake City Field Office—maybe someone from Bozeman?" Win asked.

"Not likely for something as low priority as poaching a bison."

"Okay . . . what about independent contracting? Can I reach out to someone local, get someone with some expertise pulled in on this?"

"I trust your judgment on that. Hire whoever you need if it doesn't go over $5,000. I'd have to get approval from Denver if we go over that. You're thinking Bordeaux?"

"Yes, sir. If he's available. He knows much of the park like the back of his hand, and he's been a commercial guide here for the better part of five years. He could get me where I need to go if the rangers aren't available." Win paused, then quickly added, "I'm trying to avoid asking for a chopper. Do I have authorization to hire one if I need—" He heard his boss groan.

"Let's see where this goes before we start talking helicopters. Closing the Jackson Hole RA, moving everyone to Lander, not to mention those big cases in Yellowstone—our budget for the year is totally blown." Jim paused for just a moment. "Oh, and speaking of cases, the gunrunning case with ATF in Grand Teton could be moving your way."

"ATF is running that show?" Win was surprised that the Bureau would give up jurisdiction on a high-profile case in a national park.

"They lost one of their guys. So we're gonna run it jointly." Jim sighed. "That never goes smoothly. I'm going to an operational briefing on it tomorrow in Salt Lake, but you need to know that ATF is still considering the notion that the bad guys are running guns through the parks, on up the secondary highways through Montana and into Canada. They could have been using that route since all the parks' roads opened back in late May. I don't think that's ATF's primary theory, but they've not totally discounted it."

"Yes, sir, I got that from the briefing in Moose yesterday. . . . Any thoughts on why our guys were targeted?"

"Several theories, nothing firm. Mexican cartel ticked off? Competing gunrunners? Someone getting even with the informant who was in that vehicle? Oh, and the informant's name was Greg Manyhorses. He was Canadian, a Blackfoot Native guy. He had a string of priors—nothing too serious, nothing violent. Constable Lindell was his handler, had been for several months." Jim paused for a few beats to let Win take that in, then he kept talking.

"You can pull the case up on Sentinel now, but there's still next to nothing to go on. We don't know who Agent Beckett and the informant were meeting in Jackson, or if they'd met with anyone the night before the incident in the park. We do know that Manyhorses thought he'd made some inroads with the gang within the last week, but we've got no names, no leads. Except for that coded drop at Hidden Falls in Grand Teton that you and Constable Lindell reported, Beckett and Manyhorses had been dark since July 1st. Manyhorses was trying to infiltrate an established gunrunning gang, and both men had been traveling from Utah up into the Grand Teton–Yellowstone region for the last several weeks. ATF seemed to think they'd come up empty on those trips. But apparently they'd gotten someone's attention—and not in a good way."

"Agent Beckett wasn't reporting in regularly?" Win asked.

"As a rule, yes, but once they started getting some bites last week—getting some contact with the gang—both Beckett and Manyhorses really cut back on communications with their handlers. They must have felt there was too much risk of the bad guys tagging them . . . maybe they thought they were so close to a breakthrough in the case that they didn't want to do anything that might tip them."

Jim got quiet. Then he added, "Learn from this, Win. I hate to second-guess a good agent, but maybe Beckett was trying to do too much, trying to wing it instead of following protocol, instead of having backup in place." Jim didn't say it and he didn't have to. *Maybe that's what got them killed.*

"Your interview with that deputy sheriff at the Frontier Inn and his statement are about all we've got on their movements the day before the incident. It will take a good while to run all of the surveillance footage, but your idea about getting the info out to the press and on social media was good. We've already gotten a couple of tips, and I'm betting more will come in if we keep up the chatter longer. Seems your little brother wasn't the only one bored with the sightseeing in Grand

Teton that morning. There are a couple of short videos and still shots already in the case file—mostly of our guys, but the black pickup shows up . . . just nothing clear, nothing close, unfortunately. The enhanced version of your brother's tape is in Sentinel too. Well, get up to speed with the case."

"Yes, sir." Win answered. "Do I need to get the Park Service in the loop up here? Start checking the cameras at the park entrances?"

"They're already checking the entrance cameras in Grand Teton. As for Yellowstone, let's wait and see what shakes out after the briefing tomorrow. Might want to put that in motion if it's lookin' like the park route was a regular thing. It could be our guys were just meeting someone in Grand Teton because it was off the beaten path. It might have been an aberration; we know guns are being shipped out of the U.S. into Canada through Montana along Interstate 15, same as the drug route. Since the Canadians keep tightening their gun laws, the demand for illegal weapons has gone sky-high. The black market prices there are more than double what you'd pay here on many models, and that's for ammunition too. That's not likely to change, and this park route could be a new thing for the smugglers."

Win could hear background noise on Jim's call, other voices. He wasn't the only one working on a federal holiday. His boss seemed distracted as he tried to finish up. "Do what you have to on that dead bull, but remember that this gunrunning deal is the priority." Win was still taking that in when Jim dropped one last item on him. "Oh, and if this goes the way it looks like it might, you could be working with Constable Lindell and who knows who all from ATF." Jim was hurrying to get off the phone.

"Do we know anything more about Alex Lindell?" Win quickly asked.

"Not much. I did hear that she'd gone through the Bureau's National Academy last year, heard she was pushing real hard to stay on the case. I know the Canadians want one of their folks in the mix, so we'll see if they pull her and send a more senior investigator down here."

They finished the call and Win leaned back in his desk chair and thought about it. He stared at the 1904 oil painting that took up a prominent spot on his office wall. It portrayed a grizzly bear standing on its hind legs above a fallen elk. Focusing on the classic painting always calmed him, helped him sort through things. He had a few phone calls to make. He'd call Luke and see if he could hire him to take him to the site of the poached bison in the morning, then he'd call Judy Wade, his friend from the FBI Academy who could sniff out most anything within the Bureau or on the internet. He didn't want to go blindly into a case with Alex Lindell. Something about the woman was unsettling, a little unnerving.

If he was completely honest with himself, he'd admit that he wasn't all that comfortable working with women. He always seemed to find himself saying or thinking the wrong thing. He studied the bear painting and concluded that this flaw in his character was his parents' fault. From childhood he'd been taught to be a protector of girls. It wasn't that he thought men were smarter or superior in any way, it was just a role he thought he was expected to fulfill. *Care for them, protect them*—that's what he'd been taught. He had a hard time treating a female like one of the guys, and he'd caught plenty of grief over that at the FBI Academy, where nearly a quarter of his class was female. He remembered one of the Quantico instructors reminding him that the women were part of his team, but in his entire previous life, his *teams*—basketball, football, track—had been one hundred percent male. Heck, he didn't have a sister, not even a female first cousin. *Yep, it's Mom and Dad's fault. . . .*

That line of thinking brought Tory to mind. He hadn't talked to her since their awkward discussion late last night. What had Tucker suggested? *Cherish her . . . show her she's a priority.* That's what he said. Win picked up his personal phone and scrolled to the best of the grizzly bear pictures he'd taken earlier this afternoon. He sent the pictures to her phone and then typed in a short text, said that seeing the mama bear and the three cubs up close had taken his breath away, said that thinking of her had the same effect.

* * *

It's nice to be home. That thought caught Win off guard as he pushed open the screen door, unlocked the wooden back door, and dropped his bag on the tile floor of the mudroom. Tia had performed her cleaning magic while they'd been at Miss Martha's, and the house smelled of evergreens and pine-scented cleaner. The fresh fragrance reminded him of his grandmother's house; he liked that a lot. Gruff trotted in from wherever he'd been, and Win picked up the big orange cat and cradled him in his arms. There was instant purring and nuzzling and he felt that sense of surprise again. *This smells like home, feels like home . . .* and then an awareness he wasn't expecting—*and I won't be here much longer.* The sad, empty feeling that followed that thought was even more surprising. He'd pushed to get out of this dead-end assignment at the FBI's two-man satellite office in Yellowstone the entire three months he'd been here, and now suddenly the thought of leaving this place brought on feelings of loss. He set the cat down in the kitchen and tried to shake off the unwelcome emotions.

Jim West had told him that his big bosses at the Denver Field Office were still pushing Headquarters for his transfer; he knew it was a bureaucratic glitch holding it up. They'd promised him they'd work something out before the summer was over. They were telling him he'd be in Denver, maybe the Counterterrorism Squad, where he could try out for the office's SWAT team. Or he could consider joining the White Collar Crime Squad. That's what he'd done for his first three years in the Bureau in Charlotte. The brass were giving him his choice of a squad. "You've earned it." That's what Jim said.

Earned it. Win subconsciously reached for the scar on the back of his head. He'd spent days in the ICU in mid-May, he'd come back from near death labeled a hero. His next big case had left more mental scars than physical ones, and again his bosses lauded him as a role model for success. But he wasn't feeling it. What he was feeling was the continuing need to prove himself, to show others in the Bureau he hadn't deserved to be shipped off to this remote place. Deep in his soul he knew he was still fighting a battle for redemption. Deep in his soul he knew he needed to let that go and move on. He just wasn't real sure how to do that.

His personal phone buzzed and jolted him out of his moody con-
templation. He held his breath when he saw it was a text from Tory.
This could go either way. . . . His mood shifted and he smiled as he
read it: **Bear photos r amazing!! Ur so sweet! Off to the wilderness.
Hope to see u soon. Enjoy ur holiday!** He read it through again and
his smile broadened. Gruff said something, and he looked down at the
cat. "She said to enjoy our holiday, buddy. How 'bout we celebrate with
some of that watermelon Tucker sent home with me?" The cat looked
skeptical. "No? Then I get the watermelon, you get tuna fish. Happy
Independence Day!"

* * *

An hour later, Win watched Luke and Ellie Bordeaux herd both kids
in front of them as they walked across the crowded parking lot toward
Win's front porch. Win waited between the pair of large evergreens
that gave his one-and-a-half-story stone house some privacy from
the hordes of tourists streaming up the walkway toward the Lower
Cascade Terraces of Mammoth Hot Springs. Seeing Luke Bordeaux
was always a bit intimidating, even when the guy was in casual cargo
pants and a T-shirt, out for a day in the park. Luke was tall and fit; his
windswept black hair came nearly to his collar, and his close-cropped
black beard and mustache gave him a rakish look. Luke moved with
an ease that evidenced his years in the Army Special Forces—he was
never completely off guard.

Win stepped off the wooden porch into his small front yard and
greeted the family. "So you've been at a Fourth of July program?"

Abby, Luke's three-year-old daughter, was already flying to him. "A
flag! See! Got a flag!" She was waving a little American flag around as
Ethan, her five-year-old brother, pulled his own flag from a back pocket
and made a stab at his sister with it.

Ellie tried to snag the flag that Ethan had turned into a weapon.
She missed. She turned and smiled a weary smile at Win. "The ranger
program on U.S. history for the kids was great—" She deftly stepped

in front of Abby to block a retaliatory jab. "I thought you were taking more time off in Jackson this week?"

Win nodded and shrugged. "You know . . . duty calls." Win stepped toward the children just as a real fight was brewing. He snatched off Ethan's purple LSU ball cap and waved it to distract him, then finished his comments to Ellie. "Blake needed to get back home anyway; they'll be cutting hay this week. Will is staying with Tucker for a couple of weeks in Jackson. I might get back down there a time or two before they go back South."

Ellie grabbed for Abby's flag and got it. Luke stood behind his wife and tried to appear stern, but Win had a sense he was content with letting her referee the children's battle.

Ellie confiscated Ethan's flag and began moving them toward the boardwalk. "We're gonna walk off some energy and check out the Lower Cascade Terraces. Y'all get your business done and we'll be back directly."

Luke moved beside Win and they watched Ellie marshal both kids toward the wooden walkway that began several yards beyond Win's front porch. "Ellie has the patience of Job and unlimited energy . . . we've only been in the park fer five hours, and I'm worn out," Luke said.

"She is something special," Win agreed as he watched them walk away.

Ellie Bordeaux had been an all-state high school basketball player in Vidalia, Louisiana, and at thirty, she still looked the part. Luke was Win's height, six three, and Ellie came within a few inches of him. They were both of Cajun heritage, with the dark hair and eyes that lineage brought. Luke had always reminded Win of a Caribbean pirate—a very confident and capable pirate. And Ellie, well, Ellie was just plain pretty, inside and out.

She now had a firm grip on each child's hand as they headed up the walkway. He could tell by the motions of her head, how she swung her long hair, that she'd gone into teacher mode. Every time Win saw Ellie Bordeaux, he found himself smiling.

Luke moved to the shade of Win's front yard evergreens. "Ever take off fer Independence Day, Win?"

Win figured Luke was being sarcastic, but he gave the man a straight answer anyway. "When I was a kid, we'd go to Greers Ferry Lake. All the kinfolks would show up, spend the whole day at the lake—big picnic, water skiing, tubing, then maybe some fishing on the Little Red River . . . a cookout and fireworks at night. That was my Fourth of July holiday for so many years. Lots of good memories. What did y'all do?"

"Some of the same as you, 'cept we'd be camping somewhere. Sometimes up in your neck of the woods, on a lake, in the mountains, sometimes when I's little there'd be a reunion over south of Lake Charles, over in Cajun country. As the older folks passed, that became less common." He sighed. "Even after we moved out here five years ago, we'd try to get back fer the Fourth . . . but it gets harder as time passes." He watched his young family in the distance. "Things change."

There was a world of emotion in those two words: *Things change.* Win wasn't real sure if his good memories would cancel out the bad, if joys would trump past regrets, so he didn't look inside himself to see. Instead he told Luke he'd get them some sweet tea, and he left the man standing in the shade to sort out his own thoughts.

Luke had moved to one of the Adirondack chairs on the front porch when Win came out with the ice tea. Luke downed half of it. "She'll keep 'em corralled for a few more minutes, then they'll be rearing to get back home. It's been hard to keep 'em outa that tree house. I sure appreciate you boys helpin' me with that last week. We're gonna christen it tonight. Me, Tiger, and the kids are gonna camp out in it." He gave Win a sideways grin. "We could scooch together and make room fer you."

"Let's see . . . a sleepover in a tree on a plank floor with two preschool kids and a puppy. . . . Gee, that's gonna be a hard one to turn down."

Luke laughed as Win eased down in the other chair. "You sure you got time to go tomorrow?" Win asked.

"Yeah, I don't have anything scheduled for several days. I'd planned to be off this week in case we decided to drive back to Louisiana for the holiday, but since we didn't, I was just gonna work on the house and barn some. I'm good to go."

"I appreciate you helping. I know nothing about poaching. Nothing about big game hunting. Nothing about bison. And Trey isn't an expert on any of that either. You know, there's a sad history of poaching in the national parks—mostly deer and elk, very rarely wolves or mountain lions—but Trey said they hadn't had a trophy-hunt-type poaching violation inside Yellowstone in years." Win shifted in the chair. "And we don't have much to go on. Hikers reported the dead bull day before yesterday. It's on the northeast side slope of Specimen Ridge, about four miles in from the trailhead off the Northeast Entrance Road. Trey managed to get a chopper to take him and a couple of other rangers to check it out. They did a good workup on the site. . . . I know there won't be much left of the bull, if anything, by tomorrow, but I need to get up there and see the location myself. Trey said it was a professional job. He thinks they got the head out with a helicopter."

Luke took a sip of the tea and his tone turned serious. "We met Trey and Cindy at the Gardiner fireworks last night. He filled me in on some of this. It's been all over social media, it's not like it's a secret." Luke shrugged. "Trey was thinkin' the bull had been shot maybe three, four days before the hiker spotted it. Real bold to take a bull that way, especially this time of year."

"How do you shoot anything in the middle of the park, then fly part of it out, and not expect anyone to notice?" Win asked.

Luke thought on it for only a moment. "With the location you're giving me it might be a sight easier than you'd think. They've got that bridge construction project on the Yellowstone River east of Roosevelt . . . got three or four other construction projects goin' on Highway 212 through the Lamar Valley. The heavy equipment ramps up about dawn so they can shut down in the heat of the day. All that noise carries down the valley, echoes off the ridges—especially at start-up. They're workin' seven days a week, weather permitting. And the highway crews bring in lots of their supplies by chopper. The poachers may have timed it so that their shot gets lost in the noise. May have the chopper timed so that anyone seein' it just figures it fer a construction-related flight.

They'd have to know the construction schedule, but that might just work."

Sometimes Luke's ability to think like a criminal was a bit unnerving. Win blinked back his surprise at Luke's theory and just nodded. "That's really high risk, and that's probably conspiracy along with the actual offense of violating the 1894 Lacey Act, which prohibited the killing of animals in Yellowstone. And how could it possibly be worth it? One dead bull?"

Luke took another sip. "A legal hunt outside the park for that type of animal could run you $20,000 if you hire a top-notch outfitter, if you get the $6,000 out-of-state permit, if you win the lottery and get a tag. Some people just won't go the legal route, and the money isn't a factor with big game poachers. A trophy mount from a big bison bull, bragging rights that it had been shot in Yellowstone National Park, right under the nose of the Feds . . . it could easily be a $30,000 to $50,000 payout to the poachers, and that's on top of expenses paid." He shrugged. "There's plenty of folks who would jump at the chance fer that kinda money."

Win hoped his neutral expression hid his shock at the huge potential payout—and at Luke's detailed knowledge of it. "Anybody you know in the guide community who has those kinds of connections, who could pull that off?" he casually asked.

Luke waved to Ellie and the kids, who were now walking back their way. He didn't look at Win when he spoke. "I know what you're thinkin', Win Tyler. Thinkin' that boy knows too damn much about this gig. You're wondering how that is, why that is. . . . You're thinkin' that boy has those kind of connections, the know-how. You're thinking that boy, Bordeaux, he coulda pulled it off."

Before Win could respond, Luke rose and jumped down off the porch, as fluid and quick as a cat. He scooped Abby up in his arms and headed toward the parking lot. Draping his free arm around Ellie's shoulders, he called back, "Meet you at the hotel lobby at five in the mornin'!"

CHAPTER SEVEN

It was another early morning. Too damn early. He liked things a bit more spread out, a little time to chill in between. But here he was again.

He leaned against the dirty pickup and pulled the tarp back over their prize. "Seems like a lot of effort to go to for such a small haul."

The bulky man was tying down the tarp's straps on the other side of the pickup's bed. "You're the boss, but it wasn't just your call . . . it wasn't just my call either." They both glanced up and their eyes met for a moment. The voice was as hard as the man's face. "We agreed this was the thing to do, we was doin' a job." He paused for a moment, then spit to the side. "And you know it ain't just the haul—we were staking our claim on this route. Damn Feds are cutting things off on the interstates, we're gonna use the park route. But we don't need no competition."

"Yeah, yeah, we agreed. It's done." He glanced back down at his work as he finished the thought. "We might have called too much attention to ourselves is all." He strapped down another corner of the tarp, then slammed the tailgate shut. He watched his partner walk over to the camper's trailer hitch and retrieve the drink he'd left there. The guy downed the rest of the sixteen-ounce energy drink in one long swallow and wiped his brow. It was likely only forty-five degrees, but counting out the twenty-nine handguns, repackaging them in plastic, stashing them in the container, and then moving the heavy aluminum box to the guy's truck had worked up a sweat. The man crushed the can in his hand and dropped it to the ground.

"Can't believe you drink that stuff—it'll kill you."

The man scoffed. "You worried 'bout my lifespan all a sudden?"

"We may all need to be worried about our lifespans if this deal goes sideways on us. . . . You just told me Roadie may be a little shaky."

The other man shrugged. "It's his first serious gig. He's a hard worker, he's not a fool."

I'm the boss, dammit! How'd I let him talk me into this! He squared his shoulders and told the guy what he was really thinking. He raised his voice. "Well, you damn well know that takedown was a fool's stunt! Out in the open, middle of the morning, on a road full of tourists! We probably got made, and now we gotta stash this haul until we see if there's any blowback. Can't even run it to the border for a payoff. We just gotta sit on it." He was more than a little hot.

The other guy shrugged again. "We just keep our boys buying down in Nevada, in Utah. There's a big gun show going on in Salt Lake soon, and another in Las Vegas this month. Roadie is giving some kid down around Ogden fifty dollars a pop for every stolen handgun. He's come up with some nice pieces." He shook his head. "I ain't in a hurry . . . you shouldn't be either. The Canadians are paying top dollar, and if our border route gets dicey at Piegan, then we pick another spot. Going through that Indian reservation has worked."

"I just don't feel good about this . . . we don't even know who we tagged."

"Whoever they were, they were cutting into our business, they were using our route, they were playin' with fire." He laughed that wicked laugh of his. "No pun intended." He laughed again and pulled out his keys. "You still gonna take that vacation you keep telling us about when we wrap up this haul?"

"Hell, yeah. Someplace warm where I can just lay around with a beer and stare at the ocean. I'm thinkin' Cabo."

"Mexico? Seriously? Don't you ever watch the news? American tourists are droppin' like flies in Mexico. It's scary dangerous!" The man shook his head and waved as he climbed in the truck. "You won't catch me south of the border . . . there's some vicious dudes down there."

He considered the irony of that statement as he watched the pickup back out of the campsite and take the service road toward the entrance to the Bridge Bay Campground. He stood and watched until the truck passed on the Grand Loop Road headed north toward the Lake Yellowstone Hotel and the inner reaches of the park.

He needed to close the trailer up and get on the road himself, but he just stood staring at the sparkling blue lake that lay just beyond the main highway a few hundred yards away. The massive snowcapped Absaroka Mountains stood to the east, across seven miles of open water. It was quite a view. But his actual view was now inward. It wasn't that he felt any remorse for killing the competing gunrunners, it wasn't that. A man has a right to protect his business, has a right to protect what's his.

He thought he'd hit the passenger with the AR-15 right after the fools realized the meetup was a setup and took off down that dirt road. They didn't get any return fire, so he figured he'd put one guy out of commission. Then the wreck, where they'd been damned lucky to pry up the lift gate and get the gun box out before anyone showed up. If there hadn't been three of them, it wouldn't have happened. He knew his partner had finished off the two losers while he and Roadie were working on the lift gate, knew the flare gun they'd used to ignite the gunpower would fuel an intense fire that would consume the evidence. It might take the cops weeks to identify the dead; nothing much had made the TV news.

No, it wasn't remorse or guilt that he felt. But it bothered him that he'd agreed to such a reckless plan. It bothered him that he'd gotten greedy, hadn't been more cautious. He watched the early sunlight shimmering off the expansive lake, he took in the imposing mountains that stretched toward the sky. He sighed. Maybe he was slipping, maybe he did need that time off, that vacation, just a short trip to leave a bit of a trail in case this venture went off the rails. He liked what he'd seen of Cabo San Lucas on the internet. He smiled to himself as he opened the door to the camper trailer. His partner was right. *Mexico is full of vicious dudes, damn straight it is. And pretty soon they'll have one more.*

*   *   *

Win stood there in the trees near the edge of the small clearing and took it in: three large blackish-brown humps lying in the short grass. The turkey buzzards didn't even pause with the men's arrival—they just kept up their task as dozens of ravens flared to the surrounding trees. Four coyotes trotted toward the opposite tree line, each one glancing back longingly at the feast they'd been forced to abandon.

Trey shifted his rifle and chambered a round as Win started to step toward the carcasses—Luke's strong arm blocked his way. "Kin smell 'em a little—likely bears or wolves will be nearby. Get ready . . . keep your head up." Win eased the Bureau-modified M4 rifle off his shoulder, clicked off the safety, and cradled the gun. With his free hand, he reached for the binoculars that hung around his neck.

"You don't need those . . . the coyotes ran off to the east. They won't be running into any other hazard. Any other predator will be on the opposite side of the clearing . . . 'bout where we are," Luke said.

Oh geez, that's just great.

The adrenaline in Win's system went up a notch. He'd been on high alert since they'd hiked the last hundred yards to the spot where they now stood. They'd detoured to the Lamar Valley from Specimen Ridge after a wildlife photographer had called in a second possible poaching incident this morning. The detour from Specimen Ridge to the Lamar River Trailhead, then the hike into this remote spot, had taken hours. It was closing in on mid-afternoon, and now it was apparent that the photographer had told it right. Win knew that three buffalo didn't just fall over dead. *Maybe a lightning strike? Maybe poisonous plants? Don't they have hemlock out here?* His mind kept running through different possibilities before they arrived, before they caught a glimpse of the headless forms lying in the clearing. He couldn't fathom a person simply taking the lives of the big beasts for selfish gain or bragging rights.

This was a big-time crime—a big-time problem. And now another problem was lurking just behind them.

Luke shifted at Win's side and nodded with his head toward the dense undergrowth in the trees to their right. All three men slowly pivoted away from the clearing and faced the deeper woods. The cool wind was fanning his face but Win felt sweat running down his back, his hands were moist on the rifle. Luke now had his big Wilson Hunter 10mm in his hand; he squared himself on Win's right. Trey was on Win's left side, still as a statue.

Win swung his head to scan the thick brush on either side—something moved in the thicket of short pine forty yards to his right. The creature huffed a loud warning.

"Oh, crap," Trey said as he leveled his rifle toward the thicket.

"Back slowly toward the clearing . . . be ready if it decides to charge us," Luke said.

"What is it?" Win whispered.

"A grizzly . . . but maybe it's eaten its fill . . . maybe it ain't up fer a fight."

Win pointed the rifle in the general direction of the thicket and took a step back through the timber. Nothing moved in the underbrush. "What about the bear spray?" he whispered to Luke.

"What about it?" Luke replied, his big pistol aimed at something Win couldn't see.

"Shouldn't we get out the bear spray?" Win asked quietly again.

"We're downwind from the bear—stiff breeze. Spray that stuff and it comes right back on us."

"Oh."

"And don't whisper. It knows exactly where we are, knows exactly what we are. Talk loud and it may decide to move on." Luke and Trey both took another step back, their guns didn't waver. Luke's voice was loud and hard. "Win, don't shoot quick, it might fake a charge, might bluff. If you do shoot, go for the head."

Maybe it won't charge. God, please don't let it charge, Win prayed silently.

But it did.

*   *   *

Dex Pierson sat in his big Dodge pickup and watched the dust cloud in the distance announce Jesse's arrival. It was half past two, and Jesse was taking his good slow time 'cause he was driving that fancy rig and didn't wanta get it dinged up on the rough dirt road. This time they were meeting in a spot more to Dex's liking—far off the beaten path on a dirt two-track that ran beneath a power line north of Gibbon Falls.

Dex rolled up his window to let the dust blow over as his partner pulled the big Infiniti SUV to a stop behind him.

Jesse was already grumbling as he exited the expensive vehicle. "Hell, Dex. I've been on the road all day. Couldn't you find a spot a little more outa the way?"

"You're gonna be thinking outa the way is a damn good thing if things go as bad as they could. Do you have any idea what could happen if the rangers find those dead bulls? Any idea?" Dex's voice was rising, and he was cutting the distance between them quickly.

Jesse stopped and dropped his hands to his hips. He gave Dex one of those downcast, contrite looks that Dex had seen way too many times before when one of their schemes went sideways. "You know I didn't plan it that way," Jesse said, trying to deflect Dex's anger. "Hey, I got rid of your guns, I brought your cut—that's 20K—and Mr. Yé says they're gonna wire each of us another ten thousand for the extra trouble. The chopper pilot is cool with it. All three trophies will be on a flight to China by tomorrow night. I'd say we've had a damn good payday."

Dex just stood there glaring at him. Jesse shook his head and kept talking. "You know I was just as shocked as you were. You were standing next to Mr. Zhào—how in hell could he have put three bulls down? How?"

Actually, the events of yesterday morning were still a little foggy in Dex's mind. Everything had gone perfectly up to the point of the kill shot. Everything. Jesse had rented a small, unobtrusive SUV from some low-rent car rental place in West Yellowstone. He'd driven Mr. Zhào and Mr. Yé over to the Lamar River Trailhead late afternoon on July 4th. Dex had left his nice rig at his dad's place and driven the old

man's beat-up Chevy pickup to the trailhead to meet them. They'd
hiked in the three miles from the trailhead to the confluence of Cache
Creek and the Lamar River, then they'd followed the Cache Creek Trail
northeastward away from the river to another mountain stream, South
Cache Creek. They hiked a game trail leading away from that creek and
into the dense lodgepole pine forest that hugged the lower benches of
the mountain. Their camping spot was off the main trails, within a half
mile of their quarry.

They'd avoided a few groups of hikers on the trail, but they were
dressed and outfitted to blend in—Dex didn't think anyone would
really notice them. He'd covered his face and neck tats with makeup,
and he had the two high-powered Winchester Model 70 magnum rifles
and the tripod broken down in his big pack. He'd been pleased that
Jesse had convinced the Asian clients to lose their expensive duds and
dress down for the hike—he could tell they were enjoying the clan-
destine nature of it. To a casual observer they looked like four hikers
backpacking into one of the wilder areas of the park.

Dex had taken the clients up to a high bench that overlooked the
area where the three bachelor bulls were hanging out. They'd laid on
their stomachs on top of a cliff and watched the animals with binoculars until twilight. Dex didn't have to point out the big animal that
he wanted Mr. Zhào to have in his sights at daybreak. That bull was
massive, his huge head was solid black, his horns were a good twenty
inches long, and his beard dropped nearly to his knees. A perfect specimen of an American bison bull. Dex estimated his weight at 2,300
pounds. His younger companions were probably his sons. Dex really
didn't know that for sure, but he told that tale to the clients and they
seemed to believe him. While the larger bull grazed and appeared content with putting on more weight, his "sons" locked horns and battled
with their huge heads. They pawed at the ground, practiced their bel-
lows, and rolled in the dirt. The big guy seemed to tolerate their antics;
they gave him a wide berth. Dex figured they'd gotten there just in
time, as those three would be moving down into the Lamar Valley in a
day or so to claim their share of the waiting cows.

That night Dex had prepared a big campfire dinner of bison steak with all the fixings. He prided himself on being an excellent backcountry cook. Given the language barrier, there wasn't much talking around the fire, but that suited him fine. He wasn't much into the social aspects of the job; he'd leave those to Jesse. He'd been assured that Mr. Zhào had practiced with a similar rifle, that he was experienced with guns. Mr. Yé bragged that Mr. Zhào had taken elephants, rhinos, and lions in Africa, even tigers in India. He'd told them that his boss had an immense trophy room at his home on China's southeast coast.

After dinner they'd toasted to a successful hunt. Jesse had brought along some expensive Chinese liquor; Dex figured paint remover tasted better. He'd faked a closed-mouth smile and raised his glass to their success. He was impressed that Jesse had even thought to bring crystal old-fashioneds—no Styrofoam or plastic cups for these clients. Dex figured Jesse was already working those two for another score of some sort. His partner always seemed to have several balls in the air, several schemes in the works.

They'd moved into position well before dawn, and the two clients had impressed Dex with their ease of movement on the rocky side slopes. He'd set up the scoped bolt-action rifle on its tripod on a smooth rock outcropping less than 250 yards from the center point of the small clearing. He held the second rifle in reserve, just in case of a jam. That had never happened, and it wasn't likely. Dex Pierson was meticulous in his care of the guns.

The plan was for Jesse to break down the camp. After that, he'd hike up to the clearing to take the videos and the photos and help Dex finish packaging the trophy. Removing the huge animal's head and neck required considerable skill, which Dex possessed, and disposable hazmat suits, which Jesse provided. After that difficult task was accomplished, Jesse would coordinate the load out with the helicopter pilot by satellite phone, then he'd take the guns, cutting tools, and bloody suits—all of that flew out with the chopper. As soon as it lifted off, Dex and the clients would casually hike the eight or so miles to the trailhead parking lot. Dex would drop them off at the Tower–Roosevelt junction. Jesse had arranged for a car service to pick them up at the

Roosevelt Lodge Dining Room for the drive to West Yellowstone's airport, which would probably take at least three hours due to animal jams and holiday traffic. Mr. Zhào's chartered jet was waiting at the airport to whisk them off to San Francisco.

The chopper would deliver Jesse and the bison head to an isolated landing strip near Cooke City; it would be either trucked to a taxidermist stateside or shipped overseas. What Dex thought of as the "logistic" parts of the job would be wrapped up within twenty-four hours and everyone would be happy. This wasn't their first rodeo—he and Jesse had the setup and extraction phases well scripted. That was the plan . . . but first there was the kill shot.

The conditions were ideal for the shot. The sky was deep purple just before sunrise, and if Dex had been into the beauty of the place, which he wasn't, he'd have noticed the dazzling number of stars that adorned the heavens. There was a hint of a crescent moon still in the sky as the first touches of yellow framed Saddle and Hague Mountains, which lay far to the southeast. The temperature was thirty-six degrees, wind was negligible, humidity was low. Conditions were perfect, and the kill shot at less than 250 yards was a cinch even for a novice.

The heavy rifle was loaded with three .458 rounds that Dex had packed and loaded himself. One shot to the heart was preferred for a humane kill; the heavy bullets were designed to bring down a Cape buffalo or an elephant, and it would take that level of firepower to bring down the big bison bull. The other two rounds were backup, just in case of a miss or wounding hit. But there'd be no excuse for more than one round at this range, under these conditions. One shot would be enough.

Dex scoped the clearing out with his night vision goggles. The big bull was up, stretching his huge frame, condensation rising from his nostrils in the cold air. One of the smaller bulls was also standing but was half-asleep, with its head hanging low. The third bull was still lounging. Dex glanced at his watch as the dim light was brightening: 5:25 a.m. The bulldozers and Mack Trucks were roaring to life on Highway 212 straight down the valley, only twelve miles to the west as the crow flies. He could hear the low rumbling from the spot where he stood—the noise of the heavy construction equipment would help dampen the sound of the single shot. Dex motioned for Mr. Zhào to be ready, and the man acquired the largest bull in the Leupold sight. Dex decided to go for the shot as soon as the third bull stood. They only had to wait seconds. Dex placed his left hand on Mr. Zhào's shoulder, then pulled it back. It was their prearranged signal that cleared the client to fire.

The first shot exploded in the clearing. Things went to hell after that.

* * *

The bear barreled through the brush, cleared the thicket, and raced toward them. It came at them quicker than you would think it could as it crashed through the underbrush, roaring and snapping its jaws. The creature's hair was standing straight up, making it look bigger than it was, and it was plenty big to begin with. Dried blood from its recent feast covered its face, giving it an even more terrifying look. Two-inch teeth, four-inch claws, and four hundred pounds of fury was coming straight at them.

The men held their guns steady as they yelled at the bear. Win kept hollering something along the lines of "Stop, dammit!" He had no idea what the other two men were shouting—everything had morphed into slow motion. The bear slid to a stop less than thirty feet away and bounded from side to side, still snarling, snapping, and slobbering. Then it seemed to conclude that it was a waste of energy to push the point further. The bear's dark eyes gave the tall, noisy intruders a final searing stare before it turned and slowly stomped back into the thicket.

Lordy! Win sucked in a deep breath. The adrenaline spike was crazy. After the yelling, he was at a loss for what to say.

Luke raised his dark eyebrows and nodded. "Welp, I reckon he told us." He seemed totally unfazed, but he hadn't lowered that big pistol.

Trey lowered the muzzle of his rifle. He turned toward Luke and shook his head. "Too damn close . . . I nearly pulled the trigger."

Win realized his legs were shaking and his hands were trembling against the hard surface of the rifle. He took another deep breath and finally regained his speech. "So it's gone?"

"Wouldn't bet on that," Luke replied. "Y'all get in the clearing and start workin'. I'll watch for him . . . he may circle back."

"Okay . . . okay." Win didn't have to be told twice to retreat from that spot.

Trey was already moving toward the downed bison. His fair skin was just a touch paler. Win didn't know if that was from seeing the slaughtered animals or from the bear attack. Either one could have done it.

They'd agreed that Trey would video the site with a small drone before they walked into the carnage. Trey had already gotten off a quick satellite phone call with the Chief Ranger, and was getting the drone out of his backpack, when Win moved into the clearing and took it in. It wasn't a big space, less than three acres, he'd guess. The clearing was encircled by tall lodgepole pines that were swaying in the wind. The ground was slightly sloped, not steep. He could see gray bluffs stair-stepping up the ridge on the clearing's far side. The short grass hadn't yet wilted from the summer's heat; it was still nearly kelly green. Clumps of bright-yellow arrowleaf balsamroot and purple lupine flowers dotted the field. Win was thinking how pretty this little spot would be if violent death hadn't found it.

The ravens were keeping up their annoying chatter from across the field, and two turkey vultures sat silently in the top of a dead tree and watched the men; their hairless red heads gave the big blackish-brown birds a garish look. Win wondered why there weren't more buzzards here. Vultures seemed to be few and far between in Yellowstone. Maybe they didn't like the cold weather; maybe other scavengers were more numerous or more aggressive here. A dead cow back home would have attracted twenty vultures by now, maybe more. He made a mental note to ask someone, then he dropped his gaze back to the slaughter in front of him. He literally shook his head to get his focus back on track.

Trey was just about to get the drone set up when Luke stepped to the edge of the clearing and joined them. "We need to get this done as soon as we can in case that little fella went fer reinforcements."

Win raised his eyebrows. "Little fella?"

Luke nodded toward the woods. "That was about a two-and-a-half-year-old. Likely got kicked out by his mom this spring. Grizzly cubs generally stay with their mother until their second year . . . they can get pretty big by that age."

Trey stopped what he was doing and scanned the forest behind them. "Did you see how distended his belly was? He'd been eating for hours. Fortunate for us."

"Yeah. Thankful he wasn't up for a fight," Luke said. Win knew they were talking about the bear to put off the inevitable, same as him thinking about the buzzards. None of them wanted to step forward and deal with the death of three magnificent creatures on this beautiful afternoon. The men turned back toward the clearing. There was difficult work to do. But before they started, they all got real still and quiet.

*   *   *

Win had worked enough cases in his three-plus years in the Bureau to recognize the perfect witness. And Randolph Mitchem, the guy who had called in the three dead bison on the satellite phone this morning, was the perfect witness. The man looked more like a middle-aged college professor than a nationally known wildlife photographer. He was intelligent, observant, and thorough, but modesty wasn't one of his virtues. He didn't hesitate to tell Win his photos were featured in art galleries throughout the West. It was coming up on seven o'clock that evening when they stood behind his tricked-out SUV at the Lamar River Trailhead parking lot and talked.

The man adjusted his wire-rimmed glasses, pushed his Tilley hat back off his forehead, and ran a tan bandana across his face. "I've been watching those three bulls for nearly two weeks. I usually take game trails up to overlooks so that I can set up my tripod," he said. "The big bull, he had to be close to twenty-four hundred pounds. A massive bull, still in his prime. Those three bulls had moved down from the higher slopes together. I was trying to get up there today to get some shots right at dawn, but I had a flat tire from that damn construction work, and I didn't get here to the trailhead until 7:06."

Win loved how the guy had everything timed, everything recorded. "You began your hike into the site then?" he asked.

"No . . . no, hit the toilets, had some more coffee, rechecked my photos from earlier this morning from over near Pebble Creek. . . ." He went on and on. Win was glad he was recording all this. "I decided I could still try for some shots of the bulls. The two younger ones have been sparring a bit lately, and the big guy is . . . uh . . . was amazing in the right light. So I started up the trail—"

Win interrupted for the record. "That would be the Lamar River Trail?"

"Yeah, right . . . I crossed Soda Butte Creek on the footbridge and started up the Lamar River Trail at 7:26. See, I always make a time note in my journal." He pointed to the small leather book he was holding.

"Why?"

Mitchem screwed up his mouth, as if he wasn't too sure himself, then he shrugged. "Well, some of my customers want to know exactly when the shot was taken, where it was taken. It adds to their experience when they buy the photos. I may take twenty-five hundred digital shots a day. It helps me keep them straight."

"Makes sense," Win responded. "Tell me what you saw. Anyone or anything on the trail into the site."

"This trail is busy, but only for the first mile or so. Lots of folks are brave enough to hike up to that first rise. . . ." He pointed to a barren sagebrush hill far in the distance. "They can look back and see their car in the parking lot from there. After that, it's mostly the backcountry campers and experienced hikers who go further. Even with bear spray on your belt, the average person has enough sense to realize they're out of their element when they lose sight of the parking lot or the highway in the Lamar Valley. It's pretty wild out here."

Mitchem stared across the valley and kept up the monologue. "There wasn't anything out of the ordinary really. This morning I followed a backpacking group of four—two men, two women, maybe in their mid-forties—from Illinois, they said. They asked about my cameras, and we visited back and forth some. They stopped about three miles in and I hiked on alone. I stopped several times along the river to get some bird shots, then again where the creek joins the river for a moose and her calf. I realized then that I was going to lose my best late-morning light if I didn't get on up to the bulls, so I picked it up a bit. At that point I was less than one mile from the clearing where I found them." He swallowed hard and Win could see the emotions come over him.

"Did you see any other hikers that close to the site?"

"Ah . . . uh." He cleared his throat and tried to regroup. "Uh, yeah . . . I saw two more groups before I got above the clearing. The first group was past the Death Gulch area, on a lower side slope of Cache Mountain. I didn't stop, just waved, and kept up a pace . . . was trying to catch the light. Anyway, there were several young men outfitted for overnight, with very new equipment. They were breaking camp beside South Cache Creek, just off the trail—which is illegal by the way. I spoke, but not a word back to me. They were big guys, talking among themselves, sounded Eastern European or something. They weren't friendly."

Mitchem paused and wiped his face with the bandana again. "Ah, a little further on, when I was nearly to the point where I take the game trail up to the overlook, I met three men. They weren't friendly either. Two Asians and a Caucasian. I was guessing the White guy was their guide. I spoke to them as we passed on the trail, got a nod and a grunt from the American, but not a word from the two foreigners."

"Why did you think he was American and the other two were foreigners?"

He thought about the question. "I don't know . . . ah, the White guy just *looked* American: a little rough, *scruffy* maybe is a better word. He had some kinda face paint on. I could tell 'cause he was really sweating and it had smeared his jacket. He was carrying a large backpack—twice as big as the other guys' packs. I remember thinking he looked angry, disgusted maybe. He was several steps ahead of the other men." He shrugged. "Maybe they weren't even together. But the Asian guys didn't even have bear spray, I did notice that. They looked very clean, and it's hard to stay clean when you're camping overnight—unless you have a guide to do all the work for you." He paused again. "They just *looked* foreign . . . I don't know. There are lots of Japanese and Korean tourists, even a few Chinese, here in Yellowstone. I'd bet money they weren't Americans."

They stood near the SUV's tailgate and talked for nearly fifteen minutes more. The photographer showed Win his photos of the dead bulls, of the bear and coyotes feasting on the carcasses, of the two buzzards descending. Mitchem had been fooling around with edits on the pictures after he'd saved the originals to his laptop and a flash drive. He pulled up one photo on the laptop that he'd filtered to black and white—he said he'd taken it at 780 feet with a 70-200mm zoom, whatever that meant. The three headless carcasses lying prone in the small, idyllic clearing, with the outline of the distant mountains in the background. A raven was in the foreground, its head cocked as if in question. The photo was a piece of art—a haunting piece of art.

Win took it in. "Why black and white?"

"It catches the emotions."

Yes, it does.

The man continued to talk. "Black and white, right and wrong, good and evil. I've already got this one sold to CNN. It'll get lots of play . . . maybe help you catch the scum who did this."

CHAPTER EIGHT

Win had scheduled a more formal interview with the photographer for tomorrow, Luke had caught another ride back home, and Trey had folks in place to guard the dead bulls overnight. Win finally left the Lamar River Trailhead and drove four miles before he pulled into the Yellowstone Institute's complex of cabins to make a few more calls on his Bureau phone. The Institute had the only cell phone repeater in the Lamar Valley, and he knew he wouldn't have reliable cell coverage most of the way back into Mammoth. It was well after 8:00 p.m. when he called his supervisor.

"We're getting absolutely slammed," Jim West said, before Win even launched into his report on the dead buffalo. "Every news network in the country has called, some foreign outlets as well. *No comment* isn't gonna cut it much longer!"

"I guess some photos got out," Win said.

"Yes, they did." Jim didn't sound happy. "I asked that guy, Mitchem, to hold off on putting anything out on social media, on contacting the press. Told him this morning after he'd called in the dead bison that the Bureau would appreciate some time to get investigative resources in place. . . ." Win could tell Jim was fuming. "The story started hitting the news feeds even before you made the first report back to me from the incident site." Jim took a breath. "I barely had time to brief Denver before the calls started coming in down there. Our press agent is scrambling."

Win wasn't sure what to say. Two days ago the Bureau had put out a press release that two men had been shot to death after a violent car chase in Grand Teton National Park. It hadn't been that big of a news story. Three buffalo get killed in Yellowstone and it immediately goes viral and global—the coverage is immediate and intense. While the senseless killing of the bulls was appalling, the senseless killing of two men was horrific. One story was sensational international news, the other received little notice, business as usual. It said something about the current state of humanity that didn't sit well with Win Tyler.

Win forced his focus back on his boss. "Who've we got coming?"

"The office's press agent, four ERT members out of Denver, and somebody from the Violent Crime Squad—maybe two from that squad; they all left Denver on the office's King Air at six. They're repaving the runway at that airstrip in Gardiner, so they'll have to land in Livingston. Should be touching down around eight. We're borrowing an agent who has his ERT certification outa Bozeman; he's gonna pick some of them up in his vehicle. Kirk Hampton is picking up the others. You met Kirk the day before yesterday in Moose . . . since Johnson's out, Kirk will be working the case with you. He's new to the RA, he's mostly worked cybercrime. Fill him in on the facts."

"They're coming down tonight?"

"Yeah, the plan is for everyone to drive from Livingston to Gardiner if we can find someplace for them to stay. It's almost impossible to find a room anywhere near Yellowstone this time of year."

"What about the two cabins at Mammoth that we keep empty?" Win was referring to two small cabins near the Mammoth Hot Springs Hotel that the Bureau kept on hold in case of emergencies. This certainly counted as an emergency.

"Can't use those. ATF has already requested them for the gunrunning investigation. They're supposed to have someone in place later tonight or early in the morning. I've been too tied up on this bison thing to even ask who they've got going up there."

"I guess I'm meeting with them?"

"Yeah. You're gonna have a full day tomorrow."

The clock on the dashboard said 8:22. He still had nearly an hour's drive back to Mammoth. Win controlled his breathing so his boss wouldn't hear him sigh. *Didn't join the FBI to sit around and do nothing,* he reminded himself.

"You're confident that you've got the site secure?" Jim asked.

"Yes, sir, the rangers got several folks down here. They're going to build some perimeter campfires, use some battery-powered electric fencing, try to keep the site as free of contamination as possible. But that's tough. We had one encounter with a grizzly bear when we first got up there."

There was a long pause. "Please tell me you didn't shoot a bear."

"No . . . no, sir. It just bluffed a charge and moved off."

"Thank goodness. Don't shoot *anything* or *anyone* else. . . . I don't think I can handle another shooting inquiry on you." Jim sounded exasperated. Win didn't know if his supervisor was kidding or not. He sighed. *Probably not.*

*   *   *

He'd been watching the osprey hunt for the better part of thirty minutes. It was a big bird—sixty, maybe sixty-five-inch wingspan. He was thinking it was probably a female, given its large size. She had nice color, dark brown on top, sorta off-white with lots of light-brown spots below. A brown stripe swept to her yellow eyes, and her black beak hooked sharply. But it was the one-and-a-half-inch talons that made her lethal. Lethal to fish, that is.

She had cruised up and down the river several times now. Every so often she'd light on one of the dead trees that lined the warm stream. He reckoned the temperature of the riverbank must fluctuate over the years. If it had stayed hot, there wouldn't have been forty-foot lodgepole pine growing there to begin with. But most were dead now—bare white skeletons that rose above the water. The ground got too warm from time to time to support green timber; he figured that was why the big trees had died off. Maybe it was the global warming thing that everyone talked about, or maybe a hot spring or geyser had come to life and heated the water and the surrounding ground. Yellowstone was always in flux, and the Firehole River was apt to change as well. But either way, the tall trees provided a good spot for the osprey to sit and watch the rippling current below, for her to patiently wait for a fish to swim into view. He liked how the stream was always deep blue, how the rapids were always bright white, how wisps of steam rose from the surface most days. He could identify with the osprey; this was a good spot to sit and think. To wait.

He picked up his binoculars and checked on his customers again. They were still a good 250 yards away, near Sapphire Pool. Its depth and its iridescent blue hue made it one of the park's prettiest springs, but dang, how many photos of a thermal feature can you take? He looked at his watch again: 8:24. He felt a slight stab of guilt that he wasn't out there leading the group tour of Biscuit Basin. The features along this easy three-quarter-mile boardwalk loop were self-explanatory, and he'd sent the group off with the excuse that he needed to make some adjustments to the spotting scopes. What he really needed was some time to himself to plan. Hauling a van full of old folks around for four hours on the Twilight Geyser Tour wasn't conducive to deep thinking.

He glanced off to the west, where thin, high clouds were promising a spectacular sunset. That was good. He'd make it up to the folks by stopping at the pullout that overlooked the Midway Geyser Basin before they headed back. He'd get everyone out of the van and use their phones and cameras to get photos of the three couples with the mountains and the brilliant sunset as the backdrop, with the steam rising from the Grand Prismatic Spring, with vapors floating above the Firehole River, and, if he got real lucky, a geyser spouting up. "*Christmas card photos*," that's what he liked to call them. Show the folks back home how magical this place is . . . wouldn't hurt his chance at some nice tips either. He sighed. He always got better tips when the bears showed up. But they hadn't seen a bear on the drive tonight; couldn't count on the bears being where you needed 'em to be. That big bull elk had been a crowd-pleaser, but he doubted seeing that big boy would cause anyone to throw extra cash his way. He looked up at the osprey again and sighed again. *Maybe there'll be a bear beside the road before we get back to Old Faithful.*

If he'd blinked, he'd have missed it. She dove from her high perch straight down into the blue water and her talons snatched a ten-inch trout from just below the surface. Flaring her wings, she began to climb with her supper. She hadn't gained more than sixty feet of altitude when a huge black-and-white blur dropped from the sky above her. The osprey dodged the hurling object, and the shining silver fish fell from her grasp. But it didn't drop far. The bald eagle grabbed it in midair with one talon, screeched a warning to the smaller raptor, and soared away with its stolen prize.

"Hot damn!" he muttered out loud. The eagle flew back up the river toward the pedestrian bridge and the osprey flew in the opposite direction, likely disappointed about its dinner, but probably glad to be alive.

Witnessing the birds' savage encounter was an *aha* moment. He couldn't remember what those instances of enlightenment were called, but it got him to thinking. Here he'd been working his tail off at two jobs, taking risks for months, and now he was just sitting, just waiting. Waiting was gettin' old. He could choose to wait like the osprey hoping to spot another score, or he could be above it all, let the game totally play out, then swoop down like the eagle and take it all. Let someone else do the work, then move in and take it away. The eagle was bigger, badder, and bolder than the osprey. That's what it comes down to: fortune favors the brave. *Damn right it does.*

* * *

Win locked the back door, balanced his coffee mug, and stepped off the back steps into brilliant sunshine. It was nearly six and the light was hitting the white travertine of the Lower Cascade Terraces square on; it was almost blinding. He never grew tired of seeing the hot springs at his doorstep first thing every morning. It was shrouded in near darkness when he began his run most days right after five, but by the time he returned to the house about thirty minutes later, the sky would have lightened and the draping walls of gleaming white streaked with brilliant orange would greet him. He'd only taken three steps toward his truck when the voice stopped him in his tracks.

"Four big bulls . . . damn. What a waste." There was anger in Luke's tone.

Win knew he'd flinched, been caught unaware, as he turned away from the Bureau SUV and toward the voice near the corner of the house. He tried to act nonchalant.

"A little early, isn't it?" he asked.

Luke leaned back in the old lawn chair and stretched his left shoulder. "My daddy used to say half the day had got by at nine. I notice you get up with the chickens too." He eyed Win's mug. "You got any more of that coffee?"

"Uh-huh . . . you wanta come in?"

"Naw, it's right pretty out here, seeing the light hit the terraces this time of day. You kin bring it out."

Luke was the first one on his schedule for this morning's interviews, but Win hadn't counted on doing that interview in his backyard. He went inside, pulled on a heavier parka over his light jacket, poured a cup of coffee, topped his own coffee off, and joined Luke in the small grassy area between the house and the old carriage shed that passed as his backyard. He and his brothers had drug several old metal lawn chairs and a copper firepit out of the basement when they were visiting last week. They'd spent two evenings around the firepit, telling stories from home while watching the stars and the moon and the flames. It had been nice.

Win handed off the coffee, sat down in one of the chairs facing the hot springs, and pulled the parka tighter around him. He didn't think he'd ever get accustomed to it being near freezing early on summer mornings.

Win decided not to do a formal interview. That could come later. He watched the steam rise from his mug; it seemed to blend with the vapor rising from the hot springs a hundred feet away. He started the conversation. "You've thought about it. Who killed those bulls?"

Luke stretched his left shoulder again. "That part I don't know. But based on the photos Trey showed me of that first bull they got, and on what we saw at that site, then at the other location . . . based on all that, it's the same bunch, same general methods, but one big difference."

Win raised an eyebrow and turned toward Luke. "And that would be?"

"They were in a hurry on that second deal . . . somethin' had gone sideways on 'em."

"You know that how?"

"The hiker's Instagram photos on that first kill showed a clean, professional cut of the trophy mount—the bull's neck and head. But with the three bulls you can tell someone was rushing. It wasn't as clean, not as professional. And that's a big deal in this business. The trophy mount is critical. That's a huge part of what the shooter is paying for. Gotta have that massive neck and head on his den wall, gotta look good.

"And then there was the haul out—nothing disturbed at the site with the first bull." Luke shrugged. "Mount coulda been beamed up . . . just disappeared. With the three bulls it was clear that the chopper was having a time with the load, with the haul out. Lots of sagebrush flattened, chopper swung the load wide, lots of blood spread. Each one of those mounts would weigh over four hundred pounds. So twelve hundred pounds, maybe more. Ain't no big deal fer two men to wrap and roll one mount into a tarp for a lift out. But three? It ain't the weight so much as it is the space on the lift tarp, the time it takes to wrap and move the mounts—and they can't be damaged. Even a great taxidermist can't fix some things. Either it was a different extraction team, or they weren't expecting three dead bison. I'd bet on that last option. I'd bet some fool got greedy."

Win took another sip of his coffee. He knew Luke Bordeaux had spent several months in Alaska as a big game hunting guide immediately after he left the military over five years ago. He also knew one of the previous FBI agents who'd been stationed in Yellowstone had charged Luke with poaching game in the park. That run-in with the law had only been a little over a year ago. He'd also been charged with poaching a deer last April. All those charges had been dismissed and

Luke's commercial guide licenses had recently been reinstated. But as they say in the Bureau, Luke Bordeaux had some history.

"Why'd you get out of big game guiding?"

Luke was quiet for a minute, maybe calculating how much Win knew about his former life. He finally answered. "I grew up huntin' from the time I was little"—he glanced toward Win—"and I reckon you did too."

Win nodded, and Luke kept talking. "We ate what we killed, same as with fish. If we kept 'em, we ate 'em. Taking rich folks out to kill just fer the killing, just fer their ego . . . after a while it didn't sit right with me. There's a place fer wildlife management—an important place—herds have to be thinned out or you're gonna get overgrazing, starvation, and disease. The Lord tells us to be good stewards of this world and its creatures. Managing the wildlife is a part of that. But trophy hunting? There was too much waste in it. I met too many self-indulgent folks who didn't respect the animals, who didn't respect life." He shrugged again. "It just got to the point where it wasn't fer me."

Win could hear it in Luke's voice, he knew they were getting down to the lick-log. Luke shifted in the chair to face Win. "You know about my past. . . . Is this one of them deals where you keep your enemies closer than your friends? Do you think I'm involved in this, Win Tyler?"

Win locked eyes with the man. "No. No, I don't think you're involved, but what I do think is that I could be transferred out of here at any time, probably to Denver. If I leave or even if I stay and get shifted to another case, this poaching deal will likely get moved to someone else in the Bureau, maybe even handed over to Park Service special agents. And if that happens, with your background and your recent poaching charges, dismissed or not, those new folks are gonna take a hard look at you. *A real hard look.* I want to catch these scumbags before that happens. As I see it, getting your help is the quickest way to catch them."

Luke took that in and looked back toward the terraces. "Alright. I can't argue with that. Other than drink some more coffee, whata we need to do?"

"First, give me a tutorial on big game hunting and anything you've heard or know about poaching. I've got about forty minutes before I have to get in the office," Win said as he stood. "Second, run your traps today . . . see if you can come up with a list of suspects. There can't be that many people who could pull off this kind of operation. See what you hear, and let me know. Either get back with me or with Trey if I'm tied up. We've got a bunch of folks arriving from Denver this morning, others got here last night. I'm gonna be meetin' myself comin' and goin'."

Luke nodded. "It was all over the news last night, early news this mornin'."

Win sighed. "I know, and if it's a slow news day, it could get worse."

Luke handed off his empty mug and looked up at Win. "You know, all this press could be a good thing. The boys who set up those bison kills, they probably won't be prepared fer this kinda fallout. In my experience, when you get in a hurry, you make mistakes. They've already made mistakes on the haul out of the three mounts. I'll bet ya they'll make some more."

*　*　*

She looked better than the last time he'd seen her, three days ago at the briefing at the ranger station in Moose. Alex hadn't been thrilled with his offer of an early lunch at eleven, she'd wanted to meet earlier. He told her he was booked. She was miffed and he didn't care. She was on his turf now, and by eleven it had already been a long day of tedious meetings; he wasn't in the mood to deal with her insults.

She followed the petite hostess to his table near the back of the Mammoth Hot Springs Hotel dining room. As she walked toward him in the crowded restaurant, he could tell that her dark eyes were touching everyone in the room. She was wearing navy cargo pants, a light-blue top, and a light-blue long-sleeve shirt over that. It was nearly seventy-five degrees, so he figured the second shirt was to conceal her sidearm. Maybe the Mounties were a bit like the Bureau, he thought, no need for the gun or badge to be out in plain sight. She had her hair in a severe ponytail, and she held a ball cap in her hand. No law enforcement emblems were visible, but he was guessing she was in an unofficial field uniform of sorts. He made a mental note to ask her if she ever wore one of those bright-red jackets he'd seen in the movies, if she had a horse.

He stood up when she got to his table, and he nodded to her and motioned toward the empty chair. She hesitated for a moment and seemed to be considering shaking his hand, but she sat down in the chair instead. He was sitting with his back to the wall—he always did that if he could. People thought it came from his being in law enforcement, but it actually came from growing up with two younger brothers who were always looking to waylay him.

She hadn't said anything, so he nodded to her again and started talking. *Might as well get the preliminaries over with.* "Welcome to Mammoth Hot Springs, the Park Service's headquarters for Yellowstone National Park. I understand we'll be working the case together."

She glanced to both sides. No one was listening to them, no one was sitting too close. He was thinking that she was uncomfortable with her back to the room. But he didn't care, this was his show to run.

"Yeah . . . I got here late last night. They put me in one of those little cabins behind the hotel. It's actually pretty nice."

She's trying to be pleasant. That's a nice change. But it didn't last.

"Even the dump I stayed at in Jackson had TV, had internet . . . and reliable cell service. My phone doesn't work half the time here."

"Folks who come here come to see the park, the animals, the scenery. People come here to get off the grid. Do you have a satellite phone?"

"Yeah, it's in my vehicle. It's heavy, a hassle to carry around—now I've got three phones to juggle. It's a pain."

"Goes with the territory." He didn't have any sympathy; since he was working the Lamar Valley bison case he had the same issues. "Who's ATF got here?"

She switched into business mode and ordered ice water when the waiter moved in. Win ordered the day's special; he offered to buy her lunch, but she passed on it. She told him that ATF was still concentrating their manpower in Grand Teton and down into northern

Utah. She didn't get into case details in the restaurant, but she laid out enough information that it was clear they were on their own with the Yellowstone part of the gunrunning case for at least a couple more days.

He was thinking someone higher up had decided she needed to be nudged off to the sidelines, out of the thick of the case. He figured he was probably right, but he wanted her take on it. "So if all the work is south of here, why are you investigating this angle?" he asked.

She took a sip of her water. "My informant told me the main route out of Utah and Nevada had shifted to the east, away from the interstates, up through the parks, through the Blackfeet Reservation and into Canada's First Nation Reserves. That route leads straight to Calgary, same as the interstates."

"That would be slow going," Win responded.

"Yeah, slow going for 890 miles on the secondary roads, but it would get you there. And ATF and our folks have stopped three shipments on Interstates 15 and 90 in Idaho and Montana in the last nine months. Would you rather get there slow or not get there at all? We're talking big money on these deals."

"How much?"

She glanced around again. No one was near them. "The last shipment we got on my side of the border had come up I-15 and had already cleared customs at Coutts. There were twenty-six used AR-15s and two dozen handguns. All of them had the serial numbers filed off. They were packed within pallets of potatoes. Street value was $134,000 Canadian. That would be about $97,000 U.S."

"What about the driver?"

She shook her head. "Didn't know squat. He thought he was running cocaine."

"How'd he get stopped?"

"Potatoes did him in. Canada has random agricultural inspections near the border. He passed the initial inspection and got stopped about fifty miles in. It was a fluke we got him. Canada requires a license to own a handgun, and AR-15-type weapons can't be imported, can't be owned. Hunting rifles have a less-stringent process for licensing, they're common in the western part of the country. After a couple of recent high-profile shootings, there is a move to tighten gun laws more, require periodic training, that sort of thing. But the U.S. is flooding us with black market weapons and people are dying because of it. Can you imagine how many illegal guns are getting past us? We picked up sixteen illegal weapons in Calgary last month. In a city of 1.4 million, sixteen guns in one month!" She sounded shocked at the number.

That's all? Win kept his expression neutral as he did a quick mental count of the family arsenal they'd had at his house when he was growing up. He decided not to mention the number. Obviously the Second Amendment wasn't a thing in Canada.

CHAPTER NINE

Anyone watching Win Tyler could see that he was loving it: the interaction with other agents, the rapid response to issues, problems, or requests. The teamwork. Win was a team player, and the moment he hit the office after the early lunch with Alex, he had a team. The ERT folks were still with the rangers at the site of the bison kill, but both of the Violent Crime Squad members—Kirk Hampton from the Lander RA, and the Denver press agent—were working the phones and getting set up for a 3:30 press conference. After lunch he'd sat in his office on the second floor and watched a steady stream of TV satellite vans roll past the building. It was gonna get crazy.

The *bison massacre*, as it had been dubbed by last night's cable news shows, was a hot story based on the volume of press that it had generated by early afternoon. Win knew they needed more resources. He'd made a call to the Chief Ranger, and the Park Service had sent over a law enforcement ranger to stand at the front door and halt the constant traffic. They'd also sent a seasoned support staffer, Janet Swam, who had all the required clearances to handle the phones and shuffle the paperwork in the FBI office.

Janet had worked with Win shortly after he arrived in the park, and on seeing her today, he was struck again by her similarity to his second-grade teacher. She looked to be at least eighty, with her silver hair pulled back in a tight bun. Her eyes were somewhere behind thick lenses; the glasses' green frames were holdovers from the 1980s. Her stern look hadn't changed a bit since he'd seen her last, but a positive constant was her tendency to show up with all sorts of homemade treats. She knocked on his doorframe at two and silently held out her latest stash of goodies: homemade brownies and chocolate chip cookies. Win smiled at her and figured he'd made enough choices today; no time for indecision—he took one of each. He started in on the big cookie with his fourth cup of coffee.

Kirk paused in his trek down the hall and leaned into Win's office from the doorway. "I guess the homemade cookies help make up for the remoteness of the place," he offered.

Win swallowed the last bite of the cookie and nodded down at his paper plate. "You want the brownie?"

The guy shook his head. "Naw . . . uh, no, I'm vegan. Just admiring it is all."

Win signaled Kirk in, and he slumped into one of the antique chairs. He drew a deep breath and closed his eyes for a moment. Kirk Hampton looked real young, much younger than Win. They hadn't had time for chitchat, no time to get to know each other. Kirk was wearing jeans and a sweatshirt; Win thought the clothes were way too casual for the office, but he said nothing. He told himself to let it go, could be the guy had been up most of the night trying to get the evidence response folks settled. "I'll bet you had a long night getting the team situated. . . . Did you find a decent place for them to stay?" Win asked.

"Not a clue," Kirk replied, staring down at his phone. "Dropped 'em off at that dump of a hotel Denver gave me off the GPS, then I hit a few bars." He glanced up at Win and shook his head. "Had a late night, but there's like no action in Gardiner."

Win wasn't sure what to say so he made another stab at being social. "Jim said you'd been on the Cyber Squad."

Kirk's eyes opened wider, and he straightened in the chair. "Yeah, yeah, joined the Bureau as soon as I got my degree—like, right outa college . . . you know they waive the three-year work requirement if a prospective agent is totally into computers, languages, something like that. Well, I got this job right out of Dartmouth. Thought it would look stellar on my résumé, you know. Been in two years now, kinda looking to land in an international cybersecurity firm . . . I'm trolling some of the headhunter sites, been getting some good hits already, but I may need to build my platform a bit to score a really sweet spot."

Whoa! For real? Win was surprised, and not just by the sudden flood of personal information. He knew there were work experience exemptions in the FBI for certain advanced degrees and skills, such as law, languages, and computers, but he'd never met another special agent who considered the Bureau a short-term stop, just a quick step up to something better. Kirk looked down at his phone, then eyed the brownie again. He seemed oblivious to the fact that Win hadn't responded.

"So you're new to the Lander RA?" Win finally asked.

The guy shook his head and sighed. "That was not, like, a voluntary transfer. Lander is expanding their office space since they shut down the office in Jackson, so they needed someone with my expertise to line things up, integrate all the new hardware." He sighed again. "Was thinking it was a real temporary thing, but it's dragged on for several weeks." He shrugged. "But that cow-town assignment may be the push I needed to get another gig that'll pad the bank."

"Okaaay . . . so you're not impressed with central Wyoming?"

"It's *Wyoming*, dude. Not my scene." He nodded toward Win's Indiana Jones–style hat that was hanging on the oak coatrack. "I can see you're into this, but even Lander is light-years ahead of Mammoth. They claim the population in Lander is nearly eight thousand, but that has to count the horses and cows. At least in Lander there's 5G. Here in this office, even with the recent upgrades, cell service is weak half the time. This place is, like, nowhere." He glanced down at his phone again and frowned.

Win picked up the brownie just in case the guy's appetite overruled his vegan tendencies. "Not to interrupt your job search, but you do know Jim will want a report later today on your efforts to track down the chopper that hauled those bison heads out," he said. He was wondering how much authority he had over Kirk, if any. Wondering if Kirk would do the work.

"Yeah, yeah . . . I'm on that." Kirk sighed and frowned again. "I don't really get the big push here—dead bison, really? Come on, man! I saw dozens of bison when I was driving up, whole herds. Looked like big furry cows." The younger agent locked eyes with Win. "You probably had beef for lunch . . . no one's ramped up over that bovine's demise." Kirk's flippant tone said he couldn't care less about the case.

Well, there you go. Win knew his eyes had narrowed, knew the flash of anger he felt was carrying to the man sitting in front of him. Win held his breath to keep from saying his thoughts. He had zero tolerance for a slacker, for anyone playing the system for their own gain.

Kirk was perceptive enough to see that he was fixing to get hammered. He quickly switched subjects and found a conciliatory tone. "Uh . . . I hear you're gonna get transferred to Denver as soon as they can make it work," he said. "I'll bet you're countin' the minutes."

Win tamped down his anger. *Not the time or the place,* he internally counseled himself. He leaned back in his chair and glanced away. "I was anxious about it at first, wanting to get out of here, but now so much has happened . . . met some good people, seen some amazing things."

"Yeah, but you're workin' poaching cases? The occasional petty theft or small-time drugs?" Kirk said as he started to stand.

This kid must live under a rock! Apparently, Kirk hadn't kept up with the national news the last couple of months. Win's tone was incredulous. "Haven't you followed any of Yellowstone's domestic terrorism or counterintelligence cases since May? There were some big cases here for the Denver Field Office."

Kirk shrugged his thin shoulders, glanced at his phone, and moved toward the door. "Naw, haven't gotten into the weeds on any of that . . . my world's online. . . . Speakin' of that"—he nodded down toward his phone again—"got an interesting bite on my résumé." He waved at Win as he left the room. "Later, man."

* * *

After Kirk left, Win finished his coffee and polished off the brownie as he tried to fight the sinking feeling that had surfaced during their talk. It felt too much like those recent conversations with his little brother. *Totally one sided.* And Kirk Hampton obviously had the same outlook as Will—life was all about the money. No thought of justice, honor, or loyalty, just a blatant inward focus, an entirely self-centered perspective. Win stared at the bear painting on his wall and wondered why he suddenly felt old.

He breathed one last sigh, then began reviewing the various digital reports that had begun hitting the poaching case file. The preliminary ballistic information on the dead bulls had finally shown up from the Evidence Response Team leader. One thing was clear: the poachers were definitely pros, and there wasn't much to find except for evidence of really good shooting. A clean shot to the heart, probably just three shots, but they didn't have the animals' necks or heads, so that wasn't conclusive. Win was doubtful they'd disfigure the mount with any kind of head shot. He knew Luke was right, an impressive head mount was critical in a trophy hunt.

The rifle had to be very powerful since the animals had dropped where they'd been hit. He was guessing something bigger than a .30-06. No way to know yet, since they hadn't found any brass or slugs. They did know the shots had been taken from less than eight hundred feet away, up on the overlooking bluffs. He'd suspected that location when they'd first scouted the site. It was a close shot, close enough that the shooter didn't have to be a true marksman. But three heart shots from any distance was impressive. *Lucky shots?* he wondered, as he forced himself to compartmentalize his anger and disgust.

A phone buzzed as he was closing out of the ERT report. It was Blake calling his personal phone. "Hey, Bubba. Work letting up any?"

"No, if anything, it's ramping up again," Win responded as he stood and walked across the room to close his office door.

"Don't seem to be any shortage of bad guys out there," his brother said.

"Probably not much of a shortage of bad guys anywhere else either—excellent job security. You in the hay field?"

"Yeah, just finished cutting the bermudagrass down by the river. And it's hotter than blue blazes. Radio said it's supposed to be over a hundred today. What are y'all up to at two o'clock? A sizzlin' seventy-five degrees?"

"Naw, it's a heat wave here too. Gonna get near eighty."

He heard his brother scoff. "I could get used to that. But I suppose there's pluses and minuses wherever you are. I saw a story about some dead buffalo bulls in Yellowstone on the news last night. You gonna give me the inside scoop on that?"

"No."

"You in the middle of it?"

"Maybe, can't say much."

"I'll take that as a *yes*," Blake said. He paused for just a moment. "Well, catch those scum, but be careful doin' it. After you show'd us those big buffalo herds last week—after seein' those huge bulls—I'm thinkin' someone would have to have some serious firepower to bring one of those suckers down. And if they'd kill animals in a national park, they might not be too picky 'bout other things they'd shoot. They're some dangerous dudes. . . . Watch yourself, Bubba."

"I hear you. . . . I've thought about that." But it occurred to Win as he said the words that he hadn't really given his personal protection as much thought as he should have. His brother was right. Win abruptly changed the subject. "Whata ya hear from Will?"

"Tucker's got him locked down tighter than a drum. He had to call me from a flip phone Tucker gave him—no smart phone. But you know, it's only been two days and he is sounding more normal, or as normal as a fifteen-year-old sounds. You haven't touched base with them?"

"No, I was gonna give it a couple more days."

"Well, Tucker's got them signed up for a four-day backpacking trip in Yellowstone early next week. I talked to Will last night and he seemed excited about it. And he is lovin' working with the horses. You know, if football doesn't work out for him, I could see him going to vet school. He's always been good with animals . . ."

Win leaned back in his office chair and listened to Blake talk about Will, about the crops, the cattle, the things of home that he could picture clearly when he closed his eyes. This was what that Headquarters shrink had wanted him to do more of: focus on normal things, on good things, in between the crush and pressure of the job. Ease the stress, even if it's just for one phone call. They closed the call with Win's promise to be careful and Blake's promise to FaceTime Win in a few days with his four-year-old twin nephews and Li'l Bit, his two-year-old niece.

* * *

Jesse pulled the big gray SUV into the small parking lot less than a hundred yards north of the Grand Loop Road. Terrace Spring was the first thermal feature you came to on the road from West Yellowstone into the park. He'd left town right after the Rotary lunch and made the thirty-minute drive here. He'd always liked this spot; it was a favorite of his for getting rid of *"unwanteds,"* as he liked to call them. It was just after two and he knew there wouldn't be many other people here. It was probably eighty degrees and there was no shade, no bathrooms either, and the more dramatic geysers, fumaroles, and colorful springs were just up the road. No reason to stop here unless you were hiking the seldom-used Terrace Spring Trail or stopping to view the Gibbon River valley and Three Brothers Mountains, which loomed to the southwest, or needing a convenient, reliable spot to dispose of *unwanteds.*

Most folks thought criminals just dropped murder weapons, contraband, bodies, or other evidence into a river. *Drive over a bridge— throw it off!* But it was amazing how often that didn't work. Running water eventually washes evidence up *somewhere*, not to mention that bridge pilings are often the first places cops investigate. Better to drop it—whatever *it* is—into one of Yellowstone's thermal pools, where the water temperature ranges from 140 to 230 degrees, where the depths range from thirty feet to bottomless, where the heat and acid will eat it away. This seldom-visited spot with its unimpressive hot springs and dark-blue pools was his location of choice for the job at hand.

As he expected, the parking lot at Terrace Spring was nearly deserted. He watched a man in a black Rolling Stones T-shirt and a woman in a crop top and bright-pink shorts walk ahead of two small kids on the wooden boardwalk nearby. *Wow, people can be damn fools!* he thought, watching the little boy and girl make a wild dash for the railing near a gurgling spring that was spitting water three feet into the air. The parents continued to saunter along, seemingly unconcerned. Never mind that the water below the boardwalk was likely near boiling, never mind that people died in Yellowstone's superheated pools often—the two adults were just lollygagging along with no regard for the danger. He was thinking that the animals did a far better job of guarding their offspring than many of the humans he'd seen in the park.

The only other people at the nondescript thermal feature were a couple moving toward their motorcycle. They were putting on their helmets, snapping their leather jackets, getting ready to move on. They revved up the Harley to an earsplitting level and slowly began to pull away toward the highway.

He'd just wait. He hit the switch to lower the windows of his Infiniti, then turned off the engine and the satellite radio's classical music. *Just wait.* Yesterday afternoon he told Dex that he'd gotten rid of the guns. That wasn't true. What was true was that they were now hotter than firecrackers. He'd thought he might sell the rifle that hadn't fired, maybe even sell both of them—they were vintage guns, expensive guns. But then he'd seen the news about the bison massacre. He knew the heat was on. Selling them was no longer an option. If the Feds found a slug or were somehow able to match the powder residue on the bison carcasses to Dex's gunpowder stash, they could trace it back to the rifle that had fired. He'd told Dex not to keep his reloading equipment at his father's place, and maybe Dex had listened, but he couldn't count on that. Hell, didn't seem like he could count on anybody thinking things through, doing their job. *Dammit, you can't get good help anymore.*

By some miracle, the two children and their parents made it off the boardwalk unscathed. He pulled his Stetson down lower to shield his face as the group filed past his big SUV on their way to their van. He watched them from under the brim, although hiding his identity wasn't really necessary since he doubted those fools would have noticed a fly-ing saucer in the parking lot. It always amazed him that most people saw next to nothing of their surroundings, even when their surround-ings were as amazing as Yellowstone.

Jesse knew Terrace Spring was a relatively new thermal feature. This area about a mile east of the Madison junction on the Grand Loop Road had been an open field interspersed with scattered stands of lodgepole pine not that many years ago. It was a pretty place on a slightly sloping area just to the north of the highway. The hot water had formed a deep, placid pool, with a couple of smaller, active springs nearby. All of the pools emptied into a small stream that meandered down the slope, killed a few trees, flowed under the highway, and across another open area to join the Gibbon River. The Park Service was forced to rebuild the highway every so often to keep the hot water from melting the asphalt.

In the last few years, as the blue pools grew, they'd added board-walks so that folks wouldn't be tempted to park on the side of the road and walk up to the site. It was just as dangerous as it was fascinating. Some days the water shot up two or three feet; some days it was smooth as glass. That was one of the things that he liked about Yellowstone— the landscape was always changing. Something was always new.

The young couple were handing out water bottles to the kids and trying to herd them into their minivan. He scanned the busy highway and the lot entrance. Nothing coming right now. He clicked open the vehicle's tailgate, got out, and reached into the back compartment for the army duffel bag that contained the two disassembled Winchester Safari Express rifles. These older guns didn't just pop apart like some newer, plastic models—no, these babies were smooth wood and heavy metal, built to fire the powerful cartridges that brought down big game. He laid the gun components out in the SUV's back compart-ment and studied them. He'd packaged the guns separately because he was waffling on disposing of both. They were high-dollar firearms, and Dex had been smart enough to file off the serial numbers. He still was thinking of keeping one.

"Hey, sir—"

What tha— He whirred around and his hand instinctively went to the pancake holster under his shirt, on his back hip. He stood blocking the view into the SUV.

The young man in the Stones shirt was standing right behind him. He took a step back at Jesse's sudden turn. "Uh, didn't mean to startle you . . . was wondering if you could help me?"

Jesse's attention shot from the guns in his vehicle to the pistol he was gripping to the intruder. He forced a smile and wondered how much this jerk had seen.

"Sure, sure, what do you need?" He kept his fingers on the handgun's grip as he spoke.

"We've got a flat . . . and uh, it's my aunt's van, and . . . there isn't a jack."

"Spare tire?"

"Yeah, yeah . . . tire . . . no jack."

My jack's in the compartment under the guns, he thought. *This ain't good.*

Both men glanced at the van when the kids started screaming and pointing toward the woods where a small herd of elk were emerging.

The young man was embarrassed. "I hate to bother you . . . I saw you had spotting scopes in the back. Are you a photographer or something?"

Jesse smiled again as he stepped toward the guy, hoping to block his view a bit more. He hit the remote and the Infiniti's tailgate lowered. It registered with him that the guy had no idea what he was seeing.

Jesse took another step forward and introduced himself with a fictitious name. He kept talking, "Yeah, I'm trying out some new tripods with my equipment . . . lots of metal pieces, was fixing to put them together. But no problem at all." The kids were still yelling on the other side of the lot. Jesse ratcheted up the enthusiasm in his voice. "Hey, I've got a better scope in the back seat and some great binoculars. Let's get the kids some close-up views of the elk—they'll love that! Then we'll get that tire fixed."

They carried the scope and the binoculars toward the two kids, who were being scolded by mom for the screaming. The herd of twenty or so elk ignored the humans and stopped in an open area fifty yards away to graze.

"Hey, I found us a hero!" the young man announced to his family as they approached the van. "Meet the nicest guy in Yellowstone!"

*   *   *

Win had barely closed out his call with his brother when his Bureau phone buzzed. He found himself marveling at his Academy friend's efficiency.

"Hey, Win, this is SSA Joe Shorter, Training Division at Quantico. Judy Wade reached out to me and said you needed the lowdown on Alex Lindell."

"Wow, I left Judy a message Monday afternoon—that was fast."

The training supervisor laughed softly. "Judy is amazing. She has, or can get, the skinny on anyone, so you'd better watch yourself! You're working with Alex on a case?"

"Looking that way, sir . . . it'll probably be real short-term, but things could get a little dicey and I want to know who I'm dealing with. I'd appreciate any insight you've got on her."

"I follow you. She was in one of those ten-week National Academy classes we do for other law enforcement agencies . . . that was just over a year ago. The Bureau tries to enroll about ten to fifteen percent foreign students in those classes. It's kinda a goodwill thing with our allies. As I recall the Canadians pushed real hard to get her in at the last minute. I was the lead over her class, I don't know her well . . . but I did some checking on her back then. I've got some opinions."

"Whatever you can give me, sir."

"Well, she's a Mountie and there aren't that many female field officers within their force. When she was here she was ranked as a constable, what we'd call a street agent, but she'd been busted down from the rank of sergeant—a huge demotion. She is experienced, has been in the field for several years, and specialized in what the Canadians call 'Federal Policing.' Alex is logical, intuitive, driven . . . a hard worker

. . . proficient with her weapons." He paused, and Win figured he was weighing how much personal information to provide.

Win didn't say anything. He waited the guy out. He'd learned long ago that people have an aversion to silence; it's human nature to want to fill in the vacuum, and they often provide far more information than they intend. Win smiled inwardly when the supervisor started talking again.

"I was told that she lost her partner in a gunfight in Toronto . . . some sort of raid that went all sorts of bad. She got caught in the fallout from it, lost her rank. I remember thinking then that she might have been sent to the National Academy to give her a break. She's a good officer."

"Well, she just lost an informant she'd been handling for nearly nine months, and an ATF agent that she knew. That all went down on a case she was working alongside ATF last week," Win said.

"Oh, man. That has to take a toll."

"She probably needs to step away from this case, but that's not likely to happen. I've heard that she's been in the thick of it since ATF set up a joint task force with the Canadians last fall to stop the flow of illegal weapons. She wants to be in it, she wants it bad."

Win could tell that the supervisor was holding something back. His self-interest kicked in. "Is she up for the work?"

"The last time I saw her she was down here in February for a seven-day follow-up to the National Academy. Unless she's really changed, I don't see a problem with her doing the job. Alex is a pro. She's hard-nosed, but she's a pro."

Win didn't reply, and he knew the supervisor could tell he wasn't convinced. "Her partner, ah . . . the guy who got killed in that busted takedown in Toronto . . . well, word had it he and Alex were having an affair. Word had it the affair busted up her marriage. She lost custody of her daughter."

"Whoa . . . that's a lot of baggage. What about as a person—what about *her*?"

"When she was here, she had an edge. She wasn't gonna win any Miss Congeniality contests. Never showed any interest in getting to know anyone. Maybe a chip on her shoulder, trauma over the Toronto deal. I don't know."

"I made the mistake of thinking Alex was a guy when I first called her. I was expecting a man. I called and asked to talk to the agent, asked to speak to Alex—"

"I'll bet that went over well."

"She was really ticked off. I thought she was a little over the top."

"Sounds like she hasn't changed much in that regard. She's not happy or nice, but she is sharp and capable. At least you've got that."

Yeah, at least I've got that.

* * *

Win ended the call and hurried to finish up the professional photographer's FD-302 interview report. Randolph Mitchem had driven in from his summer cabin in Gardiner at 9:00 that morning to meet with Win for the formal interview. Win had done a search for Mitchem on the internet the night before and was stunned to learn that the guy's original wildlife and landscape photos of the Yellowstone region were selling for over $10,000 each—some were priced three times that amount. Even the prints were out of Win's price range; he was impressed.

The photographer had taken the morning off from his craft and he wasn't too happy about it, but he was still amazingly helpful. He described the group of several "large men," as he called them, who were camped illegally about one mile from the incident site. He'd passed by them quickly, he said, and had few details to provide.

But Mitchem had done a rough sketch of the "American" he'd seen on the trail with the two smaller guys he'd labeled as "foreigners." The sketch wasn't great, but it wasn't bad either: wild brown hair under a ball cap, stout shoulders anchoring a short, thick neck. A broad face half covered with an unkempt beard, eyes that were wide set and angry.

In contrast, Mitchem thought the two Asian men looked relaxed on the hike, maybe even smug. The stout White guy was toting a huge backpack; he looked completely exhausted and a whole lot mad. Mitchem said again that he thought the guy had on some kind of face paint.

Mitchem hadn't seen or heard any helicopters in the Lamar Valley the morning that the three bulls were shot, but he didn't get to the killing field until mid-morning. He'd seen plenty of other choppers east of Roosevelt that summer—he assumed they were all related to the bridge or highway construction work. Mitchem had remarked that nothing ruins a true Yellowstone experience quicker than having a noisy helicopter drop into view.

Win hit SUBMIT to send the photographer's interview into the inner workings of the Bureau and glanced down at a text he'd just received from Trey: **Big group Mitchem spotted camped quarter mile up Slough Creek Trail. Jazz will make contact within the hour. Interview there?**

Win texted back a **10-4** and pulled the Lamar Valley trail maps out of his desk drawer. It wasn't yet 2:45, but he was now looking for an excuse to get out of the office. The press conference was coming up at 3:30 and things were getting wild. Trey had been working on locating the two groups of backpackers that Mitchem had spotted hiking out near the incident site. They'd had several tips on the whereabouts of the group of European guys who'd been camped illegally along South Cache Creek, and now it seemed they had them.

But the second group of three were proving harder to find. The larger group had no permits to camp. The smaller group had filed for a backcountry camping permit, but they were supposed to be at a primitive campground that was nearly two miles closer to the trailhead than the point where Mitchem had seen them. There was no evidence that they'd camped overnight in their assigned location, and the phone numbers and names they'd left on the paperwork at the backcountry ranger station weren't legible. Trey said that backpackers constantly disregarded the rules, said he was working on it.

Win and Trey were both feeling the pressure. They needed to make some progress, finish up their potential witness interviews, develop some solid leads. They were now more than forty-eight hours out from the bison killings. They needed a break in the case.

Win buzzed Kirk to tell him he was leaving the office, then he grabbed the map, a handheld recorder, and the satellite phone. He hesitated at his office door, moved back to his antique oak desk, opened the side drawer, and pulled out a compact Glock 43 handgun and its pancake holster. He loaded the gun, put it back in its holster, and sat there looking at it.

It was one of his personal guns. He'd qualified with it and had approval from the Bureau to carry it, but he hadn't worn it often. The Glock 22 .40 caliber that he wore on his belt when on duty had been standard issue when he entered the Bureau three and a half years ago. Most FBI agents now carried a Glock 19, a 9mm weapon. But Win liked the higher firepower, and his use of the older model had been grandfathered in. He shifted his focus back to the small Glock on his desk. He knew most agents didn't carry two guns, didn't need to carry two guns. He hadn't carried a second weapon since . . . well, since the last time he felt threatened. *Am I under threat now? No. . . .* But as he slid the compact holster onto the back of his belt, he remembered Blake's words: *dangerous dudes.*

CHAPTER TEN

Win keyed in the security code on the back door of the two-story stone building that housed the FBI satellite office, and quietly eased out of the heavy wooden door. He couldn't go out the front door; he'd have to dodge the frantic activity on the main entrance steps and porch, where he knew several Park Service folks were setting up a podium for the afternoon press conference. He wanted to be nowhere to be found when that circus began.

The tension and the level of activity in the small FBI building had become intense in the last thirty minutes. The poor press agent was to the point of pulling out what little hair he had left. No one had any useful information to report, so they were going to bring in the Park Service's press people, talk about the history of poaching in the park and the health of the park's bison herd, which he'd just heard some guy say numbered over 5,000 this year. He knew they'd make a plea for the public to turn in any photos, videos, or tips on the poachers. He knew Headquarters and the Park Service were throwing around numbers and trying to set an amount for a reward. He'd heard $25,000 mentioned more than once. They'd only offered $10,000 for information leading to an arrest in the killings of the ATF agent and the informant last week in Grand Teton. The disparity in the response to the two cases bothered Win Tyler—bothered him a lot.

Win swung around the corner of the building to his Bureau-issued Ford Expedition and had just reached for the door handle when he saw her out of the corner of his eye. He paused for a second and wondered what Alex was doing on the other side of the narrow street. He found out real quick what he suspected: she was staking him out, waiting for him to leave, wanting to be part of the action. He forced the annoyance from his face and turned to watch her approach.

"You're going into the park?" Her voice was borderline friendly. She acted as if she'd just accidently stumbled upon him.

"Uh-huh."

"I'd like to go . . . get a feel for the area." She looked really earnest.

"I'm working a case. Hope to interview witnesses," he began. But as she dropped her gaze from his eyes, he felt something akin to pity surface in his chest. He'd been sidelined on a case before, he knew how awful that felt. But he tried again to dissuade her. "I thought you were gonna be getting some direction from the ATF folks."

"Everyone's tied up on leads. I probably won't hear from them till tonight or even tomorrow." She shrugged her thin shoulders and motioned with her head toward the SUV. "I'll just be along for the ride."

He gave up. "Okay then." His supervisor had said to work with her, and she obviously had no work of her own to do. *What the heck.*

She climbed in the passenger side of the big gray SUV and got quiet. They took the Grand Loop Road through the old parade ground alongside Officer's Row, the stately line of brick-and-clapboard two-story houses that had housed the cavalry officers' families back in the late 1800s. He pointed out the Yellowstone Chapel, a lovely gray-stone church that had stood since 1913 and had played a significant role in his life during his short time in the park. They passed Lower Yellowstone, the rows of modest, modern houses and duplexes where the rangers and their families lived. Then they dropped off the plateau, crossed the high steel bridge over the Gardner River, and climbed southeastward into the more mountainous regions of the park.

Win didn't bother acting like a tour guide for long, he just let her take it in. He answered her questions about the road. He could tell she was studying the route. Eighteen miles and thirty minutes later, they made a pit stop at Roosevelt. He returned a couple of calls and checked his texts. There wasn't always cell service here, so that was a bonus.

Alex walked over to the shade beside the gas station and asked Win to wait while she made a call.

He sat in the truck and killed time watching a line of happy cowpokes cross the road at the beginning of their trail ride. They were waving their caps and hats back toward their friends and families—the last horseback photo op before the wranglers got serious about the trek. The horses seemed to take their riders' enthusiastic antics in stride, and as he watched them move into the sagebrush flats, Win wondered how his little brother was faring with Miss Martha's much-less-docile mounts. Will had always been good with horses, all the Tyler boys were. Growing up on a cattle farm in the Ozarks, horses, cattle, working dogs, and barn cats were all part of the mix.

Then his mind strayed into unwelcome territory. He had a bad habit of doing that lately, letting his thoughts wander down sad roads from the past. Shelby didn't like horses, never wanted pets . . . never wanted children either. She'd told him they'd hold back her medical career, told him it wouldn't be fair to the kids. She said she didn't have time in her life for pets or for children. *Didn't have time in her life. . . .* Ultimately, he reckoned he'd fallen into that category as well.

Alex slid into the truck and caught him thinking those thoughts. He didn't get his game face on fast enough.

"So I'm not the only one dealing with loss," she said.

He tamped down the thoughts of Shelby and shifted to look at Alex. She was pretty darn perceptive, he'd give her that. She didn't pull on her seat belt, she just sat there looking into his eyes. He wasn't real sure what he was expecting, but this wasn't it.

"It's not like you haven't figured it out . . . figured out there was something between Greg and me," she said softly.

"It's none of my business. Isn't that what you told me?" He knew she was talking about Greg Manyhorses, the informant who'd been killed. *And yeah, I figured that out.* Being romantically involved with an informant was unprofessional, dangerous, and possibly criminal, but he didn't mention those things. She knew all that.

She took a deep breath and just sat there for a moment, staring at him. "No, it isn't your business, but I'm . . . ah . . . I'm not dealing with this so well." She swallowed hard and he started to speak, but she beat him to it. "It's just that I'm sidelined—basically off the case, you know that." Her tone held accusations, as if it were somehow his fault. She cleared her throat and he realized she was nearly in tears. "I want to get the ones who did this. It's all I can give him now." She broke the eye contact and shook her head. "Ah, there's no one to talk with . . . I haven't talked to my ex-husband or my daughter in nearly a month . . . I've got no one to talk to." She nearly lost her composure again before she spoke. "Greg was someone to talk to."

He didn't answer. He didn't know how to respond. He started the engine and let the air-conditioning blow on them, but he knew she still had things to say, so he didn't put the SUV in gear.

"I miss talking to him," she said softly. She had turned her eyes away from his, but he could tell she was blinking tears away. "There were things I should have mentioned . . . told him . . . there were things I should have asked." She stared off into space as if she could picture it, could picture the conversations that never took place. It was another level of sadness, and all he heard for a few moments was her ragged breathing.

"I'm sorry, Alex. We all suffer losses . . . maybe not to the same degree. But I'm learning that there's no quick fix for grief." He swallowed down his own emotions. "I'm sorry," he said again.

"He was a good guy, you know. Just got mixed up with the wrong people in high school, skipped college, skipped the military, now he's skipped life . . ."

"You grew up with him?"

He could tell she was struggling to keep from crying, she nodded. "He was Blood Tribe, or Kainai. Americans would call us Blackfoot, I suppose. My mother is Kainai, and my father is half Siksika, also a Blackfoot Nation. He's a Mountie . . . he met my mother when she was in college in Calgary. That's where I grew up. I'd go back to the Kainai Nation Reserve in Standoff and stay with my grandparents during school breaks, for ceremonies. I met Greg when we were little kids, just six or seven years old. He was a different clan, but he was practically a brother. It was never really a love affair . . . not really, not like you think." Her eyes cut to his, and he saw the flinty glint reappear. "It's not what you're thinking."

"I'm not judging you."

"I think you are—you've got that Christian vibe. Friendly, nice, kind to everyone . . . but I'll bet you're always judging."

He blinked in surprise. *Geez, where is this coming from?* He started to speak, but she wasn't finished.

"My grandfather converted to Anglican . . . he carried a Bible . . . he judged me." Her voice became bitter. "It's just a crutch, you know. Religion, church, God—any god, they're all just crutches. Just something to lean on if you can't handle life yourself."

Win was taken aback by her comments on faith. And suddenly concerned that he needed an answer. "I don't agree with that, Alex. That's not my reality. I trust in God and my faith is central to me. It's my foundation, the foundation for anything good that I do."

His satellite phone buzzed before she could answer. She turned away from him and pulled on her seat belt. He figured that signaled an end to the emotional discussion, so he reached for the phone.

It was Trey and he got right to business. "Jazz hasn't called back in after her initial contact with that backpacking group. Her backup is delayed south of Tower. How far are you from her location?"

Win did a quick review of the maps, distances, and times in his head. "We're at the Tower–Roosevelt junction . . . can be at the Slough Creek Trailhead in fifteen minutes or so."

"Ten-four. Okay. She has a sat phone, but there's no cell service where she's at. Give me an update when you can."

"Copy that. We're rolling."

* * *

Ranger Jazmine Jackson didn't typically take any crap off anyone. The twenty-five-year-old was a member of the park's Special Response Team, she was athletic and professional. And right at this moment, Win didn't have to be a genius to recognize that she was afraid.

A big guy—no, a huge guy—was towering over Jazz with a club-like hand raised. She was standing just outside of his reach. Her bright-yellow Taser was in her hand, but she was pointing it down, not yet committed to engaging the giant.

Win stepped into the campsite from the trail, and Alex smoothly moved ten feet to his left, her hand on her holster. The confrontation was less than thirty feet away.

"Hold it!" Win shouted. "FBI! Back off!"

The big guy froze and turned his head toward Win, but kept his arm raised. Win's hand went to the Glock's grip, but he didn't pull it. The other campers turned toward him as one, a solid line of mammoth men in T-shirts and shorts, all with buzz cuts or shaved heads, all well over Win's considerable height, and each one scowling in anger.

"I've got this handled, Win," Jazmine called out, in a much stronger voice than he would have thought her capable of, given the throng of giants in front of her.

The threatening man slowly lowered his arm and turned toward Win with a booming voice. "You boss?" It was clear English wasn't his native language.

Win didn't answer the question. "What's going on?" he nearly yelled at the guy.

"She tell us to go . . . to go. . . . We are just here. Stay here." He motioned with the other big hand toward the scattered tents, toward the other seven men.

Win counted them in his head as his eyes scanned them again for weapons. Heck, these guys didn't need weapons. As a group, they were big enough to scare anyone to death. Win took a couple of steps closer to the men, his hand still on the Glock.

Ranger Jazmine spoke up before he could. "We're here to do a subject interview on a poaching incident. We need your cooperation, now!" She'd clearly lost her patience.

The man glanced her way in confusion, then immediately turned back to Win. "You boss?" came the question again.

Alex moved toward Win; he felt her touch his arm. "Let me try," she said quietly.

"Bonjour, monsieur, parlez-vous français? Nous sommes des policiers et nous avons besoin de votre assistance," Alex said as she stepped forward.

Darn if every one of those monsters didn't perk up and smile. They all nodded, and Alex set off into a rapid-fire discourse with the apparent leader. Win didn't understand a word. When there was a momentary break, Win quickly asked Alex, "What did you say?"

"I told them that we're police officers and we need their help. They're a professional rugby scrum, here on a team-building trip."

What's a rugby scrum? Win wondered.

Alex kept up the dialogue in French as everyone moved back toward their firepit for the interviews, and she filled Win in a bit more. "I think they need help. It's sounding as if the tour they paid for has abandoned them. None of them speaks passable English."

"They're French?" he asked.

"Probably not, they're with a Moldavian team, but French is widely spoken in professional rugby circles."

How does she know this stuff?

Alex kept talking. "I thought they looked like forwards, ah, it would be like your big linemen in American football. . . . I hope I didn't overstep."

"Are you kidding? I was dead in the water there. I appreciate your help. You speak French really well."

"Canada is a bilingual country, Win. English *and* French are the national languages."

"Oh."

Ranger Jazmine seemed impressed with Alex's methods. She managed a few basic words in French with the apparent leader. The giant smiled down at Jazz. She glanced at Win to see if he noticed; she looked extremely pleased with herself.

Now that it was reasonably clear that no one was going to get beaten up, tasered, or shot, the interviews went amazingly well. Alex translated as she introduced the men, got an apology for Jazmine, and set out their mission. Win wasn't expecting much from the interviews. He was surprised by what he got. Two of the men had seen a group of backpackers hike past their makeshift camp near South Cache Creek late on the afternoon of July 4th. The big guys reported that the two smaller men who hiked past them were clearly speaking Chinese, no doubt about that. But there were two Caucasian men, not one, and those two were carrying the larger packs. The rugby players didn't get a good look at anyone; they were intentionally staying away from the trail. But they could hear the men, and what they heard was what they called "American English" and Chinese. The four hikers were taking the trail that led to the clearing where the dead bulls were found. Win knew there were no designated campgrounds on that trail.

The next morning right at 5:25 the group reported that they clearly heard three shots—they knew the exact time because they had just begun their workout routine. They'd talked about the gunfire as they stoked their campfire before breakfast. They'd heard a helicopter as they were finishing breakfast and starting to plan for the day—that had to be around seven o'clock. They heard the chopper again less than thirty minutes later. They didn't get a look at it. It was flying low, they could tell that by the sound. The group leader thought the gun-shots and the helicopter were odd; he decided to break camp and move to a different area. The only other hiker they saw before they moved out was a man carrying camera equipment who waved to them as he passed. They didn't see anyone else hike out of the immediate area, but they were busy with their camp teardown and could have easily missed other hikers.

Since Alex was the only one who could communicate with the rugby team, she volunteered to stay with Ranger Jazmine and help move them to a legal campground and sort out their issues. Win was relieved to leave her doing something helpful. He had other things to do.

He pulled out the satellite phone and put a call in to Trey and the ERT leader. Somewhere on that trail there was a campsite they had to find. Somewhere on that trail there might be evidence left behind. And there were four men to track down, not three as they'd previously thought. The fourth guy must have gone with the chopper when it hauled out the trophy mounts. The two Asian men were very possibly

Chinese. The list of what to do was getting longer, but Win's pulse was ticking up. Evidence was coming together, facts were being confirmed, the investigation was beginning to narrow. Win Tyler was in his zone.

*　*　*

Win and Trey had just settled into the corner table at McClain's Tavern, a Gardiner beer joint with tinted windows, minimal lighting, and rough customers. The band was finishing their warm-up, and as far as Win could tell most of the mismatched tables were occupied. Cigarette and marijuana smoke was so thick in the air that Win could taste it. He didn't think there was enough light in the place to spot a bad guy if one showed up, but he narrowed his eyes to let them adjust to the gloom and hoped that the food was better than the sketchy ambiance.

Win wasn't a fan of the bar scene; it had been Trey's idea to come here. It hadn't taken Luke and Trey long to come up with a suspect list on the poaching. Trey said their number one on the list frequented this dive, and Win needed to get eyes on the guy. He'd barely had time to feed the cat and grab a shower after the afternoon trek to interview the rugby players, and now here he was at 8:30 on a rainy night on Park Street in Gardiner, hoping to at least get a meal. *Gonna be another short night.* Win checked his phone for a minute while Trey tried to get the attention of a waitress. They'd just ordered drinks and the ribeye special when Trey touched Win's sleeve and motioned with his eyes toward the front door.

"Bingo," he said, leaning back in his chair and nodding toward the couple who'd entered the noisy room.

Win followed the ranger's eyes to a broad-shouldered man who was adjusting his ball cap over a headful of wild hair while holding the arm of a scantily clad young woman. They were silhouetted against the glow of the flashing neon window sign; the guy had on the typical outdoorsman garb, the skinny girl didn't seem to have on nearly enough of anything. The man turned, scanned the room, and zeroed in on Trey with laser focus.

"Uh-oh," the ranger said softy.

The man was beside their table in five quick strides, the hesitant woman trailing in his wake. He dropped one hand on the table and leaned toward the ranger with a withering glare.

"My father tells me you people are filing a trumped-up charge against him for some ridiculous water-quality crap with his well. You know you should be going through me! He ain't in good enough health to deal with that . . . . What is it with you Feds? Can't deal with a real man?"

Trey's face had turned red, and Win could see the anger building. The guy was leaning across the table toward Trey, speaking rapid fire. *Time to defuse the situation.*

"Whoa, whoa, I don't think we've been introduced." Win stood and moved out of the shadows, his hand extended. The guy straightened and turned, and Win got a better look at him. He was maybe Trey's height, six one-ish, but he was stout. Big shoulders, short neck, and a broad face that would have been intimating on its own, but garish red-and-black tattoos marked his forehead and cheeks, and a thick brown beard covered his lower face. He opened his mouth to speak and Win had to force himself not to stare; the guy's canine teeth had been filed to points. *Vampire* was the word that suddenly came to Win's mind.

Trey was standing now too, and folks at the surrounding tables were probably wondering when the fight would start. But the stout guy just stood there, facing Win down, his mouth gapped just enough to show the fangs, his lips twisted in a snarl.

Win didn't let on he'd even registered the guy's frightening posture. He held his smile and nodded a greeting. "Oookay . . . I'm Win Tyler, the resident FBI agent in Yellowstone. And you are?"

The wispy girl at the guy's side tugged on his arm; that seemed to snap him out of it. Trey had pulled himself together too, and both men started talking at once—much too loudly to be friendly. The woman slid closer to the angry man and tugged his arm again. "Dex, let's not go gettin' yourself all worked up. We'll go over to the Bull Moose for dinner. The crowd here ain't to my liking anyway." She threw Win a sneer.

Win pulled back his extended hand but held the smile. The guy had *thug* written all over him, but his shifty eyes gave away his anxiety—facing up to two law enforcement types was not what he had in mind for the evening. Especially when one of the law enforcement types was a good two inches taller and fit as a fiddle. He might be a thug, Win thought, but he wasn't a stupid thug.

"Stay off our place, Hechtner!" He threw one last threat at Trey before he turned. He didn't give Win a second look.

The band started some country throwback tune and half the crowd stood to hit the dance floor. A potential fight couldn't top the allure of nuzzling up real close to your honey for a slow dance. The hotheaded guy and the nearly nude woman weaved through the swaying couples toward the door. They never looked back.

"Well, that was pleasant," Trey commented as they sat back down. "That was Dex Pierson and whoever his current main squeeze is."

Win sat down and leaned into the ranger, better to be heard over the music. "Why no heads-up on the Dracula look?"

Trey just grinned. "I wanted to see your reaction to the dude." His eyebrows went up. "I have to say I'm impressed. Not even a twitch. Whata you got? Ice water in your veins?"

Win smiled. "Didn't wanta give him the satisfaction. Why are you thinking this is our guy for the poaching?"

Trey lowered his voice and got serious. "Pierson has been out of the Montana state pen on parole for well over a year now. Served less than a third of his seven-year sentence. This last time he was in for aggravated robbery, felony theft, a bunch of related charges. His father lives on fifteen acres that borders the park, not far from Gardiner . . . we've got some limited oversight there because of the shared boundary. Before Pierson was locked up this last time, there was a rash of elk poaching outside the park, not far from their place. It was the Sheriff's jurisdiction, but they called us in to help. We were never able to arrest anyone, but Dex Pierson was our main suspect."

"Luke has him high up on the suspect list too?" Win asked.

"Yup, Luke said Pierson worked on and off as a laborer on the Yellowstone River Bridge construction crew, back earlier in the summer. That could give him access to their helicopter delivery schedule and the equipment start-up times." Trey paused and waited for a couple to pass their table. "And, Luke heard that Pierson made marksman during his stint in the Army. Heard the guy was good with guns."

"Can you get me the file on that old poaching case? Anything you've got on Pierson. I need to go over it tonight. Denver wants this to move fast."

Trey nodded as the waitress appeared with their food. "Whata you thinkin'?" he asked.

"I'm thinking that Pierson is checkin' all the boxes for me. He matches the physical description that Mitchem gave us of one of the guys he met on the trail the morning the bulls were shot. Plus he was a suspect in a previous poaching incident, he has a prison background, he's known to be good with guns, and he worked that construction project in the park." Win took a sip of his coke before he continued. "I'm also thinking that he's out on parole and I won't even need a warrant to pay him a visit real early in the morning. That's what I'm thinking."

CHAPTER ELEVEN

Win didn't say anything as he stepped inside the mobile home's dimly lit interior. He left the door open behind him as he did a quick scan of the cramped room. He didn't like this. Didn't like this at all. He'd assisted with office searches back in Charlotte, in his first office posting. But since he'd worked white-collar crime, he'd been on raids only twice, and there'd always been backup, another agent or two to watch over the exterior of the structure, another to stand in sight of anyone in the building—at least someone to watch his back. He'd waited for nearly thirty minutes in the dark at the wooded entrance to the Piersons' long, rutted driveway for the Sheriff's deputy and the parole officer. They hadn't shown up, and Park County Dispatch couldn't give him an ETA for anyone else. It was either go in alone at 5:45 a.m. or wait for another day. Denver wanted the bison massacre solved—Win's supervisor had told him to make it happen, he didn't have time to wait.

The room consisted of a compact living area and kitchen. The space looked worn and tired, but it didn't look dirty. Everything smelled of fried bacon and woodsmoke. The blinds were pulled on the windows, and the small living area was dark to begin with; the once-white walls were stained after years of long wear and from the ash of the black pot-bellied stove that stood in the corner. It was cold outside this morning and that thing was radiating heat.

Win's eyes settled on the shotgun that was leaning against the far wall near the kitchen counter and the hunting rifle that hung by its strap among a host of jackets and coats. *Get any weapons secured and unloaded immediately.* Win heard his Quantico instructor's voice clearly. *But I've gotta clear the dwelling, Pierson could be hiding . . . which do I handle first?* Win hesitated and turned back to the old man. "Why don't you walk along with me as I check out the house?" Win suggested, hoping that he wasn't letting a potential hostile get behind him.

The frail, elderly man had answered the door moments before; it wasn't even 6:00 a.m., but it was clear that the man had been up for a while. He was pale and stooped, and he used a long walking stick for balance as he shuffled across the rug toward a worn cloth recliner. He coughed and cleared his throat. "Look around yourself. . . . You said you's here to see Dex," he said as he eased down into the large brown chair. "I 'spect you're thinkin' he's here."

"Now why would I be thinking that, Mr. Pierson? You said he wasn't here . . . is he?" Win's right hand stayed real near his holster. "Mr. Pierson, I'm gonna put your weapons up here on the counter while I check the house. Are they loaded?"

The man glanced his way and scoffed. "What good would they be if they weren't loaded? You sound like you're from down South, boy, you should know that." He shook his head and used the cane to prop a leg up on the sagging ottoman. He tried to clear his throat again.

Win eyed the big, overstuffed chair. "You got a gun in the chair, Mr. Pierson?"

The man's eyes twinkled, and he smiled. "Well, that's more like it, boy. Now you're thinkin' more like a lawman. There for a while you's just feelin' sorry for me . . . wondering what social services you could call to help this old man, wondering if your missus could drop by a cake."

Win maneuvered behind the huge recliner, reached down beside the right cushion, and pulled a small revolver from its hiding spot. The man didn't move.

"You're sure Dex hasn't been here in a while?"

The thin man shook his head and settled back in the chair. Win's eyes swept the room again. A large television with a game console and DVD player was against the far wall. A ratty couch held folded blankets and a pillow. There was a rickety table whose linoleum top held two chipped plates and two coffee mugs. It was clear that two people had been having breakfast when he'd knocked on the door and announced himself minutes ago. There was an old Chevy pickup parked in what passed as the front yard of the ancient mobile home. The blue Ford truck registered to Dex Pierson was nowhere to be seen.

Win put the revolver, shotgun, and rifle up on the kitchen counter and unloaded them while his eyes flicked between the open door and the trailer's dark hallway. Then he took a deep breath, pulled his Glock, and made a quick and thorough check of the two-bedroom trailer. There wasn't anywhere to hide, really; the rear door was blocked by a large stand-up freezer, and the windows in the back were too small for a man of Dex Pierson's size to use for escape. Win checked the tiny pantry and the kitchen again—he saw a cell phone plugged into the wall outlet. He pulled a window shade aside and glanced out the back. The lot was mostly wooded with aspen trees and a few scroungy lodge-pole pines. He saw a small well house, piles of light-blue sheet metal that appeared to be parts of a camper trailer, and an overgrown garden. A large freestanding garage sat off to the side.

Mr. Pierson seemed to be talking to himself when Win came back into the living room and holstered his gun.

"He don't come by every day . . . you know how it is with kids these days," the man was saying. "I don't see him every day."

"Your son has this address listed as his permanent residence on his parole papers. So unless you tell me different, I assume he still lives here. Your kitchen's well stocked, your firewood is stacked. I notice your freezer's full of meat. . . . Do you still hunt?" He glanced out the front window as he glimpsed a police cruiser pulling up beside his Expedition. The deputy had finally made it.

Pierson coughed, then answered. "Naw, naw . . . I know I don't look it, but I'm turnin' eighty-six next month. I done outlived all my huntin' buddies. They used to take me, Dex used to take me huntin', but with

the arthritis in my knees and hips, I ain't gettin' out much anymore."
A cloud covered the rising sun and the room went a shade darker. The
man kept talking. "Dex, he's a good un . . . taught him to hunt when
he weren't but a little un." He nodded absently and coughed a couple
of times before he finished his thought. "Yup, Dex was a late child . . .
I was way past my prime when he was born . . . but he's a good un.
He's—"

"Who was here having breakfast with you, Mr. Pierson? There are
two plates, two cups."

A burly guy in black pants, an armored vest, and ball cap appeared
at the open door. A patch on his tan shirt sleeve said *Park County
Sheriff.* Win nodded toward the kitchen table and the guy focused on
the two plates. He unholstered his handgun and kept it pointed down.
He stepped into the room slowly.

"I've cleared the trailer," Win said.

The man glanced at Win. "Deputy Chad Maddox. Parole guy didn't
show. Big wreck on the highway, sorry I'm late. We've got another unit
comin', should be here any minute." He turned his attention to the old
man. "Hey, Pierson, where's Dex? Where's the kid?" he gruffly asked.

What kid? Win was shocked—they were doing an armed raid on a
parolee's residence and no one had mentioned there was a child living
there. "What kid!" Win directed the charge at the deputy. He was a
little hot.

The old man answered. "It's Dex's boy, my grandson. He don't like
strangers, probably run off in the woods." The man sagged back in the
chair and coughed.

Win gave the deputy a *We'll talk about this later* look and moved
toward the door. "Stay here with Mr. Pierson." He motioned with his
head to the pile of weapons on the counter, to the phone plugged into
the wall. The deputy nodded that he understood.

"I'll check the shed and the well house," Win said as he went out
the door. A second deputy had arrived; she exited her SUV with gun
drawn and moved to help Win clear the outbuildings. She had sergeant
stripes on her tan shirt, and her name tag said *Sullivan.* She looked like

she knew what she was doing. The well house was clean, nothing there but an ancient water pump and insulation.

Win motioned to her to cover the back of the big sheet-metal garage as he pulled his Glock, called out, "FBI, entering the building!" and then eased the wide door open and flipped on the lights. He slipped into the open space as the door creaked shut behind him. The rundown prefabricated building looked as if the roof might cave in any minute, but Win saw plenty of evidence that it had seen recent use. The interior was cluttered with junk, but there was no vehicle—not a working one, anyway. A snowmobile sat on concrete blocks, its hood detached and set to the side. It probably hadn't been used in years. There was a discarded snowplow next to piles of boxes and junk on the dirty concrete floor.

Win zeroed in on the Dillon gunsmithing and ammunition-reloading tools neatly stacked along the wooden workbench that ran nearly the length of the structure. Someone kept the weaponry in tip-top shape, but that tendency toward care didn't seem to translate to many other things in Pierson's garage. A metal dog pen padded with blankets was the only other clean area. A water dish and empty food bowl were on the floor near the pen, and a new sack of dog food sat on the end of the workbench. *Where's the dog?* Win turned as a scuffing sound came from a tarp-covered pile of junk near the back of the long room.

Win moved toward the sound, then crouched and flipped up the grungy tarp with his free hand. His right hand pointed the Glock at whatever was underneath—he was hoping it was just the dog. It wasn't. The black muzzle of a shotgun stared up at him, barely two feet in front of his face. *Whoa! Geez!* He fought the instinct to pull back. Any sudden movement might provoke the towheaded boy whose gaunt face stared back at him. Win eased the Glock to the side and held his breath.

"Get outa here!" the kid hissed.

The shotgun muzzle was still in his face. Win hadn't yet managed to breathe. He willed himself to stay motionless, to take a breath, to sound calm. "Your grandpa didn't mention you might be here . . . reckon he figured you'd hide out in the woods," Win quietly said.

"He figured wrong."

"Uh-huh, I can see that."

The shaggy-headed boy and half-grown dog were still staring up at him. It was hard to get his eyes off the gun's gaping muzzle, but Win forced himself to focus on the child.

"You wanta move that shotgun outa my face? Get your finger off that trigger?"

"No."

Win tried to take another breath. He could hear the deputies' voices outside the shed, and the crackling of a police radio. He could hear the soft whimper of the puppy, the rapid pounding of his heart in his ears. This could go downhill fast if the deputies barged in. *I have to get that gun.*

"Get out!" the boy hissed again. "You gonna haul me off to foster care! You're thinkin' I ain't nothin' but trailer trash!"

"Naw, I's thinkin' that is 'bout the best-lookin' bluetick hound I've seen. What's his name?" Win's eyes went to the half-grown dog; he didn't dare meet the eyes of the little heathen with the 20-gauge pointed at him. He had the kid cornered—cornered animals were prone to lash out. He tried again. "That's a fine dog. What's his name, son?"

The boy's fierce gray eyes blinked for the first time. He shifted back a little; the wild blond hair hung down in his face. His free hand gripped the dog's leather collar tighter.

"You ain't takin' my dog!" It was the same hostile hiss.

"Wouldn't even consider it. Was just thinkin' 'bout his good color, deep clear eyes. . . . My great-uncle raised coonhounds back in Arkansas. I'll bet yours is a dandy." The skinny pup knew he was being discussed. He dropped his mouth open, the big tongue rolled out, he showed all his teeth in a dog smile.

"Your hound is a sight friendlier than you are, son. What's his name?"

Win saw the kid shift his eyes to the dog for a second, saw his dirty finger come off the shotgun's trigger and go to the guard.

"It's Max," he said in a whisper.

"Alright then, you and Max, we need to get back to the house. I'm sure your grandpa—Mr. Pierson is your grandpa, isn't he?—I'm sure he's worried about you."

"No he ain't. He knows I kin take care of myself." The shotgun barrel had moved slightly to the side. Win reached up and gripped the barrel, easing it up toward the ceiling. The kid still had a grip on it with one hand, but his finger hadn't moved from the guard.

"You mind if I look this over? Huh, it's not a 20-gauge, it's a .410. Don't see many .410s anymore. . . . Is it yours?" He gently rotated the gun away from the boy and noticed the safety was on. He holstered the Glock and dropped down on one knee.

The answer was nearly a whisper. "It's mine. Dex got it for me for Christmas. I'm eight now, it's my first gun. . . . I's trying to scare you off is all."

"I can see that. But it's dangerous to point a gun at anyone, anytime. I 'spect you know that. . . . Things can get outa hand real quick. You look a lot smarter than that, son."

"Quit callin' me *son*! You're just here to hurt us."

"I won't hurt you . . . and I could address you proper if I knew your name," Win said softly.

Before the kid could answer, someone banged on the shed door and Win, the boy, and the dog all jumped. Win was real glad he was holding that shotgun.

"I'm good!" Win yelled toward the closed door. "It's clear. There's a boy and a dog in here. We'll be right out."

"We're all clear out here!" the female deputy called back.

"C'mon, we'll get you back to your grandpa." Win motioned the boy up. The hound made a half-hearted bark, but it kept up the smiling.

The boy dropped his head as he shuffled toward the door. He held on tight to the leather leash. "It's Shane," he said quietly. "My name is Shane."

Win shifted the light shotgun to his left hand and eased the boy toward the door with his right hand. "Alright, Shane. My name is Win. No one is gonna hurt you. I'll make sure of that."

"Whata we got?" Win heard as he pushed the garage door open. Deputy Maddox was standing close and looked poised to bang on the metal door again. The guy had abandoned his post in the trailer, and Win wasn't happy about that. The female deputy holstered her weapon and bent down to talk to the boy, asking him to follow her to the dwelling. The dog was bounding up and down, his eager eyes going from person to person.

Win waited until they were out of earshot before he responded to Maddox. "Seems to me it's what we haven't got that's important. We haven't got Dex Pierson and we haven't got any concrete proof that he's been here in days. . . . And why wasn't the Bureau notified that he had a child living here with him?" Win's eyes had gone deep blue and narrowed.

Deputy Maddox shuffled his feet, wiped a hand across his face, then spit to the side. "Yeah, well. My sergeant is gonna be ticked too. I forgot to mention the kid on the ready sheet for the raid." His words didn't sound like much of an apology. He shrugged. "The parole officer had heard he had a kid, but Pierson didn't have it registered. You have to have that sort of thing registered under his level of parole, I reckon." Maddox finally met Win's angry eyes. "So legally Dex is only living here with his old man." The deputy paused and seemed to be thinking it over. "I'll haul the kid over to social services in Livingston, they've got some sort of youth lockup. I'll take the dog to the pound in Gardiner. That should stir things up a bit, might force Pierson to surface."

* * *

Dex Pierson had planned to be back at his old man's place last night, but things just had a tendency of not going the way he thought they would. That little gal was a hot number and now he couldn't even remember her name . . . it was Coco, or Fudge, or Tiffany, something along those lines. He'd learned long ago to call all of them *honey*, or *babe*, or *sweetheart*, something along those lines. Simplified things.

He noticed he had a voicemail from his father. The call had come in a few minutes earlier as he was driving away from her house, and he'd let it go. A call from the old man before seven was never good news. He needed to stop at the Zippy Mart and get some coffee before he checked back into the world. He got back in the truck and sipped the hot coffee as he watched a truck pulling a trailer of river rafts go by, watched a huge tour bus across the street at the Geyser Way Motel loading eager tourists for today's trip into the park. The traffic was already a steady stream on Highway 89 through town. The line of vehicles was snaking across the Yellowstone River Bridge and heading south toward the park's entrance. Last night's light rain had cleared the haze from the sky; it was gonna be a pretty day.

The coffee began to clear the cobwebs from his brain, and he hit PLAY on the voicemail. "Dex, this is your daddy." The voice paused for a fit of coughing. "FBI agent, deputies here for you. FBI man says he wants to talk to you . . . for you to go to the Sheriff's substation"— more coughing—"in Gardiner. Turn yourself in, he says." Dex heard him take a labored breath. "They're wantin' me to go to the hospital. . . . They're taking the boy." The recording ended with another fit of coughing, and Dex sat there in his truck, staring at the phone. He let loose with a string of cussing that blew off a little steam. It was probably that agent he'd run into last night at the bar. Damn bad timing.

They're takin' the boy. Those words hit him the hardest and sobered him up right quick. He glanced at his watch, it was nearly 7:30. He pulled his face paint, as he called it, from the truck's console and smoothed the tan makeup over the tats on his face. He pulled out a container with two white rubber tabs that he pushed onto his fang teeth. They didn't look totally real, not if someone looked closely, but they cancelled out the vampire vibe. He pulled on a worn ball cap and glanced at himself in the mirror. It would have to do. He sent a quick text to Jesse. They sure as hell needed to touch base, but the guy never answered his phone this early unless they were on a job. Dex used their emergency code word, *fire*, in the innocuous text and hoped Jesse was paying attention.

He started the big black Dodge, nosed onto the highway between two vans, and headed south toward the park. The Sheriff's substation was two blocks back the other direction, and he knew all the law enforcement types in the area would stop at the Zippy Mart for coffee sooner or later this morning. No reason to make this too easy for them.

He mentally clicked off the critical items that he needed to do immediately, get as far away from Dad's place as possible, as quickly as possible, get to his stash in the park and lay low until Jesse called on the burner phone. They only used the throwaway phones when there was the potential for things to get hot. And things had damn well gotten hot. One final item on his list: avoid rangers and cops at all costs. That last one was the key, and it could be a little tricky. He couldn't use the main route into Yellowstone; the entrance booths were equipped with surveillance cameras that recorded the license plate and a visual of every vehicle that entered. Even delivery trucks and service vehicles had to pass through that surveillance web.

So he crossed the steel bridge and meandered the narrow backstreets of small-town Gardiner until he got to the big Park Service maintenance yard on the southeast side of town. He'd worked the road construction job in the Lamar Valley off and on in May and June. He knew the park's rangers wouldn't stop any construction-related traffic that used the service road behind the entrance booths. He pulled up outside the big warehouse and waved to a couple of workers who were just pulling in. He hopped out and rummaged around under the truck's back seat for the safety helmet that he'd neglected to return to the construction company when he'd quit that job. He threw his cap in the front seat, put the helmet on, and casually loaded three long hazard barricades into the bed of his pickup.

He'd learned long ago that if you acted as if you owned the place, didn't hesitate to do your thing, most folks would just mind their own business and let you mind yours. He'd stolen a lot of stuff that way— right from under the nose of someone who assumed he had the right to take it. People generally didn't want to get involved. He drove off with the big orange-and-white barricade signs hanging out of the back of the truck, visible for anyone to see. He pulled onto the service road behind two massive dump trucks that were headed for one of the many work zones in the park. They were always building, tearing down, or fixing something in Yellowstone during the summer; the few months of decent weather gave a sense of urgency to any job. The convoy cruised behind the park's entrance booths and safely passed the forward-facing surveillance cameras. Dex nodded to himself. *One down. Piece of cake.*

* * *

His eyes lit up when he saw them. Roadie had sounded excited on the crack-of-dawn phone call. He said he'd come, but he'd grumbled a bit about driving over two hours back to the Yellowstone Lake area. The guy never sounded this hyped up, so he'd raced around to get on the road quickly. So quickly that he'd screwed up and left his phone by his nightstand. He'd fumed about that, and about all the other recent foul-ups for most of the drive through the park to the Bridge Bay Campground. But when he made the early-morning drive, he had no idea the surprise would be this good.

"Damn . . . damn! How many you got here?" he asked as he stepped forward to glance down at four identical matte-black AR-15s laid out across the unmade bed. Boxes with the same model number were stacked to the ceiling in every corner of the camper trailer's bedroom.

"Thirty-seven. Every one of 'em brand-spanking new! Number one seller! Never been fired! Can you imagine what these will bring in Canada?" the younger man behind him exclaimed. The small trailer shifted a tad as the two men maneuvered to stand side by side above the bed.

"Where did—"

"You know that kid in Ogden I told you about? He'd been gettin' me a piece here and there for about three months. He called me all amped up yesterday, said he'd hit the mother lode! Said he and some buddies followed an SUV with a trailer outa that big gun show in Salt Lake, said they hit it when the dudes stopped for dinner in Ogden. Said they thought they might get five or six good handguns—bust out a window, do a smash and grab—but they got this haul! Alarms never went off in the vehicle or the trailer. Kid thought he'd won the lottery."

His mind began running the numbers. If what he'd just heard was true, they were looking at $150,000 easy, maybe more.

"What'd you pay him?"

"That may be the best part. The fool asked for twenty grand, and I sounded shocked and told him I could come up with five, get them off his hands quick 'cause they'd be hot. Fool agreed to 5K. Can you believe it?" He shook his head and Roadie kept talking. "Drove all night to get down there and back."

"Wow." He didn't know what else to say, so he turned the conversation in another direction. "The story still hitting the news south of here?"

For the first time, the mood got somber. "Haven't seen a thing on TV for the last few days. Some buffalo killing here in Yellowstone is big in the news. But you know . . . you know the cops have to be all over it," the younger man said.

"Yeah." He sucked in a deep breath. "It was a reckless play to begin with, dammit. . . . Didn't expect them to even identify the bodies for weeks, and here we are five days out and we're dealing with two dead Feds."

"Uh, saw online that one of them was an informant, a snitch. And since they was setting us up, I ain't feelin' too bad about it anymore," Roadie said.

He shook his head again. "It ain't a matter of feeling one way or another, it's a matter of staying off their radar, dodgin' the heat. If someone wastes a cop, much less a federal cop, they get all ramped up."

"Yeah well, that's why we're moving our inventory, that's why we haven't been able to make a delivery over the border. That's why I've been bored to death sitting around campgrounds in a damn national park." Roadie sighed and nodded toward the display of guns. "I got it all set up like you wanted, but with this new haul, I say we get Tank more involved. He's the one popped those two dudes anyway. I say we start moving stuff to Canada, I say we start cashing in—"

"Whoa, whoa . . . dial it back a little . . . we're not in a hurry. Let's make sure we're squared away," he said as a wave of concern washed over him. "You've moved the rest of the guns in from the other trailers

. . . what about the ones from down in Grand Teton?" He leaned down and picked up one of the new weapons, ran his fingers around the steel barrel, up the flash suppressor, along the waffled handguard, down the top accessory rail. His hands caressed the solid polymer stock, the thirty-round magazine. He lifted it higher and admired the matte-black finish. He was holding six and a half pounds of lethal. It was American made, a high-end model, top of the line. It could spit out forty-five rounds of absolute killing power per minute on semiauto. Over four hundred rounds a minute with an auto adjustment. *Sweet.*

Roadie pulled a key from his pants pocket and held it up as he answered the question.

"Rented a cabin in Canyon on Monday—one of those they were supposed to remodel this year but didn't get to it. Got it real cheap, pre-paid for two weeks. It's back away from the others, not far off the service road. Tank helped me move some guns in, but then he claimed he was tied up for a few days. I'd been moving our inventory up there for the last couple of days till this deal came up yesterday." Roadie motioned with his chin toward a row of keys hanging on the wall bracket. "It's all in place . . . we're good."

"Why didn't you call me on this deal before you drove to Ogden?" he asked.

Roadie shuffled a bit and shrugged. "Thought it was too good to be true," he said softly. Then he laughed. "Hell, you still thinkin' 'bout that Mexican vacation? This could be your ticket to that beach in Cabo. This could be your ticket out—"

He was thinking exactly the same thing as he swung the solid rifle into Roadie's face in a crippling blow. He got him with a second strike to the throat as he fell.

My ticket out. Yep, I was thinkin' the same damn thing.

CHAPTER TWELVE

Dex kept close behind the two dump trucks as they rumbled through the upper reaches of the park for five miles, then slowed down to a crawl to maneuver through the congested tourist traffic in Mammoth. Both trucks turned onto the Grand Loop Road in front of the Albright Visitor Center and headed south toward Roosevelt and the Lamar Valley highway construction sites. Dex continued west past the Mammoth Hot Springs Hotel, then past the restaurants and the general store.

He glanced at his fuel gauge—it was sitting too close to empty—and swung into the gas station at the last second. *Dammit!* He'd loaned the truck out so often, you'd think it could at least come back with a full tank once in a while. He pulled in behind a van full of more kids than he could count. The driver stopped in front of the pumps and the children bailed out of the doors and scattered like quail. Dex sat there and waited for the kids to disperse, then he eased by the van in the tight parking lot and pulled around the vintage gas station. The log-and-stone building was built in 1920—it had been modernized, but it wasn't high-tech by any means. Dex knew that the only surveillance cameras were pointed toward the pumps; he needed gas, but he didn't need to get made.

He drove slowly behind the old building, where lines were forming at the exterior bathroom doors. He checked out the back lot and smiled when he saw four disabled vehicles lined up against the fence.

Yellowstone National Park wasn't the best place in the country to break down. There were only seven gas stations in an area the size of Delaware and Rhode Island combined, and they couldn't always be relied upon to have fuel on hand, much less repair services. There were four stations with a mechanic, and Mammoth's wasn't counted in that number. Dex knew there were usually a few vehicles lined up in the station's back lot, waiting their turn to be towed to a location with better services.

Pulling the big Dodge in at an angle between the station and the disabled vehicles, he rummaged around in the truck's center console until he found a small screwdriver. He hopped out, walked around his truck, and removed the front and back plates from a newer Ford SUV that sat up against the fence. A ruined tire and warped wheel rim had forced the Ford into this line of the unlucky; the driver probably went off the asphalt, then tried to correct too quickly. Yellowstone's roads could be unforgiving. He quickly removed his rear plate and attached his new Arizona one, then waited for the last person in line to enter the restroom before he completed the front-plate switch. He tossed his old plates into the passenger floorboard and dropped his jacket on top of them. Then he eased the construction barricades out of the back of the pickup and laid them against the fence, dropped his safety hat onto the back seat, and pulled on his ball cap. He forced himself to concentrate on one task at a time. Think too far ahead, get in a hurry, screw something up. He couldn't afford to screw something up.

He'd just started to put his truck in gear when a white-and-green Park Service Tahoe pulled around the corner of the building, stopped behind him, and turned on its light bar. He could see a lady park ranger reporting something into her radio, then she opened her door and stepped out. Didn't seem to be anyone with her—he registered that. The lines had cleared up and no one was waiting for the john—he registered that. No cameras out here, no witnesses here. Those factors were processed in slow motion as Dex reached into the console for the switchblade that he always kept handy. He palmed it in his right hand as he raised his left hand in a wave back to her. He hit the power button to lower the window and waited while she walked toward the driver's side of the big pickup. He watched in the side mirror as the young Black ranger paused to pull her flat hat on over her tight braids, adjust her gun belt, and take note of his new rear license plate. He was thinking she didn't even look twenty, they were hiring them younger and younger these days.

Dex waved his left arm out the open window, shifted in the seat, and held the nine-inch blade with his right hand under the cuff of his denim shirt. His heartbeat had slowed and his breath had gone still, just like it did before a kill shot, just like it had back during the war. Something inside screamed that this wasn't the same, that she wasn't his enemy. A louder voice told him he couldn't face prison again.

"Sir, you can't park back here, this area is for service vehicles only. Can I see your driver's license and the truck's registration?" she politely asked. She was almost to the driver's door. "Sir, step out of the vehicle, please."

He heard all her commands—they seemed to be coming from far away . . . things were still moving in slow motion. She was almost below the open window of the tall pickup. His left hand found the door handle: a quick tug of the handle and a shove of the door, and she'd be on her butt and he could be out with the knife. It would be over in a heartbeat.

Then one of the exterior bathroom doors slammed just thirty feet away. "Hey, dork!" he heard a boy yell.

"You're toast!" the other teen shouted as he pushed the metal door back and it crashed into the wall.

Dex didn't much believe in Divine Intervention, but if he did, this would have been it. He raised his eyes from the ranger toward the two boys who were coming to blows outside the bathroom and yelled, "Brad! Chris! Get your rear ends in this truck! I'm moving down to the store!" His loud voice took on an even angrier tone. "You better get down there now! I mean now!"

The boys looked his way in confusion, spotted the park ranger, then ran. Dex glanced down at the ranger, who'd turned to see what all the commotion was about. "I'm sorry officer. Chris has a stomach bug—I wouldn't get too close. I'm moving right now. Will round them up at the store." He put the Dodge in gear and slowly moved forward. She didn't seem to know what to say or do as she watched him pull away; she turned just in time to see the two boys race around the corner of the station.

Dex eased the pickup in front of the pumps and onto the road and slowly headed back past the gas station and the general store the way he'd come. He turned at the junction and entered the stream of traffic moving south through the Fort Yellowstone Historic District into the depths of the park. He kept an eye on his rearview mirror until he crossed the Gardner River Bridge. *All clear.* He popped the console open and slid the knife back into its spot. He gripped the steering wheel tighter when he realized his hand was shaking, that sweat was coursing down his face. He didn't allow himself to wonder how things could have played out. He couldn't bring himself to think about it.

It was eighteen miles down the Grand Loop Road to the gas station at the Tower–Roosevelt junction; he was running on fumes when he pulled up to the pumps. After the fuel stop, his drive south past Tower, over Mount Washburn and Dunraven Pass, and into the Canyon area was uneventful—not even a major bear jam to slow things down. *Just stay under the forty-five-mile-per-hour speed limit, don't get in a rush,* he kept reminding himself.

It was nearly 10:30 when he finally pulled in front of the small, single-hitch camper trailer that sat in one of the least-desirable spots in the Canyon Campground. It was far back toward the rear of the expansive 270-pad RV and tent camping area, and it wasn't attractive. A scraggly lodgepole pine tree leaned away from the trailer, and two other pines that could have provided shade had blown down. He noticed that no one had gotten around to cutting them up for firewood.

He hadn't been down here to check on the trailer in several days, and that wasn't good. He only had six more days to move it to another spot, and he'd been so distracted by the bad bison shoot that he'd completely forgotten to make a reservation at another campground. He'd need to do some hustling to make that work. The Park Service only allowed a camper to stay in the same Yellowstone campground for fourteen days. He reckoned it made the process more fair, but hell, it was a lot of trouble to keep moving around, trying to keep track of which driver's license he'd used where, which camper he had where. And then there was the occasional busybody camp host who'd drop by and want to visit. Yeah, it was their job to make sure all was well, but hell, if all was well he wouldn't have to be holed up in the middle of Yellowstone in a damn camper trailer in the first place. He did not understand for one second how rational people could drag one of those things around the country and seemingly enjoy it.

He let out a sigh as he eased the big pickup onto the paved parking pad, nudging its grill into one of the downed pine trees. Reaching into the back seat, he found the old quilt he used to cover the seats when Shane had the dog ride with them. Then he got out and casually draped it over the back of the truck's tailgate, conveniently covering his new Arizona license. To the casual observer it looked as if he was airing out the blanket, not concealing a stolen plate.

Now he needed to move fast to make the campsite look legit. Nothing to draw attention to the vehicle or the camper. Nothing to draw attention to him. He unlocked the camper's door, dropped the metal stairs, and reached in for the two folding camp chairs he kept stashed there. He set them up over near the firepit and waved to a guy and a kid riding bicycles along the narrow, paved road that weaved through the wooded camping area. He leaned a fishing pole up against the side of the trailer—might make someone think he'd been out fishing, instead of up to no good—grabbed the small cooler out of the truck bed and sat it on the picnic table, then hooked the truck's battery up to the camper's two 10-volts. He set the truck on idle to let the camper's batteries recharge. One downside of some of Yellowstone's campgrounds was the lack of electric and water hookups. But the upside was obvious—he was nearly invisible here. It was the perfect place to disappear.

He moved into the trailer and paused. For the first time since he'd listened to the voicemail from his old man three hours ago, he took a long, deep breath. He blew out the stale, hot air and checked the burner phone again for the hundredth time. Jesse still hadn't texted or called.

He walked through the trailer and slid open the windows to air out the place. The light-blue Grand River twenty-two-foot camper was a used FEMA castoff. It had begun its life with a noble purpose: housing wildfire victims in southern Idaho. Last winter, when FEMA had no more use for the trailers, Dex bought four for a song and stole six more to make it a round number. He'd made all his money back by selling three of them, used one for spare parts, and loaned or leased out the others, so he was ahead of the game. The camper contained only a small living area, a tiny kitchen with two hot plates, an even tinier bathroom, and a bedroom that held a queen-size mattress.

He'd added a couple of custom features to make this one more to his liking. He walked over and moved the twenty-seven-inch television to an angle and checked to see that his stash of cash was still neatly stacked in the hidden cubby hole he'd built behind the electronics. After buying the new truck a few weeks back, he still had upward of $43,000 lying there. He slid the thick envelope with the $20,000 Jesse had given him for the last botched hunt in beside the stacked bills and nudged the television back into place. *All good.* Plenty of walking money if it came to that.

The jackknife Naugahyde sofa could be pulled up to reveal a gun safe of sorts; he slid the sofa seat up and a fully assembled .458 rifle appeared in its cushioned slot. There were two empty slots for the Winchester Model 70 and its backup that Jesse had taken with him on the chopper after the disastrous shoot with the Chinese guys. He hated that Jesse had to ditch those rifles, they were beautiful guns. His two best AR-15s and two Sig Sauer 9mm handguns made up the rest of the complement in his hidden gun safe. Lifting one of the handguns, he racked the slide just to hear some sound other than his own breathing. He set it on the linoleum tabletop and eased his modified AR-15 out. It was shorter than the heavier Daniel Defense rifle, easier to hide. He reached down and collected two thirty-round magazines for the rifle and a couple of extras for the handgun.

Then he lowered the sofa back into place and sat down on it. He pulled the cigarette pack from his shirt pocket, then thought better of it and put it away. It was hot in the little trailer, but he didn't have enough power in the batteries yet to run the modest air-conditioner, plus it needed some work. Just another thing he hadn't gotten around to fixing. He leaned over and flipped on the small fan that sat against the screen window. The fan sucked in the breeze as it blew the shade to the side and carried the muffled sounds of his truck idling, of children playing in the distance. He sat there holding the rifle, staring at the silent phone, and wondered how Shane was making out. Probably shouldn't have brought him out West in the first place. His effort to do the right thing was likely gonna backfire. Wouldn't be the first time.

His mind turned to other things that weren't going well. There was plenty of *not going well* to choose from, but he settled on thoughts of his father. The old man being sent to the hospital was probably a good thing; he'd been trying to get him to go see a doctor for months. Every day he got worse. They both knew the cancer had come back. Didn't take a rocket scientist to figure that out. They both knew, but neither one of them said those words. Dad had said he was done with the doctors, done with the treatments, done with the pain. He'd lived eighty-five years. He'd outlived his dogs, outlived his friends, outlived wantin' to live. Dex sighed again. Dad was done. And if things didn't improve real soon, he figured he was done too.

*   *   *

"Where we goin'?"

I wish I knew. "I'm workin' on that, Shane," Win replied. He glanced in the rearview mirror at the sullen boy sitting behind him in the big SUV. The hound was draped over the kid, drooling on the leather bench seat. Win hadn't turned the kid or the dog over to Deputy Maddox. He didn't like Maddox's attitude, and it didn't feel like the right thing to do. But it was clear that the elderly Mr. Pierson needed to be in the hospital, so Win asked the boy to get his things together while he and the female deputy stood around Pierson's yard and waited. They waited for the Bureau's Evidence Response Team to arrive, waited for the volunteer fire department's ambulance to arrive, waited for the parole officer to arrive. There always seemed to be a lot of waiting in law enforcement, and patience wasn't one of Win Tyler's strengths.

Win helped Shane load a couple of duffel bags into the rear of his SUV and they both stood and watched the ambulance pull in beside Win's vehicle. It was getting downright crowded in the rutted front yard. Win took the boy back inside to sit with the old man while the EMTs checked him over. Mr. Pierson's coughing was much worse; he seemed to be going downhill fast. Win left the small living room to give them more space. He stood on the wooden porch and noticed that Deputy Sergeant Jean Sullivan was having hard words with her subordinate, Deputy Maddox. Win heard her tell Maddox to get back to the wreck that was still jamming up Highway 89 north of Gardiner.

As Maddox drove away, she leaned against her cruiser and motioned Win over to run through the options. The options weren't good. It came down to sending the child to a youth detention center in Livingston and the dog to the pound or asserting federal authority and declaring the child a victim under FBI jurisdiction. Win made a call to the FBI's Victim/Witness Assistance person in the Denver Field Office and was told by her assistant that she was up to her eyeballs with a human trafficking bust the SWAT team had made last night in Colorado Springs. "She'll get back with you when she can," the assistant had said. "Don't hold your breath."

Alrighty then.

The ambulance crew started to load Mr. Pierson, and Win made sure that Shane had the chance to take his grandpa's hand for a moment and say goodbye before they slid the gurney into the vehicle's bay. Win patted the boy on the back, herded him back to the porch, and suggested that he work with the dog on his hunting skills. He could tell the child was fighting back tears and he wasn't real sure what to do about that. So he patted him on the back again, picked a dirty tennis ball up off the grass, and threw it across the yard for the pup to chase. It didn't seem like enough, but it was all he could think to do. Shane got into the throwing and Max got into the fetching and Win brushed off his hands and drifted back over to the cruiser where the deputy stood.

They did a bit more standing around before the FBI's ERT finally got there a little before nine. Win introduced the four team members to Deputy Sullivan, gave them a quick overview of the situation, then got out of their way. Jim West had put the team on standby earlier this morning in case Win's raid turned up anything that warranted further investigation. And it did. The lead ERT agent had already spotted bloodstains in the bed of the old man's pickup. Win started to mention that half the rural pickups west of the Mississippi probably had bloodstains in the bed from something, but he thought better of it and let them do their thing.

All four of the ERT agents seemed pleased to be back in a more urban setting, in more familiar territory. They'd spent much of the last thirty-six hours in the wilds of the Lamar Valley processing the two bison kill sites and checking out primitive camping areas for evidence. He knew they weren't accustomed to working with park rangers standing guard to keep grizzly bears and wolves at bay. Win heard one of the guys remark that he was gonna have some great stories to tell his kids when this assignment wrapped up.

Win was standing outside his SUV, wondering what to do next, when the sergeant walked over to kill the time. She reported that her department had gotten out a BOLO on Dex Pierson for parole violations, there wasn't much else to say. They were both bored, both thinking they had better things to do. A few more minutes passed and she volunteered to cut Win loose, told him she'd wait until the evidence response folks finished before she closed up the place and left. Win figured she'd made the offer because she recognized a chance to make up for the snafu with the kid; no one in the Sheriff's Office wanted the Feds coming down on them over a raid where a child was present.

"The parole officer isn't gonna show. He got stuck behind the wreck on 89 and finally went back to his office. So it's just you and me." She sighed. "I shoulda had Maddox handle this for me, but, well, it's just easier to do it myself," she said. Her anger at the other deputy was obvious.

"It's clear you don't care too much for Deputy Maddox," Win remarked.

She shook her head. "Maddox should have notified you about the child. . . . I'm sorry about that. I didn't know either. It's not the way our department normally operates." She sighed again. "Maddox is a part-timer. He got here in late April and will be gone October first. October can't come soon enough for me."

"A part-timer?"

"Yeah, just like with the Park Service, the Park County Sheriff's Office hires seasonal help for several months every year. There are only three deputies working out of the Gardiner substation most of the year, but during tourist season we bump that up to at least six."

"Huh . . ."

She wasn't finished with her explanation. "We'll have as many as two thousand vehicles a day coming in the north entrance of Yellowstone during June, July, and August—and who knows how many more staying in the park's neighboring areas. The number of residents in Gardiner doubles during the summer. We are the only local police in Park County. No way we could cover it without the seasonals. It would be great if they all worked regular shifts, but like with Maddox, he's on a few days then off a few days." She frowned. "That's the only way we can get the seasonals: sell them on working near Yellowstone, sell them on the area and let them work a reduced schedule. Most of them are retired law enforcement folks. A few, like Maddox, are police officers who are in between jobs. Some of them are top-notch . . . some aren't—"

"I'm hungry." The small voice from the back seat brought him back to the moment.

"It's not even 10:30," Win answered.

"Papaw gets me up to do breakfast at four. And we only had two eggs and bacon between us today."

"Okay then—"

"They have them buffalo burgers at Shorty's. And at them picnic tables down by the river I kin give Max a snack."

Win glanced in the rearview mirror again and saw the pup's head shoot up. *Snack* was obviously a favorite word.

"Alright." Win hit the turn signal, they were less than fifty yards from the burger place. The kid had good timing; Win figured he'd used this ploy on his father before. The small frame restaurant was adorned with patriotic banners left over from the Fourth and overflowing baskets of red and white petunias. An older couple sat outside at a wooden table. The place looked inviting and nice. Win figured he and the kid could use a little of both this morning.

Alex Lindell called on his Bureau phone before Win even got the Expedition parked in front of the restaurant. He was surprised to hear she was in Gardiner, less than two blocks away. She invited herself over for a chat, as she put it.

He handed a twenty to the kid, told the pup to stay put in the truck, and scrolled through the phone with his thumb. No word from the Victim/Witness Assistance staffer, no word from his supervisor, no word from Kirk Hampton and the Violent Crime Squad folks who were working the helicopter angle on the poaching. It was past mid-morning and he had no guidance, no direction, no orders, no nothing.

"I need a twenty," the small voice below his open window said.

"I gave you a twenty," Win said as he looked down at the boy.

"That won't cover it. She says it's seventeen dollars per burger, and Max has gotta have one too." He paused and his manners seemed to surface. "You want me to get you something?"

"Lordy! How can they charge that much for a hamburger?"

"It's a bison burger . . . you know, them big buffalo. Two meat patties." The kid stopped and seemed to be rationalizing the exorbitant prices. "Maybe they're outa season, or hard to bring down . . . I don't know, but it includes fries. And it'd make you a good dinner . . ." The kid's eyebrows went up expectantly.

Win fumbled with his billfold and handed down more money. "Okay, get me one and a coke." He glanced to the side as Alex pulled her small SUV into the nearly empty gravel lot. It was a little early for lunch, but what the heck.

They all walked down the street to the river, found a picnic table in the shade, and started in on their bison burgers and fries, which Win had to admit were really good. Win sat across from Alex on the worn picnic table under a cottonwood tree; he watched her pick at her small salad. She didn't eat enough to keep a bird alive. He worked on the last of his fries and wondered where she got her energy. There wasn't much conversation until the boy and the dog wolfed down their meal. Then Shane turned to Alex.

"Are you a cop too?" he asked.

She looked at the boy, brushed her napkin across her lips, and almost smiled.

"Why would you think that?"

"You got a gun on. . . . Never seen a social services lady carryin'."

"That's a good observation. So you're acquainted with lots of social service ladies?"

The kid looked down at the dog and shrugged. Alex paused a moment more, then answered his question. "No, I'm not a local police officer. I'm a constable with the Royal Canadian Mounted Police."

The boy's head flew up and his eyes widened. "You're a Mountie?" The tone was reverent.

"Yes." She smiled at the boy, and Win noticed that she had a pretty smile. She needed to use it more often.

"Do you have one of them big black horses?" Shane asked. "One of those red coats?"

I've been wondering that too, Win thought to himself.

"I've got the jacket—it's for dressy occasions—but not the horse. Those horses are for the Musical Ride. They're Mountie ambassadors, I guess you'd say. So how'd you know about the black horses?"

"Dex took me to see 'em at the fairground up in Livingston a few weeks ago. They were at the rodeo. They put on a show . . . it was sho nuff awesome."

Alex seemed unfazed by the constant questions from the eight-year-old; she seemed to be enjoying the attention. Win let them talk as he checked his phone again, then gathered up their trash. He suggested that Shane take Max for a little exercise while he and Alex talked business.

"Don't get too close to the river, it's fast," Alex cautioned as the kid grabbed the pup's leash and raced down the grassy slope toward the water. When the boy and dog had gotten a few yards away, she turned toward Win.

"He mentioned Dex, as in Dex Pierson? Isn't he the guy the locals sent a BOLO out on early this morning? I got the notice on my cell . . . no photo, not many details." She locked eyes with him. "I'm thinking Shane is the son of your main suspect in the bison-poaching case?"

Win swallowed a last fry and nodded.

"And why is he with you?"

Win took another sip of the coke and sighed. "I'm working on a plan . . . but he's talking to you way more than to me or the deputies. I'm not even one hundred percent sure who he is. He says his name is Shane and the dog's name is Max. He told me he's eight years old and that Dex's father, Mr. Pierson, is his papaw. That is *all* he will tell me. He has a Southern accent. . . . Dex Pierson and his father do not. Dex was raised in Rock Springs, Wyoming. So I don't know where Shane came from, but that young dog, that dog is a purebred coonhound. They are Southern dogs—"

"Surely your agency has some system, some placement service, or something," she said.

"I've called the Bureau's program in Denver, but they're over-whelmed with a human trafficking case. They're supposed to reach back out to me about where to take him, what to do. I didn't feel good about leaving him with the Sheriff's people this morning, and he couldn't go to the hospital with his grandfather. I don't have time to babysit a kid."

"No, no, you don't. But you're good at it." She smiled again. "You're a softy . . . he can tell that, even the dog can tell that. He got you here to what is obviously a favorite lunch spot."

"It's part of a case—I'm not a softy. It's part of a case is all." Win shifted the topic. "What are you doing in Gardiner?"

She took off her sunglasses and rubbed her eyes as she watched the boy, who was now skipping rocks across the fast-flowing river. "Spent the last several hours looking at surveillance footage from the two main convenience stores here in town."

"Anything?"

"No, nothing. I looked back on the dates that ATF thought Agent Beckett was working this area." She took a sip of her drink and dropped her sunglasses back in place. "Did you get anyone on the raid? Did you get a lead on the kid's father?"

"No . . . so it looks like we've both come up empty so far today." He nodded toward the river. "I'm gonna find a safe spot for the boy, then get back on it." Win pulled his phone from his pocket and slid it across the table to Alex. "My guy shouldn't be too hard to spot." Dex Pierson's latest mug shot, garish tattoos and fangs visible, stared up from the phone.

Alex straightened and sucked in her breath when she saw the photo. Win thought it was from the guy's vampire look, but that wasn't it.

"He was in the store down at that corner, the Zippy Mart, just before 7:30 this morning. He was in front of me getting coffee."

Are you kidding me! Win slowly sat his coke down and stared at her as she continued to talk. His pulse was ticking up.

"He looked kinda hungover, not quite with it . . . I watched him all the way out. He's hard to miss, kinda scary looking."

That's for sure. "Did he make you as law enforcement?"

She shook her head. "No, no, I don't think so. It was cold in the store's back room, so I'm sure I still had my heavier coat on—no weapon or badge visible." She paused and thought back over it. "He didn't seem to be in a hurry, not overly watchful. He didn't speak to anyone, just got a large coffee, paid at the counter, and left."

"No one with him?"

"Not that I saw. But I was trying to get back to their surveillance equipment—they have several good cameras. You should be able to get a view of his vehicle and the direction he took."

Win was already standing as she finished talking. "Can you watch the boy for a few minutes while I run down there and look at the tape? Just a few minutes?"

She fiddled with her napkin, but finally looked him in the eyes. "First the rugby scrum, now this kid? You think I'm just treading water here . . . been pushed to the side." It wasn't a question and they both knew the truth of her statement.

"Look, I appreciate your help . . . I do. It will just be a few minutes. It could break the case." He motioned with his head down the slope, where the boy was now throwing a stick for the dog to retrieve. "Maybe you could get some information out of him—his full name would be a good start. Like I said, I've got next to nothing, and he seems to admire you."

She sucked in a long breath and looked down the hill. The kid was laughing and the dog was barking and it seemed so normal and whole-some and right. Win saw that familiar veil of sadness drop over her face. She nodded without looking up at him. "Go on," she said. "I'll stay right here."

CHAPTER THIRTEEN

There's a saying that sometimes it's better to be lucky than good. Win didn't believe in luck, but whatever brought this good fortune his way was sure welcome. He had a lead. Zippy Mart's surveillance cameras were top-notch. They showed Dex Pierson drive up to the convenience store at 7:19 a.m. He walked into the store and went straight to the coffee, just as Alex had said. His hair was wild, his garish tats were in full view, and he appeared casual and unconcerned with the other customers. He paid for his drink and left the store at 7:27. He sat in the vehicle for nearly five minutes, then he pulled into the stream of tourist traffic that was flowing south toward Gardiner's bridge over the Yellowstone River.

Win zeroed in on the man's vehicle. It wasn't the older blue Ford truck that the Montana Motor Vehicle Division reported was licensed to Dex Pierson. They were looking for the wrong truck. This wasn't the same vehicle or license number that they'd issued the BOLO on earlier this morning. Pierson was driving a newer-model black Dodge Ram 1500, a four-door pickup with a black grill, black wheels, off-road tires—a tough guy's truck. Dex had either borrowed, stolen, or bought himself a high-priced new ride.

Win got screenshots of the truck and its plates as his mind flashed back to the videos he'd seen of the vehicle involved in the killings of the two men in Grand Teton. The Bureau's enhanced images of that pursuit showed a large black pickup, *"likely a Dodge Ram 1500 or GMC*

Sierra, four-door." That's what the latest FBI bulletin had said. Win sent
a quick email with the screenshots to Jim West before he even stood up.
He asked the store's manager for a copy of the video and was thrilled
to get it without a warrant. He put in a call to Trey to get a copy of the
morning's surveillance footage from the park's entrance booths and
to get a ranger to sit through the remaining hours of the store's video,
to see if Dex Pierson's vehicle came back north on Highway 89. But
Win was betting it wouldn't show up. He was betting Dex Pierson was
already tucked away deep in the wilds of Yellowstone National Park.

*   *   *

Ellie Bordeaux was quickly in charge. "Y'all bring his stuff in here right
now! Shane, I want you to get in the shower, turn the water on, use
soap and a washrag, and clean yourself up! Then I'm gonna give you a
haircut. Now move!"

The boy stood up straighter and glanced in alarm at Win. Win
motioned with his chin. "I'd be doing what she says. She's a really good
cook. We'll get a spot fixed for Max in the barn, and you can come out
and see him when you get presentable."

Luke waited until all the bag-laden kids had trooped into the house
behind a very assertive Ellie. "You said he *might* be Pierson's kid?" The
pup pulled at the leash, but obeyed Luke's command to heel. "Might
be?" Luke repeated.

"Shane doesn't call Pierson *Dad*, calls him *Dex*. The boy and the
dog are not from this part of the country, that's for sure. The older
Mr. Pierson, he's lived outside Gardiner for over twenty years. Dex has
lived there off and on when he wasn't in prison. The records say that
both men are from Rock Springs, Wyoming."

"Welp, that kid and that dog, they're from our part of the country."
Luke pushed back the barn's heavy sliding door. "Only I expect the
boy is from Alabama or Georgia with that accent. That what you're
thinkin'?"

"Yeah." Win reached down to pet the enthusiastic hound. "And I'm
guessing this pup is nine or ten months old, if that. I'm thinking the

boy hasn't been here too long either. One of the deputies checked with the Gardiner Public Schools this morning and they have no attendance records for him. Based on all the books and stuff he piled in my truck, I'll bet someone's been homeschooling him. Dex gave him a .410 for Christmas. That is about all I can get out of him."

"Oh, that's good—Dex Pierson has a reputation of bein' proficient with guns. Kid's probably a crack shot."

"Everything you got locked up in a gun safe?"

"I've got a three-year-old and a five-year-old. You know everything's locked up—or on me." Luke hesitated at the big door. "I volunteered to keep him here when you called. We'll keep Shane and the dog safe. You need to run down Dex, and you can't do it with his kid in tow. If anyone can get some information outa him, it would be Ellie."

"You thought of anyplace that Dex might hide out? The surveillance video showed him going south toward the bridge, toward the park. I've got the rangers running through the footage from the cameras at the park entrance—"

Luke cut him off. "There are ways around that—some old wagon roads southwest of Gardiner, that would be a long, rough ride. But there's also the construction entrance on the southeast side of town."

Win shrugged and played devil's advocate. "Yeah . . . and he may not have even tried to enter the park, he could be any number of places in Gardiner. Laying low at a friend's house, at one of the private RV camps, the list goes on and on."

"I'd bet on the park."

"Because?"

"Fewer cops there. As in *no cops* there, 'cept the rangers, and they got more on their hands than they can say grace over. Height of tourist season. Pierson has gotta think you're after him. If I's him, I'd change my appearance, get into the park, switch vehicles or plates, and make myself scarce."

Same thing I was thinkin'. . . . Maybe I'm finally getting the hang of this.

* * *

It was a little after one and he'd just wedged his muscular frame out of the trailer's tiny shower when he finally got a text from Jesse on the burner phone. The text didn't tell him a whole lot, but at least he'd clued his partner in on the fact that the heat was closing in, that he was hiding out. **Warm front still in place, may cool off in a few days. Hang tight, will be in touch.**

Hang tight! It wasn't Jesse's butt on the line, with the Feds raiding his house, hauling off his stuff, hospitalizing his dad, snatching the kid. *Hang tight!* Easy for him to say. Dex sat there on the trailer's fake-leather sofa with a thin towel wrapped around his waist, and stewed over it. The text indicated Jesse thought this might just blow over in a few days, thought killing a few bison in the park was no big deal. But Dex had known his partner long enough to realize that Jesse wasn't likely gonna sit tight himself. Jesse was already taking steps to minimize his exposure, to come up with an exit plan. Jesse wasn't no fool. And Jesse sure as hell wasn't gonna bail him out. Nope, he'd have to do that himself.

He leaned back on the stiff cushion and thought about the weak links in their little venture—this wasn't a one-man show. There was someone who met the chopper and transported the trophies to the taxidermist. Not a clue who that was. Jesse used taxidermists in several states, but those folks likely thought nothing was amiss with the trophies. Dex figured Jesse had fake hunting licenses, permits, and any other necessary documentation handy. The taxidermists might actually be on the up and up. As far as he knew, this last job was the only one that involved international logistics. How the hell do you get over half a ton of bison heads to China? He had no idea who handled those critical details for his partner.

Then there was the chopper pilot. He'd seen him several times now, but he didn't know his name, couldn't recognize his face. All he knew was that Jesse had recruited the guy after using him for some legitimate wildlife aerial tours up around Big Sky over a year ago. The guy had worn a bandana around his face each time he'd worked the haul out for them. That would be five, no, six times since early spring. Dex knew he couldn't even pick the guy out of a lineup—that was smart.

And speaking of being recognized. . . . He frowned as he glanced at his reflection in the cheap mirror that he'd hung above the linoleum tabletop. He'd done a buzz cut on his wild hair and shaved off the shaggy beard before he took a shower, but even with those radical changes, no one would have any trouble identifying him, that was for damn sure.

He wished he hadn't taken his buddy's advice and gotten the red-and-black lightning tattoos on his face or the skull and crossbones on his forehead several years ago. Yeah, his ink was a work of art, but it attracted attention, and he didn't need attention right now. He also wished he hadn't had his teeth filed down to points. He'd done those things in weak moments, after he'd gotten all nervous about dealing with some of the men he'd spent time with at the state lockup in Deer Lodge a few years back. Those boys had kept in touch, and they'd pressured him to work drugs with them when he got out. They weren't takin' no for an answer. He didn't do hardcore drugs, and he wanted nothing to do with anyone who was into that mess.

He thought the badass look coupled with an equally threating attitude might scare the drug dealers off. It did. It also intimidated some unpleasant dudes during his last three-year stint in prison—saved him from some fights. He sucked in a breath as he looked back at the reflection of who he had become. *It scares everyone else off too.* Well, most everyone. He'd been surprised that some women considered the evil look to be a turn-on, but then those weren't the girls most men would want to take home to mama. Even Shane was terrified when he first saw Dex's new look a few years ago. Dex laughed it off and told the little boy to pretend it was a Halloween costume. Shane had gotten used to it; kids were adaptable. And Dad . . . Dad didn't even seem surprised. "Wouldn't expect any better from you, you hanging around with thugs. Just a matter of time 'fore you started lookin' like one." That's what Dad had said.

Dex dropped his head back and stared up at the cheap plastic ceiling. He'd always had a hard time pleasing his old man. His father had been gone a lot when he was growing up. He worked for Union Pacific before he got injured uncoupling a train; that's when he retired from the railroad on disability and moved to Montana. Not long after that Mama died, and not long after that the only woman Dex ever loved chose another man. Dex left the Army and slid back into the trouble that seemed to follow him constantly during high school. He knew his folks thought the Army might straighten him out, might give him the break he needed in life. Looking back on it, Dex figured it could have gone that way, but it didn't, and he'd been trying ever since to figure out why.

He could blame it on his daddy for being gone so much when he was little, on his mama for being sick so often during his teen years, or on Katie for choosing his best friend as her lover. . . . He could come up with a whole string of excuses. But truth was, he'd made bad choices— one after another, until they all sorta snowballed on him. *Wasn't no one else to blame.* No one else to blame. Some famous singer had sat on a beach in the Keys and written a classic song about that, made millions singing about being a loser. *Well, here sits a real loser.*

It was getting hotter in the trailer, and he moved the fan to direct the warm stream of air onto his chest. It was time to put the face paint back on, cap the fangs, and walk the three-quarter-mile trail down to the Canyon General Store and get some supplies. The park rangers were ridiculously shorthanded, and it wasn't even half past one; the raid on Dad's place was only a few hours ago. Dex figured he still had a little time before he needed to really hunker down and wait, to *hang tight*, as Jesse had ordered. But following orders wasn't his strong suit, and he was hungry for more than canned meat or chili, of which he had an abundance in the trailer. He decided that he still had time to move around a bit, to be out in public, get some things done.

He pulled a cigarette from the pack he'd laid on the table, lit it, and inhaled deeply. *Then again,* he thought, *bad decisions seem to stick to me like glue.* He blew the smoke up toward the ceiling. *My luck I'll walk right into a cop.* He crushed out the cigarette in a cup and pulled himself up off the sofa. *Hell, if I didn't have bad luck, I'd have no luck at all.*

* * *

Jim West had gotten the revised BOLO out on Dex Pierson and the black Dodge Ram before Win made it back to the office at 1:30. It was a relief to get Shane squared away and be back in the hunt. Kirk Hampton was the only agent at the FBI office in Mammoth when Win walked in the door. They walked together down the hall to the breakroom.

They were standing there rehashing the events of this morning; Win had given the other agent the CliffsNotes version. "With the other guys in Cody interviewing those chopper companies, I shoulda been there with you for backup this morning," Kirk was saying as Win poured himself a cup of coffee. "You shouldn't have been out there by yourself."

"Someone needed to be here in the office. Jim gave you that job. If everyone had shown up like they were supposed to at Pierson's trailer, I wouldn't have needed more backup."

Kirk was still rooting around in the overhead cabinet, looking for the Coffee-Mate. He turned and looked Win's way. "Like, you can't ever have too much backup, isn't that what they say at Quantico?" Kirk finally found the canister he was looking for and dumped an ample portion of white powder into his coffee. Win wondered how that fit into a vegan diet. Kirk stirred his coffee and looked up at Win as he spoke. "You coulda been totally iced if your suspect had been at that trailer before those deputies arrived. A few dead buffalo are not worth losing your life over, dude."

Win leaned back against the wall. Kirk's stretching to check in the top cabinet had pulled his T-shirt tight and revealed a problem. For a moment Win hesitated to call the other agent on the breach of protocol—he wasn't this guy's supervisor—but he was the case agent, and that gave him some authority. This breach could easily become his problem. "Where's your gun, Kirk? You know we're supposed to be armed while on duty." *And we're on duty most of the time,* Win thought.

"Ah . . ." Kirk glanced down at his clinging T-shirt, as if surprised not to see a holster riding against his hip. He glanced back up at Win and grinned. "The Glock's heavy, man . . . causes my pants to sag." He picked up his coffee cup, took a sip, and stared at Win over the top of it. Win read the challenge in Kirk's eyes; he held the eye contact and didn't respond. Kirk blinked first. The younger agent sucked in a breath and shrugged. "I'm not really into firearms. It's, like, not my thing."

Win spoke softly. "Well then, I suggest you show up tomorrow in pants that won't sag, in a dress shirt, with a jacket. I suggest you wear your gun, that you carry your creds. . . . You're an FBI agent. While we work this case, I expect you to look and act like one." Win turned to walk away.

The guy wasn't giving up that easily. "Why? For appearances? For the press that's milling around?" he called after Win's back.

Win turned toward him so quickly that the younger man stumbled backward. "No, not just for appearances, although that wouldn't hurt. You're an officer of the law, and that firearm might save your life or save someone else's life. That's why!" Win pivoted again and walked down the hall. He was getting real tired of being the only grown-up in the room.

* * *

"Mr. Prince? There's a call for you . . . it's that gentleman that does some repair work for you, a Mr. Pierson." The older woman with tight curly gray hair who'd knocked softly and cracked open the door was hesitant; she knew this would be a trying day for her boss.

Prince looked up sharply at the intrusion. The ornate clock on the wall said it wasn't even three.

"I told him you were in conference. . . . He said it was urgent. It's line two," she said.

Prince tried to look puzzled. "Ah, Pierson? Oh, yeah, right. He's the guy we've got doing the plumbing on those rental houses . . . right?" He shook his head as if he'd just placed the name in his mind.

She nodded. "Yes, he's done several of the repairs. He's been very reliable, does good work."

He smiled back at his secretary. "Not a problem. I'll take the call."

His secretary paused before she left the doorway. "I know today's difficult for you . . . losing Bree last year. . . . You really should take the rest of the day off; I'll handle this if you want."

Prince leaned back in the leather desk chair and sighed. "I'm better working . . . takes my mind off it. I appreciate you thinking of me. What would I do without you?" He faked a stricken look, drew in a deep breath, and shook his head. "How could it have been a year . . . a year ago today."

He leaned forward and his hand moved to pick up the receiver. She gave him one last motherly look of concern before she quietly closed the door.

Dex Pierson didn't waste any time on small talk. "Hey, dude. I'm not liking the lack of communication. We've got issues."

"What the hell are you doing calling me here?" his voice was low and lethal.

Dex scoffed. "*Mr. Prince . . . Mr. Prince?* Couldn't you do better than that, Jesse?"

The man laughed quietly and tried to shift the mood with his answer. "Hell, it has a nice ring to it: Jesse L. Prince. Where are you?"

"Trying to keep my head down, that's where." The tone said that was the best answer Jesse would get. He decided not to push it, Dex was hot.

Jesse leaned back in his chair and sighed. "All right. You know I'm workin' to clean everything up. We'll be back in business within the month. Already got some clients interested in a trophy grizzly . . . maybe somewhere right outside the park." He heard Dex draw in a breath. The guy was getting impatient. "Just do as I say. Sit tight till this blows over—the press will move on, the story will change. In a few weeks no one will care."

"Well, there's an FBI agent nosing around up here. Raided Dad's place early this morning. I'm hearing they took his truck and some of my hobby items, if you get my drift. This could cause us some grief."

"Okay, I'll look into it. You just chill, okay? Don't call my office again—I'll get back with you." Jesse dropped the receiver before his partner could respond.

He leaned back in the chair and sighed again. *Hell of a mess!* He didn't have to check on the raid at old man Pierson's trailer. He knew all about it—he'd gotten the report from two of his sources well before noon. The Feds being all ramped up was a problem. Could be this young FBI agent was out to make a name for himself, wanted a score on a high-profile case. Could be something that needed to be squashed, but not yet—not yet. He cautioned himself to follow the orders he'd just given Dex. *Sit tight.*

He had a lot to lose here if things went off the rails. His eyes scanned the large, opulent office with its cherrywood paneling, black iron light fixtures, and imposing stone fireplace. The bronze Western sculptures and original landscape paintings were insured at six figures. His gaze touched on the various diplomas and plaques that hung on one wall. A "*love me*" wall, he liked to joke when visitors and clients admired his achievements. It had always amazed him that people accepted without question the Notre Dame and Northwestern credentials, the civic and community awards from back East. He had an impressive résumé, that was for damn sure. What did it matter that none of it was real?

He glanced down at his expansive mahogany desk and his eyes settled on the gold-framed picture of Bree. It was too bad . . . a shame, really. She was a beautiful girl, a few years younger than him. So full of life. She thought he was dashing and fun. She thought he was intelligent and successful. She didn't realize he was also cunning and evil. He wasn't sure she grasped that until a year ago today—maybe it occurred to her while they were standing on the lip of that cliff, with his hand firmly on her back, or maybe not until she was falling. He'd never know. And he didn't really care.

*   *   *

The huge white satellite truck with WYNX TV plastered across the side was still idling near the FBI's Pagoda Building, blocking the small gravel lot where the FBI vehicles parked. Win had politely asked them to move twice already, and his patience was wearing thin. The driver saw Win coming out of the rear door, waved in submission, and put the huge vehicle in gear. It lumbered down the street, where Win figured it would meander around for a few minutes and then come right back to this open spot. Since the press hit town yesterday, there was hardly an empty parking space anywhere in Mammoth, much less spots large enough to accommodate the big satellite trucks. Win stood there and watched it pull away as he opened the tailgate on the Expedition. He'd loaned his long gun to one of the Denver agents for their morning trek to Cody; now he needed to get it back inside his SUV's gun safe.

He'd just taken the rifle out of its case when a vehicle pulled in behind him, once again blocking the lot. He swung around, ready to play traffic cop again, but this time he recognized the driver. She emerged from her silver SUV and walked toward him. Alex had changed into jeans and a T-shirt since this morning. She could have passed for a typical tourist, except for her expression. Her face was etched with pain.

Win nodded to her and finished securing the modified M4 in the Expedition's gun safe, mentally checking off the steps before he closed and locked the lid. Then he turned back to her.

She stopped a few feet from him and raised her chin in greeting. "I've, ah, just packed up . . . I'm driving to Greg's wake and funeral," she said. He wasn't sure what to say. She dropped her eyes for a second, then looked back at him. "They released his body yesterday—our government expedited things, I guess. I'll leave there after the feast. . . ." She faltered, then cleared her throat. "Ah, it will be near Cardston, on the Kainai Reserve. That's only a few miles north of the border."

"Alex, I'm really sorry about Greg Manyhorses, about your loss." He wasn't sure what else to say, so he switched to business. "You're off the case?"

She shrugged. "I'm not sure," she said quietly. Then she regrouped, and her face went neutral. "I'll be meeting with the Illegal Weapons Task Force Inspector while I'm in Canada—I'm sure he'll leave me on this. I hope to get back here in a couple of days."

They both stood there in silence while the big TV satellite truck slowly passed on the narrow road behind them. Win gave the driver a warning look and it moved on by. Alex had changed focus when the noise from the big engine began to subside.

"You're a gun guy," she said.

"How do you figure that?"

"That's an AR-15—"

"It's a Bureau-modified Colt M4, a law enforcement version of an AR-15. We're replacing our older MP5s with these—"

"I know what it is. My partner was killed last year in Toronto with an illegal AR-15, smuggled in from Michigan. Do you know how rare that is in Canada? Death by gunfire? Yet it happens here every day. Well over a hundred people a day die by guns in America . . . *a day*."

Whoa! He wasn't expecting this lecture.

She kept talking. "You handle those weapons like you were born with one in your hand."

He tried to make a defense. "Grew up on a farm. I got my first .22 when I was nine. We had guns at home for hunting. I did a little competitive shooting in high school." He shrugged. "But I wouldn't say I'm a gun guy."

Her raised eyebrows showed her skepticism. "Sure you are."

He lowered the tailgate on the Expedition and looked for a way out of this debate, but she was just getting started. Alex wasn't done yet.

"When we catch the scum who killed Trent and Greg, if we're lucky enough to intercept the illegal weapons—those handguns and AR-15s—you'll just turn them back on your streets for sale, they'll just go on to kill others. It will be all fine and dandy then. They'll be legal then." He started to interrupt, but she wasn't finished. "Just more casualties to add to the great American body count. Shootings are the leading cause of death in U.S. children, did you know that? America leads the world in killing off your own citizens with weapons that were made for war . . . and . . . and it's spilling over into Canada, into my country. Gun violence went up eighty-one percent in the last few years in Canada. But no one here seems to give a damn."

Win took a step back from the unexpected barrage of accusations. "Look, Alex, I give a damn or I wouldn't be in this business. I've seen the horrific damage that an assault rifle can do—seen it up close and personal. I've read all the statistics. I don't believe civilians should own a military rifle or a thirty-round magazine. There is one use for those guns, one real use: killing people." He took a breath and figured she might as well hear the rest of it. "And I don't believe anyone should be free to carry a handgun who isn't licensed and trained—the same as we do with other dangerous things, like driving a car. Heck, you've gotta have training and take an exam to sell real estate, yet we allow most anyone to carry around a weapon that could end a life in a split second without a moment of training. We don't even do background checks on a large percentage of gun purchases. I believe in freedom balanced with personal responsibility. Responsibility is critical for freedom to function. Those are my beliefs. But, and this is a big *but*, my oath is to enforce the law of the land, not to make it."

Alex seemed surprised by his answer, not sure what to say. "Maybe America will change some day—gun violence isn't real to most people here. But it's real to me. Losing two people I loved to guns . . . it's real to me." He thought she might cry, but she straightened her thin shoulders and finished her thoughts. "Maybe when enough innocents die, when enough lives are devastated, then maybe it will change." She shook her head, turned, and walked away.

Win stood there watching her walk to her SUV, watched her pull away. *Maybe it will change. . . .* Something inside him wanted to cling to that hope. But Win Tyler had taken enough history to know that when human beings are given total freedom without regard for personal responsibility, it rarely ends well.

CHAPTER FOURTEEN

They filed into the pew right in front of him as everyone stood for the first hymn. Luke raised his chin in acknowledgment as he herded his family and Shane into the row. Win had dropped the boy off at Luke and Ellie's place early on Thursday afternoon—barely three days ago—and he hardly recognized him now. Here he was at church, with a new haircut, new clothes, new tennis shoes. Totally different look. Ellie maneuvered Shane between Abby and Ethan, so as to hold down the fighting, Win figured. Shane looked back over his shoulder and saw Win. He smiled. Win gave him a fist bump and managed to smile back.

But it wasn't lost on Win Tyler that he was forcing down a sudden tightness in his chest, that pain had invaded his heart. He could no longer avoid the nice woman who ran the Denver Field Office's Victim/ Witness Assistance Program, and he couldn't keep Ellie and Luke in a bad place with Pierson still on the loose. Everyone involved in the case thought Dex Pierson would have been found and at least questioned, if not locked up, long before now. His big bosses in Denver thought they'd have tracked down the helicopter that hauled out the bison heads, wondered why they weren't much further along in the case. And there was no more progress on the investigation into the murders involving the gunrunners in Grand Teton than there was on the poaching case. It was as if both cases had hit a wall. Jim West told Win they'd regroup on Monday. He said they'd probably set up a team to take another review of the evidence on both cases so far, maybe bring in some fresh eyes, look at different angles. They desperately needed to jump-start the stalled investigations. Jim had also told him to take all day off on Sunday—*all day*—saying that it didn't help anyone to have him burn out on the cases, that it wasn't just a suggestion.

The service concluded at 11:00, and a steady stream of tourists, locals, and rangers filed out of the historic Yellowstone Chapel. Ellie had stopped in the foyer to show the kids the church's fascinating stained-glass windows, which showcased the park's wildlife, waterfalls, and geysers. Win knew Ellie had an elementary education degree, but he figured she'd be teaching regardless. It was something that came naturally to her, passing along the things she'd learned. Win's mother was like that. He remembered his father saying that he'd never known a rock could be beautiful until Win's mother had pointed that out. She was able to find wonder in the simplest things. Ellie Bordeaux was like that too, and Win found himself thinking that Tory Madison shared that special trait. *I wonder where she is today....* He jerked a little when Luke touched his sleeve and motioned him outside. They both shook hands with the pastor again and moved toward the parking lot and the remaining congregants. The kids all scattered toward the trees on the stone building's south side.

Win waved to Trey and watched him round up his wife and daughter to go meet a bunch of his relatives who were visiting the park. Win knew the family reunion had given Trey a much-needed break from the Park Service inspectors the last two days. The reprieve was short; Trey would be back on duty later today.

Win cleared his throat and turned to Luke and Ellie. He figured he might as well get it over with. "The Bureau requested that Montana Child and Family Services in Butte send someone down to pick Shane up this afternoon. Y'all gonna be home around two?"

Ellie was watching Abby, Ethan, Shane, and three other kids stalk Uinta ground squirrels near the church building. Win didn't think she'd heard him at first. But she did.

She shot Luke a look that communicated something, then smiled at Win and moved off toward the children. "Gotta go rescue the squirrels. . . ." Then she turned and gave Luke another long look. Win wished he knew someone well enough to telegraph his thoughts that way. He could only hope that someday he'd have that kind of relationship. *Maybe someday.*

Luke leaned back against Ellie's Toyota pickup and stared off toward his wife and the group of kids. "State social services? Around two, you say?"

"Uh-huh."

"Some sorta lockup?"

"Uh-huh. In Butte, I guess the place in Livingston is full. . . . I'm sure they'll take good care of him."

"You've talked to them?"

"Yeah . . . a lady called me just before church. She was all business. I'm sure they're good people, doin' their best for kids like Shane." Even he could hear the doubt in his voice. He cleared his throat again. "You want me to come at two? Meet them there? Uh, what was Ellie sayin' with her eyes?"

Luke forced back a smile. "No, don't come. And you can't deny something you ain't heard. *Plausible deniability,* ain't that the concept?" He nodded toward the kids. "The boy is from good stock. He's got manners, been brought up right. He's got people down South. . . . We just need to find 'em. That's what Ellie and I are thinkin'."

"I've got someone working on it, but no hits so far. I'm amazed that Ellie hasn't been able to get any more information out of him. You still thinking he's from Alabama or Georgia?"

"I'm thinkin' Georgia." Luke grinned. "I was runnin' some football calls by him, and he flat-out refused to say '*Roll Tide.*'" He grinned again. "'Course his people might be Auburn fans." He shrugged. "And he's been raised in the country—knows about animals, comfortable in the woods, he can swim. Ellie says he's likely fourth grade, but he's reading well above that grade level. If he was homeschooled, they were good at it."

"He seems to get along well with y'all."

"Yeah, but he's missing his daddy and his grandpa. I caught him crying in bed last night as we was putting 'em down."

Win dropped his gaze from the children and studied his boots for a moment. "I hate that I've put you and your family in a position where Pierson could come after Shane. I thought we'd have him cleared or in custody long before now. He's completely gone to ground."

Luke shrugged with his eyebrows. "I've been staying pretty close to home, so don't worry about us. And forget the social services option. Ellie won't have it . . . I won't have it. The boy needs a safe place to be. But it's sad fer him that Dex ain't come around."

*　*　*

But Dex was around. At that moment, Dex Pierson was sitting on a knoll, beneath a scrubby pine, 546 feet northwest of the church's small parking area, watching Win and Luke talk. He'd staked out the entrance road to Luke's house since well before dawn. He was hoping the woman would take Shane somewhere and he could make a run at them. It hadn't really occurred to him that it was Sunday morning and that some folks went to church. He vaguely recalled that his mother went to church from time to time when he was young. He didn't think he'd ever been in a church.

He'd followed Ellie's vehicle to the Yellowstone Chapel in the older Chevy Silverado he borrowed from the Canyon Campground. He watched them pull in, pile out, and head for the gray-stone chapel's doors. Shane was laughing and teasing with the two smaller Bordeaux kids as they all greeted who Dex guessed to be the priest or preacher or whatever they called the boss man. Everyone seemed happy, pleased to be there.

As the number of arriving attendees dwindled and the service began, Dex made himself comfortable and waited. He was a hunter. He knew how to find the best vantage point. And he had a perfect view from his high spot between the Lower Cascade Terraces and the church parking lot. He figured this hilltop was used mostly by photographers, since it overlooked the Fort Yellowstone Historic District and Mount Everts. It wasn't on a trail that went anywhere, really; he'd had the place to himself for the last hour. As he sat alone with the spotting scope, as he pretended to view the ever-present elk and the occasional coyote or fox, he felt that familiar sadness descend on him. He hated it when he had time to look inward, to become introspective. He tried to focus on the wildlife, the scenery, the sporadic hikers, but his mind kept wandering back to the people in the church. He wondered how on earth he could have turned out so different from them.

He was pleased to see Shane looking happy, playing with the other children. That was one of many things he'd felt bad about these last few months—not getting Shane involved with other kids after he brought him here. He reckoned that an eight-year-old oughta be playing base-ball or some other sport. Maybe soccer was the thing these days. Shane should be going to pool parties and picnics with other kids during the summer, not holed up in a rundown trailer in the woods with a dying old man and a shiftless ex-con. It wasn't what he'd intended when he picked Shane up from Katie's sister seven months ago. It wasn't what he'd intended at all.

He blew out a breath and focused the spotting scope back on the two men standing by the Toyota pickup. It hadn't been too hard to find out that the boy was staying at Bordeaux's place; he'd called one of his girlfriends and she'd done some snooping around for him. Someone at the Sheriff's Office had confirmed that Shane had gone with the FBI agent after the raid on the trailer. He discovered that the agent had gone by the town's veterinarian to check the hound for a microchip that morning. Someone had seen Ellie Bordeaux with her kids and Shane at the local library two days ago. It paid to date a girl who worked down at city hall, who had access to the police records and all the local gossip.

He wasn't dumb enough to try to get Shane back from Bordeaux's house. Luke Bordeaux was a force. Dex had visited the local VFW post a few times when he first got out of the pen. He knew the bartender would take pity on him and set out some whiskey. After all, he'd served in the Army, been in a combat zone, gotten an honorable discharge. At least he hadn't messed that up. He'd heard plenty about Luke Bordeaux at the VFW. The guy was a true hero—Special Forces, someone had said. Purple Heart, Silver Star, Bronze Star. *Whoa!* He focused back on Bordeaux through the scope. The man was six three or four, about the height of the FBI agent. He was probably one hundred percent muscle, and he had that Louisiana Cajun swagger. Even leaning back against the little pickup, he looked alert and lethal. Dex had learned enough in the military and in prison to know what kind of man you didn't mess with. Luke Bordeaux was that kind of man.

He shifted the scope slightly to better view the agent. His opinion hadn't changed since the first time he'd seen him at the bar last week. He was sharp; you could see it in his eyes. He was also confident and capable; he hadn't flinched when Dex stared him down. Most men didn't stand up to him that easily. The FBI man was tan and fit and built a lot like Bordeaux. Both of them probably ran, probably lifted weights, either of them could easily beat him in a fair fight. Dex smiled at that thought. Might not be a problem since he never fought fair. He watched the agent pull off the light jacket he'd worn in church. Now Dex could clearly see the black handgun holstered on his right side, saw the pouches on his belt that contained an extra magazine and handcuffs. He might have been at worship, but he was ready for work.

Dex leaned back against the big rock for a moment and blinked to clear his eyes. It would be smart to let Shane stay where he was—the boy seemed well cared for and safe. But *smart* had never been his MO. He wanted the kid with him, wanted to prove to Shane that he could take care of him, that he could get them both out of this mess. He'd accomplished the first three things on his list: he'd gotten away from Dad's place, he'd made it to his hideout at the camper in Canyon, and he'd laid low for three days and managed to stay off the cops' radar. He added two more tasks to the list: get Shane back and get the hell out of Dodge.

* * *

Win had eaten a ham sandwich, gotten two loads of laundry done, cleaned the litter box, and made it through the pile of mail that had accumulated that week on the granite kitchen counter. He tried to get Gruff to play with his fake mouse, but the big orange cat was stretched out on the bedroom rug in the afternoon sun. He yawned and closed his eyes when Win tried to summon him. "If you were a dog, you'd jump up and play," he called to the cat. Not even an ear twitch in response.

He'd had a good phone visit with his grandparents, and he'd left a message for Blake, who he figured was still in the middle of the hay-field, Sunday or not. He was avoiding calling Mom and Dad. He knew they would be disappointed in him for not reaching out to Will before now. He'd been back in Mammoth for nearly a week, and he'd made no effort to call his little brother. He finally sucked it up and called them; thankfully, Dad was hauling hay and Mom was leaving to visit a sick neighbor. She only had a couple of minutes to talk, but in that short time she managed to point out that Will was barely fifteen and Win was the adult, that Win was required to act like one. She'd talked to Will twice this week and she was sure he was anxious for Win to call. Before she hurried off the phone, she told Win to call back tonight for a longer visit after Dad got in from the field. Win knew what she really wanted was an update on his reaching out to his little brother. She wanted to make sure her eldest son was acting like an adult.

He sat in the leather reading chair in his bedroom and thought about it. He agreed with everything she'd said. *I am the adult.* He won-dered how other twenty-eight-year-olds felt on gorgeous Sunday after-noons after being lectured by their mothers, when there was no one to talk to except a sleeping cat.

That got him to thinking about Tory and wondering what she was doing on this spectacular summer day. He knew she was somewhere in the backcountry north of Yellowstone Lake. The grizzly bear research along Pelican Creek was in full swing during July. She'd told him they'd be out of cell phone range for several days, but once they set up a base camp she'd be able to use the satellite phone occasionally. He wished that would be soon. He wanted her to call. It had been a week since he'd talked with her, six days since he sent the text and the photos of the bear family. Tucker had told him to do something to make her feel special. *How do I do that when she's in the middle of the dang wilder-ness?* He sighed and leaned back in the chair.

Then he zeroed in on the heavy satellite phone that sat on top of the dresser. It was a Bureau phone. He really shouldn't use it for a personal call. But he knew the Bureau allowed agents some latitude in phone calls; they were often on duty for days at a stretch, and their personal phones weren't always available. He stared at the sat phone again. He knew it wasn't regulations or policies that were keeping him from calling the number for the Interagency Grizzly Bear Research Project. It was pure old fear. He was afraid she wouldn't talk to him—and if she did, what would she say? He knew the researchers often took a break from their work on Sundays. She'd told him that. He knew her last short text to him had been encouraging; he'd reread it at least a hundred times. But he'd also replayed their last, long conversation down at Miss Martha's. She'd called him out, she'd said that he was still holding on to someone else, that she deserved better. He was thinking she was right.

But how do you move past loss, past grief, if you don't step forward? He had no idea. But it occurred to him that God knew, God knew how he should move forward, God knew His plans for Win Tyler, for Tory Madison. *Trust God, step out in faith,* his heart told him.

He got up, reached for the satellite phone, powered it up, and punched in the number he'd memorized. The guy who answered the phone at base camp came in clear as a bell. He thought Tory was available. "Hold on, I'll get her," he said. Win only had to hold for a few moments before he heard her cheery voice in the background, heard her thank the guy who handed her the phone.

"Oh Win, I'm so glad you called!" Tory said. "This morning was absolutely amazing! You wouldn't *believe* what we saw . . ."

* * *

He was on the call with Tory for ten minutes or less, but it was good, real good. She had a limited time that she could use the sat phone, and she'd already called her parents back in Tennessee this afternoon. She was upbeat and happy and seemed thrilled to hear from him. As Win got off the call with her, he figured he could channel some of that buzz over to the obligatory call to his little brother. He was wrong about that.

"Hey, bud, how's it going?" He tried for an enthusiastic tone.

"Hey," was Will's tepid response.

"Y'all still heading out tomorrow to go backpacking?"

"Yeah. Maybe. Tucker's run into some issues on his legal work. He was gonna call you . . . he's right here, I'll let him tell you." Win could hear the disappointment in his brother's voice.

"Whoa, whoa . . . how are you doing otherwise? Y'all go to church? You working out? How are the horses?" Win threw out questions, hoping to keep the conversation going.

"Tucker went to church. I'm good, don't need that. Horses are awesome. A man is flying in from Colorado to look at an awesome filly this afternoon. From Colorado! He's gonna pay $25,000. How cool is that! She's a sorrel two-year-old, can turn on a dime. Make an awesome cuttin' horse. That's what the guy's lookin' for. It's awesome." Win registered the uptick in enthusiasm, noted no improvement in Will's vocabulary. They talked horses for a couple of minutes more, but the conversation started to lag—no questions for Win, no interest in his job or his life. Win could hear that lack of concern in Will's voice. He didn't protest this time when the boy handed the phone off to Tucker.

"Will tells me there's some glitch in the camping trip?" Win said. He heard Tucker sigh into the phone.

"Yeah. Aunt Martha's former attorney forgot to file my reciprocity papers—*pro hac vice*—for bar standing here in Wyoming when he semiretired a few weeks ago, so it seems I've been practicing law without a license. I've got to go plead my case with the Wyoming Bar Association's counsel, then explain the foul-up to a circuit judge Tuesday afternoon in Cheyenne."

"Uh-oh. That doesn't sound good."

"It sounds worse than it is. The attorney has filed an affidavit stating that he's at fault. But I'll still have to appear, probably pay a small fine, and amend a boatload of documents that I've already prepared on several real estate deals. It's a pain and it's gonna keep me from going on the backpacking trip." Tucker paused. "I don't suppose you could shake loose for four days and go with Will? He's really been looking forward to it."

"No chance in the next few days—wish I could. I'm covered up on two big cases. Can he go by himself? I'll foot the bill," Win responded.

"It's already paid for . . . but I honestly hadn't thought that far ahead. I'd hoped it would work out so that I could go. Will wasn't the only one excited about it. I don't see why he can't go alone unless they have some age limit policy. Let me check that out, and if he still wants to make the trip, I'll send you the particulars. It's a top-tier company, they come highly recommended. I don't think your folks would have any problem with the outfitters."

"Hey, buddy, if you've set it up, I know it's first-class. That isn't an issue. See what Will thinks after you talk to the company and let me know. How's it going otherwise? Is he behaving himself?"

Win heard Tucker laugh. "He's taking his workouts seriously: running, sprints, weights. . . . The kid is disciplined. And he's great with the horses and the folks here. Since he's not on his phone, we're watching one classic movie a night and competing to see who can read the most novels in two weeks." Tucker paused, and Win could tell his friend was smiling as they wrapped up the call. "Will is a lot like you. He has the smarts, the work ethic, the curiosity. Maybe that's why y'all butt heads, you're too much alike. He's in a rebellious stage, but he'll outgrow it. I predict y'all will be tight in a year or so."

They closed out the call and Win set the phone to the side. *I really hope you're right, Tucker, I really hope you're right.*

* * *

Win was still thinking about his conversation with Will, or more accurately the lack of conversation, as he dug through the drawer for his flag football uniform. He had agreed to play quarterback for the Fightin' Pine Martens this afternoon, since Trey was tied up showing his cousins the park. The embarrassing yellow jerseys and silly rodent mascot aside, they had a pretty good team. Two of his teammates were park rangers who'd played Division I or II football. One of the women on the team had been a star volleyball player in college, and Jazmine Jackson was a pure athlete; she could play anything.

As he pulled on his shorts, he wondered if football was at the core of Will's razzing him. Maybe the kid was ticked that Win had turned down a big NFL signing bonus for a career in public service. Will seemed to think life was all about the money. *Where is he getting this crap?* It wasn't at home. Win's folks were salt of the earth: hardworking, frugal, happy that he'd followed his heart and his true calling. No one in his family had ever brought up the money. So why was his little brother so focused on material things, with no emphasis on the spiritual? *Why does he see me as a loser?*

The knock on his front door was loud. Gruff raised his head and glared toward the intrusion. Win pulled on his football jersey, stepped over the cat, and walked toward the door. The impatient rapping started again.

"Coming!" Win called as he strode down the hall in his sock feet. He opened the heavy wooden door and stared through the screen door at three men standing shoulder to shoulder on the porch. They were dressed in identical khaki cargo pants with navy blue T-shirts under black tactical vests. *ATF* was emblazoned on the front of the vests and on their blue ball caps. Their firearms were low on their thighs, and their badges and some type of ATF name tag hung around their necks on lanyards. All three looked remarkably the same: same short haircut, same scruffy beard, same scowl. Win didn't open the screen door, he just stood there.

Win caught a glimpse of Kirk jogging across the parking lot toward the house. The young agent slowed and held up his hands in a *What could I do?* gesture. Several tourists had stopped in the lot to check out what was going down. A couple of them had their phones or cameras out. Win shifted his focus back to the three guys standing in front of him. It was weird that none of them had spoken.

"Can I help you gentlemen?" Win asked.

"You're Win Tyler." The one in the middle didn't really ask it like a question, and he didn't sound friendly.

"Who's asking?"

"Group Supervisor Gene Cranford, ATF."

"Yeah, I got the ATF part. I see y'all are trying to be inconspicuous."

The middle guy ignored the comment. "We understand you've got information on a suspect vehicle and a suspect in Trent Beckett's murder. We want that information *now*."

Seriously! Win knew his eyes had narrowed, knew his anger was rising, knew his usually long fuse had suddenly gotten shorter. He didn't open the screen door.

"Well, Group Supervisor Gene Cranford, ATF, I'm Special Agent Winston Tyler, FBI, and today is my day off. You would have received any report I filed on a suspected subject vehicle, subject, or person of interest directly from the FBI field office in Denver or our RA in Lander, Wyoming. That is where I file my reports. I don't discuss my reports or any other confidential case matters on my front porch on Sunday afternoons, in sight of twenty gawking tourists. I assume you know what proper channels are—I suggest you follow those."

All three men were still glaring at him. Win figured he didn't look terribly imposing with a smiling weasel on his yellow jersey, but he really didn't care. Kirk had finally made it up onto the wooden porch; he moved behind one of the Adirondack chairs and tried to catch his breath. At least Win now had an ally, he was thankful for that. And he figured the ATF guys might drop the intimidation tactics since there was a witness. He was right about that.

The middle guy held up a hand. "Hey, look . . . we lost a man, a good man. If you've got information we can use, we need it. We don't need to wait till tomorrow for another drawn-out briefing in Jackson where nothing but infighting gets done. We're eight days out and Trent's killers are still out there."

Win was still hot, but he eased open the screen door. "I can meet you at my office at 5:45. Kirk can make you at home there, or you can see the sights until then." Win looked at Kirk and his colleague nodded. He turned back toward the leader. "Oh, and I'd recommend a bit more discretion in the park, your raid gear is drawing a crowd."

Win didn't wait for them to agree to his terms; he started to shut the screen door. The others turned to leave, but the middle guy held up his hand again. "Agent Tyler, we want justice for our man—"

"I get that," Win said, and he stepped back inside and closed both doors. He listened to the men tromping down the porch steps as he leaned back against the wooden door and drew in a long breath. *I get that. . . . I really do.*

CHAPTER FIFTEEN

Win called his supervisor on the way to the park's makeshift football field at Mammoth's abandoned elementary school near the entrance to the Lower Mammoth employee-housing area. Jim didn't sound happy about the Sunday afternoon call; Win wondered if it had been his goal to take the whole day off as well. Jim said to cut the meeting short with the ATF agents. He thought this was a rogue deal—no one had informed the Bureau that ATF was sending a team to Yellowstone. Win could tell his boss was angry, that he thought the other agency was totally out of line. Jim told Win to get to his game, said he'd make some calls, he'd handle it. They ended the call just as Win pulled up to the field. Win waved to a few of his teammates as he jumped out of his old Explorer and hustled to get in warm-ups. He put the annoyance of the work intrusion behind him and soon was enjoying the sun on his back, the camaraderie with the other players, the feel of the leather ball in his hands.

The teams broke for halftime and Win jogged toward the orange water coolers. When he saw Alex Lindell sitting by herself at the end of the modest wooden bleachers, he sighed. Now another interruption on his day off. He hadn't seen her since she'd left town to go to Manyhorses's funeral late Thursday afternoon, but she'd called him Saturday morning to let him know she'd be in the Jackson area for several days, running down case leads. He'd noticed that her voice was strong on that call. Her tone told him that ATF was finally letting her back in the game, that she was a part of the investigation. *So why is she here?*

Jazmine pitched him a cold bottle of Gatorade and gave him a thumbs-up. "You're killin' it, Win! Trey's gonna lose his quarterback slot!"

Win caught the bottle and saluted her with it, but his attention went back to Alex. He turned and walked toward the bleachers. Alex was wearing what he thought of as her field uniform, the gray-and-blue garb, and she looked more relaxed than usual. He wondered again why she was back in Yellowstone, but before he could ask, she started talking. "That ranger, Jazmine, she's crushing on you in a big way, Win."

Win wiped the sweat from his face with his forearm. "She's a good ranger, a nice girl . . . is it that obvious?"

Alex hopped down off the bleacher, waved to Jazmine, and turned back to Win. "Yeah, it is. You need to tell her you're not interested."

"How do you know I'm not interested?"

"Oh, that wistful expression that crosses your face when you think no one is looking. Your heart is somewhere else . . . with someone who isn't here. I'm sure Jazmine has figured that out, but you still need to tell her."

He made a mental note to guard his emotions better, to hide his feelings. He'd always prided himself on being cool, calm, deliberate. He knew that sometimes he came off as aloof and detached, but with Alex he was having the opposite problem. She was reading him far too easily.

He downed half the sports drink. He was hoping he could dodge Alex on the appearance of the ATF boys, but he knew better.

"I'm hearing from my people that ATF may start moving on the Yellowstone angle on the gunrunning case," she was saying.

Win sighed and took another step toward her. "An ATF supervisor and two of his guys showed up at my house a little over an hour ago. I'm meeting them in my office at 5:45."

She stood up straighter, but her face didn't give her surprise away. "Okay . . ."

Win didn't like that they were stringing her along, asking her to do the grunt work but not keeping her in the loop. The Canadians had lost a guy too; it didn't matter that Greg Manyhorses was an informant. He deserved justice just the same as Agent Trent Beckett. And Alex deserved to be treated better than this.

"Can you clear it with your folks to be in the meeting?" Win asked. "I don't like them ridin' in here heavy-handed, trying to take over the case after blowing us off for days. I'm good with you being in the meeting if your people can clear it with the Bureau."

"Okay," she repeated, and she turned toward the dirt parking lot. He could tell she was having to work to hide her disappointment from him.

Win watched her thin shoulders sag as she moved away from him. He knew it was compassion he was feeling when he called to her, "Hey, hey! I've got something to give you . . . almost forgot I had it." He held a finger up to signal a teammate that he'd be right back. He jogged to his parked vehicle and waved for Alex to follow.

Win opened the Explorer's passenger door and reached into the glove box. He'd nearly forgotten it was there. Alex stood behind him as he dug through the pile of extra napkins, the little packets of salt and pepper, until he found the SUV's worn owner's manual. He let it fall open to the middle where he'd stuck the bright-yellow arrowleaf balsamroot blossom one week ago. The delicate flower was folded inside a Kleenex, now dried flat, now a deeper gold.

As he gently lifted it out of the book, his mind's eye saw the flat, dried jonquils his mother sent him each spring. *The first jonquil on the farm,* her note would often say, or *the prettiest one near the hay barn,* or something of the sort. They were always delicately laid out on wax paper so as not to tear or decay. He'd thought for years that the only purpose for wax paper was the laying out of flowers—flowers that were a precious gift, a reminder that his mother thought of him when spring's new beginnings took hold. The flat yellow blossoms reminded him that someone far away loved him enough to send a tangible token. For just a second, he let himself wonder how he'd feel when the expected spring flower didn't come, when late February or early March passed without the card or letter that held the first flower of spring.

He held the deep-yellow blossom gently in his hand as he turned toward Alex. He was holding the last flower Alex Lindell would ever receive from Greg Manyhorses, the last expression of love. Her dark eyes were on it, and she took it from him with the same reverence he felt. She knew what it was. She pulled it close to her, turned, and walked away.

*　*　*

What the hell! He was running straight toward the commotion, one hand on the grip of the Glock at his side. He'd just gotten out of his football uniform, grabbed a quick shower, and decided to walk the quarter mile down the street to his office for the 5:45 meeting with the ATF posse. It was a beautiful summer day, and on his drive back to his house from the game, he'd spotted a small herd of elk grazing on the parade ground. He'd be able to stop and see them on his stroll to the office—he never got tired of watching the wildlife. He'd made it halfway to the office, just past the gas station and the general store, when everything erupted.

A big black Dodge pickup with Kansas plates had just parked facing the parade ground, across from the Terrace Grill. Win could see that a stout guy had just gotten out of the driver's door. The man's orange T-shirt registered, the gray ball cap, the unkempt brown beard, but it was the silver item in the man's hand that held his focus. *A gun?* The guy was swinging it wildly—no control. The late-afternoon sun was hitting whatever it was, Win couldn't be sure. Win saw one of the ATF guys moving between the cars near the black pickup, heard him holler "Gun! Police! Gun! Drop it!" Win's eyes darted back to the flashing object in the guy's hand again. "*Gun!* Drop it! Hands up!" Win's mind screamed, or maybe it was the second ATF guy who yelled that. Everything was happening so fast. Alex appeared barely twenty feet from the gunman near the pickup's tailgate, holding her pistol in a two-handed grip. She was balanced on the balls of her feet, leaning forward, shouting something toward the guy. Win could see several faces in the background, horrified faces. The parking area was jammed with onlookers watching the elk that were lounging thirty yards beyond them.

"Drop it! Drop the gun!" Win heard Alex shout. Then, "I've got the shot!"

Win was a firm believer in Divine Intervention, and this was a perfect example. Trey Hechtner had gone into action an instant after Alex ran across the street toward the back of the pickup, just as the guy exited the truck, moments after she'd pulled her sidearm. Trey had been standing between the crowd of photo-hungry tourists and a huge bull elk. He'd been doing his ranger thing: keeping the tourists at bay, keeping a close eye on the bull, answering dozens of questions about the animals, all with good humor and grace. But Trey had a better view of the man exiting the pickup than Alex, the ATF guys, or Win. Trey was the one who began to yell, "No gun! It's a phone! No gun!" Trey was the one who saved the day—who potentially saved a life. The ranger ran toward the front of the truck, kicked the driver's door shut while grabbing the silver phone from the man's hand, and gripped him around the chest. An ATF agent was now on top of them, his gun was still drawn, but he'd pointed the muzzle toward the ground. He grabbed one of the driver's hands and pulled it down and behind him.

Win saw Trey's calm face as he pushed the truck's driver up against the pickup's fender, saw another of the ATF guys emerge from behind other parked vehicles and pull out his handcuffs. The elk were all standing with their heads raised high, ears up, alarm in their eyes. "It's over . . . move back across the street," Trey called out to anyone within hearing distance. "Move back across the street, now please!" Trey's voice was measured and direct. The tourists who'd been filming the ruckus on their phones began to retreat as the third ATF agent appeared and moved toward the pickup.

Win got to Alex just as she was lowering her firearm. He was as shocked by the expression on her face and in her eyes as he'd been by the chaos that had erupted moments ago. He saw rage—pure fury and hate. *I've got the shot!* That's what she'd yelled seconds ago. She was fixing to kill the guy, Win had no doubt about that. If Trey hadn't made his move, if Trey hadn't jumped into action, they'd have a dead man instead of a furious tourist from Kansas who was now shouting to the ATF guys that he wasn't about to drop the newest iPhone to the pavement. He was yelling that he would sue them for cuffing him, that they had no right to accost him. He didn't know he'd come within seconds of dying. All he had to do was obey simple commands: *Drop the object. Raise your hands.* Win drew in a deep breath and shook his head. So many tragedies happen every year in police encounters because people refuse to obey simple commands, because humans make mistakes, because any mistake with a gun can be deadly.

Several Park Service folks were crossing the street from the Terrace Grill, and a ranger's Tahoe with its light bar flashing pulled up and blocked the road behind the pickup. The elk trotted a few feet away, then lost interest and dropped their heads to graze.

Win stood beside Alex at the rear of the big black pickup and tried to decide what to do. The Park Service folks who'd walked over appeared to be honchos, and Trey was deferring to them. Win went over to the stone-faced ATF supervisor and told him that he could positively identify the person of interest in the case they'd come to investigate. Win told him that the cuffed man was not that person. Win announced to the law enforcement group that he wanted everyone involved to meet in the FBI conference room as soon as they wrapped up this unfortunate situation.

One of the ATF guys was trying to explain to the man in cuffs that he fit the description . . . , that his vehicle fit the description . . . , and so on and so forth, but Win could tell the apology, such as it was, wasn't getting through to the angry tourist. There was still a large crowd congregated on the sidewalk across the street—shooting video, snapping photos, and calling out questions. Apparently a police takedown was way more interesting than grazing elk. *This could get ugly,* Win thought. He leveled his gaze back at the ATF supervisor. "This is your deal," he said. "I'll be waiting for you in my office." Then he turned and pulled out his Bureau phone, hitting the speed dial for Jim West as he walked away. *So much for all day off.*

* * *

The 5:45 meeting at Win's office wasn't going to go well. Alex was fixing to get into the ATF supervisor's face. Win could feel it. He hung back a little, watching her storm down the hall from the breakroom as the three ATF guys entered the small foyer. Win's granny would say Alex "wasn't no bigger than a minute," but she was tough, she'd had enough, and she was primed for a fight.

"I've been working this case for months! Months! And you show up and totally shelve me . . . and this isn't the first time. What was that cowboy play with the guy in the black truck? There was no planning! No surveillance! No investigation! No assurance you had the right man! And right in the middle of a crowd of tourists! Are you gonna do an armed takedown on everyone who drives a black pickup in Montana?"

We're technically in Wyoming, Win thought, but it seemed a moot point and not worth mentioning. He sure couldn't argue with the other points she was making. He moved to her side to try to calm her down, but his effort to defuse the situation didn't help. She was still raging, going toe to toe with the ATF supervisor.

"What in hell do you think you were doing!" she nearly shouted. "Your stupid play will force our subject to go completely to ground. What were you thinking!"

We don't really have a subject, Win thought, and to his credit, Group Supervisor Cranford didn't respond to Alex in kind. He stood there and let her finish her rant. Win figured he'd had enough time to conclude that ATF was going to catch hell over this screwup and that he was fixing to be in deep trouble. *And he should be. This could have been a tragedy.*

Win decided to take Jim West's advice and cut the meeting short. He blocked the door to the conference room and addressed Alex and the agents. "I've already talked with Chief Ranger Randall about the incident with the tourist. He wants to meet with Agent Cranford in his office, and since Constable Lindell was also involved in the altercation, I suggest that she accompany him to that meeting. Ranger Trey Hechtner was also actively involved, and he will be there."

Agent Cranford took a step forward and started to say something, but Win cut him off. "This isn't an FBI matter . . . not at this point." Win glared at the senior agent. "I assume that you had some legal reason for stopping that man." Win shifted his eyes to Alex. "And I assume that you had some contact with ATF before the takedown began. Whatever those factors are, they need to be shared with the Park Service. The Bureau has no oversight or jurisdiction since no crime was committed and no charges have been filed." He paused. "At least, no crime was committed by the individual who was stopped, cuffed, and questioned." Win let the veiled threat hang in the air.

Another of the ATF guys started to speak and Win stared him down. "I suggest y'all take up your issues with the Park Service across the street. The FBI has no arrest warrant for any individual in the case related to Agent Trent Beckett or Greg Manyhorses. Let me repeat: we may have a person of interest, but we do not have a suspect." He let his words settle before he continued. "We want to see that case resolved as badly as anyone, but I know you'll all agree that cooler heads need to prevail right now. We have to work together to follow the evidence, to bring the killers to justice."

Win raised a hand and pointed toward the front door. "Chief Randall is waiting for you in his office in the park's Administration Building."

The ATF group turned and filed out of the building without another word. Alex lagged behind.

"What were you doing? You left my ball game, spotted the ATF boys in Mammoth, and followed them, didn't you?"

She didn't respond.

"That wasn't smart, wasn't smart at all," Win said.

"What would you have done?"

Maybe the same dumb thing.

"I thought we had him . . . I thought we had the guy who killed Greg." Her voice wasn't much louder than a whisper.

"You were going to shoot him."

Her voice turned cold. "Yeah, yeah, I was." With that she turned and followed the men out the open door.

Win just stood there staring at her retreating back, wondering how she'd gotten to that point—to the point where she didn't care about shooting a man, where she didn't care about ending a life.

CHAPTER SIXTEEN

Win stood in the open door of the hospital room and looked in at the frail form lying under the thin sheet. He couldn't see Mr. Pierson clearly, but what he could see looked much worse than when they'd loaded him into the ambulance at his trailer last Thursday morning. A young dark-haired nurse in blue scrubs was hanging an IV bag on the other side of the bed; she glanced over at Win but continued her task. Win's eyes did a quick sweep of the monitors for the man's vital signs. They didn't look good.

Win had taken a call from the charge nurse at Livingston Healthcare just after Alex and the ATF guys cleared out of his office nearly two hours earlier. The nurse told him that Dex Pierson's father was alert and refusing his pain medication. He was asking to talk to FBI Agent Tyler, asking for Win by name. During Pierson's hospital stay, the Bureau hadn't been able to interview him because of the medications, but now it seemed he was willing to talk. The poaching case was stalled. Win desperately needed the old man to fill in some of the blanks.

Both Win and his supervisor thought the trip to Livingston to meet with Mr. Pierson might move the poaching case along. They also concluded that getting Win out of Mammoth while the Park Service and ATF hashed out the incident with the tourist couldn't hurt. After Jim called Kirk back in to cover the office for the evening, Win hit the road.

The old man stirred and seemed to sense Win's presence. He turned his head. "You comin' in?" his weak voice asked. Win took off his hat and stepped into the dim room. The man nodded slightly as his hand tried to adjust the oxygen tube under his nose. He choked back a cough before he asked, "Where's Shane?"

"Took him to stay with friends of mine. They've got some kids, a dog; they're good people. They'll take care of him till we get this sorted out. You wanta help me sort this out, Mr. Pierson?"

The old man answered Win with questions of his own. "You talk to the doctor? Doctor tell you I's dying?"

"Yes, I spoke with him. . . . Yes, uh, it's a HIPAA thing, a privacy thing . . . but yes . . . I'm sorry."

"Don't be . . ." The man struggled to draw a deeper breath. "Don't be sorry."

Sorry. . . . Why am I hearing that, saying that, so often lately?

The old man shifted his head on the foam pillows, then he latched hold of the nurse's hand and commanded, "Stay." He lifted his eyes back to Win. "You a lawyer?"

Win was puzzled. He'd come here to ask the questions, but he hadn't expected the dire announcement from the doctor regarding Mr. Pierson's health. He hadn't expected to interview a dying man. "Yes, I'm an attorney. But I—

"Don't need no more'n that. I figured you FBI folks to be lawyers or such . . . I got need for a lawyer now." He drew another shallow breath. "It's a legal will if it's written and dated, if it's signed and witnessed by two people, ain't it?"

"Yes. In most states, yes."

"Then you write this down, just as I say." Win pulled out his pen and wrote the few sentences word for word on the back of a blank medical work order that the nurse handed him. She didn't seem to think the odd exchange was unusual, or maybe she was just accustomed to accommodating the last wishes of the dying. Win wasn't sure which it was.

The old man got his hand up to initial the provisions, then to scribble a signature. Win gave it to the nurse, and they both dated it and added their signatures below Mr. Pierson's scratches.

He collapsed back into the pillows and grimaced as he tried to stifle a cough. Tears were in his eyes when he opened them. "You kin give me that painkiller now. . . . It's done now." The voice got softer and Win wondered if the tears were from the pain or from the reckoning.

Win asked the nurse to leave as he turned on his tape recorder and hurried through some basic information. He stood over Mr. Pierson and slowly asked questions that the man ignored. That went on for a good five minutes before the nurse stuck her head back in the room and said she needed to administer the pain medication since he'd requested it. She hurried down the hall to get the meds, and Win stared down at the silent patient. The old man shifted and finally spoke.

"Open the curtain," he commanded in a stronger voice than Win expected.

Win walked around the bed and pulled the curtain back. The room was on the second floor of the small, modern hospital. Win knew that Livingston Healthcare contained only twenty-five beds, that there were relatively few specialists. But it sat near the Yellowstone River, and the views of the mountains from the windows had to aid healing. It was after 8:30 and the sun was on its downward trek; it was struggling to poke through a bank of gray thunderheads that were draped across the Absaroka and Gallatin Ranges. The nurse injected the painkiller into the IV line; she did it without saying a word and quietly left the room. Win turned off the recorder, drew a deep breath, and concluded that he'd made the long drive to Livingston for nothing.

"You come here asking about Dex. . . . Dex ain't gonna go back to prison . . . says he ain't gonna go back to prison again."

"I need to talk to him. We haven't issued a warrant for his arrest. I just need an interview, to follow up with him on some things."

The man's weak eyes found his, and Win saw his features relax slightly as the morphine began to hit his system. Bureau policy, not to mention plain old humanity, wouldn't allow him to question the man any further once the painkillers kicked in. He only had a few seconds more.

"There were weapons at your house—"

"They're mine, not his. Dex has to record his guns. . . . Ask him."

"Where is Dex now?"

"Don't know."

"Shane? Where is he from? He won't tell us anything."

Pierson seemed to rally at the mention of the boy; his eyes brightened, and his voice suddenly grew stronger. "He's my grandson . . . ain't he a fine one? Hadn't had him around much till this year. Been good . . . been good to have him. To see I got something that'll live on. . . . Seems important now to have someone to live on, to have someone hold the things I held, read the things I wrote, smile ten years from now at things I said. All a sudden, it's important to have someone remember me . . . was real good of Dex to have him come stay with us." The old man blinked several times to try to force his eyes open. "We had us a right good visit." He tried to smile as his eyes found Win again. "Good Book says there's a season for everything. . . . I'm in the season for goodbyes . . ."

Win straightened and drew in another deep breath. He knew the man was fading. He wasn't sure what to say, so he asked if he could call the chaplain. He hoped the hospital had one.

Pierson's pale features softened more. His eyes were nearly closed. Win didn't expect him to speak again, but he did. "No . . . no preacher. I've made my peace." He struggled to breathe, then added, "Dex come to see me tonight . . . we said our goodbyes. Dex is a good un." He nodded and fought to keep his eyes open. "He'll get Shane and leave, more'n likely. That's what he said."

Win moved closer to the bedside and stared down at Pierson in disbelief. *Dex Pierson was here!*

The man's hand found Win's arm and his dim eyes locked on Win's. "You go get my important things tonight . . . my things I'd want 'em to have. . . . Will mean somethin' to Shane someday. I know it will. . . . If you don't go, word gets around I'm in the hospital, some trash will steal me blind. You'll go tonight?"

Win started to protest. The young nurse had come back in; she looked into Win's face, then busied herself with the IV bags again. The thin fingers tightened on Win's arm. Win leaned in slightly and nodded. "Yes, sir. I'll get those things for Shane. You rest."

Win watched as the man lapsed into drug-induced sleep. He processed what he'd just been told and what he'd not been told. His first question was for the nurse. "He said his son visited him earlier tonight. Is that possible?"

She shrugged. "He's not had any visitors that I know of. . . . I didn't come on shift until 7:30."

"Cameras in here?"

"No. No cameras in these observation rooms."

Then why are they called observation rooms? "Surveillance cameras anywhere at the hospital?" he asked.

"Privacy is very important . . . there might be one covering the parking lot or maybe the entrance." She moved toward the door and nodded down at Mr. Pierson. "I put five milligrams of morphine in his IV. He should rest comfortably until at least mid-morning."

Win just stood there and frowned.

"I'm working five rooms, it's been pretty busy . . . I guess someone could have come in." She shrugged again.

*   *   *

Win smelled cigarette smoke the moment he stepped out of the Bureau SUV. He hesitated and then moved away from the vehicle so as not to be silhouetted against its interior lights. If Dex Pierson had visited his father at the hospital tonight, he'd managed to evade the surveillance cameras covering the front entrances and the main parking lot. The building's rear cameras were offline for some reason no one could explain, but the thought that Dex was bold enough to use the staff and physicians' entrances was a stretch. Win had convinced himself that the old man had dreamed the farewell meeting with his son.

But he still wanted to be cautious. He'd called Deputy Sullivan before he left Livingston nearly an hour ago, and he'd called her again before he drove down the gravel county road that led to Pierson's long, wooded driveway. She told him that deputies had driven by the place as often as possible in the last three days, that they'd checked the locks and made sure the exterior lights were on, that they'd found nothing out of order. She said she'd meet Win there tonight—she'd try to make it before ten. She assured him that everything should be fine.

But it wasn't fine. He felt it even before he smelled the cigarette. The deputy's cruiser wasn't here, and there were no exterior lights on at the trailer or the garage. There were no other vehicles in the rutted yard. He'd swept the area with his headlights before he parked. His plan had been to get here before dark, but the evening had gotten away from him, and he couldn't bring himself to pass on the visit to the old man's place. He'd told Mr. Pierson that he'd come—it was like a deathbed request—and he didn't have it in him not to go. Pierson had said Dex was at the hospital earlier that night; it should have occurred to him that Dex might go to the trailer in Gardiner before he headed back to his hideout, wherever that was. It should have occurred to him to demand some backup before he drove up to the trailer, or to simply wait and come here tomorrow. Fatigue and impatience were poor companions for good judgment.

He moved beside a scrawny pine tree that stood in what passed for the Piersons' front yard. "You wanta come out where I can see you?" Win asked into the darkness.

The question was met with silence, but Win smelled the smoke faintly again, then saw the bright-red dot as someone inhaled on the cigarette. The person was at the side of the garage, not even thirty feet away. Win shifted behind the thin tree to give himself some cover. He knew it wasn't enough—he was far too exposed. He slowly slid the Glock from its holster.

"My daddy said you wanta talk to me," the voice from near the shed said. "You ain't got nothing on me. You ain't got an arrest warrant. You don't need the gun if we're just gonna talk."

"So this was a setup? Your father sends you down here, knowing I'm coming to see him at the hospital, and then he sends me down here to fetch things for the boy."

"Daddy can be right sly about things . . . I guess that's what this is. Where's Shane and what is it you wanta know?"

Win ignored the questions. "Step out where I can see you."

"I don't think so, not with that piece in your hand. Put it up and we'll talk. I ain't got nothing to hide."

Win couldn't see if the guy was holding a gun. His eyes were beginning to adjust to the darkness, but he still couldn't see much. "Move out where I can see you, Mr. Pierson." He kept the Glock near his thigh, he kept his finger on the trigger.

"Don't call me that, that's my daddy's name. You can call me Dex."

"Okay, Dex. Shane is fine, he's in good hands, but I'm sure he'd like to see you. I can arrange that, but I need you to come out in the open now. I'm getting tired of asking."

"Put the gun up. If I had a gun . . . if I's gonna shoot you, I could have done it when you stepped outa your rig."

That's for darn sure, Win thought to himself.

The man kept talking. "You know the sayin', you bring a gun to a fight, you got a gunfight. Is that what you want?"

"I don't want a fight. I'm not here for that."

"Well, I'm here to talk if that's what you want. If not, I'll be on my way, and you can tend to those things Daddy sent you for."

"Alright. I'm putting the gun away." Win holstered the Glock and hoped he was making the right move. "You step out where I can see you and we'll talk," he said again.

The man stepped forward a few paces and Win could make out his silhouette in the faint light filtering through the trees from the three-quarter moon.

"Where were you on the night of Sunday, July 4th, and the morning of Monday, July 5th?" Win asked.

Dex lifted the cigarette again. Its tip glowed red for a moment, then he dropped it to the ground and crushed it under his boot. "Huh . . . well, let's see . . . that's a week ago. I can't hardly remember what I've done day 'fore yesterday. . . . Can't say as I remember. Why?"

"I'm investigating the poaching of bison in Yellowstone National Park. I suspect you know that, and I suspect you know that I visited your residence here last Thursday morning under the authority of the Parole Board, and that I confiscated a vehicle, gunsmithing tools, ammo reloaders, and other items that could be related to the poaching—"

"I noticed the stuff was missin'. . . . Figured some lowlifes took advantage of Daddy being gone, figured we got robbed."

"Those items will be returned if no evidence of wrongdoing is found. You're a felon who isn't allowed to own a firearm. Why do you have ammo reloaders and gunsmithing tools?"

"It's a hobby. But I know the rules . . . maybe better than you do. I ain't carryin' a concealed gun, but this is Montana, dude. I was in a state lockup, not federal, and state felon or not, I got a right to own guns. Check it out."

You gotta be kidding me!

The silhouette took several steps closer, arms spread wide. Win could tell that Pierson's big hands were empty. Win's right hand hadn't strayed far from the Glock's grip, but he hadn't pulled the weapon again.

"You don't seem to have an alibi for the incident time, so I need you to come in for formal questioning."

"Huh. . . . That so."

"You can call your attorney to attend. We can do this at the Sheriff's substation in Gardiner or at my office in Mammoth. We're doing this tonight. It's not optional, Dex."

The man didn't respond. The tension was already high, but Win felt it rising.

Win squared his shoulders and took a slow step toward Pierson. "I'm going to handcuff you and we're going to my office tonight. I need you to raise your arms, get to your knees, then drop forward to the ground, keeping your arms raised above your head at all times. I need you to cooperate with me."

Dex Pierson didn't move. His voice was icy. "I don't think so . . . it's just you and me here. I ain't goin' back to prison. Whata you gonna do?" A cold chill went through Win as the man's daggerlike teeth flashed in the moonlight. "Whata you gonna do?" Pierson snarled again.

What am I gonna do? Win had handcuffed a wanted man exactly twice in his three years in the Bureau. The first time the criminal had been a terrified accountant surrounded by two other agents at a Charlotte bank two years ago. The second time was exactly three weeks ago. Win had nearly lost his life in that encounter. This was way too similar to the second time. This was dangerous. Real dangerous.

They both froze when the sound of a car engine carried down the ravine from the gravel road less than a quarter mile away. *Lordy, I hope that's the deputy.* Just as that thought went through Win's mind, Dex stepped into Win fast, and Win caught the hard right jab with the back of his forearm. He raised his right hand to block another blow, then regained his balance and landed a solid punch to the man's midsection that literally bounced off. Dex Pierson was wearing ceramic body armor under his shirt—it was as solid as a rock. Win hadn't been able to see it in the dark, and he was suddenly at a serious disadvantage.

Dex was stout and strong to begin with, and while Win was taller, that didn't count for much. Dex got in two blows to Win's ribs, and another to his stomach that took the breath out of him. Win tried to dodge backward but lost his footing on the rutted driveway. He staggered to the side, fighting for air, and Dex got him with a hard jab to the chin. As Win went down on one knee, the guy kicked him to the ground. He rolled to the left, his right hand grasping for the Glock in its holster; Dex kicked him in the shoulder before his hand could find the grip. The flash of pain nearly shut down his senses, but his mind registered lights skimming through the trees from the approaching car. Win lay in the dirt beside the Bureau Expedition and tried to focus on breathing. His aching arm finally found his weapon, but he didn't have the strength to pull it. He dropped his head into the cool ground and groaned as he fought for a breath. The cruiser's bright lights washed over him and he immediately heard car doors slam. He tried to roll over but couldn't. He was still struggling to breathe.

"Are you okay? Wow, don't move, can you talk to me?" It was the female deputy, Sullivan. She was beside him, then shouting something that Win only caught part of: "Get . . . people here, Maddox! . . . on that radio!"

He was vaguely aware that she was trying to pull him back toward the cover of his big SUV. "Are you okay?" she repeated for maybe the third time.

He managed to suck in some air, to choke out an answer. "Yeah . . . yeah . . . think so."

"What in the world are you doing here without backup! You could have been killed!" She nearly shouted the accusations at him.

Her flashlight was out now and directed toward his face. He shifted to try to sit up, to avoid the blinding glare of the light. He blinked to clear his eyes. The deputy's words stung. Everything else just hurt.

*   *   *

Luke and Ellie were sitting out on the side deck near the firepit. Win's mind flashed back to mid-April when he first came to their house, when he first arrived in Yellowstone, when the stars were just as breathtaking as they were tonight. It had been less than three months, but it felt like a lifetime. *So much has changed.*

Luke stood and motioned for him to join them. Win realized he was limping as he stepped up on the deck.

"Whoa, son, what happened to you?" Luke asked.

Win stood there for a second too long, and Ellie looked him over in the flickering firelight. "Win Tyler, you've been in a fight," she declared. "Come in, let me fix those scrapes." She shook her head. "You boys . . ."

"I'm fine," Win protested as she took his hand to examine his knuckles. He knew he'd flinched when he lifted his arm. "I'm fine," he repeated. "I'm sorry to call y'all so late . . . to come by so late. I wanted to see how it went with social services, I wanted . . ."

They knew better than that. He knew better than that. He knew he'd count three little heads asleep in their beds tonight. He knew Luke and Ellie would have sidestepped the well-intentioned social service folks. He didn't really know why he called Luke after he'd dusted himself off, glad to be alive; after he'd finished up at Pierson's trailer; after he and the deputies concluded Dex was once again on the run. He didn't know why he was here. Maybe to get some reassurance, maybe to have someone say he was on the right track, maybe just to have someone offer to patch him up. He wasn't sure why he found himself at Luke Bordeaux's house at 11:45 on an evening when he'd just gotten outfoxed by an elderly man, whipped by his prime suspect in the poaching case, and lectured by a deputy sheriff. He hadn't had a good night.

Luke took ahold of Win's other arm. "Hey, Ellie. I need to check on the pups one more time. Win can come with me, you get the lidocaine out. We'll be in directly."

They walked down the two-track path to the big wood-sided barn that looked like it belonged on a farm in the Midwest, not in the wilds of Montana. Luke reached for the battery box at the side of the heavy sliding door and turned off the electric current to the wires that protected Ellie's chickens and the dogs from the other animals who called this place home. He flipped on the lights and walked over to an enclosed stable where Tiger, the yellow Labrador puppy, was piled on top of a sleeping Max. Neither dog raised its head as the men peered into the pen, and Win knew this errand had nothing to do with the pups.

Luke moved away, motioned for Win to join him on the other side of the wide center aisle, and slid back another tall wooden door. They entered a room that ran the length of the barn. Much of the floor was covered with workout mats, braces of free weights were lined up in front of a mirrored wall, and an assortment of climbing ropes and a well-used punching bag hung from the high log beams. This was Luke's training gym; Win had heard Trey talk about it. The lights were bright, and Luke was looking him over.

"You must have found Dex."

"Yeah."

"He jump you?"

"No, I went back to his father's trailer near Gardiner tonight. I shouldn't have gone until my backup got there. I was gonna pick up some things Mr. Pierson wanted given to Shane—stupid of me. Dex was there. He coulda taken me out when I drove up. So stupid of me. . . . He said he wanted to talk, but things went downhill when I told him I was going to handcuff him, bring him in for questioning."

"Un-huh. I kin see that." Luke was taking in Win's obvious dings: the torn shirt, the red welt on his jaw, the cuts on his knuckles.

"He got me pretty good with some body blows. I haven't been taken down that hard since SEC play back in college." Win sighed and cut his eyes to Luke. "Then again, there was that time back in April when you whipped me. . . . I don't seem to be winning many fights out here."

"Could be cause you're pickin' the wrong boys to fight. You go to the clinic?"

"No."

"Take off your shirt and raise your arms," Luke ordered.

Win struggled to comply. He got the tattered dress shirt off, then pulled his T-shirt over his head; he fought to keep from groaning. He tossed the shirts on a bench and slowly raised his arms.

"You're carryin' two Glocks . . . I'm guessin' you didn't pull 'em."

Win shook his head. "He didn't appear to be armed. What was I supposed to do? Shoot the guy in his driveway?"

Luke moved behind him and ran his hands over Win's ribs, along his shoulders and back. Win closed his eyes tight, clenched his jaw, and fought to keep from flinching from the steady pressure.

"If he was tryin' to beat me to death, I would have shot him," Luke said. "Having trouble breathing?" he asked as he stepped around Win and looked into his eyes.

Win shook his head.

"You will. I'm thinking some bruised ribs, bad bruising on your right shoulder . . . probably nothin' broken. How do you feel?"

"Like fifteen miles of bad road."

Luke grinned. "Well, you're gonna feel worse tomorrow." He threw Win his shirts. "Did Pierson get away?"

"Yeah."

"Well, there's always next time. Learn anything?"

Win tried to draw in a deep breath. It hurt. "Learned not to get in a fistfight with someone wearing plated body armor. . . ." He tried to pull on the T-shirt and gave up. He settled for buttoning up his once-starched dress shirt. "And I'm still thinking Dex is our guy for the poaching. But we both know he's not the logistics guy, probably not the brains of the deal. There are at least two others involved."

Win paused, then decided to tell Luke his suspicions. "And I was thinking Dex might be involved in another case, a case where there was some killin', but I don't know. . . . Dex was intent on getting away tonight, not so much on hurting me. He could have taken me out the minute I stepped out of my truck. He didn't. He could have really hurt me when he had me down. He didn't."

Luke was standing near the punching bag, appraising him. "Be careful trying to think like the bad guys. Could be he didn't take you out 'cause he didn't need to take you out tonight. Under different circumstances Dex Pierson might not have hesitated to kill you, or anyone else. And then there's other factors. If he was lit, or high, or paranoid, or any number of other things you can't anticipate—if any of those factors were in play, he mighta killed you." Luke shrugged. "He might not do it if he's in his right mind, but you're gonna run into a lot of *not in their right mind* if you stay in the business of catching criminals. So I wouldn't be reading too much into you still being alive tonight, at least not as it comes to Dex Pierson's intentions."

CHAPTER SEVENTEEN

Luke had told him he'd feel worse in the morning, and Luke was right. For a few minutes Win didn't think he could make it out of bed to the shower, but the Tylenol he took during the night and the lidocaine wrap that Ellie had put around his ribs probably helped. He couldn't imagine how awful he'd feel if she hadn't patched him up. He slept through his alarm, stayed under the hot shower far too long, and sipped coffee while he fed the cat. Gruff wouldn't get near him since he smelled like horse liniment. The cat kept walking through the house on stiff legs, sniffing the air, and swinging his long tail. Win had gotten four hours of sleep, but his time for exercise, prayer, and Scripture fell by the wayside this morning—he had to hustle to get to the office by 7:30.

He'd already fielded three calls on his Bureau phone before he sat down at his desk with his third cup of coffee. The Park County Attorney called to tell him that the Sheriff's Office had filed a warrant for Dex Pierson's arrest for assault. Deputy Sullivan had told Win last night that she'd deal with the warrant—she'd told him that after chewing him out a second time for being at the trailer without backup, before sending him on his way. Win forwarded a copy of the emailed warrant to the Assistant U.S. Attorney's office down the street in the Justice Center and to Jim West in Lander. He knew the federal justice system would also crank out a warrant for Pierson for Assault On A Federal Officer, but the U.S. Attorney would have to work out jurisdictional

issues. Win didn't need to interject himself into his own assault case—
he had enough on his plate this morning. On a positive note, they now
had a solid reason to go after Dex Pierson. He wasn't just a person of
interest in a poaching case or a guy who'd missed a check-in with his
parole officer. Nope, now he was a fugitive wanted for a violent crime.

The Evidence Response Team leader called to report that their
samples on the dead bulls had finally been pushed to the top of the pile
at the FBI Lab in Quantico, and while the results weren't conclusive
yet, it was looking like Dex Pierson's reloading equipment was going
to be a match for the gunpowder residue they'd collected on the carcasses. The old pickup that was registered to Dex's father had been
thoroughly searched for evidence, and numerous spots of blood and
hair had been collected from the pickup's bed. The team leader told
Win that the samples were being analyzed for a DNA match on the
bison at a U.S. Fish and Wildlife Service Lab. *Who knew there was a lab
to test bison DNA?* Win thought, as he listened to the ERT guy talk. It
was now one week out from the bison massacre, and the reports were
finally encouraging.

The third call was Trey saying he needed a meeting later that
morning if Win could squeeze him in. But it was a message that had
been left on the office landline at 6:14 a.m. that really caught Win's
attention—a very hesitant-sounding officer from the Ogden Police
Department, saying he needed to talk with someone in the Yellowstone
FBI office. Win searched for Ogden on Google Maps: the town was in
northern Utah, 38 miles north of Salt Lake City and about 250 miles
southwest of Jackson. Win snarfed down two of Janet's huckleberry
muffins and half a cup of coffee while he waited for the Ogden Police
Department's dispatcher to connect him with the officer who'd left the
message. When the guy answered, Win was surprised to be talking
with someone in the Juvenile Detention Division.

The man sounded nervous when Win introduced himself. "Uh,
this may not be anything," the man said. Then he launched right in.
"We picked up a sixteen-year-old last night who was strung out on
Ecstasy. He was pretty messed up . . . uh, I'm sure none of this is admis-
sible in court. . . . This kid is from a prominent family, a good family. He

was panicked and tried to talk us out of locking him up. . . . Anyway, he thought he could trade some information for a get outa jail card."

Win didn't respond and the guy kept talking. "He kept saying he'd overheard another kid at a party talkin' big about swiping boxes of brand-new AR-15s from a trailer parked at the Grand Steer Steakhouse. Uh, that's at Exit 344, off I-15. . . . It was after the big gun show down in Salt Lake last week. He had no idea who the braggart was . . . they were all at a drinkin' party up at Pineview Reservoir two nights ago. Our boy overhead the name of the buyers. The names he gave up were Roadie and Tank—sounds like street names—well, anyway, this kid said he was told the guns were on their way to Yellowstone. He claims he didn't see any of this, so no descriptions. It was one kid bragging to another."

He paused to let Win digest all that.

"That's interesting," Win said, but he was thinking, *Whoa, this could be big!* "You think the kid's legit? Did you get any reports of a major gun theft? Are those street names in your system?"

"Kid's legit. I go to church with the boy's grandparents. He was terrified that he'd be charged on the drugs, that his family would find out." He sighed. "Of course, they found out. We kept him overnight. Maybe it will scare him straight . . . maybe." He cleared his throat. "On the other questions: no and no. No reports of a big robbery or theft after that gun show, and the names *Roadie* and *Tank* don't show up in our system."

Win thought about it. "Okay." He hesitated. "Okay . . . I'm wondering—"

"You're wondering why you're gettin' a call from some low-level cop in Juvenile Detention from small-town Utah?"

"No, sir, I'm not thinking that, I'm thinking these tips could be key leads in a very big case. I'm wondering what led you to make the call."

Win heard the guy take a deep breath. "My uncle was with ATF before he passed away. He was really proud of his service. I saw the news story last week about ATF losing an agent in one of the parks north of here, up in Grand Teton. Uh, I haven't read that they solved that case. Since the kid mentioned Yellowstone, I thought there could be some connection."

"Can you give me the boy's contact information, his parents'—"

"No, I can't give you a thing. I took this upstairs to my supervisor and she blew me off. You'll have to have some government lawyers go through all the hoops with a juvenile judge. It could take weeks just to get permission to meet with this kid, not to mention track down the young thieves. But I made this call because I'm thinking the family of that dead ATF agent doesn't deserve to sit for weeks for you to deal with the bureaucracy while some thug gets away with murder, while some thug sells those guns to other thugs, while other people get hurt. I could lose my job over this phone call, I know that."

"Sir, I'll consider this phone call confidential. It's part of a federal case, a significant federal case. There shouldn't be any repercussions on your reaching out to the FBI. I'll—"

"Whether I get in trouble over this call or not, it was the right thing to do. I believe the Lord works in mysterious ways, and maybe this kid telling me what he overheard, maybe that's the Lord's way of pointing you people in the right direction—finding out who killed those men in Grand Teton, getting those guns off the street."

Maybe it is.

* * *

"We've had four stolen vehicles in the northern half of the park in the last two days—that is not typical. Not at all." It was nearly 9:30 and Trey was balancing his coffee and a paper plate with two muffins as he moved into Win's office. He sat the plate on the edge of the antique oak desk, took off his flat hat, and dropped it into the second chair. "Do you know that over three hundred thousand vehicles came through the park last year in July—three hundred thousand. Not one was reported stolen. It doesn't happen often here."

Win looked up from the map he'd been studying and eyed the ranger. "Don't you ever have thefts?"

"Hardly ever. If we do, it's normally seasonal workers filching something out of someone else's locker or dorm room. Lots of the seasonals are housed in communal barracks, maybe fifty folks in one building. That's usually where we have issues with theft, drugs, and fights, and even those issues are relatively rare. Considering we have around four million visitors a year, crime isn't that common in the park." Trey took a sip of his coffee and nodded toward the muffins.

"Brought you one . . . those agents downstairs were devouring them. Don't y'all even stop for meals?"

Win grinned. "Not often enough these days." He reached for a muffin, having decided not to tell Trey he'd already eaten his share. "We've finally got something on Pierson, but the stolen car thing interests me. I think he's in the park. Luke thinks he's in the park. That black-on-black Dodge Ram that's registered to him . . . it stands out." Win glanced up at Trey and shook his head. "That truck *really* stands out—we know that. What was the fallout from Chief Randall's meeting with the ATF boys yesterday?"

Trey smiled. Not the response Win was expecting. "Our folks and ATF are still hashing it out, but you wouldn't believe all the *attaboys* I got from the inspectors—all of them were eating at the Terrace Grill when ATF tried the foolhardy takedown of that poor guy. The inspectors had a front-row seat for the show, and now they seem to think I'm some sort of hero for breaking it up."

"You *are* a hero for breaking it up," Win said. "That guy was a heartbeat from gettin' killed for not following commands."

They both got quiet for a moment. Then Trey spoke. "Yeah, he was. That woman officer, she was intense. I didn't see her while it was going down—everything happened so fast, I was on autopilot—but I've looked at a few videos we've gotten in from bystanders. The ATF guys were playing it by the book, but she had this look on her face. . . . If I hadn't yelled at her to stand down, I don't know . . ."

"Uh-huh, I saw it. I think she's too close to the case," Win said.

"Speaking of that. I'm guessin' you didn't run into a door to get that bruise on your jaw. Luke and I had breakfast this morning in Gardiner. He told me you and Dex Pierson had a scuffle last night."

Win shrugged with his eyebrows.

"Your main suspect in the poaching case attacks you and gets charged with assault."

Win raised his chin. "How'd you know about the charges?"

"The revised Montana state BOLO came over our wire early this morning. Why haven't they pulled you off the poaching case?"

Win sighed. "Well, that was fast." He sighed again. "As for the case, I'm sure they'll pull me. My boss is tied up on the murder investigation down in Grand Teton. We're getting a federal warrant drawn up on Pierson now, but I haven't even been interviewed on last night's incident. Everyone's out of pocket, most everyone is focused on the killing of those two guys down near Jackson."

Trey didn't ask any more questions because he knew Win wasn't free to give him any more answers. Everyone in the Park Service knew there was something else going on—ATF agents in raid gear didn't just show up in Yellowstone out of the blue, much less a female officer who wouldn't identify her agency. Trey suspected this was tied to the murder of the two men last week in Grand Teton, but the Feds were keeping the details to themselves.

Win switched their discussion back to Pierson. "Dex could be moving around in those stolen vehicles—"

"You and Dex on a first-name basis now?" Trey was grinning.

Win scowled at the ranger and finished his thought. "We're concentrating on a black pickup that he's probably not even driving at this point. You got the sheets on the missing vehicles?"

Trey pulled a printout from his back pocket. "They aren't really missing . . . someone hot-wires a vehicle then drops it off somewhere else. Nothing taken out of any of them, and two vehicles had expensive cameras, camping supplies—valuable stuff." He frowned and shook his head. "Nothing taken."

Win ran his finger down the list: gray Chevy Silverado stolen from one of the Canyon area lodges sometime Sunday morning, before 5:00 a.m., found behind the Albright Visitor Center in Mammoth early this morning; white Kia stolen from the Mammoth Hotel parking lot on

Sunday afternoon, found at a residence outside of Gardiner late Sunday night. . . . He read through two more nondescript vehicle reports.

"Can you get the GPS on these newer models, see where they've been taken? Can you check the surveillance cameras at the park entrances, see if they've come in and out?"

Trey finished off his muffin before he spoke. "Sure could. Sure, I could do all that if I had two or three other bodies on the case. But I don't."

Win sucked in a breath. "I'll see what I can do." With the gun-running case ramping up in Grand Teton, the Bureau was suddenly shorthanded in Mammoth as well. The two Violent Crime Squad agents who'd been sent here when the press went wild over the bison massacre were leaving for Jackson today. The FBI's ERT had driven to Jackson yesterday, and Jim's plan for a second look at all of the poaching evidence was on the back burner. Kirk was still working the phones on the helicopter angle, but he was it. Win really had thought they'd have a solid lead on the poachers through the helicopter's involvement long before now, but instead they had nothing.

Trey downed the rest of his coffee and reached for his hat. "I gotta go track down some scumbags who thought walking around on the thermal features down at Mud Volcano while taking selfies was fun."

Win stood and winced from the pain in his ribs. "That's not your district."

"Like I said, we're shorthanded." Then Trey smiled again. "Gets me outa the office and away from the inspectors, plus the fools were dumb enough to post themselves all over social media this morning, so I shouldn't have any trouble finding them."

The ranger paused in the office doorway. "Watch yourself with Pierson. Luke said you were lucky to come outa that fight in one piece."

Win shrugged and it hurt. "Doubt it had anything to do with luck. God's protection . . . even for the foolish." He shrugged again. "I shoulda handled it better, but now we can really go after the guy. Now we've got a warrant."

Win walked down the oak stairs with Trey and noticed that the two small downstairs offices were now empty. His watch said 10:02;

the two Denver agents were probably on the road south. Janet Swam was in the conference room, intent on her computer screen, and Kirk was getting another cup of coffee in the breakroom. The flurry of activity had passed, the tension and intensity that had permeated the small building for several days was gone. Win glanced out the window, not a TV satellite truck in sight. Six days ago, the trophy killing of three bison bulls in Yellowstone National Park had been the lead story throughout the nation. Now the press had moved on to other stories; now it was old news. America's short attention span continued to amaze him.

*　*　*

He snapped awake when the Westland Adventure Excursions van pulled in beside his pickup in the nearly full Canyon Visitor Education Center parking lot. He was instantly alert and angry with himself for having taken that late shift at his other job. He needed to be on his game today and he'd had barely two hours of sleep. His manager had said that some in the group they were taking out today were potential big-time tippers. He immediately plastered a broad smile on his face as he wiped the sleep from his eyes and jumped out to help them unload. He waved to Ginger, the second guide on this gig, as she jogged over from the Canyon Deli.

He took in the group with a practiced glance: two women in their mid-sixties who looked like sisters; an affluent-looking couple who were probably in their late fifties; another, much younger couple; and a tall, lanky kid who'd already retrieved his backpack and stood off to the side. The kid looked like an athlete. He also looked vaguely familiar. *That's odd . . . where have I seen him?* He knew he wasn't hitting on all cylinders this morning. He needed more coffee. It would come to him.

One of the group had to cancel at the last minute, his manager was saying as the folks gathered around for first-name introductions with the two guides. They usually did first names or nicknames on this job. Often Westland's customers were Hollywood celebrities, big-time sports figures, or TV or political personalities—names anyone would know. Their customers paid big bucks for the rustic backcountry experience, but they expected anonymity, they expected discretion.

As the customers streamed toward the restrooms, he walked back over to his pickup and made sure he had everything squared away. He pulled off his jacket and stuffed it into the top of his pack. It was going to be a beautiful day; it was already high sixties, and it was just coming up on ten. Today was the warm-up day, a gentle hike of six miles down the north rim of Yellowstone Canyon on parts of the North Rim and Seven Mile Hole Trails. Nothing too strenuous, nothing too challenging. They'd reach the primitive campground around five, plenty of time to stop along the way to admire the stunning views of the canyon's two magnificent waterfalls. Plenty time for a fancy picnic lunch on the canyon's rim with one of the best views in the universe. They'd see a few bison, elk, and maybe a bear, if they were lucky. Later a big gourmet dinner on the campfire. His manager would be with them during the first day and night. Having three staff members was always helpful during the initial twenty-four hours—it wasn't unheard of for someone to bail and ask to be walked back out. Thinking about a four-day backpacking tour in the wilds of Yellowstone and doing it were two different things. It always surprised him how quickly folks quit before they really got into it. Some people never learned that anything worthwhile required some effort.

He shifted his attention to the activity in the parking lot. Ginger was trying to get the attention of the younger couple—a huge tour bus had just pulled in, and the crush of folks near the Visitor Center's high glass doors was chaotic. He clipped his bear spray to his belt and slid his Colt 1911 handgun into his pack. The .45 caliber was heavy, but it was as reliable as a Swiss watch. He double-checked to make sure he had two extra magazines and his night vision optics, then hoisted the pack, locked the truck, and turned back toward the group. He smiled to himself as he eased the hefty pack onto his shoulders. *Shoulda been a Boy Scout. Always prepared.*

The boss was getting ready to go over the agenda for the day—this was the second time that the folks would hear it. He knew from trips past that most of them would have slept in the van on the three-hour drive after breakfast from the pickup point at Jackson Lake Lodge in Grand Teton National Park. He knew most of them would have missed the stunning views of the Grand Teton Range as they'd driven north toward Yellowstone. They'd probably slept through a dozen great wildlife encounters along the way. The van driver had the discretion to pull over and wake them if the attraction was a significant sighting: grizzly bear with cubs, moose with calf, bison sparring, those sorts of things.

But when he drove the groups in, he hardly ever stopped. It just opened up the grousing about no Wi-Fi, no cell service, and on and on. This was the first day of "out in the middle of nowhere" for most of these folks. A new reality had to take hold: *I'm just a small speck in a grand universe. It isn't all about me.* What amazed him was how often that reality never connected, how many people paid big money to come to this fascinating place and still didn't get it. So often they couldn't wait to get back to social media, business deals, or the crush of fame. For some the four-day detox didn't work, but when it did— when someone realized there was more to life than their self-absorbed world—it was beautiful to see.

He and the driver drank coffee out of their thermoses while they waited for everyone to make their way back over to the van after they'd hit the facilities. He slowly scanned the group a second time. His manager was holding up the map showing the older couple their location in Canyon, pointing out the first trail they'd be taking this morning. Most of the others were putting their jackets in their packs; it was going to be warm.

He often used this initial downtime to try to guess who would be *the problem*. There was always one. The two older women from Vermont looked pumped; he was guessing this was a bucket list trip for them. They'd probably been wide awake on the way up here. They'd be thrilled to see a deer. The middle-aged couple were likely here because they needed an adventure to brag about at the county club . . . the usual luxury cruise to Greece was now too commonplace. The young couple were still taking selfies over near the entrance to the Visitor Center and Ginger was failing in her attempts to get their attention. They didn't fit the MO of the usual clients. They were late twenties, wearing lots of spandex, sporting ink and piercings—they were a bit of a wild card. Maybe they'd gotten the excursion as a company bonus, maybe they needed a break from the kids, maybe this was a gift from wealthy parents, maybe they were bored. They were supposed to be gathering with the group, but they weren't. They could be *the problem*.

Or it could be the tall kid standing off by himself. The kid puzzled him. The driver had said the adult scheduled to be with him had cancelled yesterday and that the company had to scramble to email all sorts of waivers to his parents, since the boy was only fifteen. He didn't look fifteen. He was nearly six feet tall, and he looked fit, capable, and watchful. The kid turned and their eyes met for a moment. *Uh-huh, he looks real damn capable.* Then it hit him. *Oh, hell.*

CHAPTER EIGHTEEN

Win had just gotten back to his desk after walking Trey out of the building when he heard a soft knock on his open door.

"I've got something." Kirk Hampton was leaning into Win's office with his hands braced against the doorframe. There was an intensity in his voice that Win hadn't heard before. "Come see this." Kirk gestured with his chin back toward the communications room.

They'd had relatively little real interaction since Win had lectured him in the breakroom last Thursday afternoon, but the younger agent's clothing choices had improved and he was carrying his firearm, at least occasionally. Kirk spent most of his time hunched over his laptop in Johnson's office or in front of the communications room's monitors. Win kept reminding himself that he wasn't this guy's supervisor; he just hoped Kirk was actually working the case.

Win hit his feet and followed Kirk down the hall. Kirk slid into a chair in front of the three large monitors. The image that was frozen on the center screen was a photo of a silver helicopter with a blue stripe, and below the chopper hung a dark tarp enclosed in a cargo net. Win could tell it was an enhanced image.

"Show me the original," he said. Kirk hit the keys and a much-longer-range photo of the chopper appeared on the second screen. It was clearing a tall, dark mountain; there were three still shots in a row. The date stamp on the photos said 07/05, the day the three bulls were shot. The time said 7:58 a.m.

Kirk nodded toward the screen. "The photographer took the photos on an older cell phone that didn't show GPS locations."

"Without the GPS, can you tell where this is?" Win asked.

"I've gone through like a zillion photos of mountains. This one is in the northeast part of the park. . . . Looks like the background mountain in the photo is Abiathar Peak—that's a 10,928-foot peak about two and a quarter miles southwest of Yellowstone's northeast entrance gate. If I'm right, this chopper is about eleven air miles north of the bison kill. Nearest town is Cooke City, it's tiny."

Win leaned back against the wall and faced the monitors. "Could it be a construction-related flight?"

"Nope, already checked, and there are no commercial airfields in the Cooke City area." He looked up at Win. "But there are, like, a half dozen private airfields within a few miles of the northeast entrance. And it's a helicopter, it could put down anywhere flat." Kirk switched back to the enhanced shot on the main screen.

"Where'd you get this?" Win asked.

"A lady from New Jersey called the Newark Field Office early this morning. They sent me her contact info and I called her about an hour ago. She and her husband had been in Yellowstone the week of the Fourth. She said she didn't hear about the bison incident until they got home and she was going back through old newspapers. She read the news story on the poaching since they'd just been in the area. It said that the FBI was trying to confirm helicopter traffic in Yellowstone on July 5th. She remembered the chopper 'cause it messed up a photo she was trying to get of a moose that was standing near . . . uh . . ." He glanced down at his notes. "Uh, standing near the Warm Creek picnic area."

Win looked at the original photo that Kirk had pulled up—terrible photo of a moose, great photo of a helicopter. "Can you read the chopper's numbers?"

"They've been doctored," Kirk replied. "I guess the dudes thought completely covering up the registration numbers would be too obvious, but it looks like they've used tape to change the numbers. I can't make them out. I'm gonna get this to Denver and see if someone there can enhance it more."

"Wow, this is a game changer. This is good work, Kirk."

The agent nodded as he stared at the screen. His voice was subdued when he finally spoke. "It's been seven days—seven days. Man, you know those trophy heads are, like, gone . . . maybe even in China by now. You know whoever set up and paid for this little massacre is out of the country. Once the heat got turned up by the press, they were long gone. You know we'll never get the real bad guys."

"Yeah . . . maybe. We may just catch the small fish—"

"If we get anyone at all."

"We will."

* * *

Win had just finished updating Jim West on the helicopter lead in the poaching case. He thought the conversation with his boss was over, but it wasn't.

"Yesterday's screwup with those ATF folks trying to arrest the tourist in Mammoth could blow up on us," Jim said.

Uh-oh. "I really wasn't involved in that, Boss."

"Yeah, well. The tourist has already hired an attorney. Lawyers come out of the woodwork on deals like this, and videos of the takedown are all over social media." Jim paused. "The press hasn't really jumped on it yet, but they probably will."

"I was just a witness," Win said. "You've read my preliminary report."

"I know, I know." Jim sighed. "Eventually somebody is going to have to explain why a Royal Canadian Mounted Police officer was pulling a gun in one of *our* national parks. Oh, and stay clear of Alex Lindell, Win. ATF is trying to get her shipped back across the border. She coulda gotten someone killed yesterday . . . I understand she's basically under house arrest there in Mammoth."

Win stopped his coffee halfway to his lips. "She's still here?"

"Yeah, everyone will need her statement, but as of right now, ATF is shifting lots of resources into tracking down those tips you called me with early this morning. That could be the break we needed. If a stolen shipment of AR-15s moved through Yellowstone just days ago, then the gunrunning route has definitely moved to the parks. Whoever has those guns could have killed Beckett and Manyhorses. And finding those killers is job one right now."

"Do you want me to touch base with the ATF folks here? Get more involved in that case?"

"Not until we see who's going to have jurisdiction over it. There's a high-level briefing in Denver later this afternoon. Honestly, some of this depends on how much bad press is generated over the incident with that tourist. We're trying to let ATF and the Park Service take all the blowback on it, but at some point we'll have to get involved. We do have sole investigative jurisdiction in Yellowstone, and you'll need to give a formal statement, but for the next day or so I'd like for you to lay low, maybe be unavailable until we see what shakes out."

"I've got to go to meet the Park County Attorney in Gardiner for a noon interview, and at some point I'll be called in to give a statement to the Assistant U.S. Attorney here in Mammoth. Both of those interviews are on Dex Pierson's assault warrants."

Win heard his boss sigh again. "Speaking of that."

Here it comes, Win thought.

"You can't be on the poaching case now that we've got the assault in the mix. I want you to know this isn't a reflection on your work or your judgment."

Maybe it should be. "I understand, Boss."

"Kirk's gonna take over as case agent on the poaching deal as soon as we get the paperwork in order. Kirk hasn't had a lot of field experience—his focus has been really narrow in cybercrime—but this type of case could help him branch out. Bring him up to speed on anything you've got that he can't see in Sentinel." Jim paused. "And you and I . . . we need to go over the altercation with Pierson. We need to go over it in detail. But right now, with the gunrunning case getting hotter, let's focus on it. You okay with all that?"

Of course it wouldn't have mattered one bit if Win wasn't okay with being removed from the case, but it was nice of Jim to give him a chance to protest. He didn't challenge the move. He'd seen what *being too close to the case* looked like. He'd seen the hate in Alex Lindell's eyes when she nearly pulled the trigger on an innocent man yesterday afternoon.

* * *

Win Tyler wasn't the only one shocked by the hate in Alex Lindell's heart. She took another sip of her tea and closed her eyes to focus on it. Greg had warned her. He'd been telling her for months that her spirit was out of balance. He'd told her that the positive, confident woman he'd grown up with was becoming bitter and pessimistic. Two weeks ago, he said she was on the verge of letting the darkness overtake her. They'd agreed that she'd go with him to see his mother in Standoff, let her get an Elder to perform a healing ceremony: the five-hour sweat lodge, the incense burning with sweetgrass, sage, and cedar, maybe even chanting and drums. She wasn't sure what all was involved. She'd stalled Greg as long as she could, pointing out that her grandparents had passed on, that her father couldn't care less, that her mother hadn't lived on the reserve since college.

Alex stretched back in the comfortable chair and sighed. She glanced over at the ATF agent sitting only fifty feet away on the small covered porch of the adjacent cottage. He was watching her, pretending to read. He was also probably frustrated and bored to death, keeping tabs on her instead of doing anything productive on the gunrunning case. She knew ATF had requested that she be recalled to Canada, she knew the Park Service was fighting that because she was a witness in the mess with the tourist yesterday. Her Corporal in Calgary was shocked at the developments; he likely thought she was a total screwup. A formal reprimand, if not worse, was coming her way. Alex knew there wasn't a thing she could do about any of those issues right now.

She sighed again and tried to force her thoughts in a different direction. She tilted her head back and basked in the warmth of the sun, letting the cool breeze move her hair. Sitting here on the cream-colored cottage's porch at the Mammoth Hot Springs Hotel took her back to the last time she and Greg sat together on sun-warmed boulders, high above the Hidden Falls Trail at Jenny Lake. They'd been talking about her estrangement from her husband, about the days that had turned to weeks since she'd talked with him or held little Lacy. She couldn't face her family—she'd failed them all in too many ways.

Her mind went back to Greg's words, some of the last intimate words they'd shared. "You need to find God," he'd said, as if that was the solution. He was a believer in the spiritual realm. He pointed out that the cleansing ceremony would honor Alex's grandmother, who would have wanted that, who would have wanted Alex to find solace through her heritage. He said the women of her clan would walk her through it, she wouldn't be on her own. She'd given in to his concerns and they'd agreed to go before the summer powwow in August, as soon as this case wrapped up. She remembered standing up from the warm rocks and telling him, "Fine! You win. I'll go with you to look for a god." She remembered him looking up at her and smiling.

Then Greg had gone and gotten himself killed. She felt herself grow smaller as the reality of that loss swept over her again. Her brother, her best friend in the world, was gone. For all his faults—and Greg had many—he'd been a stabilizing force in her life. Now she was adrift again, now the hate had returned to her heart. And not just the hate. Now there was a raging thirst for revenge, a hunger to destroy the ones who'd taken him away. If they took her off the case, any hope of that was gone.

What had Agent Tyler said the other day? *"Justice, we want justice."* But that wasn't what she wanted at all.

* * *

Win had expected to be removed from the poaching case, but he hadn't figured on being taken off the gunrunning case too. He knew the Lander RA was shorthanded. He knew Jim West didn't have much choice in naming Kirk as case agent on the poaching investigation. Still, it bothered him that an agent with no apparent interest in the case, or in the Bureau for that matter, was taking over *his* job. He sucked in a breath and reminded himself that it was *his* fault the job wasn't still *his*. Win also reminded himself that he'd had very little field experience when he came to Yellowstone three months ago; he told himself Kirk deserved the chance to develop that experience. Still, he had to force down his frustration and fake some enthusiasm when Kirk swung into his office a few minutes later with an expectant look and announced, "Hey, man, guess who just got named case agent on the dead buffalo deal! So cool!"

It was coming up on eleven when Win wrapped up a short meeting with Kirk, which should have taken much longer except for the fact that Kirk's interest in the poaching case was almost exclusively confined to what he could find on the internet. Kirk left the offered stack of notes and file folders sitting on Win's desk when he stood to leave. He never even opened Win's comprehensive hard-copy files, except to dismiss the numerous typed and handwritten pages as "Waaaay too old-school."

"Not to worry," he told Win. "The case is in good hands! If I have to, I can still reach out to those two dudes from Denver who were up here for a few days, and to that ranger, Hechtner—he's on top of this thing. I think we're gonna break this case by running down that chopper, that's what I think. Like, find the chopper, find the pilot, then *boom*! We nab some of the players—case closed!" The young agent grinned and headed out the door. Win frowned at Kirk's retreating back. He noticed Kirk's casual jeans and tight T-shirt, noticed he wasn't wearing his gun today. Win sighed. Kirk was sharp, he'd seen flashes of that focus and intelligence, but Kirk had the same attention span as his fifteen-year-old brother, Will. Win sighed again. And speaking of Will . . .

Win checked his watch: it said 10:58. He needed to text Will before they set out on that backpacking trip. He stood up and stretched his sore shoulder, flinching as he tried to draw in a deep breath. *Better, it's getting better,* he thought as he pulled out his personal phone. As a

condition for Will going on the backcountry trip without Tucker, their
mom was making Will send text updates to Win. She understood that
cell service would be sporadic at best on the four-day trip, but she also
understood that occasionally text messages go through when voice
messages or calls will not. Win was thinking that his mother's recent
foray into understanding technology had its drawbacks; he didn't have
the time or the desire to keep up with Will's camping trip. He knew
Will didn't want to be monitored, and he sure as heck didn't want to be
doing the monitoring. But he sucked it up and filed it under the *be the
adult* category as he sent a quick text to Will. He got a reply five minutes later. His little brother was all business: **Hiking from N rim Canyon,
7 + 3 guides. Camp at 4C4.**

Win quickly typed **10-4, have fun. Love you!** The seconds ticked
by as Win glared at the phone—no response. *Be the adult,* Win told
himself again.

* * *

Win was sitting on the edge of Luke's side deck, watching the gangly
blue-gray hound run circles around Shane. He'd been playing with the
kids and the pups for the last twenty minutes and they'd worn him
out. He drained the last of the sweet tea he'd been sipping, pulled
off his sunglasses, and wiped his face with his dress-shirt sleeve. He
figured it was over eighty degrees; the sky was azure and cloudless.
There was only a hint of a breeze moving the tops of the tall spruce
trees that surrounded the yard, and low humidity or not, it felt like
summer. He wiped his face again. He hadn't dressed for a romp with
the kids and the dogs. He'd only planned to stop by briefly, but the
earlier conversation with his boss made him hesitant to get back to
the office. He'd brought Ellie two bags of groceries from the Gardiner
Market, figured it was the least he could do since they were keeping
Shane, since they'd patched him up last night.

It was nearly three, and Luke was supposed to be back from a
wolf-watching excursion with clients anytime. Win had spent two
hours at the Park County Sheriff's substation, which consisted of two

desks pushed together at Gardiner's volunteer fire department building, giving his formal statement on Dex Pierson's assault. It had been more than a little embarrassing recounting the altercation to a gruff prosecuting attorney who seemed amused that a federal agent had been dumb enough to get beaten up by his prime suspect in a case. Win got out of their office as quickly as he could, thankful that he hadn't run into Deputy Sullivan and gotten another tongue lashing about last night's recklessness.

Ellie was sitting in one of the front-porch rocking chairs. A wide-brimmed straw hat shielded her face from the sun. She had a book, looked like she was reading, but every few moments her eyes swept between Shane in the yard, Ethan in the tree house, and Abby making castles in the sandbox near the woodpile. Win pushed off from the deck and walked toward her. "Do you actually get any reading done?" he asked as he put his empty glass on the porch.

Ellie looked up and smiled. "You'd be surprised."

"I don't think I'd be surprised at anything you're able to do," Win said as he climbed the two steps and sat down in the empty chair beside her. "You amaze me."

The exhausted puppy, Tiger, lay near Ellie's feet beside a pot overflowing with yellow and purple flowers. The fawn-colored pup raised his head, yawned, then dropped his head back down to the wooden porch with a thump.

"You and Shane wore Tiger out," she said.

Win glanced down at the pup. "Who names a dog *Tiger*? That's a cat's name."

"Not if you're an LSU fan, it isn't."

He motioned to the purple and yellow petunias. "Purple and gold . . . it's a theme here."

"You've noticed?" she said in a teasing voice. "Luke would have named Ethan after the team mascot if I hadn't vetoed that idea."

Win sat back in the chair and nodded. *She's probably kidding, but maybe not.*

Ellie gave him a sideways glance. "You're in a good mood this after-noon, and I'm thinking it's not just playing with the kids and the dogs. What's up?"

He blinked in surprise and wondered how every woman in his life could read his thoughts and his moods as if they were plastered on his forehead. He shrugged with his good shoulder and gave her a sheepish reply. "Well, that girl I've told you about, uh, Tory Madison. She called me on the sat phone right before noon. She's camped somewhere in the Pelican Creek Valley, that's down north of Yellowstone Lake, with the grizzly bear research group. She told me she's hiking out to the Lake area tomorrow, wanted to see if I could get off, come meet her for dinner."

"And?"

"My boss wanted me out of Mammoth for a day or two anyway—we've got an issue with another agency—so he was good with me tak-ing leave for parts of two days." Win paused and smiled to himself at his sudden good fortune. "So we've got a dinner date tomorrow night at the Lake Yellowstone Hotel."

"Nice place," she said, nodding her approval. "Luke took me there for our anniversary last year. Your friend will love it."

"Catch it, Mr. Win!" Shane yelled from the yard as he launched the dog's slimy tennis ball toward them.

Win snagged the ball out of the air just before it hit Ellie. Dog slob-ber flew everywhere. Ellie hardly flinched. Win figured raising two kids must have given her nerves of steel.

She laughed and closed the book. "You're moving pretty quick for someone who had such a rough night." She took in the bruise on his jaw, glanced at the scrapes on his knuckles. "You heal fast."

Win grinned back at her. "That's a darn good thing, seein's how often I get hurt out here."

She waved back at Shane and Ethan, who were whooping it up below the tree house with the hound. "It's good having Shane here, been good feeling like we're making a difference in someone's life. Not having close family here . . . I miss that," she said.

"I've been working with a woman who's enraged over something, who said she hadn't talked with her daughter or her ex-husband in several weeks—" Win stopped in midsentence. He glanced at Ellie. "I have no idea why I just told you that."

She didn't look puzzled, she just nodded. "Maybe you should ask her to consider calling the daughter, to call the man, to start the healing."

"She'd tell me it's none of my business."

"She'd be right. But it is the Lord's business, and sometimes He leads us to get into other people's business on His behalf. Don't expect her to take your advice or to take it well. Maybe you're just being led to plant the Lord's seeds."

Win looked skeptical.

Ellie's eyes swept the yard again and then focused back on his. "You said you had no idea why you just told me that. Well, I 'spect the Spirit is nudging you to do something. To help." She paused. "You know what it says in 1 Peter 3:15, *be prepared to give an answer for the hope that is in you in a gentle and respectful way.* Your hope is in Christ as Lord, same as mine, but this woman you work with may not have hope . . . in anything."

Before Win could respond, Shane and Max came running. Shane wiped the sweat from his face and told the dog to sit. Max responded with two earsplitting howls that Win figured carried two miles.

"Lordy, that dog is loud!" Win said.

Shane beamed with pride. "Been workin' on his baying. He'll use that when he's chasin' raccoons. Mr. Luke said he's gotta have a deep, strong bay. Max is catchin' right on."

"Uh-huh, I can see that," Win replied. The hound was pleased to be the center of attention; he gave them a dog smile, rolled out his tongue, and shook his long black ears. Win dodged backward as slobber went flying. He made a mental note to rule out coonhounds when he finally got a dog.

"Miss Ellie says she's takin' me to see Papaw this afternoon at the hospital. She says as soon as Mr. Luke gets home, we'll go."

Ellie glanced down at the side table and checked the time on her phone. "Oh, we need to get ready! Shane, go put Max and Tiger up in the barn and run and get in the shower. Luke will be here soon, and we'll be going."

The kid gave Win a grin and a fist bump and called for the dogs to follow him. Little Ethan trailed along behind them.

As soon as the boys were out of earshot, Ellie turned to Win. "I checked with the nurse this morning. Mr. Pierson will be moved to hospice tomorrow. She said he'd likely be alert late this afternoon and it'd be okay to bring Shane by for a visit."

Win frowned.

"It's okay, Luke's going with us. Oh, and I know about the deputy you've had stationed down on our road by the highway. Patrol car has been there since you left here last night. You were afraid Shane's daddy might show up here?"

Win shrugged. "Just wanted you to be safe. Since there's a state warrant out on the man now, the Sheriff's Office was glad to stake out your road for several hours. They won't be there if Luke's at home. I appreciate y'all taking care of Shane. But now that I've got a little more time on my hands, I promise I'm gonna try harder to find out where he belongs."

* * *

It was after four o'clock when Win rolled into Mammoth, pulled into the gravel side lot of the Pagoda building where his office was housed, and began fulfilling his promise to Ellie. He punched in the back entrance security code and hustled up the stairs to his office. He closed his door and didn't even look at the landline. He didn't want to be there long, since Jim West had told him to make himself scarce. He had no desire to end up in a jurisdictional dispute with ATF and the Park Service; he had even less desire to run into Alex Lindell. He dug in his front desk drawer for the business card he'd stuck there several days ago. If he couldn't trace the boy, maybe he could trace the hound. He found the card and made the call.

"Yello! Donnie Sawyer!" was the answer on the second ring.

"Deputy Sawyer, this is Win Tyler with the FBI. I'm sorry to bother you again on your trip, but I wondered if you could help me out with something?"

The man ignored the question; he sounded cautious. "You get that burning vehicle thing solved?"

"No. We're still workin' that case, but ATF has taken the lead on it, and I've got another issue."

He heard the man sigh. "There's always another issue, ain't there? Whataya need?"

"We've got a boy, says his name is Shane, says he's eight years old. He's been living with Dex Pierson, a person of interest in a case. We can't get any information out of him, but I'm thinking he's from Georgia, maybe Alabama, based on his accent. He's got a bluetick coonhound with him, looks like a purebred dog, maybe eight to ten months old. I ran the dog by a vet up here and there's no microchip, so that's a dead end. I can send you a photo of the man the boy's been living with."

"Okay, we're still wandering arounds the parks . . . I ain't busy."

Win texted Dex's mug shot to the deputy. Win heard Sawyer suck in a breath. Dex had that effect on folks.

"Whoa, he'd be hard to forget."

"Yeah, that's what I'm thinking too. My late great-uncle raised coonhounds, and those breeders were a tight bunch. You know anyone I could call and maybe track down some hound breeders in your part of the country?"

Sawyer didn't hesitate. "I kin do it for you. I'm just sitting in the shade, waiting for the kids to get back from their horseback ride here in Canyon. We did that big loop of geysers and hot springs over at Norris Basin this morning. I'm ready for a rest. I don't mind sitting here makin' a few calls. If I don't move, I got a connection . . . kinda nice to have phone service."

It didn't take long. Win barely had time to walk down to the break-room, grab one of Janet's homemade fried peach pies, and pour another cup of coffee, before his phone buzzed.

"We hit pay dirt," Deputy Sawyer said as soon as Win answered. "Got a hit on the third call. A breeder outside of Rome, Georgia, sold that man a pup last year, in mid-December. Said the guy sent him a PayPal deposit the month before to hold a bluetick male out of his latest litter. The breeder advertises on the internet. That's how they initially connected." The deputy paused; Win guessed the man was glancing at his notes before he continued.

"Well, anyway, Pierson picked up the pup on December 19th. And yes, Pierson had a young boy with him. The breeder said the boy was polite, real excited about the puppy. The man was thinking it was a Christmas present from his father—said the father looked scary as Hell but seemed nice enough once they got to visitin'. Pierson paid him eighteen hundred cash, plus the two-hundred-dollar deposit, plus the amount for the pup's initial vaccinations and registration papers. Those are not inexpensive dogs. The boy said they were going to Montana and his new pup would get to see some snow, but the guy didn't get their address. The breeder said he's real picky who he sells his dogs to—he was concerned about the dog. I told him I'd call him back. Is the dog okay?"

"This is exactly what I need, and, yes, the dog is fine. He slobbered all over me this afternoon."

The man chuckled. "I'm texting you the breeder's contact information now."

"This helps, this helps a lot," Win responded as he swiped to check the contact information that came in on his phone. "I really appreciate it."

"Glad to help," Sawyer said. "We're gonna be here another three, four days, then head on back home. You need anything else, just holler."

Win started to rush off the call, but his manners kicked in. "Y'all having a good trip?"

"Youbetcha. I gotta say, this place is amazing. My brother and his family are headin' back home after the kids get done with their horseback riding this afternoon. We're staying in one of them four-unit cabins here in Canyon, gonna drive down and see that Mud Volcano area again later today. My boy Cabe has really gotten into the thermal features—boy might become a geologist. You seen that Dragon's Mouth Spring thing? It's fascinating . . . and kinda spooky."

"Yeah it is." *You have no idea,* Win thought as his mind flashed back to his up-close and personal experience at that spring just over three weeks ago. They wrapped up the pleasantries by hashing out Arkansas and Georgia's football prospects for the coming season. The Bulldogs were gonna have another good year.

CHAPTER NINETEEN

This wasn't a good time for Tank to be out of pocket. Not a good time at all. He'd decided to move the camper trailer with the AR-15s out of the Bridge Bay Campground before he disposed of the body last Thursday night. He'd cursed himself a hundred times for being hasty, not thinking it through, not having a plan. It would've been way smarter, and a hell of a lot less work, to let Roadie move the new rifles up to that rented cabin at Canyon. Let Roadie drive with the trailer to the next campground, let Roadie package the new guns for transport over the border, let Roadie run the risk of getting caught. But no, he'd acted without thinking it through and he'd acted at the worst possible time, when Tank was off on his other gig, when other ventures were falling apart, when several loose ends were dangling.

And it was time to tend to more of those loose ends. He quickly calculated how much it could cost him to hire some muscle to eliminate his other problems. The chopper was a done deal, no worries there . . .

He raised his eyes and smiled at the cute barista who held up a cup to see if he needed a refill. That sweetheart took good care of him here; he was a regular. He glanced in his tumbler, smiled back at her, and shook his head *no*.

Between ten and twenty grand, that should do it. It wasn't like he was gonna have to hire a professional assassin—there were plenty of meth heads and losers who'd be up for the job. Might even get it done for five grand, but there again, no need to get greedy. Generally speaking, you get what you pay for.

He leaned back in the comfortable seat in the far corner of the coffee shop and sipped his latte from its stainless steel tumbler. Good of them to let him get their pricey coffee in his own container—kept it hotter, made it go down smoother. He took another bite of the huckleberry scone and washed it down with more coffee. It was after ten, a little late for breakfast, but he'd had a busy morning. He dabbed his mouth with the napkin and noticed the discoloration under two of his manicured nails. He frowned down at them and paused. Either hydraulic fluid or Semtex. Neither one was good. *Gettin' careless, dammit.* He carefully cleaned under the nails with a plastic butter knife. He wiped whatever it was off on his napkin, rolled the napkin into a tight ball, and launched it into the nearest trash container, ten feet away. *Nothin' but net!* He smiled to himself as he saw the little cutie behind the counter glance his way and flash him a thumbs-up.

He scrolled down the screen of his laptop and mentally calculated how much to transfer to the offshore account in the Caymans. He currently had too much sitting in his local bank accounts, but the damn Feds were making it harder and harder to transfer too much cash offshore. His Grand Cayman banker had warned him about deposits over 100K; some new antiterrorism initiatives to dry up sources of illicit funds were flagging those higher amounts. Damn terrorists were making it harder to do business. He'd have to split the transfers, and that carried risks of its own. He leaned back and looked at the screen. He took another sip of the latte. *Uh-uh. . . . No need to get hasty. Hasty had already caused some problems.*

He'd checked one thing off his list this morning, so what to do next? He'd come to the conclusion that he needed to wipe the slate totally clean. He'd also concluded it wouldn't be easy. Tank was a pro—a dangerous pro. The guy hadn't hesitated to shoot the two competing gunrunners, who turned out to be Feds. And Tank hadn't even seemed too concerned about the fact that they were law enforcement, that the heat was on. The guy was steely, solid, steady. Tank was the kind of guy he wanted around, the kind of guy who'd come in handy if he decided to restart the business here once the dust settled. But that was a long shot and he knew it. Plus Tank knew too much. Tank had connections, and he'd apparently been using those recently. Somehow Tank had found out about his condo in Grand Cayman. The guy probably suspected that the Cabo San Lucas line was just that—a line, a bit of misdirection. If the Feds fingered Tank, he could point the authorities toward the stately powder-blue condo on Seven Mile Beach instead of some thatch-covered cabana on a Mexican shore. So, risky or not, Tank had to go.

Then there was good ole boy Dex. He had to admit that Dex had turned out to be a lot sharper than he'd given him credit for. When he'd told Dex to go to ground after those Chinese fools screwed up the trophy hunt, Dex had *really* gone to ground. He didn't know where Dex was, and the guy was using burner phones so his sources couldn't track him. He figured Dex was probably holed up in one of those damn FEMA trailers, but there were 2,218 official RV camping spots in Yellowstone, never mind the hundreds just outside the park. He didn't have the time or the inclination to drive around and look for the guy. And he couldn't very well hire a hit man to go after a target if he had no idea where the target was. That was a recipe for disaster. He closed his computer screen and sighed as he thought about it.

He and Dex went way back—all the way back to elementary school. Tight as brothers in junior high and part of high school. Played on the same teams, chased the same girls, even took their first drink together. *And now Dex has disappeared.* He sighed again. *Dex has lost trust in me.* He took another sip of his coffee and reflected on that. *Losing trust in me is the smartest thing Dex Pierson has done in the last few years.*

*   *   *

It was past mid-morning and Win was counting his blessings at not being called in by the Chief Ranger or ATF on the tourist takedown disaster. He'd left his Bureau Expedition parked near the rear of the Mammoth Hot Springs Hotel so that it wouldn't be obvious that he was in the office. Trey had called him from near Roosevelt last night to let him know that the tourist had officially filed a lawsuit against the ATF and all sorts of unnamed codefendants. Neither he nor Trey wanted to be among those codefendants. The Assistant U.S. Attorney who was stationed in Mammoth was right in the middle of that mess, but she managed an early meeting with Win at the Justice Center regarding the Assault On A Federal Officer charge against Dex Pierson.

As part of her due diligence on the complaint against Pierson, the woman sent Win across the street to the Mammoth Clinic to have his injuries confirmed by the doctor, pointing out that he should have gone to the clinic immediately after Pierson attacked him. Win didn't appreciate the scolding and told her the Sheriff's deputies had plenty of photos of his injuries taken just after the fight. He sucked it up and dodged the traffic as he crossed the divided street. He admitted to himself that she was right. The young doctor confirmed what Win already knew: contusions on his jaw, ribs, and shoulder, minor lacerations on his knuckles. All in all, no big deal, but it still hurt like hell if he moved too quickly. His exercise schedule would have to stay on hold for a few more days.

He left the office in the care of Janet Swam after downing three pieces of her sour cream pound cake and headed for his Bureau vehicle. He knew he was pushing his luck if he stayed at the office much longer—someone from the Park Service was going to call and rope him into the tourist crisis. If he wasn't sitting at his desk, at least he'd have a better chance that his excuses of being unavailable would ring true.

He gave several elk cows and their calves a wide berth as he walked up the crumbling asphalt street toward his vehicle. The cows were grazing on the Historic District's watered lawns and the calves were running and playing, like all baby things do. The sky was crystal clear and the breeze was gentle. He figured it was going to be another warm day by park standards. It'd probably hit eighty today, but at 10:30 the air was still crisp and cool. He pulled his light jacket off and draped it over his arm. The sun felt good on his back.

He stopped to watch a flock of cliff swallows diving and soaring near the eves of an ancient two-story building that sat near the street. They'd built their gourd-shaped nests of mud tight under the eaves. He knew they were closely related to the barn swallows he grew up with in Arkansas, but these were a little darker and lacked the forked tail that distinguished the Southern birds. But their dizzying acrobatics were the same, their mastery of the air identical.

His commune with nature was far too brief. A massive tour bus, with a colorful Western landscape covering its side, slowly swung around the corner of the street and rumbled toward him. The modern bus seemed completely out of place on the narrow street, in the middle of hundred-year-old buildings. The elk moved away, and the birds all flared and disappeared. Win sighed and opened the door to his SUV. *Woulda been nice to stand here a few minutes more.*

But where he really wanted to be on this beautiful summer day was in West Yellowstone with Kirk and two other agents who had a raid on a helicopter charter company lined up for this morning. It hadn't taken long for Denver's analysts to decipher the real registration numbers on the helicopter that was suspected in the poaching. The Bell 206B-3 was registered to Vista Transport Services based at West Yellowstone's airport. They'd learned that the pilot Kirk was focused on, a guy named Phil Jimson, was scheduled to work today. Two agents from Denver's Violent Crime Squad had flown into that airport late last night and Kirk had driven over to meet them. They'd planned to go in at eight, right as the company opened, so by now they either had their man or not—he'd been hoping someone would call to clue him in. Staying out of the case was hard, not going on the raid was hard, waiting for an unofficial update was hard.

And it was even harder knowing that it was his own stupidity that had taken him off the case, his recklessness in rushing to get to Mr. Pierson's trailer before his backup arrived. Never mind that his backup was late. He should have waited. Maybe the fight with Dex could have been avoided and they could have taken him into custody. Win knew from his upbringing on the farm that being in too big of a hurry usually led to trouble. He remembered the verse from Proverbs: *'The plans of the diligent lead to success, but the one who is hasty comes to ruin.'* It went something like that. His boss hadn't chewed him out over the mistake yet, but it was coming . . . and he darn well deserved it.

He pulled the door shut as the huge bus slowly moved past. Its roaring engine spewed a cloud of diesel fumes that engulfed his SUV and permeated the interior. He coughed and sat back to wait for the bus to pass. He had a few hours to kill before he left on the long drive to meet Tory at Lake and he needed a plan. He'd set up shop at his house and continue to track down leads on Shane's real identity. He'd also text his little brother again and try to quit fuming about the kid's lack of responsiveness. He hadn't heard a word from him since the short text yesterday morning as the backpacking excursion began. Their mother was going to be worried. *I'll probably get the blame.* The bus was finally making the turn in front of his office, so he put the Expedition in gear and followed it. He had a few other calls to make, he had things to do, but his team was hopefully closing in on the bad guys and he was on the bench . . . *and I don't like that one little bit.*

* * *

He'd just pulled up into the gravel parking area behind his stone house when he spotted Alex Lindell sitting in a lawn chair near his back steps. *Oh, geez!* She wasn't in the field uniform he usually saw her in. She was dressed more like a tourist, in jeans, a light blouse, and tennis shoes. Her hair was pulled back in a tight ponytail, and the look on her face was as severe as her hairstyle. She might not be the last person he wanted to see today, but she was way up that list.

He didn't know why she was here, but he had orders to stay away from her and he intended to follow those orders. Ellie's advice to talk with Alex floated through his mind, but he filed it away. He didn't want to be in this woman's business—the Lord could find a more willing servant to plant His seeds in Alex Lindell's heart.

She stood up and walked toward him as he got out of the Expedition. Her voice was bitter. "I imagine they've told you I'm stuck here doing nothing while ATF runs down Greg's killers," she said. Her dark eyes were as hard as her tone.

Whoa. Gettin' right to the point! "Look, Alex, I'm on my way outa here soon, and I don't have time for this—"

She took a step closer and got in his space. He had to look down to meet her angry eyes. He didn't like this. Not one damn bit.

He drew in a shallow breath and took a step back. He softened his tone. "I hear you're stuck in Mammoth waiting to be interviewed on the takedown of that guy from Kansas."

"I'm sure you've also been told ATF has me locked down at the hotel cottages so I can't get into any more trouble!" He started to respond, but she kept talking. "Well, they couldn't watch me 24/7 so I'm here wanting some answers on the case."

Win quickly regrouped. "You know as well as I do that I'm not authorized to give you answers on the case. And even if I could, I'm not working the gunrunning case any longer." He tried to keep his voice calm. "Look, I've been told you're a good officer, a real professional." Win remembered a similar conversation not so long ago that had helped him. *Maybe I can help her.* She started to speak but he cut her off. "Listen to me! I expect you to act like the professional you are! We both have a job to do. We should both be pleased that the gunrunning case is getting legs, is moving forward. We both want justice for Agent Beckett and Greg Manyhorses, we both want illegal guns off the streets. We should be thrilled that ATF and the Bureau are gaining traction."

She shook her head, her anger barely controlled. "ATF's sending agents here, but I'll probably be ordered to Jackson, then back to Canada tomorrow. You aren't the one being pushed aside!"

He stepped toward her and raised his voice. His tone became harsh as he glared down at her. "This isn't about you. This isn't about me. This is about justice, about doing the right thing—a just cause!"

She stood there and took the lecture, likely shocked by his sudden aggression. He stepped to the side and walked past her to the back door. When he pulled out the key to open it, she was still standing in the same spot, facing him now, looking defiant.

For some reason, he gave her one last parting shot before he climbed the last step and walked in the door. "In my opinion, Alex, you need to do some serious soul-searching, and yes, I believe God helps us with that if we ask Him. I also think you need to consider calling your daughter and your husband. There's no going back, but based on what you told me, you've made some mistakes. You need to mend some fences, make peace with others and yourself."

She didn't respond, and he started inside. He paused for a moment, lowered his voice, and met her angry eyes. "And I'll pray for you, Alex."

"Don't bother!" she shouted as he closed the door.

* * *

It was coming up on 2:30 and he'd managed to eat a good lunch, play with the cat, get a few bills paid, and catch up on his laundry. He hadn't made as much progress on running down Shane's identity as he thought he would have. In fact, he hadn't made any real progress at all. He'd left a boatload of messages, but there were just some days when no one was in.

And he still hadn't heard a word from Will. He'd sent a second text early that afternoon, but no response. He reminded himself that cell phone coverage, even text service, was hit or miss in Yellowstone. It didn't help to fret about it; he'd give the kid a break and assume they were camped out of range. He thought about calling the company, he was sure the group checked in every day by satellite phone, but that seemed like overkill. He called his mother and she agreed that they might be trying to hold the reins a little tight on Will. He teased her and reminded her that Will was a Tyler and that she'd raised her boys to take care of themselves.

If he hadn't been so excited about his dinner date with Tory, he would have been really miffed that he hadn't heard a word from Kirk or Jim West about the raid on the helicopter company this morning. They needed a break in that case, not a dry hole. He'd left a message for Jim to let him know that Alex had shown up at his door and that he'd sent her packing. He'd hoped to score some information on the raid from someone in the Lander RA, but that hadn't happened. He knew Kirk wasn't likely to call. Win was off the case, period. Kirk was probably totally overwhelmed. He'd told Win this was his first FBI "action," as he'd called it—the first raid in his short FBI career. Win had started to remind him to take his gun, but he decided not to push it. Win knew Jim West had insisted that two experienced agents accompany Kirk. They weren't expecting trouble, but trouble is notoriously unpredictable, and Win wished he were there.

Win shifted into packing for the overnight trip, thinking of Tory and her beautiful smile, wondering how to lose the nerves that had suddenly appeared. He stood in front of the full-length mirror that hung on the back of his bathroom door. He knew why he was so nervous about his date with Tory tonight. He was on thin ice with her, he was aware of that. She'd called him out on not being over Shelby. That serious talk had been ten days ago, and while their texts and short phone calls had been positive since then, if the relationship was going to move forward, he needed to make that happen. Back in early June, they'd agreed to go slowly. They were both coming off long-term relationships—they'd both been hurt. But going slowly and being at a dead stop were two different things. He needed to up his game. Tucker said to make her feel special, feel cherished. *I can do that.*

He had tried on three shirts and hadn't been happy with any of them. They were going to dinner at the Lake Yellowstone Hotel Dining Room; it was a nice place, a white-tablecloth kind of place, that's what Trey had said. Ellie told him the restaurant had great food and a classy atmosphere, and that Tory would like it. Win had made a reservation for seven and was supposed to pick her up at her cabin at six. He pulled on a deep-red shirt and turned in the mirror. *Too much like I'm goin' to a Razorback game . . . too bright, maybe?* Gruff sat down nearby and stared up at the cardinal shirt.

"What?"

The cat frowned, then dropped his head and casually licked his paw.

"Okay, maybe the blue shirt . . . Shelby said it matched my eyes." *Geez, that's all I need, thoughts of Shelby!* He retreated to the closet, then buttoned up the cobalt shirt, tucked it in, and pulled the belt with its small silver buckle into place. With his cowboy boots and the belt, he looked a little Western but not over the top. *I am in Wyoming, after all.*

The small Glock 43 was in an ankle holster. He hated wearing that holster, it wasn't comfortable, but he wasn't about to draw attention to his weapon on this date. He knew lots of women thought dating an FBI agent was exciting, but there was a vast difference between casual dating and serious dating. Win Tyler didn't think Tory Madison did the casual dating thing; she was looking for a life partner, a marriage partner, same as he was. She might have already been thinking about the downsides of life with a man in law enforcement. He reached down, pulled at his khaki pants leg, and adjusted the ankle holster. *Yeah, there are downsides, like being armed most of the time, and being on call 24/7....* He straightened, squared his shoulders, and flinched from the pain. *And gettin' beat up by scumbags.*

* * *

There was a lady playing the grand piano in the atrium of the Lake Yellowstone Hotel. There were comfortable places to sit and look out of the high windows at the silvery-blue lake and the towering mountains in the distance. There were waiters in uniforms serving drinks, and there was a nice, upscale, civilized vibe to the whole place. If the clothes had been different, he could have been walking in on the predinner crowd from 1920, or maybe even 1891—that was when it opened. It was the oldest hotel in the park, and its colonial revival architecture mirrored the grand hotels of the East Coast and Great Lakes in the late 1800s and early 1900s. It was like walking into a history lesson with scenery—incredible scenery.

He went over to the massive fireplace and took a closer look at the beautiful handmade tile that surrounded it. The sign at the front said it was added to the hotel in 1923. His mind did the math: more than ninety-five years of watching over this spectacular room. He tried to imagine the conversations that had taken place in this comfortable spot, around the tile fireplace—talk of the stock market crash, the Depression, World Wars I and II, men on the moon, Vietnam, and on and on. Or maybe the travelers who'd made so much effort to come here long ago came to forget those worries, came here instead to marvel at the geysers, gasp at the bears and the bison, lose themselves in the vastness of the place. Same as folks today.

Tory had texted him to meet her in the lobby, she was running a few minutes late. He was thrilled to have even limited cell service here since he'd had none on the long drive from Mammoth. He turned away from the remarkable fireplace just as she came past the reception area. Tory was just as lovely as he expected. She was wearing the blue sundress that she'd bought in Jackson and worn to Tucker's Fourth of July cookout at Miss Martha's house. She had a dark sweater draped across her shoulders and her long brunette hair was tied back with a soft-blue ribbon. She saw him and smiled, and he felt his knees go a little weak. He wondered for a split second why she had that effect on him. He'd practiced what he was going to say on the two-and-a-half-hour drive down from Mammoth—he had a clever and sharp opening. But the practiced words somehow evaporated as she walked toward him, and all he could think to say was "Hey, Tory."

By some miracle he snagged a couple of plush armchairs for them in front of the tall windows overlooking the lake. The view of the lake and the mountains with the early-evening sun hitting them was simply jaw-dropping, he couldn't think of a better way to describe it. The waiter swooped in and took their drink orders. The pianist was playing a lovely version of "Somewhere Over the Rainbow," and his mind got stuck on the part about dreams coming true. He couldn't understand why he seemed incapable of intelligent thought each time he saw Tory. He made a mental note to figure that out.

She was talking about the seven-mile hike to the Yellowstone Lake area from the research group's base camp in the Pelican Creek Valley. Tory said it had been slow going since she and another woman had escorted one of the researchers to the Lake Medical Clinic. The guy had been bitten by a bear cub and the wound became infected. They'd arranged for a ranger to meet them at the trailhead, near the north end of the lake, and take them to the clinic earlier this afternoon. Tory confessed that she hadn't made it to her cabin until four and was scrambling to get cleaned up, get her dress ironed, and get herself together before he arrived at six. She said she was sorry if she seemed flustered.

You're stunning, not flustered, he wanted to say. But he just smiled and asked an innocuous question about their lengthy hike, then another question about her work. He watched her eyes sparkle when she talked, watched the small gold drop earrings gently sway when she moved her head, watched her delicate hands amplify her words. Realized before the maître d' called their table that he'd fallen in love.

CHAPTER TWENTY

They'd paid $450 for the three-hour sunset fishing trip on the highest, coldest lake in the world, or was it the largest, highest lake in North America, or . . . she couldn't remember now. She was trying to keep from getting seasick, or maybe *lakesick* would be a better word for it. She'd forgotten to take the Dramamine. It was sitting in her purse in their car in the Bridge Bay Marina parking lot. It hadn't been windy when they'd started out, and the boat wasn't tiny. The twenty-two-foot aluminum boat had a deck chair fore and aft, a small covered cowling with a young guy driving, and a fishing guide who looked as rugged as the mountains. The water in the inlet where the marina was located was as calm and glassy as a mirror. She'd thought the trip would be smooth. But as soon as they motored under the highway bridge and out into the expanse of the big lake, the wind picked up, the whitecaps appeared, the rocking began, and she was immediately green at the gills, as the guide pointed out.

But she wasn't about to go back. This fishing trip was her gift to Jeff, it was part of their forty-year anniversary trip across the West. He'd grown up fishing, he talked about it often, but with work, with children, and now with small grandchildren, he never got to go. Fond memories became the distant past far too soon. She didn't want Jeff's thoughts of fishing to be just a memory. So she was determined to ride this out and pretend to have a great time. This was important to him and that mattered.

The guide waved toward her and shouted something—he was pointing at Jeff and making reeling motions with his hands.

"You got another one! Woo-hoo!" she called out over the steady swoosh of the wind.

The fish flashed to the surface a few yards away. Water splashed as it tried to shake off the hook. "Nice fish! That one will be eight pounds!" the guide yelled.

She tried to smile, tried to show some tiny bit of enthusiasm, but for goodness' sake, her husband had landed at least twenty fish while she'd caught none. Not that she really cared. Her line was in the water, she assumed the bait was still there. They were fishing for the native cutthroat trout with its distinct red slash on its jaw, but Jeff was mostly catching the larger, whitish-gray lake trout. The guide had told them they could keep as many of those as they caught, that they couldn't be released back into the water. Lake trout were an invasive species that competed with the native fish—some were over thirty pounds, he said. The Park Service was trying to exterminate them, and Jeff was certainly making his contribution to that effort. He was loving this, and she was loving that he was happy.

She turned her attention back to her line, where nothing was happening. The boat took a slight roll as the driver turned it to better land Jeff's latest catch. She focused her mind on the trip to get her thoughts off her rumbling stomach. The Lake Yellowstone Hotel was off to the northwest; it looked beautiful in the glow of the late afternoon. She absently wondered why they'd painted it bright-yellow back in 1891. Maybe to stand out against the dark evergreens that lined the lake? Maybe a color trend back in that day? There were historic markers everywhere. Someone would know.

They'd made their reservations nearly a year ago and were staying in one of the lakeview rooms in the historic hotel. When they checked in yesterday afternoon, she had to stifle a gasp when she saw the room rate. But instead of showing her shock, she'd taken Jeff's arm and told him how wonderful it was to be enjoying the premier accommodations in Yellowstone's oldest hotel. And it really was nice, very nice. The desk clerk said those rooms had been completely renovated just last year, but many of the Gilded Age touches remained.

The vintage soaking tub had been a treat after their flight from Indianapolis to Cody, then the meandering journey to Cooke City, then along the park roads from the northeast gate. They'd pulled over to take long-range photos of mountain goats on Barronette Peak. The clerk at their Cody hotel said it was worth the stop to see the mystical-looking white creatures hop around the cliff face, thousands of feet above the highway. They'd stopped again on the shoulder for a few minutes to glimpse a cow moose standing chest deep in a lily pond at the side of the road. She seemed to pose for the pictures each time a photographer came near. A harried ranger was having a terrible time keeping the crowd in check. Then they'd seen what had to be hundreds of bison grazing in a broad watershed that a sign said was the Lamar Valley. The sheer number of them was nearly overwhelming.

She'd fallen asleep somewhere after that point and awakened when Jeff pulled up in front of the grand old hotel. It looked just like it had on the internet: a stately yellow four-story wooden building with towering white columns and trim. One of those refurbished 1936 yellow tour buses sat outside the main doors, and a few guests were disembarking. She felt as if she'd awakened in another time—a slower, more peaceful time.

The boat lurched a bit when a white-capping wave connected. That jolted her back to the present. Jeff finally had the darn fish up to the side of the boat, and the guide was getting it in the net. It would be another minute before she had to get her phone out and take a picture of this particular trout. The photo would be filed along with the dozens of other photos of nearly identical fat, silver fish that Jeff would proudly sort through tonight to send to the grandkids whenever they found a spot with reliable cell service. In a weird way it was nice not to be connected, not to be distracted every few minutes by her phone.

She drew in a breath and tried again to force her queasy stomach into submission. She glanced at the guys again—still fighting that darn fish! She'd read somewhere that one could subdue motion sickness with positive thoughts. It was worth a shot. She refocused on the western horizon, where the sun had just dipped below the mountains. The sky above her was still a soft hue of blue, and the high clouds began to hint at color. Soft violets and lavender transitioned to a dreamy pink. She smiled when she remembered what her Aunt Jean used to call it—a cotton candy sky.

"You've got one!"

She nearly jumped out of the deck chair at the guide's shout. She instinctively pulled back on the heavy rod and tried to remember his instructions from two hours ago. He was quickly by her side, and she heard Jeff cheering her on. She had to admit their enthusiasm was contagious. The guide had one hand on her rod now—she saw him signal something to the guy driving the boat and the engine dropped to an idle. The line in her reel was squealing then going quiet, then squealing again. "Take up the slack, easy does it, take up more slack. . . . It's a real big one, it may be trying to go deep . . . or it could be you've snagged a log . . . lots of sunken logs in this lake," the guide was saying. Jeff threw his fish in the live well, put down his rod, and was holding on to the back of her chair, offering more encouragement. This was, after all, her first ever Yellowstone fish.

The guide had retrieved the net from near Jeff's chair; he was leaning down toward the water, trying to see what she had. Jeff put his hand on her rod to steady it. She was suddenly reeling as fast as she could, it had to be near the surface. It had to be close. The guide shifted the net to get a better angle, and Jeff moved closer to her side. "It's coming up, keep reeling!" he said. She looked down into the icy blue water just before it broke the surface, her eyes probing the dark depths for the silver flash of a fish . . . saw a dark shape, then white, it was almost up . . . almost here. . . . She strained harder with the rod . . . almost up! Her scream echoed across the water.

*   *   *

He was holding her hand as they walked back toward Tory's cabin. Darkness was beginning to settle around them, and there were only a few people still out and about. The warmth of the day hadn't totally gone, and he could hear muffled voices coming from inside the open windows of every small yellow cabin they passed. No air-conditioning, no television, no Wi-Fi, no cell service to speak of—it was early to bed for most everyone at the park.

It had been a perfect evening, really. The dinner was fantastic, and when they'd finished, he and Tory had walked down below the hotel to the lakefront and sat on a bench and watched a few distant fishing boats bob in the choppy water. They'd talked about the mountains that stood sentry around the huge lake; it was nearly twenty miles to the southern flank of the Absaroka Range and the Red Mountains that stood across the shimmering water to the south. She'd told him that there were dozens of geysers and hot springs just below the lake's surface, that the lake bed was near the center of Yellowstone's volcanic caldera, that the last major eruption 640,000 years ago had formed the lake. Win had learned more about the volcano and the park's thermal features on his last case than he'd ever wanted to know. But it pleased him that he had some knowledge of the park, of its history, of its magic. He was glad he could make more than a cursory contribution to their conversation.

The after-dinner crowd had drifted down to the front of the hotel to better take in the view and the sunset. He wanted her more to himself, and he took her hand and led her down the narrow paved road along the lakeshore. Other couples and families with bands of children had the same idea—there was no privacy at the height of tourist season in this beautiful place. He and Tory found another bench and watched the distant clouds catch the last rays of sun. The sky took on the same hue as the blue lake, and the wispy white clouds transitioned to soft shades of red.

"My mother would call this a pink-and-blue sky," Tory said as she leaned her head on his shoulder. He'd heard his grandmother call it that and he smiled at the memory. He turned his head and nuzzled his chin against her hair. Her hair smelled like flowers.

"What are you thinking, Win Tyler?" she asked when he didn't respond.

"I'm thinking that I love to hear you talk, that I love to look into your eyes, that I want you to know how special you are. . . ." She sat close to him and he pulled the sweater over her shoulders and held her tight with his arm. They sat like that for a good long while, and he didn't even notice the folks who were also taking in the sights around them. He was at peace.

It was deep twilight now and they were nearly to her cabin's steps. He knew he couldn't go in; she'd told him that Tracy, one of her research partners, had already turned in for the night. He'd scanned the surrounding cabins and vehicles, no one was in sight. He was determined to get that first kiss. It would be a perfect way to end an evening that he didn't want to end—

Whoa! Geez! A gigantic black head swung around the corner of the cabin, then stopped. The massive bison bull was just steps in front of them. Win gripped Tory's hand tighter and pulled her back toward his body with his other arm.

"Don't move," she whispered as they both stood motionless. They were so close they could see the dirt on its horns, smell its musty odor, hear its raspy breathing as it chewed. Its ebony eyes settled on them and then seemed to dismiss them. It lowered its huge head, made a snort that sounded more like contentment than anger, and snapped off a tuft of grass at the corner of the cabin.

Win and Tory took a slow step back, and then another. A woman who'd come out of her cabin to retrieve something from her car froze in place a few yards away. Win and Tory continued to slowly step back up the paved lane as the bison stepped forward and moved into full view in front of Tory's steps.

Out of the corner of his eye, Win saw a man jogging through the twilight toward them. "Sorry folks, I thought this big fella had moved on for the night. . . . Ease on back up . . . twenty-five yards away, that's right, nice and slow, no sudden moves." The guy had a flashlight, but he didn't really need it. The sky hadn't gone completely dark.

The security guy, or whatever he was, didn't seem too alarmed. "You did just the right thing, slowly backing away." He signaled with his flashlight for a couple of kids to move back as he kept talking to

Win. "Had to airlift a lady to the trauma center last week who got too close to one—threw her twenty feet in the air. Horrible injuries. They're unpredictable for sure." Win pulled Tory closer into him; he noticed that she didn't resist. The guy was still talking. "This big fella is one of the bulls who keeps the grass mowed around the cabins. He usually moves down to the lake before dark."

Seriously! Mowing the grass? Win didn't know if the guy was kidding or not, but what he did know was that his respect for Tory had gone up another notch. She hadn't flinched, or panicked, or overreacted. She'd done the correct things and expected him to do the same. He reminded himself that her current gig was studying real live grizzly bears, that she'd hiked for miles today right through the heart of one of the continent's most concentrated bear populations. That she'd been camped in a tent for days, that she looked feminine and soft, but she had to be tough as nails.

"Isn't this cool!" she whispered as the bull continued to devour the short grass in front of her cabin.

"Uh-huh," was his soft answer. But as much as the unexpected close encounter with the buffalo was exhilarating, his plans had once again been derailed.

He'd thought he would kiss her goodnight, darn it. He'd pictured himself holding her and kissing her right there on those steps. But now there was a one-ton buffalo standing there, contently chewing its cud. Now there were at least a dozen onlookers who'd appeared from their cabins to see the resident lawnmower. He pulled her close to him, dropped his chin down onto her soft hair, and sighed.

* * *

He was trying to figure out a plan B for a goodnight kiss with Tory when his Bureau phone began vibrating in his jacket pocket. "Let's move back a little more," he whispered to her. "I need to check a call." They walked up the lane toward the hotel parking lot. Win fished the phone out of his pocket and caught the call on the last ring. It was Trey.

He didn't mince words. "Hey, got an issue. You still at Lake?"

"Yeah."

"Well, the boat ranger from there, Buck Harris, just called here and Chief Randall asked me to track you down. Looks like a murder victim was fished out of the lake—"

"For real? I read that y'all often have drownings down here. What makes you think it's a homicide?"

"Well, the ropes that were used to tie the body down to what I'm guessin' would be an anchor or concrete blocks—the ropes were a clue," Trey answered sarcastically.

"Okay, I get it. I'm still here, was planning to crash in the ranger's sleepover room tonight. I'm in my personal vehicle—I don't have a satellite phone or radio. Uh, why is the cell service suddenly so good?"

"'Cause most folks have given up on their phones and turned in for the night. The load on the cell towers has dropped and the coverage is better. It'll go back to next to nothing in the morning, so borrow someone's sat phone or radio while you're down there."

"Okay." Win checked the contact information that Trey had just texted him. "I've got Harris's info."

"You know where the Bridge Bay Marina is?" Trey asked.

"Yeah, I've seen it from the Grand Loop Road. About three miles south of the hotel?"

"Yup, go south from the hotel, then turn on the west side of the highway before the bridge, drive past the Bridge Bay Campground, you'll run right into it. It's the primary marina for the entire lake. We have a secondary ranger station there; it covers the permitting for any lake activities and boating."

"Got it. Can you touch base with this guy, Harris, and tell him I'm on my way, to keep any witnesses there, not disturb anything. The usual stuff. Give him an ETA of twenty minutes?" Win took a breath and looked up at the star-studded sky. He ran through a list of *to-dos* in his mind. "I'll call my supervisor as I drive, and we'll get the coroner and an Evidence Response Team in motion," he quickly added.

"Copy that. Buck is good, he'll handle things right. Oh . . . and Win, I'm sorry I had to call you in on this, had to screw up your time with Tory."

"Don't worry about it. It's what I do." Win stared off into the fading twilight toward the big bull that had finally begun to lumber away from Tory's cabin, toward the security guy's bobbing flashlight, toward the shadowy silhouette of the most beautiful woman in the world. She had her back to him, just out of earshot, watching the bison. He didn't want to leave her, but it was time for her to know the sacrifices required by his calling in life. He swallowed down an unexpected wave of fear. *This might not go well.*

CHAPTER TWENTY-ONE

The ranger station, bait shop, general store, and marina boardwalks were lit up like Christmas trees. It took a minute for Win's eyes to adjust to the bright lights as he stepped out of his old SUV. He flinched from the pain in his ribs as he pulled on his heavier jacket. A Park Service ambulance was idling near the boat ramp, its light bar flashing crimson strobes across the still water of the small bay. The EMTs and a couple of rangers were standing alongside a few onlookers at the entrance to the boat slips.

A tall ranger moved away from that group and waved with his ball cap for Win to join him. The ranger looked like an athlete; he was wearing body armor and a gun belt—clearly in law enforcement. Win had found Buck Harris. They shook hands and got the introductions out of the way. Win told Ranger Harris that he wanted to view the body before he began the interviews. They both walked down the steep concrete boat ramp onto a wooden boardwalk leading to the dock where a fishing cruiser was tied up near the gas pumps. The boat was a much smaller version of the deep-sea fishing cruisers Win had been on in Florida back in the days of vacationing with Shelby and her well-heeled parents. Win was surprised to see several nearly identical small cruisers resting in their slips. He took a moment to scan the connected docks and slips; he estimated that there were over a hundred boats of various types and sizes in the water. He wasn't expecting such a big operation at a marina in a mountainous national park.

Ranger Harris was talking as he walked ahead of Win toward the floating dock. "All of the witnesses—that would be a couple from Indiana, the boat pilot, and a fishing guide—are up at the marina ranger station waiting to give their statements." It only took a few moments to get to the cruiser. Someone had rigged a bright light beside the boat; they wouldn't have any trouble viewing the body. They stopped near the cruiser's stern, and Harris grabbed a handrail and deftly hopped down onto the deck. Win stepped down more gingerly and took a wide stance for balance as the boat gently rocked from the men's movements. The only sounds were the lapping of the water against the side of the boat and the idling of the ambulance's engine at the ramp. Win figured all the folks on the shore had gone quiet to watch them. The air felt damp and cold; the boat smelled like fish.

"Trey said you weren't down here on official business, said you might not have your gear," Ranger Harris remarked as he handed Win a pair of latex gloves.

"That's right . . . thank you," Win replied. He pulled on the gloves as he took in the still form that lay below the white sheet. He wondered for a moment why they always used white sheets, wondered if there was significance to the color. He made a mental note to research that as he drew in a shallow breath to steady himself for the difficult task of viewing the body. This wasn't something he'd done often—it wasn't something he wanted to do often. He tried to swallow and couldn't.

Ranger Harris pulled on his blue gloves, crouched down beside the still form, and took hold of the corner of the sheet. He started to pull it back, then glanced up at Win to make sure he was ready.

Win nodded and wished he'd thought to hold on to the deck railing as he looked down at the pasty white face. He fought down his queasiness and blinked to focus on the victim below him. Someone had closed the man's eyes and cushioned the head with a beach towel. *A kind thing to do,* Win reflected. The ranger pulled the sheet completely off the body and they stood side by side and studied the corpse. It was a young man. Maybe mid-twenties. . . . Caucasian, buzz cut, trimmed beard . . . deep, purple wounds on his lower face and his neck. He was on the shorter side, maybe five nine. Not a big guy.

The ranger bent down and lifted the man's hands for Win to see. The skin was stark white and puckered, but not damaged. *Should be able to lift prints.* No wedding band, no jewelry of any sort, no visible tattoos. The clothes were intact—blue T-shirt, cargo pants, work boots. It all looked perfectly normal. Well, except for the heavy hemp rope tied around the lower legs, one length of the rope extended. No fraying on the ends, no sign of a cut. Looked like a knot had simply come undone.

Harris was speaking. "He hasn't been in the water too long, would be my guess. But at this water temperature, it's hard to know. The extreme cold can preserve a body remarkably well. The lake stays close to forty-seven degrees this time of year within ten feet of the surface. Much colder at depth."

"Did you look for an ID?"

"Yes, sir. Nothing in the pockets. Not even a dime. Tried not to disturb too much, but no ID, keys, nothing. His clothes are basic. Nothing expensive, nothing out of the ordinary. With the work boots, I'm thinking he might be a seasonal employee here in the park." Win nodded and the ranger pulled the sheet back over the body and they both stepped off the boat and onto the dock. Win pulled off his gloves and stuffed them in his pocket. He hadn't touched anything, and he didn't intend to until the Evidence Response Team got here.

"What do you think?" he asked.

Ranger Harris looked surprised by the question. "Well, our killer or killers went to some trouble to hide the murder . . . but they didn't go to enough trouble. Rope came loose, from an anchor, I'd bet. I'd do a check of every boat in the marina and see who's missing an anchor. Everyone who docks here has to sign a search release, so we won't need a warrant."

"You've got surveillance cameras on the marina, on the boat slips?"

The ranger frowned and shook his head. "No, but that sure would help. We've been requesting them for years, but, you know, budget issues." He cleared his throat and looked back down at the boat's deck and the covered corpse. "I'd also look for the weapon. Someone laid into him pretty good with maybe a wrench, metal pipe, heavy flashlight, something like that. The area where the body was recovered is about eight hundred feet offshore, depth is less than forty feet. If it had been another hundred feet further out, the lake floor drops beyond three hundred feet. . . . No chance of recovering anything. Might be able to do a weapon recovery at forty feet with a commercial magnet."

It was Win's turn to be surprised. "You do many weapon recoveries here?"

"Not here, no . . . but I worked for the San Diego Police Department before I joined the Park Service. That's how we'd handle a potential weapon recovery. I was amazed at how often killers dump the body and the murder weapon in the same spot."

Win took a deep breath of the cold air—it hurt. "Okay, let me reach out to my boss again. He's already put a call in to the Teton County Coroner, and we've got an FBI Evidence Response Team working out of Jackson right now—they're scheduled to fly back to Denver tomorrow, but we're checking to see if we can get them shifted up here. Can you get some folks to start looking for a boat without an anchor? What about missing persons reports? We'll need to cover that. And the weapons check is a good idea. Can we make that search at first light?"

"Sure, sure. Oh . . . one more thing," the ranger added. "If your people approve, I want to get the body into a bag and get it under ice. They pulled him out of the lake at 9:22, shortly after sunset. It's 10:49 now. If the body has been in the lake for several days, it can start to decompose very quickly once it's outside of the water. The coroner won't be here until after midnight at the earliest if he's coming out of Jackson."

"Okay, let me clear it and we'll get photos. Won't take me but a minute." Win pulled out his phone and made the calls.

It was a professional body recovery given the circumstances. A woman had snagged the victim's shirt with an eight-pound fishing line; the body may have been floating free, or easily came loose from the anchor or whatever was weighing it down. Win was hoping the ERT folks could figure that out. The boat driver had the good sense to record their location on GPS, and the three men had managed to get the body on board their boat with minimal trauma. Minimal trauma to the body, that is. The poor woman who'd snagged the body was falling apart when Win interviewed her in a ranger's small office fifteen minutes later. The rangers had called the clinic near the hotel and asked the doctor to see the distraught woman tonight. Win figured they'd give her a sedative, something to help her sleep.

Win finished up the FD-302 interviews with the witnesses just before midnight. He stood outside the compact two-story ranger station and watched several flashlights bob from boat to boat on the smooth surface of the inlet. Ranger Harris walked up the concrete boat ramp and stood beside Win. "We've checked every boat in the slips for a missing anchor, and we're startin' in on the ones that are moored. There are only seven boats moored right now, so this shouldn't take long."

"Anything?"

"No. And no reports of anyone missing. Not here at Lake, anyway."

Win raised his chin in question.

"The park has a recovery going up on Grebe Lake, northwest of Canyon. A couple of kayakers carried inflatable boats from the trailhead to the lake. They didn't account for the wind that comes off the mountains in the late afternoon—it can get real choppy. They tumped. The lady was close enough to shore to swim out, the guy didn't make it. The water in the mountain lakes is usually some warmer than Yellowstone Lake, but if you fall in you've still only got minutes before hypothermia sets in. Water stays real cold in this park, even in mid-summer. They're trying to find the guy's body."

The ranger sighed and seemed to be searching his mind for something positive to report. "Oh, we've got our new search-and-rescue helo up there helping with the recovery. It's got all the bells and whistles, even some thermal-imaging capacity."

Win knew the lack of a rescue chopper in the park was an issue; he'd run into that limitation in earlier cases. "The new chopper is based in Yellowstone?"

"Yes, sir, up in Mammoth. You have no idea how much that will help us. We haven't consistently had a designated rescue helo stationed here, been using one for combined rescue and wildfire suppression, also sharing one with Grand Teton ever since I've been here. That's over three years. It will be great to have our own bird in addition to the medevac chopper. It will save lives."

* * *

There wasn't anything else to do at the marina. The coroner was wrapping up and Buck Harris was organizing a detail to secure the boat until the FBI's ERT arrived. That probably wouldn't happen for hours. Win got in his Explorer and drove the three miles back to the Yellowstone Lake Hotel. He drove down the lane where Tory's little yellow cabin sat; he slowed down to a crawl as he passed it. He wanted to hold her again, wanted to feel her touch. He fought down that longing, drove another couple hundred yards, and pulled up behind the one-story structure that housed the Lake District Ranger Station. His headlights illuminated two Park Service vehicles, the seventy-foot radio tower, and the compact, nearly hundred-year-old log building, with its tall stone chimney and outbuilding. The single-bulb porch light gave off a pitiful amount of illumination. Win took a minute to scan the building's dark exterior and small parking lot. Nothing seemed to be lurking in the shadows that could eat, gore, or trample him.

Ranger Harris had given him the key code to enter the rear of the building. He punched it in, opened the back door, and was met with more darkness and the strong aroma of coffee.

A woman's voice called out from a dimly lit room in the front, "Who's there?" Win could hear radios crackling in the background.

"Win Tyler, FBI."

An older woman with wild gray hair poked her head around the corner of the adjoining room. "Buck said you were comin'. Coffee is in the breakroom, showers are at the end of the hall. You can crash in the bunk room. That's second door down on the left. A couple of gals are already asleep. Make yourself at home, but since the girls are in there, you might wanta keep your pants on." The dispatcher's head disappeared as she tended to her radio traffic.

Okay then. He wasn't accustomed to coed bunk rooms, but he was too tired to really care. His priorities were a hot shower, a clean bed, and hopefully three or four hours of sleep. Tory had texted that she could meet him for breakfast tomorrow, or rather today, it was past 1:00 a.m. Now he had a murder investigation, gunrunners, ATF, Alex . . . and why hadn't he heard from Kirk on the helicopter company raid? Even an unofficial *"We got 'em!"* would be nice to hear. And not a word from Will on the backpacking trip. And then there was Shane. . . . He stopped in the dark hallway and tried to still his racing thoughts. *Lordy.*

*   *   *

He was having a hard time getting his mind to settle. And yes, Dex knew it was his own damn fault that he was stuck in this trailer staring up at the ceiling at 1:05 a.m., stewing over how he shoulda handled something, rather than being out doing something productive to get himself out of this mess. He swatted at a mosquito that had made it past the screen windows. That's all he needed, bugs gettin' in the camper.

He'd stayed real close to the campsite since his run-in with the FBI man at Dad's Sunday night. Here it was going on Wednesday and he was still fretting about it. He'd gone over it again and again. Why in Sam Hill had he laid into that FBI agent? That was an automatic trip back to the pen—and not just the state lockup, where he could be on his best behavior and be out in a reasonable time. The Feds had no parole system. Get sent to federal prison and you were stuck for most of your sentence. And the sentence for assaulting an FBI agent was likely a lengthy stay. What was he thinking! He should have just gone in with the guy, let him do his interview, and acted dumb. That generally worked for him. Surely they couldn't match the dead bison to the gunpowder he'd used to create those big rounds. Surely, they didn't have DNA workups on buffalo? *Surely not.*

He shifted on the uncomfortably thin mattress and turned the small plastic fan toward him. Its low hum cancelled out the buzzing of the pesky insect. His mind immediately fell back into the same loop it'd been runnin' for the last hour or so: And even if they did nail him on the poaching charges, so what? It was maybe a stiff fine, maybe thirty days in the county jail . . . it wasn't likely to be real prison time. He'd actually read up on it some on those days when he'd taken Shane to the Gardiner Library to use their computers, to send Katie's sister emails and pictures from the boy, to catch up on the world's news. He'd checked out some stories on last spring's poaching cases in the national forests and parks—mostly the culprits were just gettin' fined, losing their hunting licenses for a few years. Hell, he didn't even have a hunting license, no loss there. And it wasn't like they'd taken out some rare animal, a grizzly, mountain lion, wolverine, or some such. No, they'd only gone for bison bulls. Hell, there were thousands of bison in the park. Even the dudes who'd been caught killing the endangered animals were just getting fines, suspended sentences, probation, that sort of thing. So why'd he get so worked up over this deal? Get himself in real trouble?

He swatted in the darkness at the buzzing insect again and sighed. He could generally tell the seasons by the way the critters acted. He knew without looking at the calendar that it was coming up on mid-July. He knew that 'cause Canyon was over 7,800 feet in elevation, it didn't warm up enough at night, up past fifty-five degrees, for the mosquitoes to be out until then. Bitin' flies, buffalo gnats, them was a different story. They tolerated the cold better and they'd been out for a couple of weeks in the lower areas. But the mosquitoes, they generally waited for mid-July. And mid-July meant he had even less time to get Shane back to his aunt, to get him back to school, to prove to them all that at least he had that part of his life in order. It was time to go get the boy, one way or another. It was time to move on—it was *how* to move on that was causing the lack of sleep.

He was in a fix. He didn't need a police scanner to know that they had a BOLO out on him, a warrant for assault. By now they'd probably figured out that he'd sold the blue truck and had his new ride. By now they might even know about the stolen Arizona plates on the truck. They'd probably figured out he'd been borrowing vehicles in and out of the park to get around. They probably knew he was hiding out in the RV parks; there was evidence of cannibalized camper trailers at Dad's place. That brought up another problem.

He only had until tomorrow afternoon at five to vacate the camp-site. His fourteen days in the Canyon Campground were up. He should have handled that before now. Hell, there was so much he should have handled differently that one more issue hardly mattered. Where could he go? He had a buddy from his army stint who lived down in Texas, then there was a girl he'd spent a lot of time with . . . she was divorced now, she lived somewhere outside of Sheridan, Wyoming. One of them would put him and Shane up for a few days till he got back on his feet. But then there was Shane. Because of his stupidity with the agent, he hadn't dared make a move to get Shane back yet. He'd screwed that up too.

And the latest texts from Jesse were concerning. Dex knew it wasn't smart to communicate too often, and he was down to his last two burner phones. Jesse generally kept the text threads to a bare min-imum. But here he'd received a text from Jesse each day since Saturday. He hadn't answered the last two "How ya doing?" messages during the previous two days, but it was the text late this afternoon that had him concerned.

Outa the blue he'd gotten a reassuring text that said: **Bad weather is blowing over. Clear skies! Mr. Green needs an estimate on a new roof. When/where can you meet him Wednesday?**

On the surface it looked like their code. A casual observer would think it was simply a work order. Dex had done handyman jobs for Jesse's rental company and clients ever since they'd reconnected well over a year ago. But *Mr. Green* or any reference to *green* in their mes-sages always meant there was a payout waiting for Dex. He figured this must be the ten grand that Mr. Yé was supposed to be sending his way because of the "extra" bison taken in the botched hunt last week. Jesse was wanting a meeting. But something was off. Something was way, way off.

Him whipping that FBI man had to have stirred up a hornet's nest. Jesse Gibbs had connections. Jesse had to know there was a warrant out on Dex for assault. . . . He sighed again. And at this point the cops might have enough on him to charge him with vehicle theft. He'd lost count of how many vehicles he'd *borrowed* since this mess began. It wasn't just the FBI involved—no, a Park County Sheriff's cruiser had pulled up at Dad's that night. The locals were on it. If the locals were on it, then Jesse was on it.

Jesse had the reputation to uphold, him being a respectable businessman and all. Dex had read in the local paper weeks ago that Jesse was now president of the West Yellowstone Rotary Club, that he'd been selected to be on the small town's planning commission. He knew Jesse rubbed shoulders with folks in city and county government, in both Gallatin and Park Counties. Jesse woulda had his nose to the ground from the moment that bison shoot went sideways. Hell, Jesse probably knew about his fight with the FBI man before he even got back to his camper in Yellowstone that night. Nope, weren't no *clear skies*. And Jesse Gibbs had to know that. Either the Feds had nailed Jesse and were forcing him to finger Dex, or Jesse was making some other play. As much as Dex didn't want to admit it, as much as it weighed on his soul, it was that last possibility that was feeling for real.

* * *

He'd been at the marina well before dawn and out on the water for over an hour working the unsuccessful attempt at the murder weapon retrieval, so he was a few minutes late when he walked into the hotel restaurant just before 6:45 and saw her seated at a table near the window. Her pack was leaning against the wall beside her; she'd already checked out of the cabin. She was in her hiking garb, as she'd once called it: brown cargo pants, hiking boots, a T-shirt under a tan safari shirt. Her hair's auburn highlights were gleaming in the early-morning light that streamed in through the windows; she had it pulled back loosely with a beaded barrette. She looked relaxed and refreshed . . . and downright gorgeous.

She glanced up from her phone and saw him walking toward her. She smiled that amazing smile and he suddenly felt lightheaded. Could be the lack of sleep last night, could be the stress of the job, he reasoned. But he knew better. He had fallen in love with Tory Madison and every time he saw her, he fell that much further.

"Hey, Tory . . . glad you could meet me this morning," he said as he pulled out a chair. "Again, I'm sorry I had to leave so abruptly last night." He hadn't told her exactly why he'd had to cut it short, just that it was a work emergency. He'd been thankful that she had no pointed questions. She simply said, "I understand. Go do what you have to do. Maybe I'll see you before we leave tomorrow—just let me know." Then she squeezed his arm and smiled at him before disappearing into her cabin.

He still wasn't totally convinced by her remarkable level of understanding. Apparently that was obvious. She picked up her teacup and nodded at him. "Really, Win, no worries. I'm sure you could tell I was really tired last night. It had been a super long day." She raised her chin and smiled at him. "The evening was perfect."

Not quite perfect, he thought. *I didn't get that goodnight kiss.* She blushed a bit and he figured she was reading his mind. He gave her a sheepish grin. "You sleep okay?"

"Oh, yeah! Sleeping in a real bed after nine straight nights in a tent, I slept like a dream. Did you get any sleep?"

"Enough," he said as he dropped his ball cap down into the empty chair next to her wide-brimmed hat and jacket. He nodded at her phone. "Enjoying being back in civilization?"

"Playing catch-up." She held up her phone and nodded. "We've got a girls' group—friends from college, even high school friends from Franklin—we do devotionals or short blogs a couple of mornings during the week. I've been so out of touch with no cell service that I'm behind . . . I just added my contribution. I attached some photos, kinda making it like a series of short stories with pictures."

"May I see it?" he asked as the waiter appeared, brought him coffee, and refreshed the hot water for her tea. He read the three short paragraphs, looked at the four photos of baby grizzly bears. Her brief devotional on God's provision was touching and sweet. "You're a good writer."

She grinned. "You think so?"

"Uh-huh. This is great . . . I'm serious."

She dipped her head and shrugged. "Ahh . . . Lauren and I have talked about doing a series of children's books. Maybe use my photos and some of her illustrations . . . make it about God's wild creatures." She blushed again and he thought how attractive the color on her cheeks made her look, how he kept getting lost in the depths of her soft-brown eyes, how—

"Oh, Lauren and I talked this morning for a few minutes. Did you know she and Tucker are seeing each other? Did you know they've been out several times?"

"No . . . no, I didn't know that." *Seeing each other*, he noted that phrase.

The waiter interrupted them with an invitation to join the breakfast buffet. The food was fantastic, and the company was even better. He was a breakfast guy, and she teased him when he piled three more huckleberry blintzes on top of his second helping of scrambled eggs and bacon. He knew this might be the last time he'd have a chance to eat real food today. Since he'd gotten to Yellowstone, he counted himself fortunate if he managed to snag one decent meal a day.

She was finishing up another cup of tea, and she apologized for checking her phone again when it dinged. She glanced at the text and looked back up at Win. "The guy we brought out to see the doctor isn't going to be able to go back to camp," she said. "The doctor is gonna keep him here and treat the bite with IV antibiotics." She shook her head. "Soooo looks like I'll only be hiking back in with Tracy this morning."

He immediately felt his chest tighten in concern. "Just the two of you in that restricted area? Is that safe?"

Her look became serious, and she studied him for a moment before she answered. "The area we're working in, the Pelican Valley Bear Management Area, it's over forty thousand acres, and it has one of the highest grizzly bear densities in the lower forty-eight states. We try to hike in larger groups, three or more, but sometimes you have to do what you have to do." She could tell Win wasn't liking that answer. She shrugged. "Tracy will be carrying a rifle in addition to our bear spray. We take precautions, we don't take unnecessary risks, but we're working in the bears' territory." She paused and locked eyes with him. "I've seen the cop shows. Is *your* job always safe?"

"Yes, usually it's safe. . . ." *Except when it isn't,* he thought as he felt a twinge of pain in his shoulder from the beating he'd received three nights ago. "I'm an investigator, not a cop. The local and state police, SWAT teams, game wardens, even the park rangers, all those folks have dangerous jobs. Mine? Not so much."

She cocked her head and gave a playful sideways look at the fading bruise on his jaw. "Ah, so you're clumsy. . . . Just walking into trees? Didn't you spend a few days in the ICU in May? And most times when I've seen you since, you've had a few scrapes and bruises." She lightly ran her fingers across his skinned knuckles and glanced into his eyes again. "Just clumsy?"

"Maybe," he replied softly, and he tried to deflect her valid points with his best slow smile.

He wasn't sure if she was buying it or not, but she reached over and touched his other hand. Her gentle eyes were locked on his when she spoke. "Life is full of dangers, that's why we depend on God's protection. Our trust is in Him. I'm not saying there isn't fear or doubt, but we lean on our faith." Her voice was confident, and he realized she was saying that she understood the dangers of his job and had accepted them. She was green-lighting a relationship with a good man who carried a gun.

CHAPTER TWENTY-TWO

They walked out of the restaurant into the busy lobby. When she excused herself to go down the hall to the powder room, he stood by the magnificent tile fireplace, dropped her heavy backpack at his feet, and checked his phones. Tory's ranger escort and her research partner would be here any minute to pick her up for their short drive to the Pelican Valley Trailhead on the north side of the lake. She would be back to tent living for the next couple of weeks, and he wouldn't see her again until who knew when. He fought down the sharp sense of loss those thoughts brought on. He tried to shift his attention.

He glanced at his personal phone first. Still nothing from his brother, darn it, but his Bureau phone held a half dozen texts and voicemails related to the body in the lake. There was also a short text from Alex Lindell—she'd been correct when she confronted him at his house yesterday—she was being pulled off the gunrunning case. Her curt message said she was heading to Jackson for a debrief this morning, then flying to Calgary. But it was a short text from Kirk that really got Win's attention: **Not good on the chopper. Real bad. Talk later.**

Tory was walking toward him when he glanced up from his phone. He must have been frowning.

"Bad news?" she asked as she stopped in front of him.

He pocketed the phone, shrugged, and tried to smile. "Just lots going on . . . one of those days where I'm not sure where to start." But suddenly he knew exactly where to start. He took one step toward her, pulled her close with his left hand, and framed her delicate face with his right. Her soft eyes were locked on to his and the surprise that he saw there shifted to longing as he pulled her to him and kissed her.

Win Tyler had no idea how long they held that kiss, no idea what everyone milling around the lobby thought, no idea what else was happening on his jumbled list of critical concerns. What he did know was that for just a few moments he was telling this beautiful, kind woman how he felt, telling her far better than his fumbling words could. He also knew from her response that she'd gotten the message loud and clear.

He finally pulled back just a little and rested his chin on her soft hair. Then he kissed her gently on the forehead before whispering in her ear, "Be careful out there, Tory Madison. Don't forget me."

* * *

It took a good portion of Win's willpower to force his mind off that lingering kiss, to force his thoughts off the beautiful woman who'd completely captured his heart. He stood at the back entrance of the hotel and waved as Tory, Tracy, and the ranger pulled away. He had to physically shake his head to get his focus back on the job, to compartmentalize his thinking. He was normally very good at that—at separating his work from his emotions—but every nerve was tingling. The air he was breathing even felt different. *Whoa! Get a grip, Win!* He took a shallow breath and held it, then a deeper breath, then he opened the back door, walked past the reception desk and down the hall to the café for more coffee.

His watch said 8:05. He checked his phone for service and found no bars; there'd been cell service minutes ago. He sighed with frustration as he walked back into the hotel's reception area. The bellman pointed him to a spot in front of the reception desk where you could sometimes make a call. Win walked back over and tried it. It worked.

He touched base with Ranger Harris first. Harris said that he was discontinuing the attempts to find a murder weapon in the lake, and that the four ERT members had finished up with the boat and the victim's personal effects. They had gone to employee housing to find a place to crash before they drove out later this morning.

Win knew that the body would be in Jackson by now, probably got there a few hours ago. His meeting with the Teton County Coroner last night wasn't long. The guy just did the required certifications and told him the body could have been in the lake several days—he unofficially guessed more than three but less than ten. With the lake's temperature so low, he wouldn't have a firm answer until he'd completed more tests. Win wouldn't get an official cause or time of death or anything else that wasn't obvious until an autopsy was completed. The autopsy could be done in Jackson or be moved to the Wyoming State Crime Lab in Cheyenne. Harris didn't know where the body would end up; that decision would be made somewhere up the ladder.

There were still no leads on any missing persons in the area, and Harris was devoting more time to that issue today. *Somebody has to be missing the poor guy,* Win thought as he wrapped up the call with the ranger. Before leaving the marina last night, Win had asked that the man's fingerprints be transmitted to the FBI's Criminal Justice Information Services Division, or CJIS. He'd hoped to get a hit on the prints before dawn, but he was still waiting on those results as well. Waiting on results never seemed to get easier.

His next call needed to be to his supervisor with an update, but a text from his boss changed his plan. **Call Kirk.** That's all it said, but it told Win that Jim had too much on his plate. It also told Win there was fixing to be more on *his* plate.

Kirk answered on the third ring, sounding exhausted.

"Jim just texted me to reach out to you," Win said by way of greeting. "Problems?"

"Yeah . . . like I'm not even sure where to begin. . . ." The voice sounded far away. "Has anyone told you what happened in West Yellowstone yesterday?"

"No." Win held the Bureau phone tight to his ear as he walked to a less-crowded corner of the reception area. The phone signal got weaker.

"Someone in the judge's office screwed up the paperwork on the search warrant and we—me and two agents outa Denver—we didn't get into Vista's office at the airport until right after ten yesterday morning." Win heard the guy take a deep breath. "There wasn't anyone there except a receptionist . . . she looked, like, just out of high school. I think we nearly scared her to death. Anyway, the pilot, Jimson, and the chopper we were trying to track down had flown out at 8:30 to pick up two clients at Big Sky Resort. That's in southwestern Montana, about fifty-five miles north of here."

"Yeah, okay."

"Anyway, I had no more than handed the warrant to the receptionist when she picks up a call from their clients in Big Sky. No helicopter. Over an hour overdue to get them." Kirk paused.

Oh, geez. A sinking feeling hit Win's stomach. He knew from Kirk's tone where this was going.

"Found the wreckage in a ravine just before dark last night, about three miles east of Highway 191. Only the pilot on board. I came back to West Yellowstone this morning to wait for the NTSB investigators to fly in." Win heard Kirk suck in a deep breath.

"Chopper we're after, pilot we're after, both going down just before we raid the business. . . . I take it we're treating it as a crime scene," Win said.

"Oh yeah. Like, no one believes in coincidences in the Bureau. And we've got a webcam from a construction zone on Highway 191. Uh, that's the highway that runs north from West Yellowstone to Big Sky. Jimson, the pilot, he was like, paralleling the highway at about 4,000 feet . . . we're guessing at the altitude. Anyway, at 8:46 yesterday morning we have a webcam shot of two small simultaneous explosions on the chopper—one near the tail, another in the cockpit area. Then it drops like a rock."

They both paused for a moment and Win felt a wave of sadness wash over him. He wondered if someone had notified the pilot's next of kin, but he stuck to business.

"Witnesses?" he asked.

"Not that we've found yet. It's, like, really rugged up there. The rangers said it went down in the Grayling Creek watershed in the Gallatin Range. The crash site is within Yellowstone's boundary—the highway jogs through the park for several miles along the Montana-Wyoming border, so no houses around. It's a two-lane road, not even much traffic. Having the highway webcam footage is a gift." Kirk took a breath again. "And before you ask, the chopper didn't have a flight data recorder, and someone disabled the surveillance cameras at Vista's office near the helicopter pad. As of this morning, they'd been offline for at least twenty-four hours."

Okay then, the bad guys are thorough, Win thought. "What's the plan?"

"Jim wants you back on the poaching case, at least until we can get more resources in play. The crash happened in Montana and within the park, so our office still has jurisdiction. One of the Violent Crime Squad agents who was with me when we got to the wreckage said she smelled C-4 on a piece of the tail section. So Win, it's real obvious these dudes have upped the ante. This isn't just about dead bison anymore."

"No . . . no, it's not," Win replied. "You're the case agent, Kirk. What do you want me to do?"

Kirk didn't hesitate. "Pierson is our only known suspect. He was in the military, we know he could have worked with explosives on that Lamar Valley construction project—we know he's dangerous. Jim wants him brought in. I'm trying to get some other bodies to Mammoth to help you, but like half the Lander RA has that norovirus, that stomach flu that's going around. We may have to get the Marshals and the rangers involved. . . . You may be on your own for a while."

"Okay. I've been dealing with a murder at Lake Yellowstone since last night. I'm in the *waiting-for-results* phase here. I need to meet with our ERT folks, who I'm sure will be coming your way, and then I'll hand this case off to the rangers for the day."

The phone connection was starting to break up. Kirk's response was garbled. ". . . homicide? Seriously? . . . real crime doesn't . . ."

"I'm losing you," Win replied into the static. Kirk repeated his last thought. "I'd heard nothing happens in Yellowstone—" Kirk said just as the call dropped.

Yeah, I'd heard that too.

* * *

Dex Pierson knew he wasn't the sharpest knife in the drawer, but he also knew he'd always been bullheaded. When he set his mind on a thing, he tended to keep moving toward it, moving forward. Unfortunately, during his forty-two years on this earth, so many of the things he went after weren't his to begin with. He'd always been inclined to steal things. Some folks thought it was because he was lazy, but that wasn't it. Often the theft took way more effort than acquiring the object by honest means. Maybe it was the thrill of being on the wrong side of the law. He wasn't sure. But he was sure that he could be single-minded about reaching a goal, and on Wednesday morning that goal was getting Shane back.

He relaxed into the tight seat of the older gray Camry he'd borrowed and watched Ellie Bordeaux herd the three children into the old clapboard depot building that housed the Gardiner Community Library. He'd forced himself out of bed at 2:00 a.m. last night and finally made his move. He'd been scouting the gravel road to the Bordeaux place since well before dawn with his night vision optics; he'd seen Luke turn onto the near-empty highway and head south toward Mammoth in his Ford F-150 just after 5:30. He figured Ellie would be home alone with the kids. As he watched Bordeaux's red taillights fade, he'd waffled back and forth on his next move. It was a bad tendency of his, thinking just one move ahead. He'd never be good at chess.

His plans got firmed up when a Park County Sheriff's Office cruiser pulled off the highway and stopped at the entrance to the gravel road. Luke's truck wasn't even out of sight on the highway when the cruiser pulled in. Dex sighed in disgust. *Some sorta handoff, dammit.* He'd made himself more comfortable on the ridge where he could overlook the road, reminding himself that he was a hunter, that waiting was part of the game.

He'd been sitting on that ridge a long time when Ellie Bordeaux finally drove up to the Sheriff's cruiser in a cloud of dust and waved. She stopped and talked to the deputy for a few seconds and then pulled her little four-door Toyota pickup onto the highway and headed north toward Gardiner. He sprinted down the ridge to the car that he'd borrowed from the Canyon Campground around three last night. He managed to follow Ellie and the cruiser out of the park and into Gardiner. They were far enough ahead of him that he didn't see where either went, but there weren't a lot of places to go in the community of nine hundred. He'd slowly driven down Main Street, then toward the high school. He spotted her vehicle in the library's tiny parking lot on the far end of Park Street, across from Arch Park.

He knew the town's modest library was only open a couple of days a week, and this morning there wasn't much activity. Just four other vehicles sat in the compact lot. He'd pulled the Camry to the side of the street and watched as Ellie Bordeaux lifted computer bags from the back of the pickup and shooed a little girl toward the front door. Shane and the Bordeaux boy were standing in front of the truck watching ten or twelve elk graze in the mostly barren park that lay between the depot building and Yellowstone's famous Roosevelt Arch. Finally the woman had all the kids rounded up, and they headed for the library's front door.

This was the perfect spot for what he had in mind; the long, narrow frame building was isolated. The volunteer-run library was in an old railroad depot that was a good two blocks from any other buildings on the far west side of downtown. The Gardiner High School football field was a couple hundred yards north of the library—not a soul in sight there. The school complex and the modern Yellowstone Heritage and Research Center were much farther down the street, but there was little traffic on the road. The historic stone arch, which was dedicated by President Theodore Roosevelt in 1903 as the north entrance to Yellowstone National Park, sat less than one hundred yards up the slope to the south. It was crawling with tourists, but their focus was on getting the perfect photo. Nobody was going to be watching the goings-on at the isolated library on the other side of the small park.

The cool air rushed in as he powered down the window. He turned off the ignition and stretched his legs out under the steering wheel to wait and watch. Dex had heard that the townspeople wanted the depot building to be designated as a National Historic Site. After all, it had welcomed the park's first visitors back at the turn of the century. But the Northern Pacific Railway's track was long since gone and the 1903 building was showing its age. He'd come to the library a few times to check out books for his father and discs for the old man's ancient DVD player. He'd thought then how nice it was that folks gave up their free time to make things available to others. He supposed that was something he should do someday—volunteer for something. Help someone out without expecting anything in return. *Won't be happenin' anytime soon,* he mused.

Time slipped by as he sat watching the library entrance, no police in sight. He figured she'd brought the children here to use the internet for a better connection. He figured the Wi-Fi wasn't any better at her remote house than at his father's trailer outside of town. He glanced at his watch. It was 10:02. A few more cars came and went. He'd wait another few minutes, let them get settled in at whatever they were doing. He wanted to walk in and get Shane out of there with as little drama as possible.

He checked his face paint and tooth caps in the rearview mirror again. He shifted the 9mm in its holster and pulled the ball cap down lower on his buzz cut. He started the car, raised the window, drove fifty yards down the street, and eased the vehicle into the library's gravel loading zone, where he could see the building's entrance. He angled the Camry for a quick getaway and pulled the handle to open his door. That's when something totally unexpected happened.

* * *

Sometimes it was like the intricate jigsaw puzzles that his elderly great-aunt prided herself on being able to complete in hours. Dozens of pieces of information floated around in his head, each competing for a connection, for a slot that filled in another part of the puzzle. This is how he'd solved cases before, this is how he did it. So Win let his mind wander as he drove the busy Grand Loop Road north toward Mammoth, back to his office to retrieve the Bureau Expedition and his needed work gear, back to meet Kirk later today and await orders from Jim.

During the drive he let his subconscious sort through all the data, find the right spot for the critical intel, discard the unimportant. He'd used this method of analysis on other cases, mostly financial or securities fraud, back in his first office in Charlotte. Seeing the whole story, fitting those clues into the proper slots—those were areas in the investigative process that he knew he was good at. But for some reason, the poaching case wasn't falling in line. Something was off and he couldn't put his finger on it. He was missing something big. He could feel it, but he had no idea what it was.

His thoughts kept drifting to the ghostly white face that was frozen in time . . . back to the sounds of the gentle waves lapping at the edge of the cold, dark lake, back to the smell of fish. He wondered who was missing the young man who had no defensive wounds on his arms or hands, who apparently had been caught unaware by his killer. Win knew the prints they'd taken from the puckered fingers weren't in the best condition, but still he'd been hoping for results from CJIS before now. It was coming up on mid-morning and he had dozens of questions and very few answers. The clues and leads, such as they were, weren't falling into place.

He'd driven for more than thirty minutes and thankfully hadn't been slowed too much by animal jams. A glance at his fuel gauge told him he needed to fill up. He pulled into the Canyon Service Station and checked the texts on his personal phone. Mom had texted last night wanting to know how Will's camping trip was going, and Win had intended to text Will then, but Tory was a wonderful distraction. So he'd sent Will a simple **Hello?** before he left the Lake Yellowstone Hotel, and he texted his mother that he'd call the guide service on the satellite phone tonight if Will didn't touch base. Win double-checked his calls and text messages again. Nothing from his little brother since the backpacking trip began two days ago here at Canyon. Nothing.

* * *

The two women who barged out of the library's front door to its narrow porch were in a heated argument, wasn't no doubt about that. Ellie Bordeaux had been an all-state basketball player, Dex had learned that during his internet search. Those competitive days might have been twelve, fourteen years ago, but she looked fierce as a wildcat right now. She was waving her phone and shaking her long black hair as she glared down at the compact woman facing her. The other woman's messy brown hair was the same color as her clothes; she was wearing what his mama would have called a "pants outfit" with heels that didn't suit the uneven concrete landing. The shorter woman had a notebook in one hand, and she was motioning back toward the open door with the other. That lady was pale and plain and just as ramped up as her Cajun competition. She was yelling something up into Ellie's face.

Dex shrank back in the seat a little, kinda glad he was out of earshot, and wondered if this was comin' to a fistfight. Just as the Bordeaux woman threw up her hands in apparent defeat, Shane sprinted out the open door and went flying past the women, dodged the metal book drop box, and dashed around the corner of the building. Both women stopped and stared.

Dex started the car, slung gravel with his acceleration, and he swung around the old structure, hitting the power button on the window as he went. He skidded to a stop about twenty feet in front of the running boy. "Get in!" he yelled out the window. Shane dodged, then stopped, then looked totally panicked. The boy didn't know who to run from now—the two angry women, or the wild man who'd nearly run him down with a car. He pivoted and started to head for the parking lot. It suddenly occurred to Dex that Shane hadn't recognized him. He let go with a two-finger whistle. Shane stopped his escape in midstride and rushed back toward the car. Dex had been training Max with whistles; he knew Shane would understand.

The kid piled into the passenger seat, and Dex had them moving down the dusty street before the door latched. Dex glanced in the mirror and saw both women standing beside the building, staring at his taillights. He was hoping his quickie job of smearing caulk on the license plates would make them impossible to read. He took a breath and turned to look at the boy. Shane was halfway down in the floorboard, staring up at him, his flushed face a study in joy. Dex focused on that face for a long beat, then his eyes went back to driving.

"Good to see you, Shane. Stay down and cover up with my jacket." That's all he said. He wasn't trusting himself with words right yet.

He slowed and pulled through the stone archway that heralded the entrance to Yellowstone. None of the dozens of tourists jockeying for a photo at the arch even glanced his way. The official entrance booths to the park were less than a half mile beyond the arch. His dusty gray Camry eased into line behind three other vehicles. The seconds ticked by as he waited his turn to enter; he heard a distant siren just as he pulled up to the booth. He fished forty bucks out of his billfold, handed it to the smiling lady ranger in the enclosed booth, and thanked her for the park's newsletter and the map of Yellowstone that she held out with his change.

She touched her flat straw hat with one hand and waved down at him. "You have a great day, sir!" she said in a chipper voice.

"I already have" was Dex's reply.

* * *

It's about time! Win glanced at the text notification from Will as he poured himself a cup of coffee at the Canyon Service Station. He pocketed the phone, grabbed a candy bar, and walked up behind another customer to pay. Now he'd be able to let Mom know that Will was fine, one box checked off his ever-expanding list. Since he temporarily had cell service, he needed to touch base with his supervisor, check back in with Ranger Harris, see if Trey—

He said a greeting and held the door open for an older couple to enter before he walked to his truck. After settling into the Explorer,

he pulled his personal phone from his pocket and looked at the photo
and the short text his little brother had sent minutes ago. A so-so
photo of Will in front of a high, ropelike waterfall, with a smiling, out-
doorsy-looking young woman hanging onto his shoulder and, behind
them, the blurry image of a burly man. All three grinning hikers were
drenched in the spray.

Win picked up his coffee to take a sip, then stopped and looked
closer at the photo. The man in the background looked familiar; Win
used his fingers to zoom in. His breath caught as he read the text: **Me
Ginger and Tank in the wild!** *Tank?* The juvenile detention officer in
Ogden, Utah, had told him the street name of one of the gunrunners
in Yellowstone was *Tank.* And the grinning man in the background
looked a lot like Deputy Chad Maddox of the Park County Sheriff's
Office. A lot like him. Kirk's words from this morning flashed through
Win's mind: "No one believes in coincidences in the Bureau." *And neither do I.*

*   *   *

At that moment, several miles northeast of where Win sat in his old
Explorer at the Canyon Service Station, Chad Maddox, a.k.a. Tank, was
once again repositioning the pop-up tent for what had to be the two
most narcissistic human beings on the planet. After the very early-
morning hike to the waterfall, Ginger had taken most of the group to a
stunning overlook called Dawn Point, on the rim of the Grand Canyon
of the Yellowstone, while he was stuck at camp babysitting these two
fools.

He'd learned that the young couple had made their considerable
fortune as internet influencers. They'd booked the backpacking trip
at the suggestion of their business manager, who felt they needed to
change focus, reconnect with nature and other human beings. *Not
like that's gonna happen,* Tank thought as he glanced at the two twenty-somethings who were stretched out in the shade, intent on their
downloaded video games, while he moved their tent, sleeping bags, and
packs to the spot they'd requested. Each morning they'd complained

that the ground was too hard under their tent, and each morning he'd nodded and smiled and moved their tent to a *better* spot. Never mind that the ground felt hard as a rock because, for the most part, it was solid rock cushioned by a couple of inches of sandy dirt and their sleeping pads. Never mind that all the spots in the primitive campgrounds were the same: same dirt, same slope, same rocks. But he moved them each morning, just as they requested. Not once had either one of them offered to lift a finger to help or thanked him.

He tried to shift his mood as he went about his practiced tasks of reorganizing the camp for their second night at this backcountry campground. Overall they'd had a very good trip. The weather had cooperated, there'd been no mishaps, and the wildlife viewing had been above average. They'd seen a black bear and her two small cubs on the way back from the waterfall this morning, and they'd watched two grizzly bears digging for roots along the river yesterday afternoon. A couple more of the big bears had crossed near them on the slopes of Mount Washburn. Dozens of elk, deer, and bison, in addition to several coyotes and foxes, had made appearances. Still no signs of a wolf, but since there were fewer than one hundred in the entire park, spotting wolves wasn't a slam dunk. All the usual critters had appeared, and the two sisters from Vermont seemed thrilled to have photographed a badger the first evening out. They kept showing the big weasel's photos to anyone who'd look. A badger? *Go figure.*

He normally wouldn't be comfortable with Ginger leading the group of five by herself to the canyon's rim, given the dangerous terrain, but having the Tyler kid with the group was a huge plus. Everyone called him *Tyler,* and no one except the staff knew whether that was his first name or last. He was cool with it; in fact he was cool with most everything. He obviously didn't come from the entitled background that most of their clients were products of—he was good-natured, appreciative, and always quick to help. The two older ladies had taken to Tyler like mother hens. He was amazed that the kid never seemed to tire of their endless questions about his life on a Southern farm. He'd been a little concerned about the kid at first—knowing his big brother was the FBI agent he'd dealt with at old man Pierson's place initially had him on edge—but the kid had actually been a lot of help around the camp, and after the first day Tank's concern had subsided.

He moved to the fire ring and stirred the banked coals until they glowed red, then he repositioned the metal tripod that held the kettle over the smoldering fire. A glance at his watch told him the rest of the group should be arriving soon. He wanted to have the coffee and tea waiting before their early lunch. This afternoon's hike was to a backcountry thermal area just beyond Sulphur Creek that included Inkpot Spring and several active steam vents. That portion of the Mount Washburn Spur Trail was more challenging than any they'd attempted so far, but an exceptional thermal field in the middle of nowhere was worth the effort. He dropped some kindling on the embers, blew on them a couple of times, and sat back on his heels as the flames caught. He glanced up when one of the gamers approached.

"Hey, dude, when are we gonna hit the grid again?" the spandex-clad young man asked. He gestured to the mobile battery pack he was holding. "Not much juice left—I'm gonna need a charge to finish my game. Can you scoot up to the park and get me a fresh battery?"

Tank forced himself to smile up at the guy and act contrite. "I'm sorry, but that's not possible, we're still in the park. We won't get back to the facilities at Canyon Village until tomorrow afternoon." He made himself sound upbeat. "But we'll be there before you know it! Just one more night in the woods. Can I get you a snack? Not long till lunch. The coffee and hot water will be ready in a minute. Coffee, maybe?"

The man just screwed up his face and scratched at the piercings on his earlobe. He seemed to be thinking. "Then give me one of your battery packs . . . okay?"

Tank shook his head *no* and wished he could arrest the entitled jerk for something or maybe beat him to a pulp. Since those two options weren't possible given the circumstances, he smiled up at the guy again. "I sure wish I could help. Canyon is several miles from here, but we'll be there tomorrow," he repeated.

The guy finally shrugged and glanced back toward spandex girl, who was still intent on her video game. "Wow . . . that's lame. Can't get good help," he muttered as he turned away.

Tank watched the guy's retreating back for a moment with narrowed, flinty eyes. *Forget an arrest. Beating him to a pulp is the better option.*

CHAPTER TWENTY-THREE

Win was on the phone with the Park County Sheriff's Office as soon as he got the Explorer rolling out of the gas station parking lot. He asked for Deputy Maddox and was told that he was out for the day. He caught a break; Deputy Sullivan was in the office.

Win didn't want to jump right in on his suspicions about Maddox, so he began his questions with the search for Dex Pierson.

"Nothing on Pierson," Deputy Sullivan said. "But apparently you were right about him moving around in stolen vehicles. We've got two more to add to the list. And we did get his fingerprints off one of those. The confirmation on the match came in earlier this morning. He's picking models that he can hot-wire easily . . . he apparently uses them to come in and out of the park and then abandons the car and steals another one. That's how he got away from us so easily the other night at his father's place. Stole a pickup from a neighbor about a quarter mile away and left a stolen Kia in their driveway. That vehicle came out of the park on Sunday afternoon, and the rangers found the neighbor's pickup at the Norris Geyser Basin Monday afternoon. Nothing was reported missing out of the vehicles. No sign of the black Dodge he owns now." She sighed. "Dex Pierson is real good at disappearing, but we're keeping an eye on Bordeaux's house, where his son is staying. We'll stay on it."

"Okay, thanks. I'll call you if I hear anything on Pierson from our folks," Win said. Then he switched gears, trying to sound nonchalant.

"Oh, I'm curious about something. My little brother is on a backpacking trip and he sent me a photo . . . had a guy in it who looked a lot like Deputy Maddox. The text says the guy's nickname is Tank."

"Ah . . . well, Chad could be out hiking. . . he does have a second job—not sure what it is. Second jobs aren't uncommon with our seasonal deputies," she said. Win stayed quiet. "Do you need something on this?" she finally asked.

"Yeah, if you don't mind . . ."

He could tell she was puzzled. "Hold just a minute and let me get you what I've got."

Win drove around the huge lot, searching for a parking space near the Canyon Visitor Education Center, while he waited on hold. He needed to find the Park Service's Backcountry Ranger Station and see if the rangers could tell him where the photo Will texted had been taken.

Deputy Sullivan eventually came back on the line. "Sorry that took so long. It's ah, Westland Adventure Excursions, out of Jackson," she said. "I'm not sure what Chad does for them. They're registered as park concessioners, so I guess they operate all over Yellowstone. I'll text you the company's office number in Jackson and Chad's personal cell phone number. I looked at Chad's schedule and he won't be back at work here until this weekend. He took a double shift last Sunday, July 11th, that's the night we saw you up at Mr. Pierson's place. He got off duty at midnight that night."

She was kind enough not to mention Win's stupidity on the night of the 11th, so Win kept up the questions. "Any buddies that he runs with?"

"Chad sticks to himself pretty much. When he's off duty we never see him."

"Have you ever heard him called by the nickname *Tank*?"

"No, I've never heard that." She was getting suspicious. "Is there a problem?"

"Probably not . . . I was just surprised to see him in the picture, and I—"

She cut him off. "Ah . . . ah, hang on—"

Win could tell she'd turned away from her phone. He could hear someone in the background but he couldn't make out the words.

"This isn't good," she said. Before he could respond, she added, "We think Dex Pierson snatched his kid from the Gardiner Library eighteen minutes ago and was headed toward the park."

* * *

They'd driven past the turnoff to the Bordeaux place. His plan was to keep Shane under the jacket on the floorboard until they cleared the high-traffic area around Mammoth, and then switch vehicles at some isolated trailhead and head south on the Grand Loop Road to his hideout. But that wasn't Shane's plan.

"Where we going?" the small voice asked from beneath the coat.

"I got a camper at a spot you're gonna love. It's down at Canyon . . . down near those big waterfalls that I took you to see a few weeks back. We'll stay there tonight."

The small voice was tentative, wavering. "What . . . what about Max? We gonna get Max?"

Well, Hell. Dex closed his eyes for a second, then glanced ahead at the busy road. *We leave the dog behind. . . . Shane will understand. Just explain it to him.*

"Whaaat about Max?" the small voice asked again. Dex knew this was coming, but he thought he could handle it. He was wrong about that. He drew a deep breath and slowly eased the car off the highway onto the next gravel turnout. He glanced at his watch. They'd cleared the park's entrance booths five minutes ago. They were less than a mile past Bordeaux's road.

"Just missed the turnoff," he lied. "You keep down till we get off the highway. We wouldn't leave Max behind." He waited for a break in the traffic, swung the Camry back on the road, did a U-turn, and headed back down the hill toward Bordeaux's property. *This ain't smart,* he thought. But smart or not, it was the right thing to do. Maybe he'd find favorable karma, or plain old good luck, if he aimed more often at the right thing to do.

They crossed the wooden bridge that spanned the narrow Gardner River and separated the gravel road from Highway 89. They bounced along the rough track for a minute before Shane popped his head up and bounded into the seat. The boy fastened his seat belt when the car's alarms started dinging. He glanced up at Dex and smiled. "I'm glad you come to get us."

"You knew I would."

The boy nodded and turned to look out the window. He nodded again.

The first mile of Bordeaux's entrance road was across a sagebrush flat, no trees to speak of now that they'd left the stream behind. Dex knew from his reconnaissance that the gravel road turned to dirt and climbed into a lodgepole-and-spruce forest, then up to a plateau where the ranch-style house sat. He knew Bordeaux owned a forty-acre inholding within the park; he also knew the rough road was two miles of one way in and two miles of one way out and they were on it. He kept glancing in the rearview mirror and saw nothing but dust.

"When'd you get a haircut? A different car?" Shane asked.

Dex grinned down at him. "Lost the beard and the shag—needed a summer look. Borrowed the car from a nice lady in Gardiner. My rig is down in Canyon." He slowed to a crawl to miss a deep pothole. He didn't need to bust the oil pan; he wasn't used to driving off-road in a passenger car.

"We're gonna get it real dirty," Shane said.

Dex glanced over at Shane, who was suddenly subdued.

"We'll wash it good before we give it back to her—you kin help me do that. . . . Something on your mind?"

Shane nodded slowly and drew a deep breath. He was looking straight ahead at the approaching forest.

"Miss Ellie and Mr. Luke took me to see Papaw yesterday evenin'," he finally said.

Dex sat up a little straighter in the seat and looked over at the boy. There was a tear sliding down the child's cheek.

Shane sniffed back more tears and kept talking. "Papaw said he was gonna die soon, said that was okay with him, that he had Heaven comin' up next and I'd see him again. He said the medicine they were givin' him for the pain would be taking him away, said how much he appreciated me coming to stay with him."

The child paused and Dex felt his grip tighten on the steering wheel, felt his heart tighten in his chest. He started to talk, but Shane wasn't finished. "Papaw said I needed to get on back to Aunt Stacy's, said you had things you needed to tend to and that'd you'd be comin' around to see me when you could." Dex blinked a few times, there was dust in the air. The boy cleared his throat and sniffed again before he kept talking. "Said it was gonna be okay . . . said Aunt Stacy was real anxious to see me and Max, that I needed to enroll in school, they'd be startin' school middle of August." He sniffed back more tears. "You know what he said? Papaw said I's smart . . . says I's a hard worker, says he thought I could be a railroad man like he was, or maybe a soldier like you and Mr. Luke was, or even an FBI man like Mr. Win."

Dex dodged another pothole, then gunned it a little to climb the wooded hill. He looked down at Shane and tried to smile. "Your papaw is right about all that."

*　*　*

Win had just walked out of the Backcountry Ranger Station at Canyon Village, where he'd pulled out his creds, introduced himself, and asked for assistance. The office seemed to be the only quiet spot in Canyon. It was empty except for a very helpful young park ranger who told him Will's texted photo was shot at Whispering Falls, a remote spot about six miles northeast of Canyon, just off the Seven Mile Hole Trail. There was no time stamp on the picture, but she'd pointed out that it was taken early in the morning, given the angle of the sunlight on the falls, and that it could have been any morning this week, since they'd had no morning cloud cover.

She'd confirmed that the Westland Adventure Excursions group of nine were scheduled to camp at 4C6 Primitive Campground tonight for a second night, and that they'd arrive back in Canyon sometime tomorrow afternoon. She'd handed him a trail map where she'd written the tour company's emergency satellite phone number. Chad Maddox and Ginger Sayers were the guides on this week's trip. She said she didn't know either of them, but she'd only worked the backcountry desk for a couple of weeks.

Win stood on the wide sidewalk outside the ranger station and dodged the tourists trying to make their way to the Canyon General Store, the sporting goods store, the grill, or the ice cream shop, all of which were just down the walkway. Win needed some help and he needed it quickly. Unfortunately he also didn't want to go through channels. This could look like a personal deal—his little brother was on the camping trip—and he could be jumping to conclusions. This might be nothing, probably was nothing. Still, his internal alarms were going off, his senses were on red alert.

Win stood there and whispered a prayer for guidance, for wisdom, for some much-needed help. Some of the stress lifted with the prayer, and he took a couple of deep breaths and scanned the expansive parking lot, hoping to spot an angel. He didn't see one, but he did realize that most everyone within a hundred feet seemed to have a dog on a leash. This seemed to be the dog walking area for Canyon Village; there was a whole lot of sniffing going on. He tried to move away from two particularly friendly shih tzus, whose owner was oblivious to the leashes that were entwining Win's legs. Win said a greeting, untangled himself, and drifted closer to the front of the huge A-frame Visitor Center and stood under its overhanging roof. The dogs got him thinking about Shane and Max and how to deal with that expanding problem, but his concern for his brother was beginning to intrude on the multitude of other issues he faced. He fingered the map with the Westland Adventure Excursions emergency satellite phone number. He was considering calling it.

But someone beat him to it.

*   *   *

"Hey, Ginger, this is Tara in the backcountry office at Canyon. You okay out there? . . . Cool. Anyway, an FBI agent just came in asking about your group. . . . No, no, nothing too specific, had a few questions about you and your partner, Chad, but I just thought I'd give you a heads-up before you come in. . . . Yeah, yeah, no worries. . . . See you tomorrow afternoon. . . . Enjoy!"

That's how one side of the brief conversation went. Tara, the new backcountry ranger, didn't know Ginger or Chad personally, but she knew her boss had a thing for Ginger. Tara figured she could score a few points with him by tipping his friend off that the Feds were asking questions. Some folks carried a few pills, something to smoke, just to take the edge off on a long trek—Ginger might want to lose those items before she got back into Canyon. *No harm done,* Tara thought, as she punched off the sat phone, leaned over the counter, and watched through the window as the tall, drop-dead good-looking FBI agent moved up the sidewalk.

*　*　*

Dex pulled into the empty parking area in front of Bordeaux's frame house and couldn't believe his good fortune. No other vehicles were in sight. But Dex knew the heat would be on them soon—either the cops or Luke Bordeaux or both would be coming up that dusty road in minutes. He amazed himself and projected calm as he sent Shane running to the barn to fetch Max and a sack of dog food. He remarked to the boy that it was good to live out in the country where folks didn't have to lock their doors. Shane didn't have to know that it took him only seconds to pick the lock, then jimmy and force the deadbolt to get into the house. Shane didn't have to know everything.

They'd been there less than ten minutes. Shane was down the hall in a bedroom, stuffing his books and clothes into duffel bags. Max was raising a fuss about being tied to a chair on the front porch, and a black-and-white cat was crouched on an armchair, hissing at Dex every time he got too close. *Probably serves me right.* He gave up on trying to calm the cat and checked the living room again to make sure Shane wasn't leaving anything behind. Dex had already told the boy that Mr. Luke would ship his .410 to him when they got back to Georgia. He'd told Shane that carrying a shotgun across the country wasn't a good idea. Dex hadn't mentioned that the gun was likely in Bordeaux's gun safe, and he wasn't about to tamper with foolproof locks and five hundred pounds of solid steel.

As soon as he walked in, Shane had insisted on writing a thank-you note in the notebook that sat by the cell phone booster in the kitchen. Dex dropped two hundred-dollar bills down beside the note. Shane had new clothes; he figured that should cover the cost. He hesitated, then pulled out another bill when he considered the door lock he'd just broken. *Least I can do,* he reflected. He told Shane to get his packing finished, and he did another pass through the rooms.

He found the two boxes that came from his daddy's trailer stacked against the wall in the mudroom. The FBI agent had them labeled and organized—that Fed was efficient, he'd give him that. He opened the top box and stared down at the old pictures and mementos of his family through the years. He picked up a gallon ziplock bag that held Daddy's Purple Heart, a small, framed Army photo, and a shoulder patch from 25th Infantry. Dex got down on one knee to look at the items more closely. *Wow, I'd nearly forgotten Daddy served in Vietnam.* There was another small picture in a silver frame—a smiling young couple, his mother and father at their wedding. Dex held the bag up to the light and saw the gleam of a gold wedding band and two years-of-service pins the old man had gotten from Union Pacific. At the bottom of the lot was a tarnished pocket watch that had belonged to the old man's father. *My grandfather.* The watch had been wrapped in a yellowed linen handkerchief and had come free.

Dex dropped down lower and tried to breathe. He knew it was possible that Daddy was gone . . . if not now, soon, real soon. And here he was, holding his father's life—an entire life in a ziplock bag. This time the tears that came to his eyes couldn't be blamed on the dust.

* * *

Chad Maddox needed to touch base with Roadie. He'd been out of touch with the kid since the early part of his last stint with the Sheriff's

Office, then he'd immediately started this gig. . . . *Whoa, how could it have been nearly a week?* He needed to make sure all their inventory had been moved to that cabin in Canyon, he needed to see if Roadie's sources in Utah had scored any more weapons. Surely Prince would give them the go-ahead to start moving the stash across the border soon. They couldn't sit on it forever. It'd been eleven days since he'd taken out the two Feds in Grand Teton. The heat should be beginning to let up. And speaking of that, he needed to run his traps and make sure ATF and the cops were still focusing on the interstate routes, not zeroing in on the park route. Prince would want his advice on how to move the guns. He needed to have a clear and concise plan for their next shipment.

He sat on a yellow boulder that was perfectly balanced on the brink of a vertical cliff. It was just after 10:45. He'd left the camp after the group returned and began their early lunch. Afterward, the clients would get into their hour of "personal time," as they called it. He knew the two older sisters would be napping—they'd done that every day of the trip. The twenty-somethings were still playing games on their iPads when he'd left camp; he wasn't sure who'd supplied an extra battery to Spandex Dude. The kid, Tyler, was always into his exercise routine whenever there was a spare moment.

The couple from Austin were likely scrolling through dozens of phone photos and texting them to impress friends and family. They knew the texts wouldn't actually go anywhere until they got much closer to Canyon, until they reached cell phone service. But occasionally a rogue service band swept over them and every device dinged and buzzed. He knew those odd occurrences were caused by radio waves bouncing off clouds or mountains or something. He knew it was highly unpredictable, but once in a while a text did go through. You couldn't count on it, though, and that's why he was cradling a Garmin inReach Mini—the expensive little sucker could send and receive text messages when there was no cell service for miles. It had no voice capability, but that was okay. He didn't want most of his sources hearing his voice anyway.

He stared down at Yellowstone River, a green ribbon nearly a thousand feet below him. The river's roar was a gentle rush from this height. The wall of lodgepole pines that lined the south rim stood only six hundred yards from him across the chasm. This spot was dramatic. It was one of the narrower stretches of the twenty-mile-long canyon, a good place to escape from the demands of the tour. There was enough of a breeze at the canyon rim that the biting flies hadn't found him, and an overhang on the boulder provided just enough shade to make the spot comfortable. He forced his mind off the demands of the clients, off the day's schedule, off the jobs coming up. He tried to relax—he'd picked the perfect spot to do just that.

He never got tired of watching the rock's colors change as the sun marched across a cloudless sky above what folks called the Grand Canyon of the Yellowstone. He'd heard that the deep-yellow, pink, and white of the near-vertical walls were composed of rhyolite lava that had been altered by exposure to hot water and steam to create its brilliant colors. He'd also heard that the Native people, who hunted here long before the White men came, named the river and its fascinating canyon after the yellow sandstone found along the stream. Whatever the true reason behind the naming of the place, as he watched the late-morning sun change the scene to golden, there wasn't any question why those early explorers had found *Yellowstone* a fitting name.

He took in a deep breath as his eyes scanned the beauty before him. He shifted the bear spray on his belt and ran a hand through his thinning hair. *Time to get down to business.* He powered up the small device and waited for it to lock in on the satellite feed. He should have received at least three updates from Roadie since he'd been out in the boonies, but there were none. That was concerning. He hadn't talked to Roadie since real early on July 8th, the day he and Deputy Sullivan had raided old man Pierson's place with Tyler, the FBI agent. After he cussed Roadie out for calling him that morning while he was on duty, the kid had said he'd scored something big, said he'd fill him in later. That was nearly a week ago.

He sighed as he stared down at the empty screen for Roadie's contact numbers. The kid was normally dependable. He sent a quick text to Roadie's current burner phone: **You at Canyon Village?** Maybe they could touch base when he got the tour group back in tomorrow afternoon. Maybe Roadie was overwhelmed with moving all those guns to the fourplex in Canyon. Tank knew the kid wasn't happy about having to handle the transport of most of their inventory by himself. Maybe he was pouting, hadn't texted because he was ticked off—Roadie could get that way. Maybe that was it.

He checked his other texts on the device. Prince had texted yesterday afternoon, short and sweet: **All Good.** That was his style. Tank sent back **Ok** to acknowledge the contact. The final text was unexpected. It had come in early this morning from his source in the West Yellowstone Police Department. They rarely communicated on the phone or on any device that could conceivably be traced. *That's weird.* The message was even weirder: **Vista bird down. T-Bone in play. Am out. Watch yourself.** *What the hell?*

Texting the guy back wasn't an option. Their code word *out* meant the source wasn't open to contact now. He stared off into space. The West Yellowstone Police Department was tiny, just a few officers to cover the town of fourteen hundred that nosed up against the west side of the big park. His source was a newer patrol officer; he needed to be cautious. The officer had a checkered background that Tank had been able to dredge up. It had only taken a little cash and the threat of blackmail to turn the guy into an asset. He didn't need to push it. But he did need to figure out what the hell the message meant.

Vista? The only thing that came to mind was Vista Transport Services, a helicopter company that did shuttle and transport work for guide trips in the backcountry of the surrounding national forests. He'd seen their choppers at Gardiner's little airstrip every so often. The word *bird* fit, since lots of military and police types referred to helicopters by that term. But recreational helicopter trips weren't allowed in Yellowstone National Park, so he wasn't sure how that reference related to him. Vista was the same company Prince had mentioned as a possible method for shipping the guns, but they'd decided months ago that any movement of the weapons by air would be too risky.

And *T-Bone*? That thug was a lowlife loser who hung around the periphery of the park and orchestrated the sale of meth, Ecstasy, and who knows what all to the seasonal workers who flocked to the area during the summer. He'd run the scumbag out of Gardiner more than once this year after confiscating the dude's inventory of pills and cash. He'd managed to pay his rent for two months with that last take. He smiled to himself. No point arresting the guy when he could handle the resale of the product himself. He leaned back on the big boulder and thought about it. T-Bone Dawes had reasons to want payback, but no, he couldn't see it. The dealer wasn't stupid, he probably thought losing a little product to a dirty cop was just part of the cost of doing business. But Chad had heard that Dawes could be bought for muscle, knew most of his prison time had been for assaults. But how did T-Bone tie in with a chopper going down? Or were the two items even related? How did those two apparent warnings relate to him? What did the text mean?

He glanced at the short message again. His hand went to the bear spray, then to the fanny pack that he wore every waking moment when he was off duty. He felt the firm outline of the Colt 1911 through the fabric. *Watch yourself,* he read again. He knew exactly what that meant.

CHAPTER TWENTY-FOUR

If Win was expecting an angel to appear in the Canyon Village parking lot, it came in an odd form. Alex Lindell's little silver SUV pulled right past him as he stood mulling over his options in front of the Canyon Visitor Education Center. Her vehicle miraculously scored a parking spot right across from the entrance. The small woman hopped out as soon as the SUV stopped moving.

She hadn't seen him amid the crush of tourists, and he watched her hurry for the restrooms at the other end of the building. He crossed over to her SUV and waited beside it. He didn't have to wait long. Alex was scowling at her phone as she walked toward him. Alex was in go mode.

"What are you doing here?" she demanded as soon as she saw him. It wasn't a friendly greeting.

"Good to see you too," Win said, trying for a neutral tone. "You're headed to the debrief in Jackson?"

She sucked in a breath that came out as a sigh. "Just got some cell service, just got a text. They moved it to early this morning, and I missed it. Stuck for nearly two hours on the highway—two different places—with bison standing on the road. On. The. Road!" She was fuming and he wasn't sure if it was because of the bison jams, missing the meeting, or her life in general.

He shrugged. "Happens here. It's a national park, not a thoroughfare." For some reason his mind went back to the Quantico training supervisor's description of Alex: *a good officer, sharp, capable, proficient with her weapons.* Win had prayed for help; he knew enough about his God to realize that answered prayers often came in unexpected forms.

He took a step closer to her and lowered his voice. "Maybe there's a reason you missed that meeting. We may have something here. Dex Pierson now has a federal warrant out on him for assault. I got word that he nabbed Shane in Gardiner this morning and drove toward the park." Her head came up a little and he figured her eyes behind the dark shades were steely.

"And it's looking like he could be involved in the sabotage of a helicopter and the death of the pilot in the bison-poaching case I'm working. . . . That happened yesterday morning." Her head came up a little more as he kept talking. "And Pierson does have that black-on-black pickup registered to him—"

"You're thinking he's tied to the poaching *and* the gunrunning? You're thinking he's mixed up in both?" She was using her Mountie tone of voice now. She was dialed in.

"It's possible . . . he could be anywhere in the northern part of the park by now. But during the time that Pierson's been on the run, two vehicles have been reported stolen from the Canyon Village area, right here. Pierson has a history of selling camper trailers. Mammoth has an RV camping area, but it's fairly open, relatively small. I can't see him hiding out there. Canyon has one of the largest RV campgrounds in Yellowstone and it's totally wooded. It would be the perfect place to disappear."

"Have you gotten the BOLO on what he's driving now? Where he was last spotted?"

"Waiting for it to come in before I call my supervisor, before I get the rangers involved. Can you make some calls, get the okay to work with me on this?"

Alex pocketed her phone. She popped the back gate of her SUV and dug through her bag for hiking boots, a ball cap, and a long-sleeve shirt, then she reached into another bag for her body armor. She was pulling her handgun box out of the passenger seat as Win walked to the shade of the Visitor Center overhang to make another call. He knew she wasn't taking a chance on being told to stand down. She wasn't making any calls. Constable Alex Lindell was gearing up.

* * *

Dex grabbed a pair of Bordeaux's binoculars and walked out to the side deck to look though a break in the big trees toward the highway. He knew they were cuttin' it too close. They'd pulled away from the library at about 10:15, and here it was going on 11:00. He could see the sun reflecting off at least two vehicles near the wooden bridge that led to this house. It was a long way off and he couldn't make out much, but he figured it was Ellie Bordeaux and maybe a Park County Sheriff's vehicle. They were probably waiting for more backup or for Luke to arrive. Neither of those things was appealing. His getaway route was totally blocked. It was time for plan B. Problem was, he didn't have a clue what plan B was. Walk out? Not a realistic option with a dog and a little kid. He'd seen a four-wheeler near the barn, he could hot-wire that, but they'd have to leave the dog and their stuff behind.

"We leaving?" Shane had come onto the deck behind him.

Dex told the lies smoothly as he continued to watch the vehicles in the far distance. "The car is broke down, won't start, but we need to get moving. I want Miss Ellie to be surprised by your nice note and the money we left them. We might walk—"

"Why don't we take Mr. Luke's four-by-four down the river trail to the road?"

Dex whipped around so fast that it startled the child. "What?"

Shane took a step back, then tried again. "Uh . . . uh, Mr. Luke's got one of them Bad Boy Bandits, you know, them four-by-four off-road little truck-like things. It can carry all our stuff and us too. Miss Ellie said they got it a while back. We took it once to go swimmin'."

"You know where the keys are? You know where the trail is?"

Shane nodded. "Yes, sir! I even know how to drive it!"

* * *

Ranger Buck Harris's call came in before Win ever reached the shade of the Visitor Center's portico. "Hey, we got a hit on the man in the lake," Harris said. "Word got out among the seasonal employees about a body, about a drowning. You know how rumors spread. Well, anyway, a young woman who works at the restaurant here at Lake Yellowstone came in about an hour ago. She described the deceased to a tee, said he'd been living with her in employee housing off and on since late May. She hadn't seen or heard from him since last Wednesday, July 7th."

"I'm in Canyon now, hitting the phones, but I still have nothing on the fingerprints," Win said. "Who was the guy?"

"She says his name was Wayne Benson. She said he worked construction and maintenance for one of the concessioners here in the park, but she didn't know which one he was with. . . . She said he was often out of touch for two, three days at a time, but after the seventh, she's heard nothing and her calls have gone straight to voicemail."

Harris lowered his voice. "She figured he was just ghosting her, dropping out of their relationship. She told me that he'd been gone a lot during the two weeks leading up to July 7th." Harris paused. "She was thinking he might have shacked up with another girl."

"Well, if her calls went directly to voicemail, it means the phone was either turned off or the battery was completely dead. We'll need his phone number and her phone records, might be able to narrow down the date of his death based on that data. Did you check out their living quarters?"

"Yes, sir, that's where we are now. I came over here with her to the duplex they shared. He left a few items of clothing here, nothing much really. . . . I've got one of our evidence response folks coming over to collect things. She's given her permission for all that." He paused. "I've bagged a couple of burner phones, but I'm not sure they've ever been used. He left a Cordoba classical guitar. That's why she thought he'd be back. That's why she didn't report him missing, thought he'd come back for the guitar."

Win's professional detachment began to crumble at the thought of the woman staring at an abandoned guitar, hoping and longing for the man in the lake to return. The milky white face drifted through his mind again. He had to clear his throat a couple of times before he asked, "Uh, is she okay?"

The ranger's voice got even lower. "She's in shock over the news. She still thinks it's a drowning, that's the talk down here. I've got a female ranger coming over to sit with her. . . . I figured you'll want to interview her this afternoon."

"Yeah, let me get with my supervisor, see how he wants the interview handled. I'll get back with you, or have someone get back with you, shortly. Find anything else?"

"There are some things we need to check out. Like I said, she thought he might have moved in with some other girl, so she kept some papers she thought might be clues. She showed me a couple of notes our guy scribbled on a notepad, first one said *#5678 Canyon.* That could be one of the older cabin numbers up there, or maybe an overflow campground site designation. It's not in our current lodge unit numbering system, so I'm not sure. Maybe someone at Canyon Village could tell you." Win heard him shuffling paper before he continued to talk. "Uh . . . then there's another note with *37 boxes* scribbled on it, like he was doodling on the paper, maybe listening on a call, then *Ex 344, I-15.* . . . That looks like an exit number off Interstate 15. If so, that would be down in Utah, the northern part of Ogden."

Win paused for a long moment to take it in. At least one of the jotted notes was a clue all right, but not of another woman. Exit 344 on Interstate 15 in Utah was the area where the Ogden juvenile detention officer had told him numerous guns were reportedly stolen by a group of teens.

He asked Harris one final question, "Ask her if Mr. Benson had a nickname, an alias that he used, anything she'd heard him called?" Win heard the ranger talking in the background as he turned away from the phone, heard a female voice responding, clearly heard *Roadie.*

* * *

Dex couldn't believe his string of good luck—maybe there was something to this positive karma concept for doing the right thing. They'd loaded up their stuff on the back rack of the four-by-four—there was even a strap-down tarp to keep the boxes and bags from getting dirty. Shane was bouncing up and down in the seat beside the dog, thinking this was a great adventure. Clearly it hadn't crossed the boy's mind that they were stealing Bordeaux's vehicle. Dex hesitated at the Camry, then he grabbed his daypack out of it. He thought about wiping it down to remove his prints, then decided there'd been plenty of witnesses who'd seen him in the getaway car, that he'd be wasting time. And they didn't have time to waste. He glanced at his watch as they drove the small off-road vehicle down into the deep spruce forest that surrounded the house. He knew the cops would be coming up the gravel road just as soon as they got their ducks in a row. He took a deep breath, told Shane to fasten his seat belt and hold the dog close, then slowly maneuvered down the slope through the big trees.

Bordeaux had done a fine job building the trail that led westward off the plateau; it meandered down the side slope of Mount Everts toward the Gardner River and Highway 89. There were switchbacks and crude log bridges, they didn't even have to dodge any limbs. They reached a point along the park boundary where the trails diverged after several minutes of *"Hang on tight!"* driving. Dex knew from the detailed map in his head that they could continue to the west and end up at a park trailhead or cut to the southeast over the top of Gardner Canyon and wind up at the Boiling River swim area. He stopped the vehicle to think it over.

The Boiling River wasn't really a river, it was a 140-degree hot spring that cascaded into the shallow Gardner River not far north of Mammoth. It was one of only two officially sanctioned swimming areas in the big park, and he knew it would be teeming with bathers in late morning in mid-July. He also knew they kept a ranger stationed there in case of trouble. He had no intention of being that trouble, so he opted to head down game trails to the Rescue Creek Trailhead. He put the vehicle in gear and started to ease forward. Shane wasn't having it.

"We have to park here and walk on in," Shane said firmly as he pointed to a short brown post that marked the boundary between the Bordeaux inholding and Yellowstone National Park. "Mr. Luke says they don't allow no vehicles on the park trails. I reckon the swimming hole is a ways further on down—more'n a mile, maybe two." Shane nodded to his left. "We gotta walk it."

Dex never missed a beat. "Normally, Luke'd be right about that, but we've got stuff we're carrying, and we've got Max, and the rangers don't allow dogs on the trails in the park. That's a big no-no. Havin' Max on the trail is a bigger deal than the vehicle." The pup straightened at the mention of his name. He gave Dex one of those goofy dog smiles, and Dex couldn't help but wonder if the dog knew he was lying.

"So having a dog on the trail trumps having a vehicle? We have to stay in the Bandit?" the boy asked.

"Yeah, that's right."

Shane seemed to be thinking on the reasoning for that fabricated rule. He perked up considerably as they continued to drive westward around knee-high sagebrush, up and down shallow ravines, and through small pockets of pine and aspen. They spooked a small herd of pronghorn antelope, which scattered into the sagebrush and then quickly trotted back to the shade of the trees with their short white tails still flicking in alarm. Shane had to hold the pup's muzzle to keep him from raising Cain at the startled animals.

"There's a hiker's bridge over the river, maybe we can catch a ride there," Dex said as they inched down a steep slope. The rough game trail finally merged into the official park trail after about a mile of tough going. Dex could hear vehicles on Highway 89, and he knew they were nearly to the river. He had no idea if the rangers and deputies had any kind of organized search going for them, if they'd made it to Bordeaux's house, if they'd discovered the four-by-four missing. It had been thirty minutes since they drove away from the barn. Maybe the law would be waiting at the trailhead, maybe they wouldn't. He shifted in the seat and subconsciously reached back and touched the pancake holster on his back. He was ready either way.

* * *

Prince was getting antsy. He'd hired another lowlife to handle Tank, but that wasn't a done deal yet. Dex had finally surfaced—well, more or less. Prince's sources in Gardiner had messaged him mid-morning, saying that Pierson was suspected of snatching his kid from social services or from someone—that part wasn't real clear—at the town's library. The source thought the cops had tailed Pierson into the park.

He leaned back in his leather chair and drummed his pen on the mahogany desktop. He thought about it. He didn't really want to hire this hit out. He'd already hired that drug dealer, T-Bone Dawes, to handle Tank; adding someone else to the mix wasn't a good idea. He'd moved most of his assets to his Cayman accounts over the last several days. He'd had a bad feeling about this whole operation since the deal went south during the Chinese trophy hunt. The poaching deal was done, and he'd been well paid. At least there was that.

And his other venture was still solid, no crisis yet. The guns were all consolidated at the rented cabin in Canyon, but they didn't do him a damn bit of good just sitting there. It was over a seven-hundred-mile run from Canyon to Calgary on secondary roads. He'd drive up through the park, past Bozeman, Helena, and Choteau, then through the Blackfeet Reservation to the out-of-the-way Piegan border crossing. From there he'd drive through several First Nation Reserves, then on to Calgary, where the buyers were waiting. They'd already used that route three times this summer and it had gone off without a hitch.

He drew a deep breath as he leaned forward over the park map he'd laid out in front of him. He had to concede that their previous runs had been successful because Tank had run interference with the law and Roadie had driven the transport vehicle. Now Roadie was at the bottom of Lake Yellowstone, and Tank would soon be meeting his end somewhere along the slopes of Mount Washburn. He frowned down at the map. The helicopter wasn't an option any longer . . . he'd second-guessed that move a time or two. *But hell, what's done is done.* He stared down at the map and blew out the breath.

Maybe just cut your losses and leave now, a voice whispered in his ear. He glanced at his ostrich-leather go bag that sat in the corner of the office. It contained everything he needed to get on a plane. He could drive out to West Yellowstone's airport, get on standby for one of Delta's puddle jumpers to Salt Lake City, then catch an international flight. He had standing visas for Ecuador and Bolivia tucked in the bag with his array of fake passports. His consulting work as a financial adviser opened lots of doors and gave him tons of access. Convenient that neither country typically honored its extradition treaties with the U.S. He could simply fly to one of those destinations and lay low for a few weeks until he could change identities again and move on to his condo in Grand Cayman. He loved it there—beautiful beach, great climate, no crime, accommodating bankers—his kind of place.

But leaving with things hanging wasn't how he wanted this chapter of his life to end. All he really had to do was find and eliminate Dex, make sure T-Bone took care of Tank, then get those guns to the buyer in Calgary. The gun sale would add at least another $250,000 to his coffers, and flying overseas from Calgary might raise even less suspicion than trying to get out of an American airport. He glanced at his Rolex: 11:35. His plan was in motion, just sitting here thinking about it wasn't doing him any good.

He glanced up from the map at the soft knock on his door. The gray-haired woman stuck her head in and smiled at him. "Mr. Gibbs, the dealer just called, they're dropping off the coach in the next fifteen minutes. He's asked a couple of volunteers from the club to help you load the boxes. I told him you'd take it for a spin in the park, then drive on up to the reservation. I said you'd get back with him over the weekend."

He returned his secretary's smile with a sly grin and nodded. "He's wantin' to sell me that high-dollar coach, that's what he's wanting! Hey, is he attaching a small SUV, something I'll like?"

Her smile broadened. "The dealer says it's a new black BMW, says you'll love it." She shook her head in mock disapproval. "You only go first-class, only the best!" Then she straightened and beamed at him with pride. "It's such a good thing you're doing—taking time away from your business, taking books and toys to those children who have so little." He thought she might cry as she began to ease the door shut. "You are an absolute saint."

* * *

They were getting ready to start the strenuous hike to Washburn Hot Springs when Ginger pulled Chad aside to fill him in on the call she'd gotten earlier from the ranger in Canyon. Chad knew his face hadn't given away his surprise and dismay—he was well practiced at hiding his thoughts and emotions.

"What do you think an FBI agent would want with us?" Ginger asked as she sipped her water.

He managed to shrug indifferently. "Probably just one of those routine inspections, you know, making sure all the paperwork's in order, making sure we've got our permits in line."

She looked puzzled. "The Park Service should be handling all that."

Chad shrugged again and shook his head. "Probably nothing," he said as he turned to rein in the spandex couple, who were drifting away from the trail and too far from the rest of the group. While his words to Ginger were reassuring, his thoughts were anything but: *What the hell! Yeah, could be big brother, the FBI agent, checking on little brother, Tyler, or could be something else.* The *something else* had him worried. After the warning from his source at the West Yellowstone Police Department this morning, he was smart enough to know that the timing of the ranger's satellite call wasn't good. *Not good at all.*

* * *

Dex was making his second trip across the log hiker's bridge that sat just downstream from the Rescue Creek Trailhead parking lot. Shane and Max stood on the narrow bridge and watched for fish. Shane was still catching up on his talking after the mostly silent ride down from Bordeaux's house. "Miss Ellie said it's real important to git your spellin' right. . . . She said the town of Gardiner and the Gardner River are spelled different cause some mapmaker in the pioneer days got the spellin' wrong. They didn't have spellcheck back then. . . . Ain't that something?"

"Uh-huh," Dex responded as he balanced the two boxes, wiped sweat from his eyes, then moved quickly up the bank toward the lot.

"Ain't much of a river," Shane remarked for maybe the third time as Dex moved past him a few minutes later with the last of the duffel bags. "These folks out here, they count every little creek as a river. They need to come South and see what a real river looks like." Shane was still staring down into the water, hoping for a fish. Max was bounding up and down, anxious to see more action.

Dex stooped to rub the dog's head and the pup shook his long black ears; the man pulled back from the flying slobber. "You take Max up to the parking lot. Keep him on the leash, but run off some of that dog's energy. We'll be leaving here soon," Dex told the boy.

There were only five vehicles in the parking lot. Apparently the Rescue Creek Trail wasn't a big attraction on this hot summer day. He'd stashed the boxes and their gear behind two scraggly pines that hugged the edge of the small gravel lot. He'd already done an inventory of the available transportation—it wasn't looking good. Every vehicle in the lot had been manufactured in the last few years. They would all have a push-button ignition and a sophisticated security system with a kill switch. He needed a vehicle that was a lot less high-tech.

Then the good karma thing rewarded him again. He turned and pretended to watch several bighorn sheep trotting along the berm on the far side of the river as an older Chevy pickup pulled into the lot and parked not twenty feet from where he stood. He pulled the cap lower on his forehead, kept his eyes on the binoculars, and touched his teeth to make sure the white tabs were in place. He hoped he hadn't sweated enough to make the garish tats on his face visible. This wasn't the time to attract unwanted attention.

He moved away from the truck to the far side of the lot, where Shane was dutifully reading the *No Dogs* signage. He watched out of the corner of his eye as two young women got out of the pickup, pulled on sun hats and daypacks, and moved past the trailhead sign down toward the bridge. They were both carrying hiking poles and bear spray; it looked like they'd be gone for a while. But they were drinking from water bottles and taking their good slow time getting into the hike. The sound of a distant siren reminded him that he didn't have time to wait.

He thanked his lucky stars as one girl pointed out the distant sheep that were heading downriver to the water. The girls quickly moved across the bridge and disappeared into the thick willows and sagebrush to follow the sheep. They'd see Bordeaux's four-by-four along the trail soon—no real place to hide it—but that was okay. He turned toward the older Chevy truck and smiled. He was now one step closer to getting them back to Canyon, one step closer to getting them in the clear.

* * *

Win stood under the shade of the overhanging roof at the Canyon Visitor Center and considered his options. His supervisor was out of pocket; he'd left a message for him as soon as he'd gotten off the phone with Ranger Harris well over thirty minutes ago. He figured Jim was tied up with the downed chopper—he might even be in West Yellowstone. Win had finally gotten a text from Deputy Sullivan saying they had Dex Pierson and Shane cornered at Bordeaux's house and were waiting for authorization from someone before they flew a drone up to see if they could confirm that the stolen Camry was there. A hostage situation with a little kid was dicey, even if it was Pierson's own kid.

Win ran through the timeline in his head. If Pierson entered the park at Gardiner at 10:18, as Deputy Sullivan had just confirmed, he could have been at Luke's house well before 11:00 . . . it was now noon. Way too long for the guy to just be sitting there aware that the cops were on him. Win knew there was a good view of the highway turnoff from Luke's side deck. He also knew Dex Pierson was a hunter and a marksman. He'd be looking for another way out, if he hadn't already found it. Sullivan said they had a cruiser stationed on the north bank of the Yellowstone River, across from the cable bridge that Luke had constructed near the corner of his property. With the river running low and slow in this mid-summer heat, that might be an option for getting away. But Win knew that wouldn't be an easy route with a little boy and a dog in tow.

Surely Pierson wouldn't have driven into Luke's place on a dead-end road if he didn't have an exit strategy in mind. *What would I do?* Win asked himself. *I'd take Luke's new four-by-four down the hiking trails to Highway 89 and steal another car. That's what I'd do.* Win knew Luke had constructed trails off the high plateau where his house sat. The house was on the northern reaches of vast Mount Everts, a twenty-two-mile-long flat-topped mountain that formed the east side of the Gardner River Canyon and towered 2,000 vertical feet above Mammoth. But it wasn't that steep or rough near Luke's place. It wouldn't be impossible to drive the four-by-four all the way to the Gardner River, ford the shallow water, and steal another car somewhere along the highway.

Dex Pierson had already shown that he was adept at disappearing. Win thought back to Dex's angry words before their fight at the trailer three days ago: *I ain't goin' back to prison!* But surely Pierson wouldn't put Shane in danger, surely he'd leave the boy at Luke's when he realized he was trapped. That would be the smart thing to do—the right thing to do. But Dex Pierson wouldn't be in this situation to begin with if his actions were smart, if his actions were right. Win hit the callback number to give Deputy Sullivan his thoughts. He waited for the call to connect and sighed. If he were a betting man—which he wasn't, but if he were—he'd bet money his main suspect in two cases was once again in the wind.

CHAPTER TWENTY-FIVE

T-Bone Dawes prided himself on being an outdoorsman. He grew up in southern Idaho, he'd done his fair share of hunting and fishing, he knew how to get around in the woods. But he had to concede it'd been a while since he'd done an extended hike—been a long while. And he was feeling it. He'd parked his car at the busy Dunraven Pass parking lot; the last, worn sign a while back said Washburn Hot Springs was still two miles ahead. So two miles to go, then he'd do the job and backtrack another several miles to the car.

He leaned against a large rock and let four hikers march around him. Everyone was friendly and upbeat. He mumbled his greetings and wiped his face with his bandana to better conceal it. Not like anyone was noticing him, really. He was good at blending in. He just faded into the wallpaper—his mother had always said that. Being unremarkable looking came in handy in his line of work—few of his victims could pick him out of a lineup.

He leaned back against the rock again and took advantage of the shade from a lone, scroungy pine. The hike along the side slopes of the 10,219-foot mountain had been mostly across open meadow, high above the tree line. The trail was well-worn and had been almost crowded on the three-mile uphill climb toward Mount Washburn's fire tower, but once he began the downward trek to the springs, the number of folks had diminished considerably. There wasn't much shade on the upper reaches of the mountain, and the 1,400-foot elevation change from the trailhead to the fire tower weeded out most of the late-morning hikers. The view from the top was spectacular, he'd concede that, and there were entire fields of yellow, red, and purple wildflowers, but he wasn't here for the scenery. Nope, he wasn't here for that.

He pulled one of his two water bottles out of his daypack and drained the rest of it. His watch said it was straight-up noon, and it was hot; he figured the temperature was well over eighty. It occurred to him that he should have brought more water, he should have realized there wouldn't be much shade on the upper reaches of one of the highest mountains in Yellowstone. He decided to drop the daypack and rest a while longer. He had all day to do the deed.

And speaking of that, he wasn't real sure who was paying him for this gig. That was a bit disconcerting. Then again, he had $5,000 in a manila envelope hidden under the driver's seat of his car, along with typed instructions that he should have destroyed by now. But he hadn't. The note told him to begin this damn hike at Dunraven Pass before 9:00 a.m., that a tour group of several hikers would be at Washburn Hot Springs by early afternoon. That group would be coming to the springs from the west, and after seeing the thermal features, they'd loop back the same way they came to a primitive campground called 4C6. They were scheduled to be back in Canyon Village tomorrow afternoon.

The typed note said that Deputy Sheriff Chad Maddox would be one of the guides for the group. T-Bone had wondered why Maddox was leading a tour group, but he didn't really care and it didn't really matter. What mattered was that Deputy Sheriff Chad Maddox wasn't going to make it back to Canyon Village alive. The means of his death was up to Dawes, but the note said that an accident in the backcountry was preferred and would result in a $2,000 bonus. T-Bone had his eye on an epic dirt bike, and 2K extra would make it his. The note said that within two days of the confirmation of the deputy's unfortunate demise, either $5,000 or $7,000 would appear in Dawes's mailbox in West Yellowstone. Simple as that.

His employer had requested an accident. That shouldn't be too hard given the territory. There were dozens of cliffs, rockfalls, and washes to fall from, and there were the steaming hot springs that lay just ahead. He could see steam, smoke, or some kind of vapor rising over the landscape to the southeast. He knew those hot springs killed folks in Yellowstone most every year. That was a possibility for the deputy's accidental death.

And T-Bone had no qualms about making this hit, that was for damn sure. The deputy was a dirty cop, a crooked scumbag who'd robbed him of $4,000 in product and a good Taurus handgun after roughing him up in Gardiner last spring. He'd had to scramble to replace the meth and the pills. He had to keep his customers happy, but most importantly he had to make sure his supplier knew he was good for the payout. You didn't mess with the Mexican cartels—they were rapidly becoming the dominant force in Montana's drug trade, and they didn't play nice. He breathed a deep sigh and took a sip of water out of his second bottle.

He wondered again who'd hired him. He knew enough about Chad Maddox to know that the guy had to have plenty of enemies. Small-town dirty cops were usually running blackmail schemes, selling drugs or guns, or offering "get out of jail" cards to folks they'd pick up for minor infractions. They'd stop a tourist for reckless driving or DUI and take a couple of bills to tear up the ticket. Dawes could see Maddox playing that game. There'd be plenty of folks who'd be thrilled to see the deputy dead.

He took another sip of water and told himself he just needed to get his second wind, that this hike would get easier, not harder. He started to pull his daypack back onto his shoulders, then he looked with dread down the long, meandering trail as heat waves shimmered in the high-altitude air. He closed his eyes and sighed. Why couldn't this hit be in a convenient spot—in town, maybe, or just off the highway? Why had he agreed to this hike through the backcountry? *Because I'm a greedy fool, that's why.*

His pulled the pack onto one shoulder, but the aching in his legs trumped his temporary surge of motivation and he leaned back against the boulder. His mind wandered again. His employer could be a woman, he mused. The deputy looked like a complete loser, but he might have ticked off some woman. If he had a list of who not to anger in the world of crime he ran in, the Mexican drug cartels would be at the top, but right below those dangerous thugs, he'd have to list *women*. There was that old saying: *"Hell hath no fury like a woman scorned."* Based on his considerable experience, it was true.

* * *

Alex was standing beside Win in the shade when Deputy Sullivan called back with a report from Luke Bordeaux's empty house. She sounded frustrated. "We've gotten no reports of vehicles stolen in the park so far, but if Pierson got to a trailhead or parking lot and hot-wired a car, the owners could be on a backpacking trip and might not know it's missing for days." Win heard her sigh into the phone. "We've got no idea where he is . . . but he's not at Bordeaux's place and like you suspected, their four-by-four is missing." Win started to ask a question, but she kept talking. "He's one step ahead of us. He's either deeper in the park, or he doubled back and headed up Highway 89 into Gardiner. The Sheriff is trying to decide whether to issue an Amber Alert—that would get a lot more eyes looking for the boy."

"How long will that take? To get out the Amber Alert?" Win asked.

"No idea. I know the Sheriff is dealing with someone at the State Attorney General's Office and at the Child and Family Services Division. . . . It may be a family custody thing, don't know. That decision is above my pay grade."

It was above Win's pay grade as well, and he had no idea how it worked. What he did know was that it was now 12:30, he'd been told by the support staffer at the Lander RA to wait at Canyon Village until Jim called him, but he was burning daylight, getting nothing accomplished. He told Deputy Sullivan to give him a call when something was decided or if she developed any leads.

Alex was leaning against one of the building's stone pillars, watching him finish the call. She closed her eyes and shook her head. "Other than eating protein bars and drinking cokes, we haven't done anything productive in the last hour. You're waiting for callbacks, I'm waiting on nothing, I say we move on *something*. Now."

"I can't go off half-cocked without some direction from my supervisor. I've told you that. I've requested backup and assistance from our
RA in Lander, and they're supposed to get back with me. We can't go
into a confrontational situation without adequate backup, especially
since Shane may be involved." Win tried to project confidence, act as
if the delay wasn't a big deal, but internally he was chomping at the bit
too. He was thinking Alex was right, but he wasn't free to admit that
just yet.

She put her sunglasses back on and shook her head again as she
spoke. "We don't even know if we have a potential confrontational situation. We don't know anything at this point. Pierson could be here or
not."

* * *

They'd made the thirty-seven-mile drive from the Rescue Creek
Trailhead parking lot to Canyon Village in record time. No bear
jams, not even a bison on the road to slow them. It was half past one,
probably eighty-five degrees, and sunny; most of the critters and a
good percentage of the tourists had the good sense to get in the shade
and take a nap. The older Chevy pickup he'd borrowed was running
smoothly and had plenty of gas, and if his luck held, the two hikers
wouldn't even miss it until late afternoon.

Dex had tried to be upbeat and show Shane the sights. He pointed
out mountain ranges with their scarred ridges where the big 1988
Yellowstone wildfires had scorched nearly a third of the park. He
talked about the vast areas where twenty-foot lodgepole pines were
struggling to repopulate some blackened areas. He slowed the truck
to a crawl so Shane could see the pronghorn antelope and bison they
passed. He mentioned the lingering snowbanks as they crossed over
Dunraven Pass and headed down the southern-side slopes of Mount
Washburn into the Canyon Village area. But the most he'd gotten was
a nod or a grunt or a halfhearted *uh-huh* in response. Shane had been
moody and quiet ever since Dex loaded the boxes and duffel bags into

the borrowed truck. There was no hiding the fact that he'd stolen the Chevy. The boy was eight years old now, he was catching on.

Dex waved to the campground host as they drove into the huge, forested RV and tent park at Canyon. When they pulled up to his spot on the backside of the big campground, Shane climbed out of the truck without a word; he pulled the dog close with the leash and stared at the camper. Shane had a sulky attitude and Dex was letting it get to him. This fatherhood thing wasn't for the faint of heart.

He glared down at the child. "Hey, look, dammit, I'm trying my best to get us out of here, to get you home." He pulled one of the duffel bags out of the truck's bed and laid it at the boy's feet. He hardly ever used cusswords around the kid, and Shane seemed a little shocked.

"We stole a truck." Shane stood his ground and made the accusation.

"No, I stole a truck, you's just along for the ride. You didn't steal anything, so get that outa your head."

"Fine! So now what are we supposed to do?" Shane was still defiant.

"We're gonna get something to eat in the camper right quick, and then we're gonna pack up and head out. We can be south of Jackson by nightfall. We'll rent a spot in a nice RV park that has a pool and get fried chicken for supper." *That might all be overly optimistic, but it sounds like I have a plan,* Dex thought.

The boy just stood there glaring at him.

"C'mon, Shane, I'll bet Max is hungry. How 'bout you get the dog food out and feed him, get him some water and walk him around. He'll be stuck in the truck for a good while when we pull out." The boy still didn't look convinced. "Tell you what. I'll park this pickup we borrowed in the shade and leave some money in it for the owner's trouble. I'll call tomorrow and tell the rangers where to find it. How is that? Will that work for you?"

Shane shrugged and stared down at Max, who was whining and pulling at the leash. The words *dog food* hadn't been lost on him. "Is that the best we can do?" the child asked.

Dex went down on one knee and pulled the boy close to him. "Yeah . . . yeah, right now that's the best we can do." He brushed back the boy's hair and looked into his face. "We good?"

Shane nodded slowly, then hugged him as he mumbled his reply. "I'm sorry I's mad at you. . . . Yeah, we're good." The boy pulled away and began to dig through the duffel bag for the sack of kibble. Dex stood and reached into the truck bed for a box. He fought the sinking feeling in his chest. *Just started an eight-year-old on a life of crime, dammit.*

*   *   *

He'd started his life of crime at a very early age. Hell, he'd gotten the street name *T-Bone* when he was only nine because of his ability to slide two or three choice steaks down the front of his baggy jeans and walk out of the grocery store unnoticed. They'd always eaten well at their shabby rentals, and his mother had been so proud of him. He smiled to himself and wondered how much of a dent he'd single-handedly put in the bottom line at the Pocatello Albertsons when he was a kid.

He was thinking back to his childhood just to get his mind off the drudgery of the trail. He knew a wandering mind wasn't a good thing out here—there were bears, wolves, all sorts of hazards. He hadn't actually seen any animals, except a few elk and two or three ground-hog-like things, but he wasn't really looking at anything except the endless path that snaked downward toward the springs. He pulled off his orange cap, wiped his forehead, and tried to force his focus onto something other than the misery of this hike.

A group of several backpackers were coming up the trail toward him. He lowered his head and continued to trudge toward them through another in the seemingly endless string of meadows teeming with wildflowers. *I've gotta be getting close,* he told himself.

"You're almost there!" the cheerful voice said as he waved a weak greeting to the lead hiker in the group. He realized that he must look whipped or he wouldn't have gotten her shout of encouragement. He stepped off the path to let them pass. The hiker in the rear stepped off the path too.

"Do you have enough water?" the young man asked. "It's really got-ten warm today." The kind stranger had noticed T-Bone's flushed face, the sweat dripping off his chin. He called for his crew to wait up, then turned back to the assassin. "I've got an extra bottle of water in my pack if you want it, sir. I'm not gonna need it." He had already taken off his big backpack and was digging in it.

T-Bone was out of breath. He just stood there and nodded.

"The steam vents and the springs are just on the other side of that bunch of dead trees." The friendly hiker motioned with his head toward a stand of white, skeletal trees several hundred yards away, as he continued to dig in the pack. "It is so worth the hike, you'll be amazed!"

"Lots of folks down there?" T-Bone asked as he finally caught his breath.

"We camped down below, so we got to the spring mid-morning. There were more people then. But there are still a few folks . . . not as many now in the heat of the day, but more than I'd expect. Height of tourist season, I guess." He finally produced the bottle of water and handed it over.

"Hey, thanks . . . maybe I wasn't as prepared as I should have been." T-Bone opened the plastic bottle and drained half of it.

"Glad to help. I've done this trail several times—the sun is really intense at this altitude, lots of open grassland up here. Not as much shade as you'd think."

"Any rangers down there?" T-Bone asked, then quickly back-tracked. He didn't need to make this guy suspicious. "Uh, you know, any educational things going on at the springs?"

"No, no, we're on the edge of the wilderness here. But there is one group that just arrived a few minutes ago. They do have guides, a guy and a gal. They were herding several folks together and describing the features. You might tag along and get some good info. I'm sure they won't mind." The guy hoisted his big pack and waved back as he started off. "Looks like your timing is perfect!"

"Thanks." T-Bone saluted with the bottle and the guy turned and rejoined his party. T-Bone drained the rest of the water and smiled to himself. *Nothing like perfect timing.*

* * *

The Newmar London Aire Motorcoach was a dream to drive, even on the winding two-lane roads of Yellowstone. Prince found himself daydreaming about handing the dealer a check for half a million and driving it off the lot. He loved the power of the big Cummins diesel engine, the smell of the fawn-colored leather furniture, the lavishness of the walnut-and-oak interior. The exterior color scheme of chocolate and gold was striking—classy and rich. And then there was the black BMW X5 hooked to the back, towing along behind. Add that to the deal and you're talking another hundred grand. He admired the smooth braking as he slowed to let a cow moose and her calf cross the road.

He chuckled to himself and shook his head at his silly fantasies. The dealer would be lucky to get this fancy rig back from the Canadians after this job wrapped up. In addition to his noble humanitarian venture of delivering gifts to needy children, he planned on dropping off $250,000 in American weaponry to his contact up north. Prince would distribute a few boxes of gifts at the Blackfeet Reservation in the U.S. near Canada, then he'd drive to their Blackfoot kinfolks' reserve just across the border.

There wouldn't be much of a search at the border crossing, he already knew that. He'd learned from experience that the border guards wasted little time digging though boxes of toys, stuffed animals, and books destined for the First Nation Reserves. He'd made the same trip once this year, loaded only with books and toys; the other two trips had contained mostly handguns, all skillfully hidden beneath presents for the less fortunate. No one wanted to put a damper on the international goodwill generated by his civic club's donation of gifts for children.

And the high-dollar motor coach with its luxury trappings stood out—just the effect he wanted to lull the guards into complacency. He had no doubt that the fancy rig with its hidden cargo of illegal guns would breeze through the checkpoint and on to the buyer in Calgary. Then he'd ditch the coach, take the little BMW to the airport, and catch a flight to South America. He'd be on the beach in Grand Cayman before the summer was out.

He'd driven into the park's entrance from West Yellowstone just after noon. The forty-mile drive from his office was slow going at the park's 45 mile-per-hour speed limit; he was pleased to be pulling into the Canyon Village lodging complex right at one-thirty. The Park Service had completed a major overhaul of the accommodations there over the last few years. There were now five modern lodges, and most of the remaining ninety-nine fourplex cabins had undergone renovation. With more than five hundred rooms and a near-central location in the massive park, Canyon Village was ridiculously busy during the summer months. From Prince's standpoint, busy was good. People from all over the world were rushing around to get from place to place, hustling to see the wonders of Yellowstone's Grand Canyon waterfalls, then off to find lunch or dinner, then off to see wildlife . . . yeah, busy was good. No one noticed another big motor home pulling into the lot, no one questioned the loading and unloading of boxes or the presence of serious men. Everyone was caught up in their own adventures. No one interfered with his.

He smiled to himself as he pulled the thirty-five-foot coach and its towed SUV parallel to the fourplex. *Cabins #5, #6, #7, #8*, the faded sign said. The grass along the sidewalk was wilting in the heat, and the brown frame structure looked a little sad sitting off by itself in the trees. The rustic cabins were scattered about in the woods between the big lodges and the north rim of Yellowstone's Grand Canyon. A trail led to the canyon's north rim which was less than a quarter mile away. The fourplex that Prince had pulled in front of was at the far end of the first row of cabins. A service road for the huge lodging complex ran behind it, and it was the closest unit to the complex's wastewater plant. Maybe that's why it hadn't yet been refurbished and was sitting empty, Prince thought. Well, not empty. If Roadie's last inventory was correct, there were eighteen AR-15s in addition to the thirty-seven new ones he'd carried there himself a few days ago. The inventory also included sixty-one handguns of various types, all in excellent condition. He knew his Canadian buyer would be ecstatic.

He opened the door to unit 5 with an old metal key, and the smells of gun oil, dust, and mildew enveloped him. He moved around the dim room to slide open the windows. No air-conditioning, no fans, it was downright scorching in the room. He opened the internal door to the adjoining cabin so that it could air out as well. He flipped on the lights in both shabby rooms, looked over the stacks of weapons that had to be packaged, and for a moment wished he hadn't killed off his helpers.

That thought brought Dex to mind. He'd come prepared to tackle that problem—to eliminate his old friend. Dex had brought this on himself, he had no one to blame but himself, and if he was stupid enough to drag his little boy into this mess, well, that was his problem. Prince knew he'd have some cell service at Canyon Village, knew he'd be able to connect his police scanner with the booster he brought with him, thought he should be able to get updates on Pierson that way. And he could always call his law enforcement sources in Gardiner or in West Yellowstone. The guy couldn't run forever. But one thing at a time. First he'd package and load the guns, then he'd handle Dex Pierson.

He stepped back out onto the narrow wooden porch, wiped the sweat from his brow, and pushed the door open farther to let in more air. He hadn't taken two steps when he spotted a guy in a golf cart watching him from the service road. He plastered on a smile and waved.

"Sir, you can't park the RV here," the affable voice called out.

Prince walked to the sidewalk and pretended not to understand. He took in the concessioner's uniform, the huge sacks of laundry stacked on the back of the cart. *Thank goodness it's not a ranger,* he thought.

"The RV." The uniformed man pointed at the mammoth motor coach and attached SUV that sat not thirty feet away. "RVs have to be parked in designated areas, not beside the cabins."

"Oh . . . oh, of course not." Prince nodded as if he'd just realized the worker's concern. "I'm just waiting for the rest of the family to get back from their hike. I'll be moving in a couple of hours, just unloading our gear."

The guy nodded and waved. "I didn't even know we'd rented this unit. I need to get you on my linen-collection list. A few hours should be no problem . . . have a great day!"

Prince took his hand off the waffled grip of the concealed Glock on his waistband. He smiled again and waved as he turned back toward the hot, stuffy room. He had a lot of work to accomplish in two hours. And then there was Dex. . . .

* * *

Finally Jim West returned Win's call, and when he did he was all business. "Your message said there was a lead on Pierson. Talk to me."

Win ran through what they knew on Pierson's location, which wasn't much. He told Jim that he'd pulled in Constable Lindell to help him, told him a drive-through of the Canyon Campground should be made, told him they needed some help.

Help was hard to come by.

"I'm back in West Yellowstone now, been out at the crash site. No cell service there, and we even had issues with the satellite phones. We've got the NTSB investigators there along with two of our Violent Crime Squad folks. ATF has been called in because of the explosions on the chopper before it went down—they've got their ERT coming, and we've got a bomb tech flying in from Denver." Jim paused. "Until you've got something solid on Pierson's location, I can't spare anyone except Kirk."

"I understand, Boss. Do I have the go-ahead to check out the campground, get the rangers involved on this end?"

"Yeah, pull in the rangers. Kirk should be halfway to Canyon by now, an ETA of 2:30 or 3:00. If you corner Pierson, and if that child is with him, keep him contained until we get some other folks there. Pierson could be our guy on the helicopter, he could be the guy who killed Beckett and the informant." Jim paused again. "Win, don't engage Pierson without adequate backup."

"Yes, sir." Win was about to hang up when Jim stopped him.

"Oh yeah, one more thing!" Win heard his boss take a breath, slow himself down. "This just came in a few minutes ago. Our folks finally got an interview with that kid down in Ogden who told the police about stolen guns going through Yellowstone. ATF put some good folks on it, and they ran it down—looks like a bunch of teens robbed a trailer outside of a steakhouse in Ogden after a big gun show near Salt Lake City on July 6th. Those kids got away with thirty-seven brand-new AR-15s. One of them said a guy named Roadie paid him $5,000 and picked up the guns in the early-morning hours of the eighth. The kid said Roadie told him a man called Tank was working with him. Roadie was bragging about the guns going to Yellowstone National Park."

Win's mind flashed to the photo of Tank standing behind his little brother, went to the words *37 boxes* a young man called Roadie had scribbled on a scrap of paper, went to that same young man lying motionless in the bottom of a boat. Win started filling Jim in on the updates he had on the murder victim from the lake. Jim wasn't in a hurry to get off the phone any longer.

Things were suddenly falling into place. Just not in a good way.

CHAPTER TWENTY-SIX

Win was conflicted. His first thought was for Will—the possibility that his brother could be on a backpacking trip with one of the principals in the gunrunning case was chilling. But he reminded himself that the nicknames might be a fluke, there might be nothing to it. Dex Pierson, however, was an immediate threat. Pierson might be the key that tied the two cases together. He could very well be a cold-blooded killer. He also might be hiding out within a half mile of where Win stood.

Alex was raring to do something, and now that he had Jim's okay, Win decided she might as well start with a drive-through of the campground while he checked out the mysterious cabin numbers. He told Alex he'd request ranger assistance for her search, but his inquiries at the Visitor Center went nowhere. He got a blank look when he asked to see the law enforcement ranger in charge at Canyon Village. Then the older ranger at the desk shook his head and gave Win the same answer he'd probably given others needing assistance that busy afternoon: "Everyone's tied up." He told Win that the Canyon District Ranger and everyone on their rescue team, as well as several of their law enforcement rangers, were seven miles away at Grebe Lake, handling the recovery of a visitor's body. Then there was a vehicle accident below Trout Creek in the Hayden Valley that had two of their folks occupied—oh, and an incident with a bison and someone trying to get a selfie down on the South Rim Trail. Soooo, if Win could hang around for a couple of hours, maybe he could call someone in.

But Win couldn't hang around for a couple of hours, so he took the campground maps he'd requested, and he got the location of the Canyon lodging reservations office, where he might discover what *#5678 Canyon* meant, if anything. He and Alex divided the job up. She agreed that driving around the campground looking for a black pickup beat standing around doing nothing.

The Canyon Campground was immense. Win and Alex pulled into the campground's check-in station and were told that the campground host and the manager were in a meeting off-site and should be back within the hour. The employee at the station agreed to check through all the current registrations. Win didn't think Dex Pierson would use his real name or the license registered to the Dodge Ram for his camping permit, and he was right. They had nothing on file indicating that Dex was one of the 270 registered campers. They were "full to the brim," the employee told them. He said they were free to look around, but he asked that they low-key it—the campground host ran a tight ship here. He didn't want any trouble.

Win had every intention of low-keying it. But he also didn't want to waste any more time. He walked out of the small office and handed Alex one of the plats of the campsites.

"I'll drive back over to the lodging reservations office, see if he's registered anywhere in Canyon Village and check out this cabin number—it might lead to something. I'll join you when I finish up there. If we find anything, we text each other, okay? Don't go it alone." Alex didn't respond and he didn't like it. Win repeated the warning. "Alex, if you spot the truck, do not go in without me."

She finally nodded, and he continued. "If Pierson stole a vehicle north of Mammoth, he's had enough time to get down here, but just barely enough time. When we do the drive-through, we have to proceed as if he's here, we have to use caution—and you have to remember that he probably has Shane with him." Win locked eyes with her. "Alex, we can't put the boy in danger."

"You don't have to lecture me on proper police procedure," she snapped back at him. "I know what I'm doing." She fiddled with her sunglasses with her free hand, dropped the eye contact, and stared at the campsite plat.

Win started to point out that she'd violated proper police procedure more than once since he'd met her, but he didn't see the point. He just turned and headed for his Explorer. He wished he had his Bureau vehicle. He had no body armor and only one extra magazine for his compact Glock 43. He didn't even have his Bureau-issued handgun. But then again, he was down here because he had a dinner date last night. He hadn't expected to be running a dragnet on a criminal.

*   *   *

T-Bone was standing beside a tall lodgepole pine, trying to catch his breath, and using his binoculars to scan the white thermal field that dropped off the side of the mountain below him. He wasn't sure what he was expecting Washburn Hot Springs to look like, but this wasn't it. He was guessing its size to be more than a dozen football fields—and it looked like a hellish moonscape, set on a precipitous slope. The ground was mostly whitish chert scarred with deep gullies and laced with active and inactive steam vents and pools. Bare trees were scattered throughout the landscape, as if someone had tossed their white remains onto the field for effect. Slimy blackish water and steaming sludge flowed from numerous holes in the mountainside.

These weren't the pretty green, blue, and orange pools he'd seen at Norris or down around Old Faithful. Nope, these were infernal-looking cauldrons where thick steam rose from most every fissure and purplish-black liquid with the consistency of motor oil oozed downward in narrow streams.

And the smell was worse than the sight of it. Many of the region's hot springs had the rotten-egg smell of sulfur, but this place smelled bad on a level he couldn't even explain. It almost made him gag. He pulled the bandana higher on his face to try to block out the stench.

His attention turned to the few people he could see wandering around the vast area. There were several folks grouped near a large, steaming pool of blackish water more than halfway up the rugged slope. He could see other people lounging in the shade of the trees about three hundred yards away, down near the trail. Apparently that bunch had the good sense to decide that one thermal feature was no different from the next. They looked like they were ready to move out of the superheated area and on with their hike.

He'd spotted Deputy Maddox almost immediately. The creep had on a tan field hat with one of those extensions that covered his neck. He wore a long-sleeve shirt and cargo pants that shielded him from the sun. T-Bone couldn't tell if the deputy was armed, but he noted the small red canister of bear spray and fanny pack hanging from his belt. He was standing beside an open steam vent that was spewing out scalding water and blowing steam every few seconds. He seemed to be explaining something to the small group.

This might be a little harder than I thought, T-Bone reasoned as he continued to watch the scene below him with his field glasses. There were more people here than he'd figured there'd be, more likelihood of witnesses, more possibilities that someone would interfere. And on top of that, he was whipped. His legs were still trembling from climbing up through the trees from the trail to get to this point on the higher reaches of the springs. Not to mention the nearly seven-mile, bone-jarring hike to get here. Then there was the heat—the white chert was amplifying the sun's glare, he could feel it radiating through his hiking boots—and add to that his lack of water. He hadn't come well prepared, and he had enough sense to know that dehydration could be a killer at this altitude.

And speaking of a killer . . . he forced his mind off his discomfort and zeroed in on the task at hand. He sloughed off his daypack and pulled out the black-and-yellow weapon. It wasn't much larger than a snub-nose revolver and didn't weigh as much. He'd gotten the top-of-the-line Taser about a year ago. It cost $1,600 online, but he'd stolen it, so he wasn't out any money. He'd never had to use it. Just the threat of the wicked-looking little contraption was enough to convince most of his victims to pony up whatever he was after.

The device shot two barbed steel probes that were attached to twelve feet of copper wire. When they connected with a target, they'd deliver fifty thousand volts of electricity. That was enough knockdown juice to incapacitate a horse. He just had to coax Maddox to within twelve feet of him and then he'd drop him with the Taser, a rock to the head, and a heave over the edge for the twenty-foot drop into the blackish, stinky goo. Given the acidic nature of the springs, by the time someone missed the deputy, there wouldn't be much to find. That was the plan . . . if he could just get the punk to come closer. Of course, his backup plan was always a possibility—several close shots with his 9mm. He'd even attached a silencer. But T-Bone really wanted that extra two grand, and if Maddox's body was pulled from the muck with bullet holes, the coroner would be hard-pressed to declare his death an accident.

T-Bone put the 9mm in the back of his belt, tucked the Taser in the front, pulled his shirt over both of them, and slowly began the steep descent toward the middle portion of the springs. He stopped to scan the area again and saw that most of the folks in the small group had turned and begun to walk down toward the trail, back toward the dark trees. His luck was holding. The deputy broke from the group and moved back up the slope toward two young people who were posing for photos in front of one of the billowing, steaming things. *This is good!* T-Bone picked up his pace and nearly trotted toward his target. They were on the bench area of the hot springs now, they wouldn't be clearly visible from the trail far below. The spewing, gurgling, roaring sounds of the springs and steam vents were cancelling out most other sounds. He needed to get close enough to Maddox to be heard, and he needed to do it now.

T-Bone skidded to a stop behind a massive white log and watched as Maddox waved to the two photo hogs, who seemed bent on ignoring him. "Hey, we're leaving!" he heard the deputy yell. "Come on, let's go!" he called out again. T-Bone saw the two young people finally moving down the slope toward the trees, saw Maddox turn to herd them down.

His eyes swept the top portion of the thermal field. No one else was within view. He stepped out from behind the fallen tree, waved his arms, and called out, "I need some help here! My wife's fallen! Please help!"

He watched as the two younger folks glanced back, then continued their slow ramble down toward the trail. Maddox turned, waved, then immediately started climbing the rough terrain toward him. The loser couldn't resist the chance to play the hero.

T-Bone's bandana was covering half his face, and his bright-orange hat was pulled down low. No way in hell the scumbag would recognize him. He turned to the side, scrambled over fallen limbs, and pointed up the steep incline toward the big belching steam thing. He had to convince Maddox that someone needed help, that someone was lying there.

"Help us!" he called out. "She's up here!"

The thermal feature was impressive. It was a gaping opening in the side of the mountain, about twenty feet tall and several feet wide. A worn wooden sign said *Inkpot Spring*. It was living up to its name— thick, blackish goo and steaming liquid flowed from its dark mouth to form a churning pool. Vapor swirled around the opening. It looked scary as hell, and it stunk to high heaven. There were no boardwalks here, no signs demanding caution, this was not a place for a misstep or a slip. T-Bone half crawled the last few feet to the top brink of the spring. He realized that he didn't have his normal energy, just about the time he realized Maddox was right behind him.

"Where is she?" he heard the deputy call out. "Where—"

T-Bone went down on one knee and whirled around with the Taser in his hand. It would have worked if his reflexes hadn't been slowed by fatigue, if Maddox hadn't suddenly been on guard. Maddox dodged and raised his left arm to shield his face. The first barbed probe, designed to hit the upper body, missed him completely, while the second one pen-etrated his shirt sleeve and lodged in his watch band. It still delivered some voltage, and the deputy was knocked flat. Once fired, the Taser was supposed to deliver current for thirty seconds; T-Bone figured he had a few seconds to spare. He dropped the device and reached for his gun. But he figured wrong. Since the first probe had missed and the second probe wasn't in contact with Maddox's skin, it didn't have enough punch to stop the man.

Maddox was stunned but not incapacitated. Rolling away from the edge of the steam vent, he pulled out the bear spray and sent a solid blast at his assailant from less than ten feet away. T-Bone's hat flew away with the orange spray, and he screamed as the high-powered pepper repellent hit him full in the face. Now he had no vision, no oxygen, no way to respond. One shot from the Colt 1911 was all it took. Maddox kicked the lifeless body off the top of the spring and watched it fall, then sink into the inky goo below.

The young man farther down the slope didn't see much, but he knew he'd heard a scream and a gunshot. Ginger had sent Will back to help as soon as the two techies reported that Tank was still at the spring, trying to assist someone. The rest of their group, and all the other hikers in the area, had moved down the trail into the forest. Will stood beside a downed tree and saw Tank standing in the upper reaches of the hot springs, then watched him walking through the foul-smelling vapor. He was quite a distance away, but Will Tyler knew what he saw that sweltering afternoon: his tour guide, Tank, had just secured a pistol in his fanny pack, right after throwing an orange hat into Inkpot Spring.

* * *

While Alex set off for the campground drive-through, Win drove to the Canyon lodging reservations office in Washburn Lodge. The office was closed, no one could tell him when the manager would be back, and he was losing his patience. He decided to flex a little of the FBI's muscle. He walked down the lengthy line of tourists waiting to check in and laid his credentials down on the desk in front of the clerk. It wasn't really in his nature to break into line, but he was more interested in getting some solid answers than in winning a popularity contest.

He heard grumbling behind him, and he turned to stare down the waiting horde. "This is police business," he announced in a voice that carried through the packed lobby. "Sorry to cut in, but this won't take a minute." He turned back to the clerk; the impatient tourists continued to glare at his back.

The gray-haired clerk looked startled as he glanced down at Win's credentials. "Uh . . . uh, everyone's out on a late lunch."

"You aren't."

"Uh . . . okay, right. Ah, how can I help you?" Now he was getting with the program.

"I need to know if you have Dex Pierson registered in any of your lodging units—or any Pierson registered for that matter—and if you have a rental unit numbered 5678 Canyon."

The clerk ran through some files on his computer. "Hmmm . . . no Pierson registered or arriving . . . and that lodging number is not in our current numbering system. . . ." The older man paused and looked back at the screen. "But I'll bet it's one of the fourplexes that hasn't been renovated yet. We have three of those buildings that still have the old numbering system. If you drive through the newer lodge buildings to the very end of the paved road, you'll run into the cabins. What we call *cabins* here at Canyon Village are just rustic frame buildings containing four one-or-two-bedroom lodging units. Some units are adjoining, all have private baths. . . ." The guy seemed set to go on and on.

Win cleared his throat and interrupted him. "Is it rented? Number 5678—is it rented?"

The guy refocused and turned back to his computer, punched in a few keys, and watched his monitor as he spoke. "Uh, okay . . . I'll bet that's cabin number five, six, seven, and eight—a fourplex. It's at the very end, closest to the canyon rim, kinda off by itself. There's a service road that runs behind it. It's one of the ones set to be refurbished next year."

"Is it rented?" Win asked again.

The man shrugged as he looked back at his computer. "Well, if it is rented, it's off the books." The guy glanced above the computer monitor at Win. "Happens sometimes when employees need a place to crash, or maybe contractors, or construction workers who aren't picky about the accommodations. I'll bet it's pretty rough." He glanced back at the monitor. "But it's not showing up in our system as even available for rent." He shrugged again. "Sorry. Let me tell you how to get there and you can go over and check it out yourself."

*   *   *

Dex had put their trash outside in the bear-proof metal box, he'd wrenched in the camper's modest awning, he'd loaded all their stuff, and then he'd parked the stolen Chevy several campsites away. He was within seconds of pulling out when he saw a woman in a small SUV slowly drive by their campsite. He watched through the slats in the camper's cheap blinds as the vehicle moved past, it didn't look like a cop car, no extra antennas. It had Montana plates, but he knew the Feds concealed their radios and used local license plates; they didn't advertise their presence.

Could be the campers waiting to take this spot, he reasoned. Could be someone lost and looking for friends at another site. But his hunting instincts were telling him *no*, warning him that the person in that vehicle was a hunter too—and she was hunting him. He trusted the instincts that told him he'd run out of time.

Shane was piddling with the TV remote, trying to figure out how to make it work. The dog was sprawled out under the table asleep. Dex called Shane over and sat the boy down across from him in the cramped space. The small fan was humming away, but it wasn't doing much to dissipate the heat. He shoulda fixed the darn air-conditioner. He wasn't sure where to start with this talk, but he didn't have to worry about that. Shane jumped right in.

"We're runnin' from someone, ain't we?"

"No . . . no, you're not running from anyone. I am." Dex drew a deep breath after he made the confession. "I need you to listen and do just what I say. I gotta get out of here or the law will take me back to jail. You haven't done a thing wrong. Not a thing, you understand?" The boy dropped his head down and Dex kept talking, "I've made some mistakes again, broke the law. . . . You remember the same thing happened a few years ago, I had to go to jail for a while, you was little—do you remember?"

Shane was staring down at the dog. He nodded but didn't raise his head.

"I've got some things gathered up and I'm gonna leave, but I'll get back with you when I can. It might be a few months, so don't you worry about me. I'm thinking the police and the park rangers may be coming here soon. I don't want you to be scared. You ask for that FBI man, his name is Agent Tyler, he was good to you, right?"

Shane nodded again, but his head stayed down.

"You tell the FBI man that you want to go to your Aunt Stacy's in Georgia. Can you do that?"

The head nodded again. "Uh-huh."

"Here, Shane, look at me." Dex put his big hands on the boy's shoulders. The child's eyes came up, he was biting his bottom lip to keep from crying. "Look here. You done a good thing bein' with me and your papaw these last few months." Shane started to cry, but Dex wasn't finished. "You remember what your papaw told you—you can be anything you want to be. You're not gonna steal, lie, or be mean to anyone, you hear? *'You're a good un'*—ain't that what Papaw would always say?"

The boy nodded and wiped the tears from his face. He kept biting his lip.

Dex handed him a worn leather wallet. "This was your papaw's. He wanted you to have it. It has Aunt Stacy's number and address in it. There's enough money in it to get you and Max back to her place. It's hard-earned money I made, don't let anyone take it from you except that FBI man."

Dex was counting the seconds down in his head. He didn't know how long he had before they moved on him, but he couldn't let that happen with the boy here. It was past time to go.

He pulled Shane to him in a hug, then kissed the top of his tousled hair. "Everything's gonna be fine. . . . Papaw loves you. I love you, don't you ever forget that. And your daddy would be so proud of you—is so proud of you."

"He's in Heaven, where Papaw's goin', ain't he?"

Dex was done with lying. "I don't know how that God stuff works, Shane. But Papaw would tell you *yes* that's where he's going—to Heaven. And if that's so, then one day soon him and your daddy will be sittin' around talking 'bout what a fine young man you are, what a good hound you got. How you's growin' up to be somethin' special."

He lifted the heavy pack off the end of the Naugahyde couch. He ran a hand across his eyes and touched Shane's head again. "If nobody comes by 'fore dark, you go ask the neighbors to call the camp host, you tell that man to call the rangers, you tell the rangers to call the FBI man."

* * *

Win wasn't sure he'd learned much from the clerk at Washburn Lodge. He hadn't expected Dex Pierson to use his real name on a room reservation, but he had to check just in case. He'd heard seasoned agents remark at how predictable and stupid criminals could be, and he didn't want to miss the obvious. He walked out of the lodge and had nearly made it to his SUV when his phone buzzed. He and Alex were using their cell phones to communicate, since neither of them had a radio or satellite phone. Alex's text caused Win's pulse to jump: **black pickup at K123 license covered. Small trailer.** He jogged the rest of the way to his Explorer and pulled out the campground plat. He tried to make sense of the maze of camping spots. K123 was toward the backside of the big campground, stuck a little out of the way. Each of the lettered loops had a concrete-block restroom building. He located it on the map and texted back: **10-4, meet at bathroom building K.**

He put the Explorer in gear, eased up the asphalt road to the campground, and headed in the general direction of section K. He reached around and touched the small Glock that he now carried in a pancake holster on his lower back. He wished he wasn't putting Shane in danger. He wished he wasn't going into this with a woman bent on revenge. He wished some form of backup would arrive. He wished he had a bigger gun.

He pulled into the gravel turnout that passed as the parking area for the restrooms. Alex's SUV was there, and she was standing beside the open driver's door. She held up her phone with a photo of a black pickup attached to a camper trailer. Alex had taken the photo while she was driving past, it was shot through the passenger window. It wasn't a great picture, but there was no mistaking the truck—black-on-black newer Dodge Ram. Just what they were looking for. No people in the photo, nothing other than the truck and the trailer.

"It looks like they're packed up and ready to move out," Win said.

"I called the campground office. That spot is supposed to vacate by five," Alex said. "Another trailer is scheduled to move in between six and eight. This place is humming, no empty spots here. Do we wait for him to pull out? Get away from the campground, all the tourists?"

"I don't think so. If they're moving, even more folks are at risk. I think we need to make sure this is Pierson. We need to make sure before we call in the cavalry," he said.

"Is there any cavalry to call in? Seems to me everyone except us is out of pocket. Seems to me, this is our deal."

He had to admit she was right.

CHAPTER TWENTY-SEVEN

Alex had parked her SUV about fifty yards up the road from the camper with the black pickup attached. Win had parked around the loop behind a massive motor home. He was surprised that there was no activity at any of the sites. Hundreds of campers and tents sat peacefully in the heat, but hardly any people were stirring. It was nearly 2:30, peak heat of the day; he figured anyone with air-conditioning was sitting under it, and the others were out exploring the park. Maybe that's where the occupants of K123 were, out exploring the park, down at the ice cream shop, over near the towering waterfalls. He could see through gaps in the lodgepole pines that nothing was moving around the black pickup or at that campsite.

Win cautioned himself that he didn't know for sure this was Pierson's truck and trailer. But it felt right, it just felt right—the most isolated spot in the whole campground, black vehicle identical to the one he'd seen Pierson in on the Zippy Mart surveillance footage, and the color of the trailer even matched the light-blue camper parts he'd seen back at Pierson's place near Gardiner. He knew in his gut that they had him. He just wasn't sure how to proceed. What he did know was that he didn't want to put Shane in danger. He didn't want to provoke a gunfight.

Win had made the argument to Alex for waiting for someone to come out of the camper. It was obvious that whoever was there was packed up and ready to go. Win thought it was smarter to just sit back and watch, then move in if it was Pierson, when he was out in the open, when the boy wasn't at risk. But he had to admit that Alex had more experience in this sort of thing. She'd been a police officer for more than twelve years and had dealt with cornered suspects. She pointed out that Pierson could very well be somewhere else in whatever vehicle he'd stolen to get here—if in fact this was his rig. It was only 2:30. They could sit and wait until the trailer's occupants pulled out at the five o'clock deadline and find they were staking out an elderly couple from Missoula. Waiting could give Pierson that much more of a head start. She said they didn't have time for that, they didn't have time to wait any longer.

Win grudgingly agreed, and they decided that Alex would approach the camper first. Dex Pierson could identify Win, he'd never seen Alex, and he might view an approaching woman as less of a threat. Win moved behind one of the brown bear-proof containers that provided safe food and trash storage for each campsite. He figured if the heavy metal container could deter a grizzly, it could stop a bullet. He dropped to one knee and watched Alex casually walk down the road, stop when she reached the black pickup's grill, ease her handgun from under her shirt, then advance alongside the truck toward the camper.

Win pulled the small Glock from behind his back as he moved around the bear-proof container. He zigzagged as he ran across the narrow road toward the front of the black truck. The adrenaline spike had hit and he heard the crunch of the dried grass as he crossed it, felt the sun's heat penetrate his shirt, heard the sound of generators humming but not quite drowning out the sound of children shouting somewhere in the campground. Every sense was sharpened, and as he brought the compact gun alongside his thigh, he prayed that he wouldn't have to use it.

Alex was beside the closed door to the trailer now, Win could only see the top of her blue ball cap. He made it to the side of the big pickup and flinched from the feel of the hot metal as he leaned against it. He saw Alex reach up and bang on the camper's door, heard her call out, "Police! Open the door! Police!"

* * *

Ginger had pulled the group off the trail into the edge of the deep woods as soon as they got far enough away from the nearly overwhelming stench of Washburn Hot Springs to breathe fresh air. Sulphur Creek was splashing down the mountain in front of them, giving off a faint aroma of rotten eggs, but in comparison with the thermal feature they'd just left, it was almost refreshing. Everyone found a shady spot to sit on a smooth boulder or log, and she encouraged them to drink more of their sports drinks, to stay hydrated. The two older ladies looked exhausted and the couple from Austin didn't seem much better. She handed out protein bars and told them that these short heat waves in mid-summer weren't uncommon in Yellowstone. You had to be prepared for anything.

Will Tyler had caught up with the group just in time to grab a spot on a huge log and hear that lecture. *Be prepared for anything*—that was practically a Tyler family motto. He'd jogged to catch up with the group and to stay well ahead of Tank. Will wasn't sure if Tank had seen him watching back at the spring, but one thing he was sure of was that something was off, something wasn't right.

Will called out to Ginger, "Tank's comin' behind me . . . all good I guess." He shed his daypack and slowed his breathing from the half-mile run. He pulled out his water bottle and the lame flip phone that Tucker had given him so that he could check in with Win every so often while they were tromping around in the woods. He stared at the little black phone and reflected that he hadn't exactly done a stellar job of staying in touch with his older brother. He saw no service bars, but he typed a text to Win anyway: **Something is off with guide, Tank, he may have hurt someone. Maybe. Between Washburn spring - sulphur creek. May need ur help. 2:34**

He paused before he hit SEND. Maybe he was making a big deal over nothing . . . he hadn't really *seen* anything bad happen. Something in his consciousness told him to let it pass, he didn't have to get involved. Tank had pocketed a gun, no big deal there, and throwing a hat in a hot spring probably wasn't a federal offense—well, it probably was—but it was the scream that kept replaying in his mind, then the gunshot.

Everyone glanced down the trail as Tank came into view. He waved and called out, "No problem back there! False alarm." Will looked at his flushed face, caught a glimpse of flinty eyes, saw just a glimmer of evil. He hit the SEND button and swallowed down the unfamiliar feeling of fear.

*　*　*

Win was beside Alex now, leaning against the thin metal skin of the camper, his Glock pointed down in a two-handed grip. She had just raised her hand to strike the camper door again when it cracked open and Max's black nose stuck out. A small voice called from inside, "Hey . . . Miss Alex . . . it's me. . . . It's Shane."

Her voice was measured and calm as she answered. "Is anyone there with you, Shane?"

"No, ma'am."

"Shane, I want you to come on out real slowly. Hold on to Max . . . that's right, come on out."

Shane jumped down the last step and the lanky hound bounded down beside him. Shane saw Win and tried to smile, but his eyes went to the gun.

"It's okay, Shane, move back away from the steps," Win said softly.

"Dex said y'all might come. He said to tell you he's gone for a while." The boy looked directly at Win. "He said to tell you I'm going with you."

Win glanced at Alex, saw her push the metal door wide open with her free hand. He nodded at the boy. "Move over toward the firepit, Shane. We'll check some things inside. Just over there, okay?"

Win followed Alex's lead and they cleared the trailer in seconds; Alex was a pro, there was no wasted motion. And there wasn't any-place for a man of Dex's size to hide.

Win stepped out of the trailer and walked to the picnic table in the shade of a leaning pine tree to sit down beside the little boy.

"You alright?"

"Yes, sir. Dex said you'd handle this right, it'd turn out fine."

Win patted the child on the shoulder and rubbed the dog's ears as he pulled out his Bureau phone. He wished he shared Dex's confidence in everything turning out fine.

*　*　*

It had been nearly thirty minutes since they'd raided the camper, and they'd attracted a crowd. The campground host was standing to the side, fuming that so much police activity was upsetting the tranquility of his domain. The rangers had finally pulled two law enforcement guys in from the wreck in the Hayden Valley, and they were taping off the pickup and camper as a potential crime scene. Two more rangers were checking every vehicle that came through the Canyon junction on the Grand Loop Road. Win had made calls and managed to get checkpoints set up at Tower–Roosevelt junction, Norris junction, and Lake; those had been up and running for nearly fifteen minutes, not long after they knew Pierson wasn't at the trailer. Win knew all five of Yellowstone's entrances were now on high alert as well—they'd pulled in the local cops and Sheriff's deputies to help make vehicle checks there.

As slow and exasperating as law enforcement could sometimes be, it could also move with amazing speed when the big dogs threw their weight around. As soon as Win and Alex cleared the trailer, Win had called his supervisor and Jim had called his ASAC, the Assistant Special Agent in Charge of the Denver Field Office, to say they had a solid lead on the bison massacre poacher *and* that suspect could be involved in two, if not three, murders in Grand Teton and Yellowstone. The FBI needed ranger assistance at Canyon *now*, and they got it.

Win glanced up from helping secure yellow tape on the black pickup and saw Kirk pull off the campground's narrow road in his Bureau car and nose it in between two Park Service Tahoes. Kirk practically jumped out of the car. He trotted toward Win with an expectant look on his face. "Hey, man! I got here in like record time! Put on the blue lights and siren—didn't even realize my vehicle had a siren—anyway, everybody like pulled out of my way. It was awesome!"

Win resisted the urge to shake his head and groan. His mind flew back to the only two times he'd ridden in a vehicle driven at warp speed with lights and siren going. He'd been scared to death. Kirk obviously had a higher tolerance for risk.

The younger agent was still talking. "Listen, dude, I've got something that might, well, could help. I . . . uh, was waiting for the NTSB investigators to come in this morning from the chopper crash site, and uh, I'm thinking I didn't break any privacy rules, but, whatever, you need to know this. I didn't even have to go into the Bureau's system to pull this stuff up, I was sitting in a coffee shop in West Yellowstone, and I got to thinking how we might track this guy Pierson."

Win laid down the roll of tape and gave the younger agent his full attention. "You found something?"

"You know, like you told me to look for Pierson's known associates a few days ago, and I didn't find anything in our system, but like—and this is a big *but*—I start looking for the name Dex on local social media and internet reviews. And outa the blue I get a couple of hits with *Dex* in them on a business in West Yellowstone. So I searched the business and the owner's social media. Then, get this, I searched the reviews on this business's rental properties and there are three reviews within the last six months thanking the management and Dex for showing up so quickly and fixing their roofing issue or plumbing or whatever their problem was. You know, there's not like that many folks around called Dex."

Win stood there listening and wondered where this was going. "Okay, and?" he finally said.

"Like, this guy Jesse Prince, he owns the rental properties. Dude's got his fingers in several pies—a financial planning business, a rental company, he's a partner in a high-end tour service, all located in West Yellowstone. The guy was some civic club's Young Entrepreneur of the Year last year. I'm thinking, okay that could be legit, we know Pierson has done construction work off and on, but here's the deal. Then I searched through Pierson's high school yearbooks—"

Win held a hand up and stopped him. "You can do that?"

"Sure, lots of schools, colleges, and small-town newspapers have all sorts of cool stuff archived online. Well, anyway, it appears Dex Pierson was besties with a guy named Jesse Gibbs. They were in the same class all the way back to second grade. According to the local newspaper, Pierson and his runnin' buddy, Jesse, got into all sorts of low-level juvenile trouble: vandalism, spotlighting deer, minor trespassing, breaking and entering, nothing too big, no felonies. But, and this is another big *but*, Pierson goes off to the Army after he turns seventeen. That gets a lot of his past sins forgiven. His buddy, Gibbs, moves with his parents to Williston, North Dakota. Lookie here." Kirk held up his phone. "This is Jesse Gibbs his junior year at Rock Springs High School and Jesse Prince from his Instagram page last week."

Win zeroed in on the side-by-side photos: a smug sixteen-year-old with a good haircut, and a fit-looking guy in his early forties with a manicured black beard.

Kirk really had Win's attention now. Win's eyes flicked from the photos to Kirk's face. He didn't have to say a word. It was almost certainly the same person—twenty-five years older, but the same person.

"Something tells me you found more," Win said.

"This is where it starts to get creepy," Kirk said as he pocketed his phone. "I start running my search for this Jesse Gibbs dude after he graduated from high school in North Dakota. A few years after high school the local newspaper runs his engagement announcement, and then a write-up on his marriage into what appears to be a prominent family in Williston. A couple years later, the pretty wife ends up dead in an unfortunate accident. Then a year after that, Jesse's family home burns down and his parents die in the fire. The fire was ruled arson, but that got overturned. Gibbs got the insurance money from his wife's demise and from his dead parents. The policies totaled over three million. Then Jesse Gibbs just vanishes."

Whoa. They finally had a connection between Dex Pierson and a seemingly prominent businessman, someone who might have the wherewithal to pull off an international poaching operation. Win had asked Denver for a complete rundown on Dex Pierson several days ago and gotten next to nothing. Kirk had managed to find out this much over coffee this morning. Win Tyler was impressed.

"When did Jesse Prince appear?" he asked.

"The first hits I get on him in West Yellowstone are from about six years ago. He's like an upstanding citizen . . . with a long string of bad luck. Second pretty wife died last year in an accidental fall from a five-hundred-foot cliff while out hiking in the Gallatin National Forest."

Win's eyebrows went up. *Wow, this is one bad actor.*

*   *   *

"Hey, babe," he practically purred into the phone. "Been awhile, when we gonna get together?" He heard her laugh, read the shyness that was suddenly in her voice. She was thrilled that he'd called, crazy about him, that wasn't hard to read. They talked a few minutes about nothing in particular, then he asked, "What's happened with that guy Pierson you're after? Still can't believe I had a damn poacher—a criminal—doing my plumbing jobs."

"He's outa my jurisdiction, thank goodness! Not my problem any longer." He didn't respond, and as people are prone to do, she filled in the blanks. "The FBI just found his camper down at Canyon, found his little boy, but Dex Pierson was gone. If he's as good a plumber as he is at disappearing, you had yourself a great hand." She laughed again, and he pushed it a little to get more information.

"He disappeared? Hell, then I'll have to hire myself another man. . . . Hey, do they think he's left the park?"

"No, no, the working theory is that he's hiking somewhere around Canyon. They've got any vehicle getaway locked down—there are ongoing searches, roadblocks. He may just be roaming the woods around that RV park. This all came down less than thirty minutes ago."

After he got off the phone, he was laser focused. He'd finished packing the guns in the motor home a few minutes ago, then he'd sat down on the leather sofa to figure out his next move. He'd run the cold bottle over the side of his sweaty face, then taken a long drink. Nice of the dealer to stock the fridge with premium beverages. He'd decided checking in with his sources was his best move, so he'd called her. The timing couldn't have been better. She'd just come off her shift, and he could tell from her voice she was wanting some company. That wasn't going to happen, but she didn't have to know it.

Dex wouldn't just wander around the park. He knew exactly where Dex would go. They used to sit around drinking beer and talking about the trails—Dex had a thing for the outdoors, for staying fit, fresh air, that sort of thing. He couldn't really understand why the guy didn't just hit the gym, same as he did. But Dex's wilderness wanderings did pay off with great locations for their trophy hunts. Dex knew his way around in the woods, and in this particular part of the woods, he loved that trail that had a big rock at the trailhead. It led down the north side of Yellowstone's deep canyon into the absolute middle of nowhere.

Here he was, sitting in a fancy air-conditioned coach, stressing about how to find that boy, and it turns out Dex had been right under his nose, less than a mile away in the RV park. He glanced around the posh interior of the motor home again. *I'll bet Dex ain't been hiding out in anything like this. Probably one of those little FEMA trailers he stole. . . .* He nodded to himself as he conceded that Dex's fascination with the campers had given him the ideas of using the trailers as storage spots for his gun inventory and using the high-dollar motor coach to transport the weapons across the border. He'd always seen himself as way smarter than his childhood friend, and maybe he was. But he'd admit that he'd learned a few things from Dex Pierson. One of those things was how to use a Winchester Model 70 rifle. Other things? How to ambush and kill.

CHAPTER TWENTY-EIGHT

They were within a mile of the questionable comforts of the primitive campground, and Will couldn't figure out what to do. Tank hadn't seemed weird, hadn't seemed squirrely, but Will could still feel a tension and he'd caught the guy glancing back down the line of hikers toward him more than once on the four-mile hike from Sulphur Creek. He told himself he was probably imagining that—he told himself to stay cool. He really didn't think Tank had seen him at the spring, but just in case, he sure hoped Win had gotten his text.

But Tank had seen him at the spring, seconds after throwing that scumbag's hat in the inky goo. He'd caught some movement far below him near the trail, seen a tall figure in a gray T-shirt and red cap. He knew exactly who it was, he just wasn't sure how much the Tyler kid knew. At their first rest stop he asked Ginger if Tyler had stayed with the group the entire time, and she said *no*, she'd sent him back to the spring to see if he needed help. She said Tyler jogged back a few minutes later and told her it appeared to be nothing. He hadn't seemed concerned.

But Tank wasn't sure about that. The kid might just be fifteen, but he had the same deep, watchful eyes as his older brother. He had the same confident, capable look. The kid might be a problem. And speaking of problems, he'd checked his Garmin satellite device as he hiked down the trail from Washburn Hot Springs to rejoin the group. Still nothing from Roadie and no new word from Prince. That didn't feel right. His anxiety was growing, so he took a risk. He sent a follow-up text to his source at the West Yellowstone Police Department. **What's up with T-Bone? What's up there?** Maybe not a smart move, but hell, he was tired of guessing. And hell, he'd just killed a man. He figured he oughta at least find out why.

* * *

Will's text to Win, sent over forty-five minutes ago, hadn't gone through. Win checked his personal phone again, saw nothing, and wondered if he should try to contact his brother through the tour company. He'd convinced himself to do just that, when one of the rangers waved to him and jogged over with a satellite phone. Win was hoping this was a Park Service someone telling him that Pierson had been apprehended without incident, that the search was called off. But that was wishful thinking. It was Trey Hechtner's calm voice on the other end.

"I'm hearing that things have ramped up at Canyon," the ranger said in greeting. "You know, Yellowstone was relatively peaceful before you got transferred down here last spring . . . since then—"

Win interrupted his friend. "Not my fault, and you know it. Where are you?"

"I'm heading your way with the new chopper as soon as we tie up some things here, get back to Mammoth, and fuel up. Your big boss lit a fire under my big boss and now we're at your service." Win heard Trey sigh. "We finished up here at Grebe Lake a few minutes ago, found the guy who drowned. So glad we finally got the body. At least there'll be some closure for the family." Trey paused. "These cold lakes don't release bodies quickly, sometimes not ever . . . such a damn shame. He wasn't wearing a life jacket. He wasn't prepared at all."

Win didn't know what to say to that. He'd learned during his short stay in Yellowstone that *not being prepared* didn't bode well. The weather and wildlife were totally unpredictable, the lakes and streams were icy cold, and there were rockfalls, cliffs, and deep crevasses. Those numerous hazards didn't even count the scalding geyser fields and hot springs that routinely claimed victims. There were lots of ways to die in Yellowstone, especially for the unprepared. It was a paradox he'd discovered while living in this magical place surrounded by its majesty and beauty.

"What's your ETA?" Win asked.

"We'll be taking the body to Livingston or Bozeman, I guess. With the refuel at Mammoth . . . I'm guessing three hours, maybe less. That'd put us in Canyon a little after six." He paused, then quickly added, "Hey, this helo is sweet, brand-new AStar B3—it can really move out. Take you for a ride, you'll love it!" Trey knew Win hated helicopters, knew even the thought of getting on one made him queasy.

"Yeah, right. Maybe we'll get this wrapped up before you get here. When I get the word, I'm gonna head down the trail southeast of the campground. It's the way I'd go if I was trying to escape everyone— away from the tourists, away from the buildings, away from the roads."

"Don't go after him by yourself," Trey warned.

"Constable Lindell will be with me. We'll try to rope in a ranger or two."

"Hmm . . . she didn't exactly distinguish herself up here in Mammoth with that near-fatal tourist incident. She was out to get someone, I could see it in her eyes. Not the best partner to have in a manhunt, Win."

"I've talked with her about it. I think she'll play it straight now. She can be a real professional."

"*Can be* and *will be* are two very different things, buddy. Don't get yourself caught in a bad situation trying to help her redeem herself."

Win was surprised at Trey's comment. "Seriously? What makes you think I'm trying to help redeem her?"

"Because that's who you are. That's why you do what you do. You're living out the Scripture '*To those whom much is given, much is required.*'"

Before he could answer, Win heard the whine of a helicopter starting in the background. Trey's voice got louder to be heard over the noise. "Hey, gotta go! I'm hearing everyone's spread pretty thin down there . . . good luck recruiting any rangers! I'll make a call, see if I can get you some real help." He paused and the sound of the rotors intensi-fied. "Be careful out there, Win!"

* * *

Alex was walking toward him from the picnic table outside of Pierson's camper. The area was still buzzing with activity an hour after she'd knocked on the trailer's door. Three Park Service ERT members had arrived; they had just finished going through Shane's stuff and were starting in on the camper. Another couple of interpretative rangers were stationed nearby to keep curious onlookers away. It wasn't like there was much of a crowd right now. They were definitely off the beaten path, and it was now ninety degrees in the shade. In this normally temperate climate, that was officially too hot to do anything except sit under a tree and fan yourself.

The Park Service had called in another interpretative ranger to keep an eye on Shane and the dog. Win could see them about fifty yards away, near the bathroom building. The ranger was spraying Max with a hose, and Shane was jumping up and down and shouting encouragement to the wet, bounding dog. They were having fun. Win stood in the sweltering heat near the trailer and wished he had that much energy. He also wished someone would tell him what to do next.

"My Corporal in Calgary has okayed me working this with you," Alex said as she approached him.

"Kinda after the fact, isn't it?" he said.

"What's that old saying? *Better to ask for forgiveness than permission.*" She took off her sunglasses and looked hard at him. "You do know we're wasting precious time standing around here doing nothing while Pierson hikes off into the wilderness."

Win drew in a breath, removed his shades, and looked down at her. He was aware that his eyes weren't kind. "Yes, I do know that. But unlike some folks"—he glared at her—"unlike some folks, I'm try-ing to follow procedure." He tried for a more conciliatory tone, but he barely found one. "You know all of this. Kirk is still the FBI's lead case agent on the poaching case. He is setting up the command center for the manhunt at the Visitor Center down in Canyon Village. The road-blocks are in place, park entrances are being checked, rangers are monitoring or closing many of the trails near Canyon. ATF is sending some guys, and the Bureau has two Violent Crime Squad folks coming. All of them are driving from West Yellowstone and should be here within the hour. I just got a call that we'll have a chopper here within three hours. So things are moving."

"We're not," she said.

He forced down an angry response. "Alright, what do you propose?"

"Let me move down the length of the trail from this campground to the Seven Mile Hole Trailhead. When you and I were looking at the maps a few minutes ago, I know you were thinking the same thing I was—I'd go this way, I'd drop out of sight, get into the wilds of the canyon, wait till the heat's off."

"Yes, I agree with that, Alex. . . . And I know we're losing time, but we have to do this by the book. You're not going down there by yourself after an armed and dangerous fugitive. It's not gonna happen. Period." He glared at her again. "And I'm waiting on the okay from my boss to go, I'm waiting for someone to bring me some body armor, a long gun, and a satellite phone, and I'm also waiting on the Bureau's Victim Assistance folks to get back with me on Shane. I can't just dump him on the rangers. . . . Give me a break here, will you?"

Alex took a step back, holding her hands up in mock surrender. "All right . . . all right. I get it. I'll wait."

"Look, I don't want to get crossways with you. We both want the same thing here—"

"Justice? Don't tell me you're going to give me another of your *just cause* lectures. You want justice, okay. I want that too." She shook her head, then turned and walked back toward the wooden table.

No, you want revenge, Win thought as he watched her walk away. He knew it wasn't justice or even redemption she was pursuing. The cause of justice had within its foundation the hope of light, the hope of good. Revenge had a base of hate and darkness.

*   *   *

The man lowered the window and slowed the new black BMW to approach the ranger standing in the middle of North Rim Drive, a narrow one-way road. Towering lodgepole pines grew close to the paved road, giving it a shady, cave-like feel. He'd been down this road, which paralleled the north rim of the canyon, many times. He'd often had to stop for a bison. But today there was no bison on the road, just a solitary ranger holding up his hand and waving for him to stop.

Prince noticed that the young man was wearing an orange security vest, noticed that he wasn't wearing a gun belt. *They've even called in the educational rangers to block off the roads,* he thought. *They're really shorthanded. Good to know.*

"Sir, you'll have to turn around here," the guy motioned to a gravel turnout where vehicles could pull a tight U. They were temporarily making the one-lane road serve as two lanes.

Prince stopped the car and waved for the ranger to come closer to his window. "Hey, what's goin' on? Did a buffalo hurt someone?"

"Ah, we've got an issue . . . an incident." The ranger didn't know how much to say, so he repeated his polite order. "Sir, I need you to make a U-turn, please."

Prince looked distressed. He held his phone out of the car window and waved it. "Hey, my wife . . . she had a little fall . . . just down this next road, down near the Seven Mile Hole Trailhead." He pointed to the lovely photo of Bree that served as his phone's screensaver. "She called me to come pick her up. Twisted her ankle. She can't walk back." He made his voice sound desperate. "I'll just be a minute, just a minute to pick her up."

The young man bit his lip and looked conflicted. He led the Junior Ranger programs at Canyon Village this summer, traffic control wasn't in his job description. The District Ranger had pulled anyone who was breathing in to work this afternoon. They'd sent out photos of the thug who was on the loose, of the dangerous man they were supposed to be on the lookout for. The ranger looked again at the pretty woman in the photo, at the well-dressed guy in the nice car. It sure wasn't this guy. He glanced back at the line of vehicles piling up behind the BMW. He needed to get more of these folks turned around. Some idiot honked and a motorcycle revved its engine.

"Okay, fine. The trailhead is at the Glacial Boulder, just a half mile ahead of you . . . take the turn toward Inspiration Point. It's just a short loop."

Prince smiled and nodded. "Thank you so much! We'll be right out."

"If your wife needs medical attention, take her to the Visitor Center. Ask for any ranger." The young man was being helpful. "I sure hope she's okay."

Prince put the car in gear and slowly moved forward down the empty road. He waved to the young man as he passed by. "I'm sure everything will be fine."

*　*　*

Win glanced in the Explorer's rearview mirror at Shane. The boy was looking down at the dog, petting his head. There was a mixture of fear, anger, and grief in his expression. "I'll figure something out," Win said. He got no response, just a nod. The child kept petting the dog. The ranger who'd been keeping the boy occupied had been called away to close down trails, so Win had loaded Shane's things into his SUV and was running the air-conditioning to keep them cool.

"Don't be scared, it'll be alright. I'll figure somethin' out," Win said again, to reassure himself, if not the boy.

Shane's head came up. "Dex said the same thing. He said to go with you. Maybe I can go visit Miss Ellie and Mr. Luke awhile longer, 'fore I get back to Georgia."

Georgia. And just like that, Win Tyler knew what he was supposed to do.

"Hey, uh, you wanta hang out with Max at the picnic table? I need to make a call." Win glanced in the rearview mirror again.

It took them less than fifteen minutes to arrive at the campsite. One look at the tarp over the luggage in the back of the twin-cab pickup and Win could tell they were ready to head out. As soon as Deputy Donnie

Sawyer turned off the engine, his wife jumped out of the truck, their ten-year-old son right behind her.

"Oh, you must be Shane!" she called out as she headed straight for the boy. "It is so good to see you."

Shane got up out of the camp chair and nodded. Max suddenly got uncharacteristically shy and moved behind Shane's legs.

Win walked toward the man and started talking as he pulled out his wallet. "Shane's got some money on him, but this will help, and I'll send more—"

The portly man held up his hand. "No . . . nope . . . we ain't takin' your money." Win's eyes came up in surprise. The guy wasn't finished, but his voice softened. "You ain't the only one called to do good." He glanced over at Shane, who was in the process of introducing a more enthusiastic Max to the deputy's' son, Cabe. Sawyer's voice was still quiet. "You don't need to go ruining our chance at gettin' a blessin'."

"His aunt is Stacy—"

"I know," the deputy said. "I made some calls after you reached out a few minutes ago. She lives in the next county over from us. I know that she ain't in good health and she's got three kids of her own, and that this boy, Shane, has been in and out of foster care during the last three years."

"You've got good contacts."

The man raised his eyebrows and looked at Win. "I 'spect you've got some contacts too, I 'spect you've checked me out."

Win nodded.

The man shook his head and glanced over at Shane. "Did you know his aunt had him up for adoption a couple of times?"

"No . . . no, I didn't know that."

"Lemme tell you somethin'. We was supposed to leave before noon, but we couldn't find Cabe's iPad. Then they had a foul-up with our checkout, then the battery completely died, had to get a jump, let it sit and charge. . . . Delay after delay, one of those *everything's going wrong* kinda days. Donna and me, we were killing time, sitting and feeling the loss of our youngest boy—he died real sudden two years ago, meningitis, they said—we's talking after lunch 'bout how much he woulda loved this place." Sawyer stopped and cleared his throat. "Ah, been a hard row to hoe, these last two years. We were talking about adoption . . . there are lots of children with needs." His eyes were on Shane.

"And then I called."

He nodded. "And then you called."

Win just nodded. He'd seen miracles before.

"There ain't no coincidences. In law enforcement or in life." The deputy folded his arms and stood straight. "This here"—he nodded toward Shane, Cabe, his wife, and the dog—"this here may be way more than we know."

Win Tyler couldn't argue with that.

* * *

It was a little slower going than it would usually be. The high heat at the thermal area had taken the spunk out of most of the group. The two older ladies that Will thought of as the busy bees were constantly wanting to stop and rest. The Austin couple were plodding along, leaning far too often on their hiking poles. The two spandex-clad techies even seemed tired and subdued.

Ginger tried to generate some enthusiasm. After all, this was the group's last full day in the field, she needed to get some good vibes going. This trip was supposed to be fun. "Hey, everyone!" she called out as they stepped off the trail to let another group of hikers file past. "Hey, why don't we detour for about a hundred yards down the next trail . . . just up ahead. We haven't seen this part of the canyon in the afternoon light. It will be awesome!"

Awesome sounded good to Will Tyler. He was still a little freaked out by the events at the spring, unsure about what to do. He'd checked the flip phone a couple of minutes ago, no response from Win, no service. He wondered how civilization existed before smartphones made seamless connections possible. But he had to concede he had a lot more time on his hands since his phone wasn't constantly in them. And it wasn't just the lame flip phone, no one's smartphone worked out here either. Maybe humans had somehow gotten along fine without them.

"Oh, this is so cool," Will heard Ginger say to one of the Vermont ladies. Ginger was leading the group down the secondary trail now, and Tank was bringing up the rear. She dropped her voice and signaled with one hand above her head for everyone to stop and be quiet. She reached for her bear spray, then pointed down the rocky path. Within seconds, Will heard deep breathing, slight huffing, and then the sound of something walking or running through the underbrush.

The big cinnamon-colored creature crossed the trail less than twenty yards in front of them. It was beautiful, and Will could tell it wasn't a grizzly—no humped shoulders, no rounded ears, and no top-of-the-food-chain attitude. She was a black bear that happened to be solid cinnamon brown. She stopped in the middle of the trail and stared at the humans for a moment, then turned her head and grunted for her brood. The two black cubs hadn't inherited their mother's color. They tried to tackle each other as they romped across the open area along the trail. They were each twenty-five pounds of playful energy, and they didn't even glance at the people who were snapping pictures and quietly watching them.

After the bear family moved back into the trees, Ginger directed everyone off the trail to an unofficial canyon overlook, where they could pose for photos or just stand in the shade of the big pines and admire the afternoon sun hitting the high canyon walls. Silver Cord Cascade, the highest waterfall in Yellowstone, with its twelve-hundred-foot vertical drop, was directly across the canyon. Tank held the Austin couple's phone and took a few pictures of them with the fall in the far background. Tank thought that as waterfalls went, it really wasn't much, especially in mid-summer when the snow runoff was over and the rains were few and far between. But you could still see the sliver of silver far in the distance, still see the mist rising as the water struck the rocks below. There was a nice breeze here on the canyon's rim, everyone was stoked after the close encounter with the bears, and the scenery was jaw-dropping. Positive vibes seemed to have settled back onto the group. Onto everyone except Tank, that is.

Tank got the word back from his source at the West Yellowstone Police Department much sooner than he expected—he'd only texted the guy fifteen minutes ago. He'd left the Garmin on hoping to get a fast response to his message, but he was still surprised when it vibrated in his pocket so soon. He whistled to Ginger and gave her their hand signal that meant he needed to retreat to the woods for a nature call. She nodded to him and launched into a talk about the volcanic activity that was still evident in the canyon. She started pointing out steam vents puffing scalding vapor out hundreds of feet below. Everyone except the techies seemed fascinated.

Tank silently backed away from the rim, walked a few feet farther into the thick forest, and pulled out the satellite device. He clicked on the screen for his source and read the text: **Word on street—T-Bone contracted for a hit on u. Hearing 10K, No idea who? Vista chopper down by sabotage. BOLO for poacher in Yellowstone—Dex Pierson—Canyon. ATF headed into Park? OUT I mean it!**

He let loose with a few choice curse words under his breath. This was a hell of a note. His source was getting a little snarky, but that was the least of his problems. An actual contract to kill him meant this wasn't just that thug, T-Bone Dawes, seeking revenge after he confiscated the fool's pill inventory last spring. A contract was a bigger deal, a much bigger deal. And ATF heading into the park might mean they were on to something with the guns—his guns. He thought of them that way now. ATF wouldn't be screwing around with a poacher, that wasn't their thing. But illegal guns were their thing . . . that was worrisome. He reread the message for the third time, and he still wasn't sure how the Vista helicopter tied into anything. And why in hell did Dex Pierson matter?

He nearly dropped the Garmin when it buzzed in his hand. A new message appeared on the screen just below the first one: **Also murder vic in YNP Lake id as Wayne Benson.** His breath caught in his throat. *Roadie! Ah, hell . . . Roadie.* He just stood there in the hot, closed space among the pine trees, staring down at the small screen. A wave of something akin to grief swept over him for a moment, then was quickly replaced by seething anger. He drew in a couple of deep breaths of the hot air, tried to focus on the nearly overwhelming aroma of the evergreens. He forced himself to be calm. The first message made more sense now. A contract on him, Roadie dead, and ATF moving for the guns—someone was cleaning house before the illegal gun deal went off the rails. The number of possibilities for that move dropped down to one. Prince was behind this. Prince was tying up loose ends.

Tank turned off the Garmin and pocketed it as he walked back toward the group at the canyon's rim. Prince had picked the wrong guy to mess with. *Damn right he has!* His mind went back to the confrontation he'd seen between the osprey and the eagle a few days ago over at Biscuit Basin. The eagle was bigger, badder, bolder. The eagle took home the prize.

CHAPTER TWENTY-NINE

Dex knew this wouldn't be easy and he was right. The well-worn trail from the Canyon Campground meandered through a thick lodgepole pine forest for about two miles before it intersected with lesser-used trails leading east from Canyon along the north rim. The north rim was where he needed to be, away from Canyon Village and its hordes of tourists, and away from the cops who he figured would be bearing down soon. He'd hiked this rough trail a hundred times, and it normally wasn't too busy. He was surprised by the number of other hikers he kept meeting, by how many people he had to avoid. Each time, he'd step back into the undergrowth and the trees and wait until they passed. Each effort at concealment slowed him down more.

Dex shifted the heavy backpack on his shoulders and peered out of the woods toward this latest obstacle. A group of at least a dozen teenage girls, all wearing daypacks and dressed in various shades of khaki and green, were standing right in the middle of the forked trail, blocking his way. He considered bushwacking through the forest, but the brush in this area was dense, and the ground held unseen hazards. So he'd stepped off the trail and into the forest for a few minutes, hoping they'd move on by, but they were just standing there, apparently in deep discussion. He never could understand how women could talk so much. Right now what he saw as a female shortcoming was holding him up.

What the hell. He couldn't wait any longer. The cops or rangers or someone would be coming down the trail behind him any minute. He was just over a mile from his camper, he wasn't nearly far enough along. It was almost four o'clock, he needed to be hiking. He moved back onto the path and walked toward them. They turned, almost as one, and he tried to give them his best smile. He hoped to hell that the tooth tabs were still in place, that the tan makeup still covered his tats.

The girl in the front looked a little older than the others. She waved a phone at him and smiled. "Hey, warm out here today! Stay hydrated!"

He just smiled and nodded, and they finally began to step off the trail as he bore down on them. The older girl was still talking. "Hey, we just got a call from our troop leader. . . . She said there's a criminal on the loose out here!"

"Oh, that's not good," Dex said as he slowed and looked at her. He tried his best to appear concerned.

"She told us to come back to that big visitors building," she said. "Ah, you don't know which trail goes back to the main Canyon Village, do you?"

"There's like no signs," one of the other girls added.

He pointed to the faint path that turned southwest and kept walking. "That's the way to the main parking lot and all the facilities. Follow the yellow marks on the trees. It's not too far."

The older girl stepped aside as he walked by. She was still trying to be helpful. "Our leader says the guy they're after probably has camping gear, a big backpack, Caucasian, muscular build, about six feet." He could tell she was sizing him up, checking the descriptive items off her list. "I'd be careful out here by yourself . . . they say he's dangerous," she added.

Again he wondered why women keep talking. He knew by her tone that she'd made him. He saw a couple of the other teens fingering their bear spray. For a second he thought about taking their phones; that might delay their reporting him by a few minutes. But he didn't have it in him to terrorize a bunch of Girl Scouts. He told himself he wasn't that desperate yet.

He waved as he passed them by. "You girls stay safe."

* * *

Win felt a huge weight lift off his shoulders as he watched Deputy Sawyer drive his pickup away from Pierson's trailer and down the campground road. Win felt that he'd done something he was meant to do—a mission accomplished for Shane. He and Alex had hugged the little boy, made a fuss over Max, and loaded the boxes and Shane's duffel bags into the back of the truck for the long drive to Georgia. Shane had seemed excited and happy. For just a few moments Win stood in the heat and watched their tailgate disappear into the wooded area. For just a few moments he let himself feel happiness, let himself feel joy.

And that got him thinking about Tory. He hoped she was safe, hoped she was seeing remarkable things, hoped she was finding joy today. He glanced at his watch again—a few minutes till four. Tory and her hiking partner should be back at the research base camp in the Pelican Valley by now. He wondered if she was thinking about him, thinking about that kiss, hearing his voice. . . .

"Get back to business. You've got that girl on your mind again," Alex said as she snuck up on him, interrupting his thoughts.

Geez, how does she read me like that? He pulled in a breath and narrowed his eyes as he looked down at her. He started to speak, but his Bureau phone buzzed. It was Kirk and he sounded pleased.

"We've got something!" He didn't wait for Win to respond. "A troop of Girl Scouts just reported a sighting of Pierson on the Campground Trail about five minutes ago. They called it in to their leader, and she just called the rangers. It sounds legit, Win!"

"Okay, calm down, Kirk . . . did they say where on that trail?"

"Uh, yeah, it's like at the fork in the trail . . . uh . . . the Village Trail," Kirk answered.

"Did they say which way he went?"

"Yeah, they said he continued down the Campground Trail to the southeast. Said he was carrying a big backpack, had bear spray, they didn't see any weapon. He wasn't threatening."

"Okay." Win ran through the trail map in his mind. "Alex and I are going after him from here, from this end. The fork in the trail is about a mile southeast of here. Can you get someone to the end of that trail, and to any other exit points? What about our Violent Crime guys?"

"They're stuck at Gibbon Falls, uh, on the road—"

Win didn't have time to hear the details. "What about the park's Rapid Response Team?"

"They're stuck—"

"Have you got *anybody* there?"

Kirk sighed. "No, no law enforcement rangers . . . they're all out on the roadblocks, on the vehicle searches. I'll try to call someone back in. The Canyon District Ranger just got back from some lake, he's gonna work with me to coordinate it."

"Okay, ten-four. Alex is heading out with me on foot. Get someone to that trailhead down by the north rim. And have the rangers clear the tourists out of that area. That trail ends near Inspiration Point."

There was no response. Win figured Kirk was overwhelmed.

"Now, Kirk!" Still no response. Win lowered his voice. "Okay, Kirk. Take a deep breath, just focus. You're in charge. You *can* do this."

Win punched off the call and turned to Alex. "Gear up, we're hitting that trail."

One of the park's Evidence Response Team members, who overheard the call, turned to Win. "Do you want us to go with you?" she asked.

"Have any of you had any weapons training? Are you armed?" he asked.

The female ranger shrugged and shook her head.

"No, no . . . just finish up here. Make sure this site stays secure. I'm gonna take some of Pierson's guns. I don't have my service weapon with me."

She looked shocked. "These are all cataloged as evidence. . . . You can't do that!"

"I'm declaring this an emergency utilization of evidence," Win said as he stuffed two more bottles of water in his daypack and clipped on bear spray.

"Is that even a thing?" she asked.

No, but it sounds reasonable, Win thought. "I'm not going after this guy without some firepower," he said as he turned toward the trailer. Win knew that just taking his small Glock 43 wasn't gonna cut it. He was already looking over the numerous guns that were laid out on a tarp outside the trailer; Pierson kept an arsenal. The weapons had been photographed, cataloged, and dusted for fingerprints. Win picked up an assault rifle and a Sig Sauer handgun.

"Please keep the tags on them," the woman pleaded.

He nodded and loaded the weapons, putting extra magazines into his daypack. Then he waved for Alex. The trailhead was less than a hundred feet up the campground road, and he began jogging toward it. He knew the Mountie would have his back.

*   *   *

Tank was still struggling to contain his anger when they all trooped back into camp. He was frustrated that he hadn't yet come up with a definitive plan; he wasn't normally this indecisive. Other than getting the guns out of that cabin and on their way to Canada, and killing his former partner, he couldn't come up with a thing. So he had the good sense just to play along in his tour-guide role, focusing on what was in front of him.

As soon as they got back to the primitive campsite, most everyone in the group collapsed by their tent or tried to find shade. He and Ginger got the fire going and soon had coffee and hot water available for tea. Ginger retrieved the snack bag from its twelve-foot-tall bearproof hanging pole and handed out the goodies. It was so warm that there weren't many takers for the hot drinks, but the Gatorade had been soaking all day deep in the small creek that flowed nearby, and it was a crowd-pleaser.

Will pulled his bedroll from his tent and laid it down beside a huge pine. He rolled out his sleeping bag over the pad and stretched out for a few minutes. This wasn't his usual way to spend downtime, but he needed to think some things through. The bear, the scenery, and Ginger's upbeat mood had distracted him on the hike back from the thermal area, but deep down he was still conflicted. *Should I tell Ginger what I saw? Should I text Win more of what I saw? Should I keep my head down and my mouth shut?*

He checked the flip phone again, still no response to his first text. Still no service bars. He typed in a second text just to keep Win updated if the messages ever went through: **At camp 4C6. Bad feeling about this. 4:05.** That should do it, he thought. Just keep updating Win on where they were, on what was going on. No need to panic. Tyler boys were taught not to panic. Win used to tell him to take a deep breath, slow down, think things through. Win also used to tell him to pray about it—to pray for wisdom, for direction. His mom would say that too, so would Blake, so would Dad. Will drew in a deep breath and stared up at the canopy of green high above him. The top of the pine tree was swaying in the breeze. His friends would tell him all that prayer stuff was pathetic. *My friends could be wrong.*

*   *   *

Win and Alex agreed that this was the most logical route. The map in Win's head told him that the surest way out for Pierson was the trail from the campground that ran to the southeast, then angled south toward the north rim. They jogged down the trail, careful to stay on it—the rangers had warned them not to get far off the path. They said the wooded area was pocketed with hidden fissures and cracks, evidence of long-inactive thermal fields. A walker could easily step into a dry spring or hole and come up limping. Pierson had obviously been camped here for a while; he likely knew of those hazards as well. So Win figured the guy would stick to the trail too, at least until he reached the canyon's rim. If he reached the trailheads on the north rim, he could go any number of directions.

They were making good time, and Win was impressed with Alex's stamina. He still couldn't figure out where she got her energy, but she stayed close behind him and he knew she was watchful and alert. For a time, Win thought he might need to ask her to lead, the pain in his ribs and shoulder from the beating Dex had given him three days ago had reemerged at the beginning of the run. But he kept up a steady pace, gritted his teeth, and told himself that the heat and the motion would loosen his sore muscles. Dex Pierson needed to be behind bars, and each time a stab of pain shot through his body, Win recommitted himself to putting him there.

When he and Alex passed the point where the Girl Scouts had called in the sighting of Pierson, they slowed to advance more cautiously. Soon they were less than half a mile from the small parking area near the Seven Mile Hole Trailhead. They'd met two more small groups of hikers. None of them had seen a solitary backpacker walking east, none of them had seen Pierson. And maybe even more odd, none of them seemed the least bit concerned to see Win jogging along holding an AR-15 in plain sight. He and Alex warned the hikers about the dangerous man in the woods; they simply got shrugs and nods in return. Win was experiencing a new norm, where gun-toting hikers weren't uncommon, where dangerous men were just an accepted part of a typical day. Win didn't have time to reflect on the psychological state of his fellow citizens—he saw a leaning wooden sign that said *Glacial Boulder—Trailheads .25 Mile.* Based on Pierson's last observed position, he could have passed the trailhead more than thirty minutes ago, or if the fugitive had tried to conceal himself from the others he'd met on the path, he could be getting to the trailhead right about now. Win was relatively confident that Pierson wasn't behind them, and it would have made no sense for him to take the other trail down into Canyon Village. Win was guessing the guy was right in front of them.

And he was guessing right.

* * *

Tank was trying to figure out a plan to get back to Canyon that afternoon, and one just fell in his lap. He was bringing in the last load of wood for the evening's campfire when Ginger approached him with a concerned expression on her face. Her voice was low and tense.

"Chad, I think Mrs. Olsen overdid it at the spring. I was watching her all the way back, and I made sure she got some extra electrolytes, but I just checked on her again and she's not recovering as quickly as she should."

Ginger was talking about one of the Vermont ladies, as he liked to think of them. Mrs. Olsen was the older of the two sisters. She was in her mid-sixties and had a real enthusiasm for the outdoors. He'd noticed that she seemed very subdued when they came back to camp, but he had other, way more pressing things on his mind and he hadn't followed up with her.

"What are you thinking?" he asked.

"I thought about calling the boss on the sat phone. But it's not an emergency, and you know they're on that six-day backpacking trek down in Grand Teton." She sighed. "I hate to say it, but I think it might be best if one of us walks her back to the village. We've still got hours of daylight and it's beginning to cool off a bit. We could get her to the Visitor Center and let them check her out . . . they could transport her to the Lake Medical Clinic, if necessary. She might need IV fluids, but maybe just a night under the AC would snap her out of it."

He listened to Ginger's reasoning, acting as if he was pondering it. He didn't want her to think that he was jumping at a chance to leave.

When he didn't respond right away, she added, "You could go. I've got to do the big farewell dinner tonight. You could take Tyler with you. That way one of you could walk on each side of her, keep her from stumbling . . . make better time. You could be at the trailhead in less than two hours, maybe call a ranger from there. If you check her into a lodge or leave her with the EMTs, you could be back here well before dark."

"You think her sister would let her go without her? You think Tyler would be okay with it?"

"Sure, Mrs. Olsen actually suggested it. She said she didn't want to ruin the trip for her sister, said she'd gotten badly dehydrated once before, has some high blood pressure issues. We don't want to wait until this becomes serious. And Tyler? Tyler is always up for an adventure. Plus Mrs. Olsen acts like he's her grandson. She'd love to have him along."

Tank shook his head as if he needed convincing. "Okay . . . okay, that could work. I'll ask Tyler, you get her ready to go. The quicker we leave the sooner we'll be back."

Their clients didn't know this, but Primitive Campground 4C6 was only three miles east of the Glacial Boulder trailheads and Inspiration Point. The guides liked to keep that fact to themselves, and since no one's smartphone or GPS worked out there, it was an easy secret to keep. Their company reserved this camping spot for the last two nights of their trip so that their packable coolers could be refilled with fresh food and other necessities. The gourmet meals and fine wines that Ginger served for the evening dinners couldn't be lugged around for days in eighty-degree heat. Each day a caterer and her helper packed the nights' meals into the camp and hoisted the fresh food and beverages high above the ground on bear-proof poles while the clients were off on their adventures. No one had to know that they were just a moderate hike away from civilization.

It looked and felt like the middle of nowhere, and Tank had been at the job long enough to know that if you got fifty feet off an official trail in Yellowstone National Park, you were indeed in the wilderness.

* * *

Will had rolled over on his stomach on the sleeping bag and was watching a yellowish-tan snake with brown blotches slither through the pine needles about an arm's length away. He'd heard movement in the leaves and sticks a few minutes ago and had expected to see a squirrel, a mouse, or some other kind of rodent. But nope, here he was nearly eyeball to eyeball with a five-foot reptile. He wasn't expecting a snake, not at 8,000 feet of elevation in the Northern Rocky Mountains. He had no idea they had snakes out here. But here it was, likely wondering what this big breathing thing was blocking its path. Will was accustomed to snakes, he wasn't afraid of them, but he didn't know this Western snake and he was cautious. He and the snake were both still, checking each other out. The reptile had orange eyes and an active forked tongue. It had stopped its forward movement and raised its head to better see him.

"It's a bull snake."

"Whoa!" Will flinched and rolled onto his back at the sound of the voice above him. He'd been so engrossed in the reptile that he hadn't heard Tank approach. He was glad he hadn't uttered the curse word that first formed on his lips.

"Sorry, didn't mean to scare you," the burly man responded. "Uh, we usually see them at lower elevations, but once in a while we spot one up here." He shifted his attention from the snake, and made his sales pitch. "You wanta little adventure? Mrs. Olsen isn't feeling well, and I need someone to help me walk her back to Canyon Village. They have an EMT stationed in Canyon, and that person can look her over. They may want her to stay at a lodge or be transported down to the clinic at Lake. It'll probably be slow going, helping her along, but we should be back at least an hour before dark. You won't miss the big campfire tonight, and Ginger will save us an amazing dinner."

Tank was saying all these things in a perfectly reasonable, matter-of-fact voice. Will was staring up into his face and thinking that the words of concern for the older woman did not match his piercing gaze. He was also thinking this might be an opportunity to get away from Tank, get back to civilization, get back to Win. The thought of spending the night in a tent with this creep nearby spooked him—he'd already been worrying about that scenario. He'd also concluded that he'd seen too many horror movies where things went terribly wrong in the dark woods. Hiking out with Tank should be chill. There were lots of folks on the trails, and Mrs. Olsen would be with them. He couldn't imagine Tank doing anything to harm that sweet lady.

Then again, Will didn't know Chad Maddox very well.

* * *

Win was soaked through with sweat, and he figured Alex was too. She had stayed close behind him for the trail run, which was now more of a jog. After the fork in the trail, the path angled south toward the canyon and became much rougher; now they were slowly moving down an eroded trail interspersed with rocks, roots, and logs. At least the sun was partially blocked by the forty-foot pines, that was some consolation. They'd both drained a water bottle at their last stop to quiz some hikers, and Win was tempted to pull out another one. His ribs were hurting again and his breath was coming in shallow gasps. He double-checked the safety on his rifle to get his mind off his discomfort. Blinking the sweat from his eyes, he continued to scan the trail and dark woods in front of them.

He'd turned his phone to vibrate so as not to alert anyone of their presence. He knew they had to be within a few hundred yards of the trailhead. He sure hoped Kirk had found someone to meet them there. Either Dex was between them and the trailhead or he was not—they'd know within minutes. When the phone vibrated in his pocket, he raised his arm for Alex to stop. He moved to the side of the path, adjusted the rifle, and dropped down on one knee. He heard her ragged breathing as she moved to the opposite side and slid into the edge of the trees.

It was a familiar name on the phone's screen. He answered the phone, and a thick Cajun accent filled his ear. "Hey, Win. You got someone moving up the trail toward you. I've been stopping anyone comin' west on the trail for the last fifteen minutes, but I just got a glimpse of a man who started to walk out toward the parking lot, then he saw me and walked back your way. Back up the trail." Luke's voice was soft and serious.

Win quickly got over the initial shock of having this conversation with Luke Bordeaux, who was well within the closed area that should have been evacuated an hour ago.

"See a weapon?" Win asked quietly. He kept his eyes on the woods where the trail disappeared just beyond them.

"No, but he's carrying a backpack, tan ball cap, stout guy. . . . This could be your boy."

"Where are you?" Win asked.

"Right beside the Glacial Boulder. I wasn't in position when the guy walked out of the woods. I know he saw me."

Win turned toward Alex and used hand signals to alert her to the fact that they might have company.

"We're probably less than two hundred yards from you. We've got him between us." Win whispered into the phone. Win saw movement down the trail. "Here we go," he quietly added.

The trail curved through the trees in front of them—Win and Alex had a clear view for maybe fifty yards. Win pocketed the phone and backed farther off the path. He crouched behind a weathered log and eased the rifle in front of him. A limb broke somewhere down the trail. He glanced at Alex. She had her handgun drawn and was holding it at her side.

Win felt sweat running down his chest, and his hands felt sticky on the rifle's hard plastic frame. He reached up, wiped his face, and flipped his cap around so the bill was in the back. He fingered the safety and wished for a moment that someone had given him body armor. He felt exposed here near the trail, with the high-altitude sun beating down on him. It suddenly occurred to him that he hadn't prayed for himself, for Alex, for Dex, he hadn't prayed about the outcome. He blinked the sweat from his eyes and prayed for God's protection, and for Alex—

That's as far as he got when he saw Dex Pierson jogging up the trail toward them.

Alex must have moved, or maybe there was a flash of a reflection off something she was wearing. Whatever it was spooked Dex, who dropped and rolled into the underbrush.

"Damn!" Alex said as she dodged deeper into the woods. Win held his position and offered the man the chance of surrender. "FBI! Dex, stand up slowly and keep your hands above your head!" Win couldn't see where the guy was. "Hands up! You're surrounded. Stand up slowly!"

There was no response, but Alex yelled a warning next. "He's in the trees! He's gotten into the trees!"

Win could hear limbs in the underbrush breaking. He could tell she was going after Pierson—she wasn't holding back—and he found himself running toward the spot where she'd been. He caught a glimpse of her dodging from tree to tree, maybe forty, fifty feet in front of him, running headlong after the fugitive.

"Watch your footing!" Win called out. He could see that the pines were stunted in this area, that the ground looked chalky.

She fell before he could shout another warning. He saw her go down at a bad angle and heard her cry out in pain. Her handgun discharged as she fell, and the sound seemed frighteningly out of place in Yellowstone. Officers are trained not to run with their finger on the trigger—they practice that technique over and over—but live action isn't the same as practice. Thankfully the gun was pointed at the uneven terrain and the bullet struck only the ground.

The sharp report reverberated through the deep woods and carried for miles. The sound of gunfire set in motion several unfortunate events.

CHAPTER THIRTY

"Was that a gunshot?" Will said as all three of them froze on the trail. It wasn't really a question. He was no stranger to guns. He just wasn't expecting to hear two gunshots in one day in Yellowstone National Park.

Will was holding Mrs. Olsen's right arm and Tank was steadying her other side. They'd made fairly good time in the thirty minutes since they'd left the campsite, but Will could tell the poor lady was fading.

Tank had been acting perfectly normal. If he shot someone earlier that afternoon, he sure wasn't sweating it. He was carrying Mrs. Olsen's overnight pack in addition to his daypack, and he was kind and considerate of her at every step. Will began to second-guess himself, to think that he might have imagined the incident at the spring. They took short stops for rest and water often, and Mrs. Olsen was handling it like a trooper. Although she was pale and her reflexes were slow, she was trying real hard to have a "sunny attitude," as she called it. Will was helpful with Mrs. Olsen and deferential to Tank, doing his best to pretend nothing was wrong.

But the sound of the gunshot shocked Will back to reality, and the steely look in Tank's eyes as he stared off to the west was chilling. Will knew something was off, and that look confirmed it. Tank just shrugged and made some excuse about rangers having to put down nuisance animals sometimes—no big deal, he remarked. Mrs. Olsen said *"Oh my,"* and looked shocked. But Will wasn't buying it.

At their next stop, Will took the opportunity to send Win another text while Tank stepped around a rock pile to tend to some business. **Hiking back to Canyon w sick lady and Tank. 4:40 Need you.** He started to retype the text—it sounded like he was a little kid needing his older brother—but he heard Tank moving toward them from behind the rocks and he hit SEND. He drew in a deep breath as he pocketed the phone. Maybe he was a little kid needing his older brother. And maybe there was nothing wrong with that.

* * *

Dex assumed someone was shooting at him, and it wasn't an unreasonable assumption. He'd heard the guy yell, "*FBI!*" That was probably Agent Tyler. He wasn't sure who all else was with Tyler, blocking the trail, but he'd seen a reflection off something on the upper side of the path, so there were at least two of them. And then someone had been after him in the woods—that same someone had taken a shot. He didn't like getting shot at, not one damn bit, but this sure wasn't the time for payback. They were closing in on him. Probably knew he'd taken this trail because the Girl Scouts tipped off the rangers. Women were always getting him in trouble, dammit.

He angled through the forest, trying to stick to the areas with underbrush and the taller pines. He knew how unstable the ground could be near the north rim, how a wrong step could end badly. He moved from tree to tree with precision; he needed to keep going south-east. That was really the only viable way out of here during daylight. The cops had someone staking out the parking lot at the trailhead, but he hadn't gotten a good look at the guy. He had noticed that there were very few cars there, and that wasn't normal for this time of day. They were probably guessing he'd head for the canyon's north rim, where he could take the Seven Mile Hole Trail down toward the river or up toward Mount Washburn, or even cut back toward the cabins on the North Rim Trail. He should have known they'd figure that out—he needed to get off the main trail, and he needed to do it right now. He'd been avoiding the bushwacking route and the old lanes because he knew they were so rough and overgrown they might slow him down even more. He could still hear someone in the woods behind him. It was way past time to disappear.

*   *   *

When Win reached Alex, she was writhing in pain. He wasn't an expert on medical matters by any means, but her exposed leg above her ankle was already swelling. She'd either broken it or twisted the ankle badly. Alex's tan face had paled, and she was fighting back tears.

"Gun discharged when I fell." That was all she said about it, but he could tell she was trying to pull herself together. She closed her eyes and shook her head. Then she pulled up her pants leg and surveyed the damage.

Win kept the rifle pointed in front of them as he knelt, his eyes scanning the dense woods and then flicking back to the small woman lying on the whitish ground beside him. "Why don't you lay here a minute. Get your wind back, I'll call for help."

She was blinking away tears, but she was still on the mission. "No . . . no, we almost have him. . . ." She gasped as she tried to move her leg. "Go . . . go after him!"

He hit speed dial. Luke answered before it rang.

"You okay?"

"My partner fell in a hole, hurt her leg, her gun misfired."

"Okay, that oughta let Pierson know right where you are."

"I think he's still going southeast, toward the rim," Win said.

"Go off to the north, you'll hit an old carriage road. It's not used as a trail anymore, it's overgrown and really rough. Not many folks know about it, but Pierson might."

"Okay, I'll go after him," Win said. "I'll look for the old road."

"Should I stay here at the trailhead?"

"Yeah, yeah, till I can see for sure where he's going. Anyone else shown up?"

"I haven't seen anyone, but a ranger does have the road blocked about a half mile back. I haven't had to run off any tourists," Luke replied. "Watch yourself, Win."

* * *

Win kept moving slowly forward, then he stopped and listened. The sound of limbs breaking was straight ahead—something had gone down. He moved a few yards and found branches splintered and brush flattened. Pierson was in a hurry now, plowing through the thickets, not being as careful as he should. *Either that,* Win thought, *or I'm following an elk or a bison or maybe a bear.* He pulled the rifle in close to his chest as he maneuvered through head-high huckleberry bushes—he could barely see what was in front of him—and then his foot hit the solid rock of a short wall. Win used his free hand to part the dense brush and took a step up onto the wall just as he heard a crash to his right. Something big had fallen.

He paused for a few beats, then dropped down onto the other side of the stone wall into the relatively clear area where the old carriage path once ran. The stunted bushes were still knee- to waist-high, and scroungy pines dotted what had once been a narrow dirt lane. He could see down it for a couple hundred yards before it reentered the dark forest. A huge, weathered log lay less than forty feet away, blocking much of the track. Dex Pierson was struggling to his feet on this side of it, his back to Win. He was close enough to hit with a rock.

Win leveled the assault rifle at the guy's big backpack. He drew in a breath and got still. Dex must have sensed he was there. He turned slowly. Win saw him favoring his left leg, saw him limp as he turned, then saw the gun in his hand near his thigh.

"Drop it now! C'mon, Dex! Drop it!" Win carefully took a couple of steps closer. He couldn't afford to look at the ground, to take his eyes off Pierson.

"Well, hell." The words came out as an exhale. "Didn't think you'd know about this old road . . . ain't been used much since who knows when. Used it for stagecoach tours back in 1886. . . . Goes to a point on the rim where you can see the big waterfall." Dex paused, still breathing hard. "There's old roads and trails all around this part of the park. Hard to believe folks been sightseeing here for over 130 years."

"I don't need a history lesson, Dex. Drop the gun now!"

"Where's Shane?"

"Drop the gun and raise your hands over your head now!"

The man just stood there, trying to recover from the fall. He'd lost his cap, and Win could see the sharp points on his teeth. Much of the guy's face paint had sweated off, and portions of the red-and-black tattoos were visible. Dex looked winded, scary, and mean.

"Did you take care of Shane?" he asked again. The gun hadn't moved from beside his right leg, but the muzzle was pointed down and his tone of voice was softer.

"Yeah . . . yeah. Shane and Max are on their way to Georgia. Shane is fine. Now do us all a favor and drop that gun and raise your hands. C'mon, Dex, Shane will need you someday." Win was trying to keep his voice hard; he was trying not to plead.

"On your right!" Win heard Alex call out and he flinched from surprise. How in the world had she gotten here on that leg? How had she snuck up on him again?

Win cut his eyes to the side for a split second and saw her step out of the brush and over the low stone wall. Her face was taut with pain. But her handgun was held in a steady two-handed grip, pointed right at Dex Pierson's head.

"You've got one more chance to drop that gun!" she yelled at Pierson.

Win saw the Sig Sauer drop from Dex's fingers, saw him begin to raise his hands, heard the powerful gunshot that shook the space between them.

*　*　*

They were on a short section of the trail that hugged the rim of the vast canyon. Will could catch glimpses of the green Yellowstone River far below. There was some breeze here, and the trees were providing good shade. They'd stopped to give the frail woman more Gatorade and rest. Will leaned back against a boulder and tried to figure out why they weren't meeting more hikers coming their way—it was as if someone had closed the gate on the trailhead. He had no way of knowing that the trail had been closed for well over an hour, that the hikers he'd expected to provide a little cushion from Tank weren't going to materialize. All he knew was that he'd felt very alone since they'd left the camp. Tank had just leaned over to help Mrs. Olsen to her feet from the rock she was sitting on, when they heard the loud gunshot.

Will turned to Tank with a question, but Mrs. Olsen beat him to it. "What's happening?" she asked. "Goodness, it sounds like we're in a war zone. Is this hunting season?"

She and Will were both staring at Tank. Tank could tell this gunshot was closer, could tell something had gotten out of hand. That might work to his advantage or not, but the message from the backcountry ranger earlier today said the FBI agent was asking about him. He couldn't figure out *how* they could be onto him, but if that lowlife, Prince, had put a contract out on him, and maybe fingered him with the law, then he could be walking right into a trap. A part of him still couldn't believe that Prince would play the double-cross with him, but Tank had checked his Garmin satellite device twice since they left camp and there was nothing from Prince. Nothing.

Tank had originally thought he might be able to use Mrs. Olsen as a prop to get into Canyon. But at this rate, with the old woman in tow, they wouldn't even be at the trailhead for another hour. She was giving out and slowing down. The gunshots were worrying, the lack of hiker traffic on the trail was worrying, the lack of contact from Prince was worrying. It was time to go with his backup plan.

Tank pulled out his cell phone and looked at the screen. "Hey, we just hit cell service, my phone vibrated . . . check your phones and see."

Mrs. Olsen didn't seem interested in her phone at the moment. She might have been getting faint, she was tottering on the rock. But she obediently fumbled with her fanny pack, pulled her phone out, turned it on, and waited for it to light up.

Will shifted on the boulder, reached in his pocket for his flip phone, and opened it. "Nope, no service."

Mrs. Olsen kept staring at the screen, apparently trying to will her phone to connect. "Mine's not—"

Tank used his left hand to snatch her phone and Will's with stunning quickness. Will stared at him in disbelief. Tank's right hand wasn't holding his phone any longer, it was gripping a large silver handgun.

Will jumped up. "What the hell!"

The man's expression and voice were both icy cold. He held up the two phones with his left hand and shook them. "You won't need these little items any longer, friends. Will, me and you are gonna make a fast hike to the real world. And you"—he glared down at a shocked Mrs. Olsen—"you are gonna sit here on this rock and be thankful that I left you alive."

Before they could respond, Tank threw the phones high into the air and they began the thousand-foot drop off the brink of the north rim. As soon as they cleared the dense lodgepole pines and began to fall through the open air of the deep canyon, Yellowstone's rogue cell signals, which occasionally connected, did just that. Mrs. Olsen's phone sent a great photo of the cinnamon bear to her niece in Cleveland. Will's phone sent three urgent messages to his older brother, the FBI agent.

*   *   *

Dex spun from the impact of the bullet, then staggered backward with the weight of his pack and fell face up near the log. For a second Win thought Alex had shot him, but Win knew guns and that was no pistol shot. With a regular hunting rifle or a handgun, the wound probably would have just been a serious graze, but Win knew from the sound of the shot that Dex Pierson had taken a potentially fatal blow.

Win and Alex had both frozen for a split second, unsure of who was firing. Then they dove for the ground. Win began crawling toward Dex and the relative cover of the ancient log, as Alex tried to maneuver her injured leg back over the stone wall. A second shot hit the wall where she'd been standing, and pieces of rock and bullet sprayed like shrapnel.

"I'm good!" Win heard her call out. He answered in kind, pulled out his phone, and hit speed dial again. He put the phone on speaker and stuffed it in his shirt pocket.

"Shooter!" Win said as he shifted the rifle and resumed crawling.

"Tell me somethin' I don't know," Luke replied.

"We're pinned down," Win said. "Pierson's hit." He moved through the low brush for the last twenty feet to reach the still figure in front of him.

Win realized in a heartbeat that Dex Pierson's survival wasn't a sure thing. Dex appeared stunned; he groaned and blinked when Win touched him. Win scooped up the Sig Sauer pistol that lay in an expanding pool of blood near the man's side and stuffed it in his belt. Dex was still lying on his back with the big pack under him. Win pressed down on the bloody shreds of the man's shirt. The bullet appeared to have hit his backpack and exited the front of his left side, which meant the shooter was likely farther down the old road. Of course Win was only guessing.

He didn't have to guess for long. When Win inched up to look over the log, Dex's right hand grabbed his shirt and yanked him backward with such force that he nearly dropped his rifle. The .458 magnum cartridge took a huge chunk out of the top of the log and cut down a four-inch-diameter pine thirty yards behind them. The sounds of the shot and the tree's destruction occurred almost simultaneously. The shooter was close.

Lordy! Lordy! Win lay there almost on top of Dex, fully aware that he'd nearly had his head blown off. He silently thanked God and figured he owed Dex some thanks too. That, and he needed some answers.

"Appreciate that . . . uh, who's shooting?" Win asked as he fought to calm his racing heart. He kept one hand pressed hard against Dex's bleeding side, and the other hand on the assault rifle.

The look in Dex's eyes went from pain to realization to something akin to loss. Win figured Dex was suddenly understanding Jesse

Prince's exit plan, maybe realizing that one of the only friends he'd had in his life now considered him expendable.

Any loyalty Pierson felt for his partner seemingly evaporated with that reckoning, after being gunned down with his own rifle. His answer came in a low, breathy voice. "Jesse Gibbs . . . goes by name of . . . Jesse Prince . . . outa West Yellowstone."

"Is he your partner on the poaching? Is he the brains behind it?"

Win could tell Pierson was trying to force away the pain, trying to recover from the shock. "You thinkin' I ain't the brains?" the man snarled.

"I'm thinkin' this guy is your partner . . . he's running the show. I'm thinkin' this guy wants to make sure you don't turn him in."

Dex tried to shift, but the pain curbed his movement. He groaned again and locked eyes with Win. "Jesse sets up the clients, the haul out, the payout. I do the guiding and set up the shot."

"What about the illegal guns? Is Gibbs running that for you too?"

Dex seemed to be trying to focus on Win. He looked totally confused. "Don't know nothing about that."

The blood flow was getting a little heavier. Win used his cap to try to stem the tide, pushing down harder on the crumpled shirt that was now crimson red. The man lying beside him closed his eyes. Win realized he was fading. Win hazarded a quick glance down the lane from behind the thick log's trunk, saw nothing, and ducked back down. He considered firing off a three-round burst just to keep the shooter's attention, but he didn't. He had no idea where Alex had gone. He wouldn't shoot blindly, he couldn't risk hitting her. So instead he kept asking questions.

"Is Shane yours?"

Pierson opened his eyes and stared into space for a couple of seconds then shook his head slowly. "No." It was almost a whisper.

"You just kidnap him or somethin'?"

He shook his head again, and this time he turned his face toward Win. A trickle of blood dripped from the corner of his mouth. The daggerlike teeth were red, and Win fought the urge to pull back as Dex found his voice. "No . . . no. I was in the service in Georgia. . . . Me and his mama, Katie . . . and my best friend . . . we run around together. Was hoping she'd pick me, but she picked Jordon . . . and Jordon got himself killed in Afghanistan. . . . She died in a wreck . . . and I ended up in prison."

"And Shane?"

"He's . . . he's Jordon Bradford's son . . . but I went and got him before Christmas this last year. . . . Told Katie's sister I'd bring him home in a week or two . . . but I didn't." Dex's breath was becoming raspy. He squeezed his eyes shut as another wave of pain hit him.

"So you did kidnap him?"

"No . . . he wanted to hear stories of his father . . . I owed him that. And . . . and my old man, he needed someone, uh, a grandson . . . I owed him that."

"What was in it for the boy?"

"He got to spend time with his grandfather . . . or someone who wanted to be his grandfather." Dex drew in a labored breath. "That counts, don't it? Better than not havin' one at all, ain't it? Shane's mother died when he was four, her parents aren't livin'. The sister, she may think he's mine . . . I've led 'em to believe that . . . sent her money for him since his mother died."

Dex moaned and tried to shift, but it was like he was stuck to the spot—the blood was pooling under him. "Ain't no good . . . he's got my Winchester 70 . . . a .458 magnum kin bring down a Cape buffalo." He choked on the words a little and spit up more blood. "Try to force a shot . . . then you got 4.5 seconds before he can reload. . . . He's not using a tripod or he wouldn't be missing. You get outa here while you can, or Jesse's gonna kill us all."

CHAPTER THIRTY-ONE

Tank kept his handgun out. They'd just paused to finish off a bottle of water, sweat was dripping off both of them. Tank motioned down the trail with the gun. He was keeping Will ahead of him, and within three feet; he didn't want to give the boy a chance to bolt. They'd moved at a quick jog from the spot where they left the woman. The path was well-worn and mostly smooth. It hadn't been taxing for either of them.

Tank was ready to move on and Will was still grousing about Mrs. Olsen. Will was ticked off. "Hey, dude! We just left an old woman back there alone."

"She'll be fine, we're within a half mile of the parking lot. Start moving or *you* won't be fine!" Tank growled back. The kid was starting to act like a teenager—it was getting old.

Will knew they had to be getting close to the trailhead, but he didn't realize they were that close. He kept hoping someone, maybe a ranger, would come into view and rescue him, but they hadn't met a soul.

They'd heard more gunshots a few minutes ago, and Tank was thinking more and more that it had nothing to do with him. Maybe the rangers had cornered that loser Pierson, maybe that could work to his advantage. The cabin where he and Roadie had moved the guns wasn't far off the North Rim Trail. He just had to get to his truck in the main parking lot, drive to the cabin, load as many guns as he could stuff into his pickup, then head toward Canada. If the rangers and cops were after Pierson, it might create the perfect diversion. He always carried his Sheriff's Office credentials with him—showing them off impressed the girls. He figured flashing them at a roadblock or checkpoint should give him a free pass.

But what to do with this surly kid? He'd forced him along as insurance in case that FBI agent was after him, and he was smart enough to realize that scenario could still be in play. And if anyone stopped them on the trail or at the trailhead, he could explain that they'd hiked in and back from Washburn Hot Springs today and were just coming back to their cabin. No reason for anyone to be suspicious, hikers did that every day this time of year. Shouldn't be a problem if the kid played along. And the kid better play along—Tank had already threatened him within an inch of his life. He knew Will Tyler was scared of him, and he damn well should be.

* * *

Win was considering Dex's advice on trying to trick the shooter into another shot, then making a run for it, when he heard voices yelling in the woods behind them. *This ain't good* was his first thought, then Luke's voice came over his phone.

"Sounds like two or three folks came off the main trail from the Canyon Campground. . . . You got company. Some guy in an FBI vest just walked out to the trailhead in front of me. I'm thinkin' it's your people."

Win spoke down toward the phone in his front pocket, his hands still occupied with his rifle and Dex's bleeding side. "Get with them, try to flank the shooter."

"Roger that."

Win could still hear voices in the woods. It sounded like a herd of elephants moving toward them. Someone fell and let loose with a string of cuss words. A glance at his watch told Win they'd left Pierson's trailer only forty-five minutes ago; he and Alex had first confronted Dex in the old carriage lane less than five minutes ago. It seemed as if time was standing still, it felt like hours. He didn't know which direction the shooter might come from, where the gunman was now. What he did know was that Dex was bleeding out, that he hadn't heard from Alex since that second shot missed her, and that they hadn't had an incoming round in over two minutes.

Kirk and a female agent, both in body armor, stepped out of the woods ten yards behind Win. "Shooter! Get down!" Win yelled at them.

Kirk ignored the warning, but he did crouch lower, and the two maneuvered through the thick brush toward the log.

"It's cool," Kirk said. He was completely out of breath and holding his rifle out at a weird angle, as if he were afraid it might bite him. "Uh . . . rangers circled the area. I just got a call, someone . . . someone found gloves and a bolt-action rifle further down this old road, looking for the—oh, man!" Kirk had pushed aside another bush and saw Pierson for the first time. His eyes got as big as saucers. "Whoa, I guess this is why that dude told us to call in the ambulance and the EMTs."

"Are the EMTs on the way?" Win asked.

Kirk nodded. "Yeah, I think that got done." He didn't sound convincing.

The female agent, who'd stepped into the lane with Kirk, was carefully checking out the area. She suddenly raised the alarm. "Need help here! Got a woman down! Gunshot to the head!"

* * *

Tank was holding Will's arm and limping a little for effect when they stepped off the Seven Mile Hole Trail onto the small parking lot at the trailhead. The Glacial Boulder, a five-hundred-ton, house-size rock, was a local landmark on the north rim. It sat just yards away and seemed to be the gathering place for at least a dozen rangers, FBI agents, and other law enforcement types. Ambulances and vehicles with flashing light bars covered every inch of pavement. Tank sucked in a breath and checked again to make sure his shirt concealed the Colt .45 that was stuck in his waistband.

A park ranger in SWAT gear was walking toward them with his hand up. Tank whispered the warning in Will's ear again: "Keep your mouth shut! Just coming in from a hike, taking the North Rim Trail to our cabin. . . . Behave yourself and I'll cut you loose as soon as we get to my truck. Screw it up and some of these good people will get hurt. You got that?"

Will nodded.

Tank gave the SWAT guy his line, showed him his Sheriff's Office credentials, asked what was going on, and never let go of Will's arm. Will tried to look bored. Sweat was dripping off his chin.

"We heard gunshots," Tank said. "Sounded terrible—can't seem to escape the job even on my day off." The ranger nodded that he understood. "We're movin' slow, I stepped off a rock wrong. . . . We'll get out of your way," Tank added as he tugged on Will's arm to move him forward.

The ranger stepped aside, wiped a hand across his damp face, and pushed back his helmet. "We're still looking for someone. There was an incident." He was trying to be helpful. "You can catch the North Rim Trail down below the Glacial Boulder, walk down this road about a quarter mile toward the rim, it's just before the viewing platform for Inspiration Point. You're within a couple of miles of the cabins. If you wanta hang out till this wraps up, I could get someone to drive you there."

Tank smiled and waved off the kind offer. "Thanks, but we'll keep moving."

"Take care of that foot!" The ranger called after them.

As they slowly walked across the parking area toward the canyon, Tank's grip on Will's arm tightened. The boy glanced back at the group of folks meeting in the shadow of the massive boulder. *Where's Win?*

* * *

At that moment, Win was standing in the late-afternoon shade of a massive rock that the sign said had been deposited on the north rim of the Grand Canyon of the Yellowstone several thousand years ago, when an Ice Age glacier dropped it in this spot. Win wondered how they knew that, but then he decided he didn't care. He was letting his mind wander for a few minutes, glad that he wasn't in charge, and wishing he could get the sight of the carnage out of his head.

He'd watched the Park Service EMTs load Pierson and Alex into separate ambulances just minutes ago. Neither one was conscious nor had they been since being hauled out of the woods on stretchers. Oxygen masks covered their faces, IVs were flowing in their arms; the medics' voices were soft and serious. Nobody was wearing a particularly hopeful look. He'd heard an EMT say they were going to get them both on the medevac chopper as soon as it got here from Mammoth, get them both to Idaho Falls, to the trauma center.

The search for whoever had left that high-powered rifle in the woods was going strong, more rangers had just arrived, everyone was armed to the teeth, and Kirk was trying to get them organized and in the field. They had a suspect—Jesse Gibbs, a.k.a. Jesse Prince—but they had absolutely no idea which way the guy went after he abandoned the gun.

Win figured if Kirk's information was correct, Gibbs was a con man, a chameleon. Maybe he'd just morphed into a frightened hiker, or a bird watcher, or a photographer, someone who just happened to get caught up in the vicinity of the shooting, someone who was just trying to get back to their car or lodge. Win knew the Denver office was trying to get an emergency warrant to raid Prince's business in West Yellowstone. That might provide some answers. But at the moment they had no solid leads.

Luke walked over and stood next to him. "That lady Mountie gonna make it?"

Win shook his head. His voice was subdued. "It isn't lookin' good. She took a piece of the rock wall into her skull, maybe a fragment of the slug also . . . don't know. She answered me when I called out to her after the second shot, I do know that."

"You've been there. Sometimes with head wounds a person can function for a time, then the brain bleed begins . . . then things shut down."

Win nodded. "And they don't know about Pierson either. He's lost a lot of blood." Luke knew these things; he had helped carry Pierson out. Luke was just making small talk, being a friend.

"I'm guessing Trey called you a couple of hours ago—you got down here fast," Win said.

Luke just shrugged. "I was finishing up a tour north of Roosevelt when I got his call that you was in a tight. I was already in the area."

"How'd you get through the roadblocks to get back here?" Win asked him.

Luke smiled that cagey smile of his. "Just flashed my credentials . . . FBI."

"Please tell me you didn't really do that."

Luke arched his black eyebrows. "Then I won't tell you I did that."

Win just shook his head. He was so glad to have the man here to help that he didn't really care how he got here or who or what he claimed to be.

Kirk walked over from the huddle of rangers. "Jim's gonna take over, thank goodness. He'll be here within fifteen minutes." He ran a hand through his hair and gave a tired shrug. "Like, I might be a little over my head here, maybe." Then he switched gears. "Hey, I nearly forgot—someone found a phone next to Pierson when they loaded him on the stretcher in the woods. It's got a Razorback screensaver." Kirk held it up and looked at Win. "I'm guessing it's yours."

Win's free hand went to his bloody cargo pants pocket—empty. He took his personal phone from Kirk and immediately saw the notifications on the screen. He'd swear his heart stopped for a moment as he swiped the phone open and read the texts from Will. He locked eyes with Luke. "I need your help," he said. "I need your help now."

*   *   *

Tank and Will walked gingerly down the edge of the paved road that gently sloped toward Inspiration Point and the North Rim Trail. Tank was playing the injured-foot thing for all it was worth as he hung on to Will, a pained expression plastered on his face.

It was odd to see no tourists, no one really, after they moved beyond the frenzy of activity back near the trailhead. Tank was feeling better about things. They'd left the primitive campsite less than two hours ago, the trail was closed so no hikers would stumble across Mrs. Olsen and sound the alarm, and once they made it onto the North Rim Trail, he'd be home free. Then he'd have to decide what to do with the kid. So far the boy had been toeing the line, but they'd soon be running into more and more folks. He'd already decided he needed to lose Tyler. He just hadn't decided how to do it.

Using the 1911 wasn't an option. A gunshot from the big .45 would draw the cops like flies to honey. No, he'd need to get creative. He'd worked in law enforcement most of his adult life—he'd seen bad things. Hell, he'd done bad things. Too bad about the kid . . . wrong place, wrong time. But he had bigger fish to fry. He needed to find Prince and extract a little payback. But first he wanted to get to that cabin and get those guns. He hobbled a little as they met another ranger jogging up the road toward the posse. He sucked in a breath to calm himself, to not overthink this. One thing at a time always worked better, and *first* he needed to get rid of Tyler. Too bad about Tyler.

*　*　*

Win Tyler and Luke stood there, looked over Will's messages again, and did the math in their heads. "Will is smart," Luke said. "He put the time on the texts." His dark eyes flicked up to Win's. "Based on that, they could be here now. Should be here now."

"That's what I'm thinking." Win was already walking across the road; he shifted Pierson's AR-15 on his shoulder. He and Luke headed straight for the Special Response Team ranger who was blocking the trailhead for the Seven Mile Hole Trail. It only took seconds for the guy to confirm their hunch. Five or six minutes ago, he'd sent a couple of hikers, a young man and another guy with an injured foot, down the road toward the North Rim Trail. He didn't see a sick woman.

"Have someone go down the trail and see if they can find her," Win called over his shoulder as he began jogging down the road toward the point.

If Tank hadn't been playing up the limp, Win and Luke never would have caught them, but they did. Luke was fast and Win was faster, and they spotted the pair in front of them as soon as they sprinted into Inspiration Point's small parking lot. Win split off and slowed to approach them from the right side, while Luke moved forward from the left.

Tank probably thought he was taking the paved fork that led to the North Rim Trail, but he heard running behind him and dragged Will the wrong way. He and Will were now moving down the concrete pathway and steps that led to Inspiration Point—there was no way out but down.

The Park Service called it Inspiration Point for a reason—it was a prominent outcropping on the brink of a cliff that extended about sixty feet out from the north rim of the canyon. The concrete viewing platform was surrounded with minimal fencing and strategically placed rocks that formed short walls no higher than three feet tall. A projecting point of yellow slate and rock extended another thirty feet or so beyond the viewing platform and stone barriers. It wasn't a spot to let your kids run loose. The vertical drop was eight hundred feet, the vistas of the canyon were amazing, and Win Tyler knew they had the guy trapped.

Tank realized he was hemmed in, but he wasn't ready to quit. He'd already pulled the 1911, and now he held it near Will's head. "You stop right there!" he shouted at Win.

Win found cover behind the short wall above the top stairs, fumbled for his Bureau phone, and tried to remind himself to breathe. Tank was focused on Win and couldn't see Luke crawling below the top of the rock wall. Luke inched closer to the platform.

"You pull back now!" Tank shouted as he aimed the pistol in Win's direction. Will bumped the guy hard with his shoulder, and as Tank yanked back, the Colt discharged. The unintended shot went wild. Tank started to clock Will with the pistol, then he thought better of it and just wrapped his thick arm around Will's throat. He was holding Will in front of him now, knowing his luck had just turned for the worse.

Win stood up and held up a hand. "Whoa! Whoa! Let the boy go . . . just put the gun down. There's nowhere to go, Maddox! Let's talk about this!" Win kept his rifle pointed to the side, he moved slowly down to the lower level's rock wall and continued to urge the guy to talk. He was within fifty feet of them now.

The gunshot had gotten the attention of the throng of law enforcement types five hundred yards up the road. In less than a minute, a big white-and-green Park Service Tahoe pulled sideways across the parking lot above the steps. The newcomers huddled up behind the big SUV and tried to figure out what was going on.

Win still had his hand up. "Look, Maddox. Let's do a little trade. I'm an FBI agent, let Will go and I'll be your hostage. You'll have more bargaining power . . . you'll talk your way out of this easier." Win got no immediate response, but the expression on Tank's broad face said he was considering it. Win couldn't make himself look at his brother; he kept his eyes tight on the scumbag.

Win stood up taller, set the rifle to the side, pulled out the borrowed Sig Sauer and his small Glock, and laid them on top of the rock wall. He raised both hands. "C'mon, Maddox, this will work. Just let the boy come toward me, I'll walk your way." Win took a couple of steps. "You can negotiate with the FBI, higher stakes for them if I'm with you. Better deal for you."

Win wasn't sure that was true. All he knew was that his entire world was focused on the man in front of him who was using his little brother as a human shield, who was holding a .45 caliber weapon near his brother's head, who was fixing to die if he had anything to do with it. Win's better nature tried to cancel out that last thought but couldn't do it. Instead he whispered another prayer and took several more steps down the concrete walkway.

Win caught a glimpse of Luke out of the corner of his eye. The man was very low, still slowly moving behind the rock barrier toward the viewing platform. Win swung his eyes back to Maddox as he continued cautiously down the steps and walkway.

Win believed he had the upper hand. He knew there was something to be said for waiting the guy out, but there was also something to be said for not giving the bad guy too much time to think about things. Win's mind went to the text from his brother saying that Maddox had hurt someone earlier today. And Maddox was carrying a big .45—the ATF agent and Greg Manyhorses had been shot with a .45. If Maddox was in on the gunrunning, he might be their killer. Win couldn't let Will stay in the man's grasp any longer. He thought there was a reasonable chance he'd make the trade.

But Chad Maddox had other ideas. He motioned Win to come forward, to keep his arms high and continue moving down the steps. He hissed at Will to stand still, to keep quiet. He saw the growing crowd of lawmen on the higher elevation, behind the Tahoe in the parking lot. He thought two hostages might be better than one.

When Win reached the level portion of the viewing platform, Maddox dropped his arm from around Will's neck and pushed him toward Win. They were all within three feet of each other now, and Maddox knew the proximity made a sniper shot from the cops unlikely. "Turn around, lock your fingers behind your head," he growled at Win. "You too, kid!"

They all heard the sound of a helicopter in the distance. *Odd,* Win thought, *there's no landing spot for a chopper here,* but he was so focused on the gunman that even sounds seemed to fade away. Win sensed the tension growing. Maddox sucked in a deep breath, and Win tried to calm him—he didn't need the man any more ramped up.

"It's just the medevac chopper, there are injured folks up there." Win nodded toward the slope. "Put down the gun, Maddox—it's over."

Someone had given Kirk a bullhorn, and he used it. "FBI! Stand down. Drop your weapon and raise your arms. Do it now, sir!"

Maddox let loose with a string of cuss words, as if it had suddenly occurred to him that his plan wouldn't work, that this was the end of the line. The end of what even he considered was a sorry excuse for a life. He also made the decision to not go quietly. He could at least make the national news. He could at least take someone—two someones—with him. Go out with a bang.

Win heard Maddox draw in another deep breath, he sensed what was going on. He'd walked right into one of those cases that Luke had told him about three days ago—he was staring down death with a person who wasn't in their right mind. And that person had a .45 caliber handgun pointed at his back. Win turned his head slightly, caught a glimpse of Maddox's flat eyes, and knew he was right.

"Nothin' personal, boys," Maddox said softly.

The silver helicopter came roaring over the top of the platform from the trees at a height of less than a hundred feet. Will and Maddox instinctively ducked. Win spun and hit Maddox's gun arm, and the weapon fired high. Win yelled "Run!" and landed a solid punch in the middle of the man's face. The deputy was tough—he took the lick and came down with the Colt. Win blocked the gun with his forearm, took a knee to the stomach, and nearly went down. He caught a split-second glimpse of Luke grabbing Will off the platform just as he slammed Maddox's midsection with two solid jabs. The man stumbled and dropped the weapon, but he wasn't through yet. He plowed into Win with a body blow that caused Win to stagger backward into the low railing. Win grabbed Maddox's arm and landed another solid punch to the man's already bloody face.

Maddox charged into Win to avoid another strike, his momentum caused them both to tumble over the low rock barrier and onto the loose gravel of the narrow point. It was maybe twenty feet wide and thirty feet long, but it was the eight hundred feet straight down that was the problem. There was no decent footing, no guardrail, not even a scrawny pine, and when Maddox swung at Win again, Win just ducked and watched Maddox fall into the abyss. The chopper's roar was still in his head. He didn't know if the man screamed.

Win's first thought was that he hoped his little brother wasn't seeing this . . . his second thought was that he was losing his balance. He began sliding off the top before Maddox even hit the bottom. Win tried dropping to his knees, but it was too late. He grasped at the loose rocks on the lip of the cliff until he found a small ledge, but that gave way. He fell a few feet farther to a smaller ledge that also gave way. He was at least thirty feet below the top of the projecting point, and the brittle yellow rock was refusing to hold his 210 pounds. He'd closed his eyes against the falling rocks and dust, then opened them to look down—not a smart move. His head spun from the dizzying height. He tried to hug the fragile rock face; if he struggled, the crumbling stone would simply continue to break loose.

He knew the rangers were nearby. *They can rescue me with ropes if they can get here in time.* "Please get here in time," he whispered as he prayed for his life. Someone more experienced than Win made that call and decided the rock face was too unstable, too dangerous for the rangers to climb. They'd have to rig ropes from the platform. That would take time that Win Tyler didn't have.

Win heard Kirk on the bullhorn: "Your brother is okay, hang on, we're, like, working on it!"

It seemed like an eternity, but then Win heard the deep roar of the engine, the *whap whap whap* of the rotor blades. He wasn't sure which direction the helicopter had come from, just that it was suddenly there. He glanced up to see a man in an olive flight suit and a yellow helmet staring down at him from its open door. Win could tell the man was tethered inside the chopper, could see that he was holding a rope or cable, could tell there was a blue harness attached to the bottom of the rope. The harness was swinging wildly sixty to eighty feet below the big machine. Then the chopper dropped lower. Win could see the man in the door better now, and even with the flight suit, helmet, and dark visor, he knew he was looking at Trey Hechtner. His friend had come to save him.

The updrafts in the canyon were buffeting the helicopter—it was bouncing up and down. He saw Trey pointing to the harness, saw it swinging toward him, knew they expected him to grab it when it touched him. But with hundreds of feet of open air below him, and less than full strength in one shoulder, he wasn't sure he had the courage to let go and reach for it.

But he did. The blue nylon harness hit him in the back of the head, and he grabbed for it with his left hand and tried to push off from the cliff with his boots. He used every ounce of strength he possessed to pull his arms into the webbing. Not the way the harness was meant to be worn, but all it had to do was hold him suspended until they could deposit him on solid ground. He held the harness in a death grip and had enough awareness to pray that God would help him hang on. He wanted to shout to someone: *Put me down!* But he reasoned that they knew what they were doing, that this would soon be over, that he'd be safe.

He felt air under his feet and figured the sensation was akin to flying. He was dangling eighty feet below the park's new rescue chopper, and they were flying up the canyon. He told himself that this was the experience of a lifetime, that he shouldn't be a coward, that he should open his eyes. And just as he did, they passed over the massive Lower Falls of the Yellowstone River. He forgot his fear as he looked down in awe—an immense volume of green water was coming off the top of a volcanic ledge, dropping vertically for 308 feet to rise as dancing white mist from the riverbed below. The waterfall was directly below him and for some reason the helicopter hovered. Then it moved away from the falls to a wide paved area just behind Canyon Village. He saw vehicles arriving there, saw that the two ambulances were pulling away. This must be where the medevac chopper had landed too. The helicopter began to descend and the ground seemed to move toward him. He looked up to Trey for direction. The ranger gave him a thumbs-up and his feet touched the ground in seconds.

Win saw Luke near the back of the lot—he was just getting out of his truck, he was smiling. Win untangled the harness from his arms and pitched it aside. The chopper climbed higher, and Trey waved down to him as they reeled the cable and harness up and flew off to the north. Win fought the strong urge to drop and kiss the ground. *I am an FBI agent,* he told himself. *I need to act like one.* There were lots of people milling around the area, probably wondering what was happening, what was going on. Win scanned the crowd for a familiar face, then he saw Will running toward him from a group of first responders.

"That was wild. . . . You were amazing . . . awesome." Then his voice became serious, and his eyes looked the same as Win remembered when the young man before him was just a child. "I prayed for you," Will said softly, shrugging his shoulders. "And for me."

"Me too. I prayed too," Win said.

The boy took a step closer. It was quieter now; the chopper had moved away and everyone seemed content to let the brothers unite.

"Are we gonna tell Mom?" Will asked.

"Not a chance," Win said as he pulled Will to him in a long bear hug. "Not a chance."

EPILOGUE

"Clocked me at four point five." Will's voice through the phone held an undercurrent of awe.

"Four point five in the forty. Super-good time. You shouldn't be surprised." Win had been waiting to hear how his little brother had done in the Southern Coaches Showcase Camp's initial tryouts. Waiting to see what he'd decided to do.

"I reckon I'll stay at camp, let the coaches see me. You knew I would, didn't you? You always seem to know what's right."

Not always. "You gotta make your own choice," Win said. "You're smart to give it a shot. Give yourself options." *Heard that from Dad more times than I can count.*

His brother switched gears. "When you gonna see Tory again?"

Win felt his pulse jump at the mention of her name. "Late this afternoon. I'm taking Alex to the local airport, then I'm driving to Bozeman to see Tory. Take her to dinner, take her out." He could hear the joy in his own voice.

"Awesome . . . that's cool."

There was a long pause and Win heard loud voices in the background, then a whistle—the sounds of the sport. Will had called him from the practice field.

"How's Alex doin'?" Will finally asked.

"I'm sitting at the hospital's entrance now, waiting to pick her up. They say she'll be fine, but it'll take some more time." Alex had been in the hospital for nearly two weeks—first the trauma center, then here in Livingston, closer to the case investigation. "She told me to tell you she was pulling for you in the tryouts," Win added.

"You told her I was saying some prayers for her?"

"Uh-huh, I told her." Win smiled to himself. Will had made it his mission to send Alex cards and videos since that day in Canyon when Win told him Alex had no family, no one to care for her. Win knew his brother had also talked with her on the phone a couple of times. He wondered if Will had a crush on her. *Probably.*

Another long pause. The Tyler boys weren't good with emotional topics. As the silence dragged out, Win wondered why he wasn't better at this by now.

Win heard his brother call out to someone that he'd be right there. Heard him blow out a deep breath before he came back on the phone. "I'm sorry I acted like a jerk some lately. I'm proud of you, Win. Proud of what you're doin' . . . helping people and all. Now I know it ain't all about the money, about the fame. I guess I didn't realize what you do, how important it is."

"Thank you, bud. I appreciate that . . . I really do." Win pulled in a breath, then felt himself smiling. "You go get 'em, and, hey, I love you, Will." They ended the call just as Win saw the nurse wheel Alex outside through the sliding-glass doors. He pulled the Expedition under the covered canopy of the red-brick hospital and waited. The tall nurse was glaring down at Alex, one hand on her shoulder, forcing her to sit in a wheelchair until her ride showed up. Hospital rules, he figured; he didn't envy that nurse her task. He put it in park, got out, and moved around the vehicle.

"You said you'd be here at eleven." Alex forced herself up from the wheelchair, ignoring the nurse's efforts to help. He hustled to pull the passenger door open, then reached for her arm. He noticed that the cast on her leg was now the softer kind, that the bandages on her temple and forehead weren't as large as before. She was a fighter, she was tough, and she was beginning to heal.

"It's 11:03," Win said as he steadied her on her feet.

He saw her grimace, but the displeasure in her eyes didn't fade. Win and the nurse worked together and got her onto the running board and into the seat. He started to help her with the seat belt, then thought better of it. He backed away to let the nurse take charge. He figured she'd be thrilled to have the difficult patient off her hands.

It wasn't far from the hospital to the asphalt airstrip called Mission Field. Just a short drive through the Yellowstone River bottoms, then across Interstate 90 and up a narrow winding road. The airport sat on top of a barren plateau above the river, about six miles northeast of Livingston's historic downtown.

They settled in for the brief ride and Win wasn't real sure what to say. The earlier call with his brother had zapped his quota of sentiment and emotion. He stuck to business. "How'd you score a flight on an ATF plane to Salt Lake City?"

"I told them I'd be able to testify at the initial extradition hearing early tomorrow morning in federal court. Some U.S. judges have a catch-and-release policy these days. . . . I want to be there to make sure that scumbag Jesse Gibbs never sees the light of day when they get him back to America. He's under house arrest—get that, *house arrest*—in Bolivia."

"Yeah, I heard."

Her tone was bitter. "Gibbs got away with the guns, sold them in my country. How many Canadian lives will be lost because we didn't get him?"

Win just shook his head. It wasn't really a question—she knew the good guys didn't always come out on top. He hit the turn signal for the overpass above the interstate. "It's why we go to work every mornin', it's why we keep at it. Gibbs will pay for what he's done." Win tried to sound more confident than he felt. He drew a deep breath, then added, "They came back with positive ballistics on Chad Maddox's Colt .45 for Greg and Beckett's murders. I'm sure you knew that. And the gun also ties to the death of a hiker at a spring on Mount Washburn." He focused on the road as he turned the SUV up the steep hill. "At least you can put that behind you—the man who killed Greg is dead."

She didn't say that she felt better about it, that the killer's death somehow eased her pain. She didn't say those things because they both knew they weren't true. Instead she asked, "How are you dealing with it, with killing Maddox?"

"I didn't technically kill him—he fell off a cliff. And . . . and I'm still processing it, I guess." So many days had passed, but Win had tried not to let his mind or his soul go there just yet. He switched off the emotional topic. "You gonna try to keep Dex in prison too? We've got him on the poaching—he'll plead guilty on those charges, and he did save my life. Just because his truck got used in the murders, not sure we oughta recommend that he be indicted in the gunrunning case."

He paused a few moments, then finished his thoughts. "Dex is gonna be in the hospital and rehab for several more weeks. He nearly bought it. I wrote his father's will, so I've gotta make sure he and Shane get a reasonable resolution on that . . . Mr. Pierson's ashes are going to be scattered in Rock Springs."

"And you'll probably go and take flowers."

Maybe I will.

Alex shook her head. She stared out the side window at the cows and watched a Cessna begin its approach to the landing strip. They crested the hill, and Win could see the white concrete-block office and the cluster of mismatched hangars that made up the small airport. He didn't think she was going to respond again, but she did.

"I'll get with the U.S. Attorney about Dex Pierson. You could shoot a supporting email to the prosecutor."

Already done, he thought to himself. *She thinks I'm soft.*

She drew a deep breath and looked back down the road. They were close enough now that they could see the gleaming Gulfstream G650 sitting on the tarmac with its stairs down. Two guys in sports coats were standing in front of it. Win was thinking that ATF had a pretty high priority on this deal to send that sort of ride.

The gate to the hangars and taxiway was standing wide open, and Win drove through and parked near the pricey jet. He reached into the back seat for the small bag of Alex's personal items that the nurse had stashed there. Alex didn't make a move to open the door. She turned her head to watch Win's movements, then sniffed the air. She smiled. He hadn't seen her smile often and it caught him off guard. He knew she'd caught him.

"Dog food. Tyler, you've got a sack of dog food in here."

There were actually three sacks of dog food. They were lying on the floorboard of the back seat, under her bag; there wasn't any need denying it.

Her smile widened a bit as she looked back at the sacks. "Where are you keeping him?"

"Who?"

"You know *who*. Are you keeping the kid too or just the dog?"

He shrugged and glanced away. "Well, Shane and Max are staying with some nice folks in Georgia, near his aunt. Some of us are puttin' together a little care package to send to Shane . . . a ranger who's going back East for a wedding is gonna deliver it." *Now she knows I'm soft.*

She was trying to show disapproval, but the smile had moved to her eyes.

She glanced at the ATF guys who were finally moving their way from the plane. Then she looked back at Win and shook her head. "You really are out to save the world from evil, aren't you?"

He was glad the mood had lightened. He grinned. "One little piece at a time, God willing."

One of the ATF guys nodded to them and started to open Alex's door. She held up a hand for him to wait, unbuckled her seat belt, and looked into Win's eyes. "I called Lacy, my little girl, I called her from the hospital. We talked, more than once. I'm going to try to work some reasonable custody thing out with her father. I . . . ah . . . I talked to him too." She tried to smile again. She couldn't quite make it, but there was determination on her face. "Something might work."

"I hope so, Alex. I'll pray for y'all. That is, if you want me to."

She opened the door and the guy outside took her bag from her and stepped aside. She got her leg with the cast out on the running board before she looked back at Win. She spoke softly. "Yeah, I'd like that. Do the world a favor, Win Tyler, keep doing what you do."

ACKNOWLEDGMENTS

First, I thank God for the generous blessings He has given me that allowed me to have the time and resources to write more of Win Tyler's stories. I also want to thank my husband, Bill Temple, whose thirty-one-year career in the FBI provided practical insight into the workings of the Bureau and its agents. Several of Bill's former colleagues at the FBI contributed to the realism of the text. They have asked not to be acknowledged by name, but you know who you are— thank you so much for your help! Numerous National Park Service rangers and the Public Affairs Office at Yellowstone National Park also made significant contributions to this book. Special thanks to Rangers Kevin and Melissa Moses, who provided so much insight into a park ranger's life.

I'm also indebted to Corporal Troy Savinkoff of the Royal Canadian Mounted Police, James P. Woodie, FBI Organized Crime Drug Enforcement Task Force (ret.), Game Warden Kyle Lash with the Wyoming Game & Fish Department, and James Olson with Dead On Taxidermy in Bozeman, Montana. Shilo Clark, Marketing Coordinator of Blackfoot Crossing Historical Park in Alberta, Canada, and Ryan Running Crane of the Blackfeet Tribal Historic Preservation Office in Browning, Montana, provided information regarding the Blackfoot people. I also appreciate the help of the Public Relations Officers with the U.S. Bureau of Alcohol, Tobacco, Firearms and Explosives in the New Orleans and Denver Field Offices, the Legal Counsel for the Wyoming Bar Association, the Clerk of the District Court in Park County, Montana, the Teton County Coroner's Office, and the National Park Service Division of Fire and Aviation Management.

I've had wonderful technical and procedural advisors during the writing of this book; any errors within the novel are mine alone.

I also want to recognize the invaluable input from my faithful Beta readers. Special mention goes to Anna Anthony, Sherry Holcomb, and Annette Maples.

Thank you to the associates at Girl Friday Productions, whose professionalism and enthusiasm helped me navigate the intricacies of the publishing process. Heartfelt gratitude also goes to my outstanding editors, Allison Gorman and Brittany Dowdle, who improved the text while kindly allowing some deviation from the Chicago Manuel of Style.

Lastly, I want to thank you, the reader. I've received so much encouragement from the readers of *A Noble Calling* and *A Sacred Duty*—I can't thank you enough for your kind words! I hope you enjoyed this third foray into Win Tyler's world in Yellowstone National Park. I would encourage you to go there and visit—as Win discovered, it's a magical place! Most of the locations mentioned in the book are real; a few are fictional or were modified to accommodate the story. Please join me on my website at www.rhonaweaver.com, and I'll fill you in on which is which. And I'd love to share my day-to-day writing journey with you on Facebook and Instagram at RhonaWeaverAuthor. Let's go have a little adventure!

ABOUT THE AUTHOR

Photo © Greta James

Rhona Weaver is a retired swamp and farmland appraiser who had a thirty-five-year career in agricultural real estate and founded a program for at-risk children in Arkansas. She is a graduate of the University of Arkansas, a Sunday school teacher, and an avid gardener. Growing up on a cattle farm in the Ozarks gave her a deep apprecia-tion of the outdoors and wildlife. Her novels draw on her love of the land and her profound admiration for the men and women in our law enforcement community, who truly share a noble calling. Those park rangers, FBI agents, and other first responders are her heroes. Rhona's husband, Bill Temple, is a retired Special Agent in Charge and Deputy Assistant Director of the FBI; he helped immeasurably with research-ing the books. Rhona and Bill live in Arkansas on a ridge with a view, with two contented rescue cats.

The first two titles in the FBI Yellowstone Adventure series, *A Noble Calling* and *A Sacred Duty*, have won numerous publishing awards, including the 2021 Bill Fisher Award for Best First Book from the Independent Book Publishers Association. The Next Generation Indie Book Awards honored her with the 2023 Grand Prize for Fiction and Best Christian Fiction, and the awards for Best Action/Adventure, and Best Christian Fiction in 2021. *A Just Cause* is the third novel in the series. Please visit her website, www.rhonaweaver.com, and she would love for you to follow her on Facebook or Instagram @RhonaWeaverAuthor.

Printed in the USA
CPSIA information can be obtained
at www.ICGtesting.com
LVHW090201151124
796699LV00032B/470

* 9 7 8 1 7 3 4 7 5 0 0 7 2 *